T0038532

BY SOPHIE KIM

FATE'S THREAD
The God and the Gumiho

TALONS
Last of the Talons
Wrath of the Talon

THE
GOD
AND THE
GUMIHO

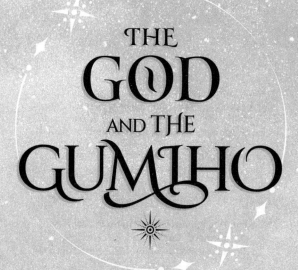

THE
GOD
AND THE
GUMIHO

BOOK ONE OF FATE'S THREAD

SOPHIE KIM

DEL REY

NEW YORK

A Del Rey Trade Paperback Original

Copyright © 2024 by Sophie Kim

Published in the United States by Del Rey,
an imprint of Random House, a division of
Penguin Random House LLC, New York.

DEL REY and the CIRCLE colophon are registered trademarks of
Penguin Random House LLC.

ISBN 978-0-593-59966-2
Ebook ISBN 978-0-593-59967-9

Printed in the United States of America on acid-free paper

randomhousebooks.com

2 4 6 8 9 7 5 3 1

Book design by Edwin A. Vazquez

Title page and chapter-opener art:
© piyaphong-stock.adobe.com (texture)
Title page and ornament art:
© Murhena-stock.adobe.com (star/frame)
Newspaper: © Lumos sp-stock.adobe.com (texture)

For my 할머니 & 할아버지.
Thank you for everything.
I love you.

AUTHOR'S NOTE

IT MEANS SO MUCH TO ME THAT YOU'RE HOLDING THIS book in your hands. *The God and the Gumiho* is nothing if not a love letter to the K-Drama, to the sparkling romance, vibrant fantasy, and lovable characters found in many of my all-time favorite productions.

Here in the city of New Sinsi, you'll encounter many mythical creatures. Gumiho, haetae, dokkaebi, gwisin, and many others wander the cherry-blossom-strewn streets and are so eager to meet you. Yet as you enter the city limits, please do keep in mind that while the stories of New Sinsi and beyond are based on traditional Korean mythology, their depictions in *The God and the Gumiho* diverge from the original folklore.

For the purpose of this story, I have taken some creative liberties. A notable example of this is that our grumpy caffeine-addicted trickster god, Seokga, is not the younger brother to Hwanin in the original mythos. It is important to me that I gently remind the audience that my books are never intended to be a complete and accurate guide to this beautiful and intricate lore. Instead, they are intended to reinterpret and retell, to inspire interest in the traditional tales through a new twist.

I often say that retellings keep stories alive. I also often say that to retell, the writer must understand the original cultural context of the folklore they work with. Please do rest assured that I have an earnest appreciation for the traditional tales of my heritage and have carefully researched the centuries of history that inspired them. New Sinsi welcomes you. The story of a grouchy god and a cheerful gumiho awaits.

THE
GOD
AND THE
GUMIHO

CHAPTER ONE

O N THE MORTAL REALM OF ISEUNG, A LONE CHERRY blossom is carried on a soft breath of wind. Its petals ripple as it rides the gust, twirling and tumbling and twisting through the narrow street of New Sinsi. It brings with it a sweet, saccharine aroma of nectar and ambrosia, so at odds with the smell of the city—the sour tang of gasoline, the greasy sizzle of frying meats, and the perpetual undercurrent of cigarette smoke that never quite seems to fade.

The city is small, but it's not quaint. As the cherry blossom flutters through the city, weaving through iron lampposts and sagging newsstands, it narrowly dodges haggard-looking pedestrians who carry battered briefcases and lukewarm cups of coffee in their ink-stained hands. Their worn shoes trudge toward the towers of smudged glass and reinforced concrete, their minds already preparing for a day of rustling through mounds of paperwork.

The cherry blossom floats through a honking intersection, past the woman selling roasted sweet potatoes, past the uniformed schoolchildren hopping over cracks fissuring through the dull sidewalks. It is so very far from its home in the city's park. The blossom sighs softly, weary and homesick.

It is losing momentum now, teetering precariously on the

supporting wind, dipping down to the pavement below. The cherry blossom has emerged in New Sinsi's shopping district, hovering just outside of a boxy black building harboring a sign reading WEAPONS, WAR ARMOR, AND OTHER WANTS in the blocky script of Hangul. In smaller lettering at the bottom are the words NO MORTALS ALLOWED.

The owner shouldn't have worried. The shop is, after all, invisible to the common men of Iseung.

With a final weary flutter, the cherry blossom begins to tumble to the sidewalk just outside the shop. Its adventure has ended; now, it is time to rest. Its delicate pink petals wither and curl inward as it floats down, down, down . . .

. . . and lands not on the sidewalk as it had so aimed, but on the shoulder of a black-haired man with cruel green eyes who stands before the shop with his mouth set into a hard, thin line.

Impatiently, the man flicks the flower away from his sharp black suit with a slender finger. He has had enough of those infernal flowers. To his displeasure, they bloomed early this year. It is not even April yet. It is the second of March.

It is clearly the work of Jacheongbi. The man mutters a curse under his breath. The goddess of agriculture has allowed the flowers to bloom early simply to spite him. She knows how much he despises the damn things. They make him sneeze uncontrollably, like some sniveling mortal. "Does she not fear me?" the man asks under his breath, adjusting his grip on the glossy black cane he holds in one hand. He tilts his green gaze up to the heavens and sneers. "Insufferable," he hisses.

There is no response.

The man returns his gaze to the shop before him. " 'No mortals allowed,' " he reads then laughs under his breath. He clucks his tongue once, twice. This statement is not a bother to him— for he is not mortal, after all.

The door is locked. The man looks at it in distaste, and with a sharp flick of the wrist, breaks the knob to allow himself entry. There's a sharp clatter on the other side.

"Jae-jin," the not-mortal calls sharply as he strides into the shop, the bell above the door chiming in a high, sweet voice to announce his presence. The shop's dark walls groan under the weight of polished weapons: sharp jikdos, small yedos, curved woldos, and an assortment of other Korean armaments that the common men have not used in quite some time. The not-mortal strides over to the counter, across a creaking wooden floor, frowning at the chubby, young dokkaebi whose cheek rests on the register's cold glass, his eyes closed in sleep. Undoubtedly, he has spent the night working himself to exhaustion.

Unlike most other dokkaebi, Jae-jin has no life.

Sighing in exasperation, the not-mortal lifts his cane slightly—and pounds it into the floor.

At the abrupt *thump* and reverberation that shakes the weaponed walls, Jae-jin lurches upward, spluttering as he rubs his sleep-bleary eyes. Their pupils expand considerably as he takes in the sight of the tall figure before him: the mouth constantly curled in displeasure, the sharp jawline harboring a pulsing muscle, the strong brow arched slightly upward as if to say *good morning.*

"Detective Seokga," Jae-jin pants, hastily rising from his perch on the stool behind the register and dipping into a respectful bow. "I—that is to say—we're not open yet . . ."

Seokga the not-mortal smiles ever so slightly, but it is not a friendly smile. It is a wolf's smile, all sharp edges and flashing white teeth. "Not open yet?" Seokga purrs, patently ignoring the door handle currently spinning in slow circles on the floor. "I suggest, then, that you lock up your shop." He watches in interest as a bead of sweat trickles down Jae-jin's neck, wetting the collar of the boy's rumpled white shirt. "And invest, perhaps, in deodorant." His grin grows.

Jae-jin swallows hard. "What . . . what can I do for you today, sir? Another sword polish, perhaps?"

"Ah." Seokga twirls his cane's hilt around in his hand, spinning the silver handle in his palm. It is no ordinary handle—it is a rendering of a snake, an imoogi. The monstrous serpent coils around the staff's glossy black material, encircling with meandering grace until it finally rests its head on the cane's hilt, content to remain underneath Seokga's fingers. Its black eyes glitter with malicious intent as Seokga ceases his spinning, instead stroking the imoogi's head with a tender, almost reverent touch. "My sword," Seokga murmurs, tightening his grip on the silver imoogi, "took a beating last night." *Snap.* With a flick of the wrist, Seokga has transformed the cane into a weapon, the imoogi hilt glinting in the morning sunlight streaming through the shop's window, and the long, silver blade shining as Jae-jin sucks in an appreciative breath. The sword's sheath, the cane, has disappeared. The imoogi now coils down the blade's length, scales as sharp as teeth. Seokga levels his sword in both of his hands and places it gently on the counter. "Fix it," he demands. "I will need it again by tonight."

Jae-jin frowns slightly, bending down to examine the weapon. "I don't see where it took a beating, sir." Indeed, the sword seems spotless, no marring in sight.

Seokga heaves a long-suffering sigh and impatiently points to a small spot on the very edge of the blade—a dent that, to the average creature, is not noticeable without a magnifying glass. "There," he says as if Jae-jin is a particularly dumb child. He wonders if the dokkaebi has lost the acute vision that all goblins possess. "Have it fixed within the hour."

"Oh," Jae-jin says hastily, squinting. "Yes, yes. I see it now."

Seokga lifts a brow, half-sure that the dokkaebi is bluffing and will reach for the magnifying glass after he has gone.

"Was it an Unruly gwisin?" Jae-jin asks eagerly as he lifts his gaze to Seokga's. "A baegopeun gwisin? Or"—here, Jae-jin's voice drops to a hushed whisper—"was it an Unruly gumiho?"

The excited tremor in his voice disgusts Seokga. His job is not as glorious as the foolish dokkaebi believes it to be. Its long hours and unending violence leave him in a perpetual state of what his haetae comrades like to refer to as *crankiness.*

"It was a dokkaebi," Seokga warns coldly, "who asked too many questions."

Jae-jin winces. "I'll have this done in a half hour," he mumbles. "Would you like to add on a sword polishing, as well, sir?"

"Just get it done." Seokga is already making his way to the door.

"Yes, sir!" the dokkaebi calls as Seokga steps onto the street outside. "I'll get it done, Detective! I promise you that!"

Seokga the not-mortal rolls his eyes and exits the shop, doing his best to hide the slight limp without the support of his beloved cane. His limbs were once mangled and ruined by his fall from grace, and although he has since healed, his right leg has never quite recovered, throbbing with a persistent, dull pain. He presses his mouth into a firm line to hide his discomfort as he continues on his way.

The mortal realm of Iseung disgusts him, but there is one feature—and, mind you, one feature only—that he finds he does not loathe with the *entire* expanse of his bitter soul.

Coffee.

CHAPTER TWO

HANI

KIM HANI HATES COFFEE.

Hates the smell of it, hates the look of it, and most of all, hates the sound that the coffee grinder emits—the insufferable *GRRR GRRR GRRR* that only ceases when the beans have been pulverized to the dark dust that resembles dirt. It smells like dirt, too—bitter and rich, with that distinct odor of mulch.

You see, then, how unfortunate it is that Kim Hani works in a café.

The Creature Café can be found just a few blocks away from Weapons, War Armor, and Other Wants. The small red-brick building is lodged between a fried chicken restaurant and a bustling noodle shop, and much like the weapons shop, is invisible to the mortal eye. Round wooden tables fill the tiny café to the brim and are occupied by creatures who slurp at their steaming coffees and teas with all the enthusiasm that one can summon on a Monday morning—which is not a lot.

Not a lot at all.

Kim Hani stands morosely behind the counter underneath the chalkboard menu, plugging her ears against the *GRRR GRRR GRRR* and steadfastly ignoring Nam Somi, her coworker, who is urging her to unplug her ears.

"It looks bad," the young gumiho insists, tugging on the folds of Hani's light brown apron. "You won't be able to hear the customers' orders when they come up, and then Boss will find out, and then you'll be fired, and then I'll have to work here all alone serving the creepy grim reapers . . ."

Of course, Hani doesn't hear any of this. She only hears a muted roaring against the fingers that are plugging her ears, and a high-pitched whining that belongs to Somi. It is only when that muted roaring finally falls to a complete silence that Hani lets her hands drop to her sides. She casts Somi a glance. "Were you saying something?"

"Never mind." Somi scowls and stomps off, her black curls bouncing as she retreats to the coffee grinder to collect the disgusting bean dust. "Aish," Hani hears Somi mutter behind her back. "One lives for one thousand four hundred and fifty-two years and forgets their manners."

Hani snorts. She is actually *much* older than one thousand four hundred and fifty-two, but she likes to keep her true age . . . secret, for various reasons. A small smile plays on her lips as she leans against the counter and observes the café.

There are only a few empty tables, the vast majority taken by the impeccably dressed jeoseung saja—grim reapers cherishing their last few moments of morning freedom before setting out to do the day's work of collecting deceased souls and filling out underworld paperwork in order to send them on their way to King Yeomra's realm. At least five black bowler hats have been deposited onto the café's hat stand, ready to be donned by the jeoseung saja as they head out on their way to work.

It is amusing, Hani thinks, that the jeoseung saja all order the same drink: a small coffee, black, no milk, no sugar. *Black,* she thinks wryly as a grim reaper enters the café and precariously balances his black hat atop somebody else's on the hat stand, *like their souls.* Corporate jobs do have a tendency to suck the life from people.

Demigods lounge back in their seats, slurping their coffees in the self-important ways that all demigods do. They may look ordinary and human for the most part, but the way that they carry themselves with pompous smiles and upturned noses clearly indicates their godly heritage.

That one there, the boy currently preoccupied with hissing at a wide-eyed jeoseung saja to put down the sausage biscuit he's eating and save the cows, is probably the son of the cattle god, Hasegyeong. Hani would place good money on it. She moves her gaze away in boredom. Demigods don't do much but wander around and sometimes slay a few Unruly creatures for shits and giggles.

Most of the time, they're just doing what normal people do—university, jobs, trips to the supermarket . . . while also trying to get their godly parents' rare attention by wrecking cars and throwing extravagant parties. Despite their divine heritage, they're probably the dullest creatures to exist. Hani doesn't bother herself with them very often, except to attend their parties when she's in the mood for some absolute chaos.

There are a few haetae within the café, too, clad in the standard precinct uniform, their walkie-talkies buzzing with static noise every few seconds to give updates on the city's supernatural crime occurrences. The guardian creatures rub their trademark golden eyes wearily as they sip at their drinks and poke at their pastries. Those eyes have always intrigued Hani. When the haetae shift into their beast form, an enormous horned and scaled lion, those eyes burn as brightly as a midsummer sun.

Dokkaebi visit the Creature Café, as well, but Hani does not see any here today. The goblins rarely emerge in the mornings, preferring instead to wreak havoc and mischief at night, dancing in the city's nightclubs, and sleeping the entire next day.

Hani sighs as the door to the café is pushed open by another group of grim reapers. Behind her, she feels Somi stiffen. The reapers are harmless (they guide the dead; they don't murder the living), but that hasn't stopped the young gumiho from flinching each time one of the creatures orders a small black coffee, no milk, no sugar. "Service with a smile," Hani reminds Somi under her breath, turning to grin mischievously down at her friend as the café's bell chimes again, signaling another entry.

But Somi is gaping at a point past Hani's shoulder. "Unnie," she breathes, "look who it is." Hani sighs inwardly. The duality of both fear and fangirl seeping into Somi's voice lets Hani know that it can only be *him*.

Only one customer has a tendency to turn Somi so pink with admiration. He has been coming for a year or two now, yet it is impossible to know when to expect him. Unlike the others, the regular jeoseung saja and haetae, Seokga the Fallen may pay a visit to the café for a week consistently, only to disappear for three months afterward. Hani is fine with this, for the fallen trickster god is as fickle a customer as she's ever seen—ordering an iced coffee with one cream and one sugar, only to return a few moments later and (wrongfully) accuse, with that cruel glint in his green eyes, that Hani put *two* creams into his coffee and demand a refund that, despite Hani's best efforts, he usually receives.

It is no surprise that the god of trickery and treachery is silver-tongued—and it is *also* no surprise that his heavenly kin threw him from the godly kingdom of Okhwang. The deity is the biggest pain in the ass that Hani has ever encountered during her very long, and very immortal, life.

She takes pleasure in the fact that if she was not retired from her time as the most notorious gumiho in Korea, she could have easily devoured Seokga's liver the first time he accused her of putting one too many creams into his drink. Alas, Hani has not been able to consume a man for one hundred and four years.

Her little binge in 1888 has left her unable to eat anything more since. She is, simply put, overstuffed.

Very, very, *very* overstuffed. It is quite clear that she will not be hungry for many more years to come.

Yet she considers taking a break from retirement as Somi turns a brilliant, blazing red—a sure sign that Seokga the Fallen is waiting at the counter. "Hani," Somi near-wheezes, her keen eyes darting from the god to the gumiho with lightning-quick speed. "Hani, he's waiting. Should I serve him? I'll faint if I serve him. Hani? Hani?"

Somi, to Hani's great disappointment, is a fangirl for all things pantheon. Her bias, as she's told Hani many times, is Yongwang—the blue-haired sea god and ruler of the underwater kingdom of Yongwangguk. But that doesn't mean that Somi hasn't written fan fiction about Seokga the Fallen. Hani saw it on Somi's computer once, and considered deleting the entire 150k-word document, if only to save Somi from herself.

It had been titled *The Smutty Prince: A Dark and Delicious Romance.*

Hani'd wanted to scrub her eyes with soap after she'd skimmed the fic. Somi used the words *bulging, moaned,* and *growled* too many times for her own good. And, of course, *sexy.*

Seokga—at least to Hani—is *not* sexy.

He's fucking *infuriating.*

Gritting her teeth, Hani turns and her hair smacks Somi in the face. "Hello," she manages to say through her teeth as Somi makes a noise of distinct disgruntlement. "Welcome to the Creature Café. What can I get for you this morning?"

"Service with a smile," Somi whispers from somewhere behind her, sounding immensely peeved. "You hypocrite." And then she giggles, looking at Seokga. "Hi, Seokga," Somi whispers.

Hani swats at her from around her back, glaring at the deity. He is dressed, as usual, in a crisp black suit and is currently examining a silver pocket watch with that sharp green gaze. Upon

Hani's words, the god glances up, snaps his pocket watch closed, and looks down at her over the length of his thin, pointed nose.

"I see that timeliness is not one of the Creature Café's strengths," he says. Hani has always found his voice strange, for it is perennially hoarse, an eternal rasp.

Perhaps he had been screaming when he fell from the sky.

Somi sighs dreamily.

"Welcome to the Creature Café," Hani repeats, clenching her jaw. She knows that if she allows herself to go off-script, then there is a very big chance that she will be fired. "What can I get for you this morning?"

Seokga sneers slightly and tilts his head up so he can examine the menu.

Hani waits as thirty seconds tick by. A minute.

Two minutes.

"If there was a line," Hani snaps, finally losing her patience, "you would be holding it up." She drops jondaemal with a certain amount of gusto. The formal speech falls and shatters on the ground. There's really no point in displaying the typical deferential manner shown to customers when she would like, very much, to kick *this* customer in a very sensitive bodily area.

The god snaps his eyes back down to her, and his lips curl in sour derision, letting Hani know that he's noticed her utter lack of respect and is *not* pleased. "The key word, there, is 'if.' If you had a line, I would be holding it up. *If* you were more pleasant to me, I might consider tipping. *If* a rabid bulgasari hadn't tried to bite my sword, I wouldn't be dealing with your questionable customer service."

Hani straightens in indignation, anger warming her cheeks. "*If* you continue to piss me off—" she bites out, and Seokga's eyes gleam in interest, as if he greatly anticipates whatever Hani plans to say next.

But Somi, ever so timidly, peeks over Hani's shoulder and whispers, half in awe, half in girlish longing, "A rabid bulgasari?"

Hani arches a brow, her anger slowly replaced by smug satisfaction at the fact that Seokga has encountered a bulgasari. The creatures do have a tendency to go rabid, which can only be expected when one eats rusted metal for breakfast, lunch, and dinner. A bulgasari had entered the Creature Café once, and had been escorted out by Hani herself after he had tried to devour the silverware.

It had been amusing and concerning all at once.

"Let me guess," Hani purrs, tilting her head. "It ate your sword for its dinner. So sorry to hear that."

Seokga scowls.

It is common knowledge that ever since his fall some six hundred years ago, Seokga the Fallen has been attempting to regain Emperor Hwanin's favor by ridding Iseung of supernatural beings with a tendency to terrorize mankind (or, simply put, Unrulies). Cruel dokkaebi, vengeful gwisin, rogue jeoseung saja, ravenous gangcheori . . . any supernatural being who disobeys the Laws of the Creature is fair game. Nothing is out of the question.

Including hungry gumiho.

But even during the peak of her terrorization of Korea and beyond, Hani had never been caught by the fallen god. *And, Hani thinks smugly, the Scarlet Fox is only an urban legend now. He doesn't know that he stands in front of her, complaining about customer service. He doesn't know that if I wasn't so full, I could make his life miserable.*

She would take such joy in munching her way through the city and cleverly evading the fallen god who would no doubt try to hunt her down. It's truly a pity that she'd overeaten in 1888.

The thought spreads a smug smile across Hani's face, even as Seokga leans forward and, in a voice cold enough to freeze over the entirety of South Korea, says, "I want an iced coffee with one cream, one sugar."

Hani cocks her head. "Fine," she retorts sweetly. "One iced coffee with one cream, one sugar, coming right up."

Behind her, Somi bustles around, snatching a plastic coffee cup and reaching for the bottle of brew. Hani sends her a pointed look. "Let me," she offers—only it's not an offer. It's a demand. Somi's eyes widen, as if she knows what Hani plans to do . . . but it's too late. Hani is preparing the god's coffee and making a point to dump three creams and four sugars into the disgusting drink.

"Hani," Somi warns in a panicked undertone as Seokga hands her his black credit card at the register. Hani ignores her.

Coffee is bad enough hot, she seethes as she stirs the ice, coffee, sugar, and cream together in the plastic cup with a plastic straw. *Why would you make it cold?*

Hani slides the drink over the counter to Seokga, who eyes it warily.

"The coffee is too light to only have one cream," he says sharply. "I said *one* cream, *one* sugar." A muscle in Seokga's jaw jumps. "You repeated it back to me. Are you daft?"

Oh, for fuck's *sake.*

Hani shrugs. "*If* you were more pleasant to me, I might have considered following your order exactly." She grins cheerfully at the seething god. "Funny how that works, isn't it?"

With a sharp, stiff motion, Seokga hands her back the coffee. He is clearly not amused. "Make it again."

Only vaguely aware that Somi is practically hyperventilating behind her, Hani grabs the coffee and violently shoves it back toward Seokga. "No," she snaps—and watches in horror as the plastic lid flies off, releasing a torrent of ice and coffee that splatters across the god of mischief's face and stains his suit.

The entire café is silent, so incredibly silent, as Seokga stands before the counter, dripping with iced coffee...and three creams, four sugars.

A few jeoseung saja shift uneasily, as if preparing to collect Hani's soul after her inevitable murder by Seokga's hand.

I've gone too far. Hani holds her breath as Seokga slowly raises a shirtsleeve to his forehead and wipes away the coffee. *I've gone too far this time.*

Drip.

Drip.

Drip.

Drops of the drink fall to the floor from the god's damp hair. He raises his gaze to Hani, and the fury burning there is enough to send Somi scuttling to the storage room, leaving Hani alone before the wrathful deity.

Hani offers a smile that is more like a grimace than anything else. "Well," she says, "at least you're wearing black."

CHAPTER THREE

SEOKGA

"DETECTIVE SEOKGA," CHIEF SHIM HIM-CHAN SAYS. Confusion, disbelief, and *amusement* flicker across his wrinkled countenance as he looks up from his desk and pushes up his thick glasses. "You . . . You look . . ."

Seokga seethes as he stalks into the haetae precinct, his knuckles white around his cane's hilt. "Do not," he warns, "speak of it." The dark markings all over his cherished black suit are infuriatingly noticeable, as is his ire. It is an effort not to stalk back to that damned café and show that girl the true power of his wrath. She is nothing, she is nobody—a mere café worker, most likely a simple dokkaebi or an inept gumiho.

And yet that *inept gumiho* had dared to throw *coffee* in his *face*.

Enough had trickled into his mouth for him to know that there certainly had not been one cream, one sugar like he demanded. And that, that on top of everything else, is the final insult.

"Apologies," Chief Shim says hastily and quickly bows his head. The swathe of gray hairs there may very well be from years of handling the trickster's dour disposition.

"Apologies received," Seokga mutters, leaning on his cane as he observes the precinct's morning goings-on. The building itself is rather drab—a concrete rectangle squashed between a massage parlor and a flower shop that Seokga predicts will be out of business within the month. The linoleum floors are scuffed and worn, covered in an eternally grimy sheen. Predictably, the overhead lights are no better—harsh and glaring, they emit a high-pitched buzzing noise akin to a fly. One would have thought that the gods would have supplied their beloved guardian creatures with a building that *wasn't* decrepit, but alas. This concrete rectangle is where Seokga is doomed to work for at least a half century more, until the building inevitably ends up crumbling into dust. And then it will be on to a new city, a new precinct, until Seokga has sent a total of twenty thousand Unrulies to King Yeomra in Jeoseung.

Seokga does not like to dwell on the fact that he has only sent ten thousand and fifty-two Unrulies to the underworld, and that consequently, his sentence on Iseung is long from being done and over with.

Officers are bent over their creaking wooden desks, flipping through manila folders and files, thumping impatiently on the sides of their slow desktop monitors. Around the corner, Seokga can hear muffled sobbing—witnesses, no doubt, brought in for questioning—and around the other corner, in the holding cell, he can hear wet hisses and vicious threats.

"What do you have for me today?" Seokga asks the chief, frowning as he adjusts his damp suit. If there's anything that he despises more than his brother Hwanin, emperor of the gods, it's not looking his best. And thanks to that gumiho, he is far from looking like his usual dashing self.

"Ah." Chief Shim rummages around in one of the many overstuffed drawers in his desk. "A mul gwisin is suspected to have been drowning people in the Han River. Two victims this morning were pulled from the water. The witness"—here, he waves to the corner around which is the sobbing—"has been drawn in for questioning."

"The water ghost will fare better, no doubt, in the Seocheongang," Seokga replies, naming the rushing red river within the underworld realm of Jeoseung. He takes the file that Chief Shim hands him and glances through the contents. Kim Min-a, age twenty. Death by drowning. Kim Jong-hyun, age twenty-two. Death by drowning. "Anything else?"

Chief Shim sighs, eyeing Seokga with what he recognizes as concern. "You work too hard, Detective. You know that, don't you?"

Seokga smirks, the portrait of nonchalance even as a part of him hisses that *of course I work too hard—that's my eternal punishment.* "Worry not, Chief. Ridding the city of Unrulies is my greatest passion."

It is not.

Chief Shim doesn't look convinced. "Have you given any thought to acquiring an assistant?" As Seokga sighs through his nose in annoyance, the old man hastens to further explain his urgings. "Somebody to get you coffee, to clean up the messes that the Unrulies leave behind, somebody to do the paperwork for you . . ."

"I told you," Seokga says coolly. "I do not like people. I work alone."

"Yes, yes." A sad smile tugs at Chief Shim's lips. "You have. But with an assistant, Seokga, your sentence could go so much faster. You would not slave over the paperwork that comes with the disposal of Unrulies, you know. Instead, there'd be more time for you to devote to your penance."

Seokga finds that he does not quite enjoy the fatherly look of weary concern that tumbles around in the chief's eyes. To him, it is ridiculous. Seokga may *look* like a twenty-something-year-old boy in desperate need of a father figure, but in *reality,* Seokga is a deity. The god of mischief. The god who snuck *twenty thousand* Unruly monsters from the Dark World into the godly realm of Okhwang, instigated a coup against Emperor Hwanin as the monsters tore into the palace, ruled on his throne for approximately five minutes, and then was promptly dethroned in a fashion that was both humiliating and highly offensive as his cowardly monsters fled back to this realm, where he's now tasked with tracking and disposing of the spineless things. Seokga closes his eyes and pushes the memory away. When he opens them again, Chief Shim is *still* speaking.

"I can put out an advertisement this afternoon—"

"Don't," Seokga snaps, finally losing his grip on his temper's already frayed and short leash. He makes it a point to speak in the informal, reminding Shim that Seokga is, in fact, much older than him. Shim always uses jondaemal around Seokga, but that warm look in his eyes has disgusted Seokga enough that he considers explicitly reminding Shim that Seokga was alive before his great-great-great-great-great-great-great-great-great-great-great-halmoni was even conceived. "An assistant would only get in my way. And, truth be told"—Seokga smirks, but it's not an amused smirk; it's a smirk that tells Shim to run while he still can—"they would probably be killed right away. The bulgasari last night dented my sword."

Chief Shim's eyes widen in concern. It is rare that an Unruly lands such a blow, and the chief haetae knows it. "Really?"

"Yes. I took it to Jeong Jae-jin this morning to get it fixed." Seokga hands the files back to him. "No assistant," he reminds the chief coldly before making his way toward where the witnesses have been gathered. "I'll take care of the mul gwisin," he adds over his shoulder. "Send anything else that comes in my way—Unruly dokkaebi, imoogi, more bulgasari, all of it. I want a minimum of ten—no, fifteen—before the day comes to a close."

Already well on his way, Seokga does not see Chief Shim watch him go with a sad shake of his head that would surely cause him disgust. Does not hear Shim's racing thoughts—that Seokga makes it so hard on himself, that he deserves to return to his home amongst the other gods, that he deserves . . . a companion. A friend. Somebody to pass the hours with, to soften his hardened heart. An assistant that could bring out the best in the grumpy fallen god, could turn his hard green eyes warm and sparkling. Seokga does not hear any of this, and perhaps it is a good thing—for if he did, Seokga would most definitely *not* be pleased.

Nor does he see the same chief boot up his computer and type, with wrinkled fingers: *Help Wanted: Detective Seokga, Haetae Precinct, New Sinsi.*

"THERE, THERE," SEOKGA SAYS HALF-HEARTEDLY, GINGERLY providing a tissue to the sobbing woman and snatching his hand away before it can touch hers. "There, there."

Consoling weeping mortals has never quite been his forte.

He watches in disgust as the human buries her face in the tissue, snuffling back snot. Humans. So weakhearted, so despicably *pathetic.*

The sniveling creature believes that she is in New Sinsi's official police precinct thanks to the glamour laid over the concrete building by a shaman and specific only to humans. Once she leaves, her memories from both her time in the precinct and her encounters with the supernatural will be erased, leaving her confused and weary.

Seokga shakes his head. *So easily fooled.*

Once, this city had been exclusive. He'd quite enjoyed the days of member-only access into New Sinsi, enjoyed that only creatures and the occasional shaman were allowed into the metropolis located just below Seoul and above Suwon. It had been the closest thing to Okhwang on the mortal realm, until humans (much in the way that they *always* do) infiltrated the streets like fat, scuttling cockroaches.

It's what they'd done to the original Sinsi, after all—the city of gods and spirits founded by Hwanung on Mount Taebak. And they've done it again to *New* Sinsi, ensuring that creatures and gods must hide in their own homes from the invading roaches.

Roaches that Seokga would rather like to step on and hear *crunch*.

He inhales thinly through his nose and attempts to gather his waning patience.

"Tell me what you saw," Seokga demands after a few moments, drumming his fingers impatiently on the silver imoogi's head. "Please," he adds as a reluctant afterthought. Humans seem to like that word. They respond to it like flies to honey.

But this human's wailing only grows louder.

Fine, then. A different tactic shall do the trick.

Seokga once had power rivaled only by Hwanin himself. He'd had the ability to worm his way into human minds, to detect their every lie, their every sin. He'd been able to sift through their shameful longings, their cruel deceits, their every trickery. It had all been so very entertaining, especially when he seized control of those minds and made the connected bodies dance like puppets on his strings.

And his illusions. Oh, his illusions. How he misses duplicating Hwanin's clothing, weaving their likenesses from nothing, and letting the emperor don the fake attire. The look on his face when Seokga waved his hand and the illusion faded, leaving the god-king naked in front of his court, is a memory that Seokga cherishes dearly.

Shape-shifting had been one of his favorite tricks out of many—particularly using it to take the form of another and wreak chaos in various realms. Pretending to be the much-beloved goddess of the moon in the heavenly kingdom of Okh-wang. Flitting as a dark butterfly through the dreary crevice of the dead that is Jeoseung to see the many lost souls collected there. In the form of a water dragon, Seokga even visited the underwater realm of Yongwangguk—although shifting into an imoogi was extremely uncomfortable as it involved sprouting *scales.*

And then, of course, there had been that other realm he'd oft visited disguised as any one of the beasts inhabiting that dark plane . . . such as the jangsan beom, tiger spirits who mimic human voices to lure mortals into their salivating maws. Ah, yes. Gamangnara. The Dark World. Realm of monsters.

A familiar, bitter feeling twists Seokga's stomach. Best not to dwell on what happened *there* any more than he must.

Yet every day that Seokga spends on Iseung is a teeth-grinding reminder of that lost realm.

Iseung. Seokga is filled with a disgust that somehow manages to be both resigned and furious all at once. The inane mortal world has always been his least favorite. Especially ever since Hwanin took over its rule in place of their sleeping mother.

For Mago, goddess of the earth, has been asleep for quite a while.

Her nap first started when Hwanin and Seokga imprisoned their tyrant father, Mireuk, in Jeoseung. "I'm tired of all these testosterone-fueled battles," Mago had grouched. And Seokga sees now that she really had been tired, because Mago has been slumbering for thousands of years. In her place, Hwanin wears the crown, placing down decrees for creatures to follow with the help of his son Hwanung, god of laws.

What would Mago say now if she were to see how much power her youngest son has lost?

Seokga sighs. Teleportation had been wonderful, too, giving him the impressive ability to commit a heinous crime and promptly flee far, far away—all while cackling maniacally to himself under his breath.

But ever since his fall, he's retained only a pale imitation of his former abilities. A few party tricks, and nothing more.

Seokga closes his eyes in concentration and lets the remnants of his power drift toward the human. He must calm her down long enough to coax a testimony from her, and judging by her hysterics, there is only one way to do that.

One entirely annoying pitfall of his capabilities has always been that he's unable to compel the truly good.

Those who have been wicked, however, play right into his hands . . . for a certain amount of time. The more sinful they have been, the longer Seokga can retain his hold over them. It's a relief, then, that so many mortals indulge in the forbidden. He will be shocked if this woman is not amongst them.

Seokga narrows his eyes as his flickering emerald tendrils, invisible to all but immortal creatures, crackle around the mortal. *Tell her to calm down,* he demands of those flickering emerald threads. *And to shut up.*

A thin sheen of sweat coats his skin as his power *listens* and wraps around the sobbing woman, restraining her shaking movements.

Calm. Down.

He grits his teeth, struggling to maintain his hold on her. If she has been wicked, it is not enough to make this easy— especially with the limits imposed on him by Hwanin. Although he has been able to keep this power in some capacity, it is utterly exhausting him. If Seokga does not pass out immediately after this heinous ordeal, he will be entirely shocked.

Finally, the woman's sobs cease, although there is still the stray hiccup here and there. "There we go," Seokga purrs, his brows pulling together tightly as he eyes the human with disdain and relief. Oh, how he wishes he still had the power to riffle through sinful minds. He'd like to know what this woman is hiding. "Now"—he reaches for a paper pad and a pencil—"why don't you tell me what you saw, and where, specifically, you saw it?"

"I . . ." the woman murmurs, barely audible over the noises of the precinct.

"Louder," Seokga snaps. He does not have the time to strain his ears. The mul gwisin is still out there, and is undoubtedly scanning the city for more prey. With something that could possibly pass for remorse if you squinted, Seokga wonders why his army had included so many water ghosts. Dealing with them often included various levels of sogginess for which he has no fondness.

Although Unruly creatures existed on Iseung long before the monstrous members of his army fled, many of the ones he hunts down are his former subjects—the Unrulies who once preferred residing in the Dark World, the creatures who composed his battalions. In their haste to retreat, the senseless things fell onto this damned plane of existence and are miserably trapped.

With him.

Forever.

A fitting punishment for all parties involved.

At his tone, the human stiffens. His powers might be restraining her from returning to hysterical sobs, but they lack the ability to bend her to his will entirely. Seokga scowls as the woman sends him a sharp, almost matronly, look.

Now that she has stopped wailing, Seokga makes careful note of her appearance. She is perhaps thirty, or thirty-five, wearing a mud-stained white turtleneck and thick black spectacles that are splattered with tears, dirt, dust, and other grime. Tear tracks run through her face's layer of BB cream in zigzag patterns, and her black mascara has been smudged in circles around her eyes. He finds, amusedly, that she reminds him of a panda.

An emotionally perturbed panda who has witnessed two drownings.

"What are you smirking at, Detective?" she demands hoarsely, adjusting her sweater's sleeves so that her hands are visible. There is a small silver wedding band on her fourth finger. It would appear elegant, had her hands not been stained with dirt and her nails not bitten down to the cuticle.

Seokga lifts a lazy brow, even as he feels his energy draining significantly. He won't be able to hold her for much longer. "Nothing," he lies smoothly, and taps the notepad with a pen. "What's your name?"

The woman blinks, but eventually draws herself upward. The emerald bands around her flicker at the sudden movement, and Seokga grinds his teeth together as he forces them to remain wrapped around the woman, restraining her tidal wave of emotions. "My name is Lee Choon-hee."

Seokga doesn't bother to write this down. All names but his own are trivial, especially human ones. "The Han River. You're the witness to two drownings. I'd like to know where, when, and how these drownings occurred. Do be specific," he adds, leaning forward. "Don't leave any details out. Especially the grisly ones."

"The grisly ones," Choon-hee repeats, her face paling slightly. The emerald bands have begun to slip.

"Yes," Seokga grinds out, sweat trickling down his forehead and his vision beginning to swim. "*Especially* the grisly ones." He will not pass out before this mortal. He must hold tightly to the little dignity he has left.

"This morning, around eight . . ." Choon-hee swallows. "I . . . I was sitting on a bench in the city park, just near the edge of the river. There was a couple close to the water. They were having a picnic. They were eating hotteok, I think. They were drinking sikhye. My boyfriend . . . I was waiting for him."

Seokga flicks his gaze to the wedding ring on Choon-hee's

finger and swallows a dark chuckle. So *that's* why he is able to control her. How spectacularly naughty.

Following his gaze, Choon-hee reddens. "I-I m-mean—"

Lazily, Seokga waves a hand in dismissal. "I am Seokga, not Yeomra." And that is a small comfort to him. The god of judgment and the dead is like cardboard personified. "I won't send you to the seven hells for mere infidelity. Continue."

She looks confused, clearly having no idea what Seokga is referencing. *It's a pity,* Seokga thinks, *that these insufferable mortals do not remember their gods.* He scowls as Choon-hee takes a deep breath. "I didn't see the first one when she was taken. I just heard a scream. A scream, and a splash. When I looked up, the water was rippling, and the man . . . her boyfriend . . . He was frozen. And then he started screaming."

"Yes, they usually do," Seokga snaps, adjusting his tie uncomfortably as sweat continues to roll down his neck. He squeezes his eyes shut, and then reopens them. The room spins. "What happened next?"

"He went into the river, screaming his girlfriend's name. Min-a. I thought that she had fallen in, and I was going to call for help . . . I had just started to scream when *it* came out of the water."

"It," Seokga repeats softly. *It* is most definitely a mul gwisin, the spirit of a drowned victim who now leads others to their own watery graves. But he has to make sure, for he is unwilling to spend any precious time chasing a false lead. "What was *it*?"

"It was almost a woman," Choon-hee whispers, "but not quite. Her skin, it was . . . bloated and blue. And when she stretched out her hand, her fingers were webbed, almost like a f-frog." The woman has begun to shake, the bonds around her struggling to remain secure. Seokga scowls, for her eyes have regained that glassy, faraway look, and her lower lip trembles violently. "And her eyes . . . Oh, God, her eyes . . . They were black, completely black. She took him, grabbed the man by his waist and . . ."

"Oh, *gods*," Seokga wants to correct her, but he holds his tongue. Most mortals of Iseung have forgotten him. It is impossible for him to wage a battle against the singular God, the one who has replaced him in human minds.

Now, the Korean pantheon is worshipped only by the creature community, who publish inane articles in *Godly Gossip* about their workout routines or raunchy speculation about their romantic liaisons, and hire sly photographers (who are usually dokkaebi) to snap pictures of Iseung's resident fallen god. These pictures typically go hand in hand with wild hearsay about his dating life. *Somebody* at the gossip rag seems to *really* enjoy pairing Seokga with whatever unfortunate individual happens to be nearby. In the past, it has been rumored that he was in a tumultuous relationship with an elderly dog-walker. He hadn't heard the end of it around the precinct for days.

Godly Gossip's photographers rarely meet pleasant fates. And although he despises his photo being taken, his ire is only exacerbated by the fact that oh-so-perfect Hwanin seems to grace almost every other magazine cover. He truly doesn't understand Iseung's fascination with Hwanin. Perhaps it's due to his shiny silver hair.

Apparently, men and women love shiny silver hair.

Even if it's bleached and dyed and fried.

And *this* woman is still babbling. Seokga returns his attention to Choon-hee. ". . . and she . . . she grabbed him and she . . ."

"And she drowned him," Seokga says instead and sets down the notepad. This information is not news to him, merely confirmation that the Han River indeed harbors a mul gwisin. He struggles to keep his eyes open as fatigue settles deep within his bones. The cost of using his power is high, but fortunately, it is nothing that a slightly sweet, but mostly bitter, cup of chilled coffee (and possibly a few hours spent unconscious) won't fix.

"*Yes*," Choon-hee wails. "She dragged him into the river and pulled him under . . . Oh, God . . . Oh, *God!*" The emerald power containing her frays, and Seokga sags in exhaustion as he loses his hold over her. Released from the bonds, Lee Choon-hee erupts once again into her waterfall of tears and senseless blubbering.

Humans.

Seokga does not bother to say goodbye as he rises unsteadily from the desk, a firm grip on his cane. He does not have the time, nor the patience, to continue talking to the mortal.

No, he has a mul gwisin to kill.

But first, a nap.

CHAPTER FOUR

HANI

"I CANNOT BELIEVE THAT YOU THREW A CUP OF COFFEE AT Seokga. I can't believe you did that to the god of mischief," Somi laments for the tenth time as she scrubs the café's glass counter with a rag and acerbic-smelling cleaning spray. "*And* that you spoke to him like that! The disrespect! Really, Hani, I cannot believe that you did that. You're so fired—so, so, so fired. Boss is going to *kill* you when she finds out."

Hani grins from where she is snacking on a cherry tart and reading Somi's *Godly Gossip* copy, tipping her chair back so it wobbles a bit more than precariously. It is a blessing that, despite being stuffed to the brim with livers and souls, human food is still *very* enjoyable to her. "She'll only find out if you tell her. Hmm. It says here that Yongwang was seen visiting Iseung and eating a fish sandwich. Isn't that sort of cannibalism?" She never would have pinned the sea god down as somebody to enjoy mackerel.

Somi shakes her head, determinedly rubbing at an invisible patch on the counter. At her silence, Hani lifts a brow and throws the magazine down. It lands face up on the table. This month's cover is a picture of the god-king Hwanin grinning with his arms around Hwanung, his son and the god of laws. In bolded letters, the headline reads: FATHER AND SON BOND OVER HAIR CARE! WHAT'S THEIR TOP-SECRET ROUTINE? Hani snorts.

Both gods have long, glossy silver hair that she would *kill* for. She wonders what salon they go to. Her hair is due for a touch-up soon. The natural roots have begun peeking out, and it's ruining the overall effect of an otherwise fabulous style.

Hani wears her hair in an expert blowout: the sort that has taken the nineties modeling world by storm, and the sort that Hani has decided looks even better on *her*. The big locks have been colored rich chocolate brown, since her ordinary deep red makes her feel naked—as if with one look, the world would point at her and announce: *The Scarlet Fox!*

She'll really need to get her roots touched up soon.

"You're *not* going to tell her, are you?" Hani demands.

The younger gumiho flushes a pale pink. "In our contract, unnie, it says . . ."

Hani rolls her eyes. "I know what it says." The contract given to the café workers by Hak Minji, the dokkaebi who founded and owns the Creature Café, explicitly states (more than once) that should a fellow employee act in a questionable manner and it somehow escapes her eye, it should be brought to her attention immediately.

Despite being a dokkaebi, Minji is anything but the fun and spontaneous type. She is the only dokkaebi that Hani has ever encountered who does not party all night. Sometimes Hani wonders if her boss really is a goblin at all.

"But the point is, Somi, that what Minji doesn't know won't hurt her." Somi's eyes widen, but Hani continues on unwaveringly, taking another large bite of her tart. "Look, it wasn't as if it was done completely on purpose. The extra creams and the sugars, yes. That god is a pain in the ass, and I daresay that he deserved a bit more lactose than needed. But spilling it all over his face, his hair, his suit? That, I promise, was at least half an accident. And the upside is, I doubt he'll be coming back ever again, so . . ." Hani grins through a large mouthful of sugared cherry. "If anything, you should be *thanking* me."

Somi makes a small, unintelligible noise through thin lips. Hani frowns, noticing that her friend has gone worryingly pale.

A dreadful realization settles upon her shoulders and she sighs in defeat. "Boss is right behind me, isn't she?" At Somi's stiff, jerky nod, Hani lets the chair legs crash to the ground and twists to meet the stare of Hak Minji. Oops.

Hani fights back a wince. She hadn't heard, nor sensed, Minji's arrival, but dokkaebi are notorious for being particularly stealthy. "Hello, Boss," she says, hastily rising to her feet and dipping into a respectful bow.

Minji does not return it.

The dokkaebi scowls instead, folding her arms and clucking her tongue in disapproval. Behind her thick, purple cat-eye glasses decorated with glittering rhinestones that probably cost more than a year of Hani's rent, dark eyes narrow to slits. They're fake glasses—Minji's eyes are perfectly acute, as are all dokkaebi eyes—which somehow adds a comedic effect. But icy blue fire dances in their black depths. Dokkaebi fire. Hani prays that it is not unleashed on her. "Kim Hani," Minji says through hot pink lips, "would you like to repeat, exactly, what you just told young Somi over there? *Hmm?*"

Minji has always reminded Hani of a gossipy aunt—quick to judge, and even quicker to spread around said judgment. Hani grimaces, her mind whirling with possible statements that could save her. Her eyes dart to Minji's handbag, an enormous pink pleather bag studded with sequins and an unholy amount of glitter. *Compliment her bag,* Hani tells herself, even as disgust makes her nose crinkle. It's the ugliest bag she's ever seen. *Compliment the bag, get in her good graces.*

Hani opens her mouth, summoning the words with notable difficulty. "I like your bag," she says feebly. "It's so—*achem*—

gorgeous?" The word nearly gets stuck in her throat, but she forces it out in a weak croak.

Minji preens. "Oh, thank you. I bought it in the shopping district last week." But then her lips curl. "Don't distract me, fox. Are you insane?" She swats at Hani with a perfectly manicured hand, the long pink nails nearly scratching her cheek. "Seokga the Fallen is a god, you idiot. When he returns to his full power and decides to blast this place to smithereens, just know that it is your doing."

Hani bristles, disliking the way that Minji scolds her. At one thousand and seven hundred years old, she is at least one thousand, six hundred and seventy years Minji's elder. But Minji is still her boss. And so Hani bows in apology, and reminds herself to use the formal tongue. "I'm sorry, Boss," she mutters. "It will not happen again." *Please don't fire me.* Hani needs this job, having not been very wise when the idea of *credit* first emerged. She supposes that she can always don a new identity, forge more files, or find a new well-paying job, like a position as a doctor or a lawyer, but all options require far too much studying. Hani does not like studying, and hates reading anything but the trashy romance novels she imports from American drugstores. "I will be on my best behavior from here on out. I promise."

Minji sighs through her nose, adjusting those ridiculous glasses. A few excruciatingly silent moments tick by, and Hani cannot help but shift guiltily underneath the goblin's gaze. "Bring me some memil-muk tomorrow," she finally demands, "and all will be forgiven. But one more strike and you're out, Hani." She scowls. "Throwing coffee all over gods. Aish," she mutters under her breath, turning away.

Hani exchanges a relieved look with Somi.

So she's not fired.

Yet.

✳

"I HAVE NEVER UNDERSTOOD THE DOKKAEBI OBSESSION with buckwheat," Hani mutters to Somi as the two girls stand in line at Yum Mart to pay for the container of memil-muk. The line is long and crawling at an excruciatingly slow pace. Tinny pop music plays from the supermarket's speakers. More than a few people are nodding along to "I Know," a newly released single by Seo Taeji and the Boys.

Somi shrugs. "Dokkaebi are born from bloodstained, discarded household items," Somi says. "They're bound to come out a little bit fucked up. I mean, that's what happens when you were a spoon once."

Hani snorts. "Not as fucked up as us," she says with a vast amount of pride. "I think that our ability to turn into a nine-tailed fox definitely exceeds a liking for buckwheat."

"And the fact that we were a fox for one thousand years before getting a human form," Somi adds in a whisper, glancing around to make sure that none of the surrounding mortals hear her.

"That, too," Hani agrees. "And our tendency to eat men's livers."

Somi gapes. "That's an outdated practice, unnie."

Ah. So it is. Hani laughs under her breath as Somi's eyes widen farther. "You've never eaten a man's liver?" she asks curiously. "Ever?"

"Of course not," Somi hisses. And then the blood drains from her face. "Have *you*?"

"Yes," Hani admits with a clandestine grin.

"How *many*?"

Thousands. But Hani just smiles a secretive little smile. "Enough to satisfy me for a lifetime."

"Hani!"

"What? It wasn't always an outdated practice. Nowadays, people are so *sensitive* about that topic."

Which may or may not have something to do with the fact that a particular gumiho treated 1888 like it was an all-you-can-eat buffet.

Somi chews on her bottom lip nervously. "What . . . what was it like?"

Hani pauses and examines Somi's face curiously. The young gumiho is as innocent a one as she's ever met, and looks the part, as well. Her eyes are wide and round, framed only by a thin coating of mascara. Her cheeks are slightly chubby, and flushed with both shock and a petal-pink cream blush. The younger girl's hair is short and curly, falling just to her chin in a cute bob, and she wears a soft white sweater that she has somehow managed to keep devoid of all stains. And yet, there is an undercurrent of morbid curiosity rippling beneath the guileless, heart-shaped face . . . One that Hani finds she quite enjoys.

"It was wonderful," Hani whispers back, her red-brown eyes dancing with mischief. "Delicious, really. The amount of power you can absorb into your fox bead by eating men is unparalleled. Regular bulgogi is nothing compared to their livers. And their souls . . ." She lowers her voice. "Their souls are the tastiest things imaginable."

Stealing souls had once been Hani's greatest hobby. A gumiho steals a soul through a kiss, holding her fox bead in her mouth and absorbing life and energy from her victim. The fox bead is a kernel of power possessed by all gumiho, and is able to expand in size and potency depending on how many souls and livers the gumiho consumes. Hani's fox bead is, needless to say, bursting with raw power.

"Did you know the Scarlet Fox?" Somi asks, her voice hushed, eyes wide. "They say that she ate the most men out of any gumiho alive and is thrice as powerful as the average fox."

Hani smirks. "I can only wish that I knew her."

The two gumiho pay for the memil-muk, Hani fishing around in her purse for some spare change and mercifully saved by Somi, who is a bit wiser when it comes to credit.

"I'll see you tomorrow," Somi offers as they stand outside the grocery store, the night air cold on their skin, and the yellow glow from the lamplight laden with fluttering moths who flock to its warmth.

"Do you want me to walk you home?" Hani asks, glancing at the darkened street before them as she tucks the jelly into her purse. Somi might be a gumiho, but the world is full of dangers for both human and inhuman women alike.

"No, no, it's fine," Somi says with a reassuring smile. "I can take care of myself, really. See?" She holds up her right fist, and with a grimace, produces three small curved claws, each one protruding from the spaces between her knuckles. *Snick.*

Hani grins. "That's my girl."

"I can use my fox bead, too, if I have to," Somi adds, retracting her claws. They sink back into her skin, leaving only angry red marks in their wake. "I'll blast whoever I need to with energy."

Hani's grin falters. For a gumiho like Somi, who has never taken another's soul or eaten someone's liver . . . Her fox bead is undoubtedly quite small. "Use the bead sparingly," she warns. "You don't want to deplete it." Because if she does so, she will die. A gumiho cannot live without their fox bead.

But Somi doesn't look concerned. "I'll be all right," she says and gives Hani a cheery little half-wave. "Tomorrow, then."

"Tomorrow." Hani winks before the two gumiho depart in different directions.

As she makes her way into the city's heart, her black boots crunching on gravel, Hani pauses to admire herself in a shop window underneath a streetlamp. Vanity has always been her sin. Even when she'd lived as a fox, she had spent hours by a lake's surface, peering at her triangular ears and red fur, grooming herself to perfection.

Now, she takes in the most beautiful woman she's ever seen in the shop's window. Hani preens, batting her angular, tilted eyes—fox eyes—that harbor a glittering mischief within their red-brown depths. She chose a matching lipstick that morning and admires the hue as she tilts her mouth upward in a satisfied smirk.

A sudden motion in the mirror's reflection catches her attention a moment later.

Two men are leaning on the lamppost a few feet away from her, watching, their hands tucked into the pockets of their black jackets, their baseball caps covering their eyes. Hani sighs in exasperation, eyeing them warily as she tightens her hold on her black pleather purse.

College boys, probably, from New Sinsi University. She can smell the alcohol on them . . . and can smell something else, something sickeningly sweet. Cheap cologne. It hits the back of her throat, coating it in a greasy tang.

Hani rolls her eyes, even as the hairs rise on the back of her neck. She may have been the Scarlet Fox, once, yet somehow, she is still not immune to the discomfort that follows being subjected to stares like these. She bites her lower lip in slight pain as she extends her claws, glossy black curves of sharp bone, from her hand and quickens her pace down Bomnal Street.

The men follow.

Scowling, Hani crosses the street to the opposite side.

The men follow.

"What happens next," Hani warns them under her breath as she increases her pace, "will not be pleasant for either of you."

They do not hear her. Or perhaps they do, and simply ignore her.

Gritting her teeth, Hani turns to face the men. She curls her lips away from her teeth and demands, in a voice of acid, "Stop. Following. Me." Her hands are hidden behind her back; they do not yet see her claws.

The men pause a few feet away. They're big, much bigger than her five foot three. She can make out identical leers underneath the shadows that their hats cast.

"Hey, sweetheart," one slurs. "Whatcha doin' tonight, huh?" His companion snickers, a wet, snotty sound that sends Hani's stomach rolling.

"I said," she repeats softly, tilting her head, "stop fucking following me." It is her final warning.

"Oh, so you're just gonna ignore his question?" the other man scoffs. "Well, that's fuckin' fine. You're ugly, anyways."

"Smile for me, baby," his friend demands. "I wanna see those pretty lips stretch wide."

"I wanna see those pretty lips around my cock," guffaws the other.

"Grab her, Beom-seok. I'll see those lips around me first—"

The men move, but so does Hani.

As they rush toward her, she spins around and narrowly avoids their grasping, hammy hands. Their leers turn into snarls as they hit air. They whirl, redirecting their attack. They are shouting now, senseless yells that send Hani's heart racing in fear.

Fear, even though she is a gumiho who has killed and destroyed and devoured.

Fear, because there is nothing more dangerous than mortal men who believe that they are entitled to the world and more.

Beom-seok grabs her shoulder, and with a feral growl, Hani slashes his hand away with her claws, drawing blood. It sprays into the air in a scarlet splatter, and Beom-seok howls.

"The damn bitch has knives!"

Not knives.

Claws.

Hani sends Beom-seok stumbling back and grins as he hits the ground hard. The other tears toward Hani, only to be blasted back by a burst of golden power that erupts from the palms of her hands. Energy sears her bloodstream as she siphons it from the fox bead within her chest. Her body hums as the bead of power begs for more of it to be released, but there is no need now.

Hani cocks her head as she stands above the two men writhing on the ground. How many women before her have they attacked? How many of those women had not had the luxury of claws, or inhuman speed and strength?

How many women?

She narrows her eyes, stomping down hard on Beom-seok's chest as he attempts to draw himself up. Slowly, she reaches into her purse and withdraws her most prized weapons, vibrant scarlet daggers that she has carried with her for centuries.

The daggers of the Scarlet Fox. The daggers from whispered urban legends, scary stories told in the dark of the bloodthirsty gumiho and her weapons of choice. Perhaps it's foolish to carry them around with her so casually, especially when she has taken pains to dye her hair, but even after all this time . . . these daggers are a part of her that is not so easily tucked away, not so easily hidden.

They are long, slightly curved, resembling in many ways talons dripping with blood. Their metal is sharp, a ruby red that gleams under the streetlamp's light. Grinning with unbridled bloodlust, Hani deftly flips them into the air before her fingers close once again around the noir handles.

Now the damn bitch has knives.

It has been a while since Hani has killed.

One hundred and four years, to be precise.

And while she's still stuffed to the brim . . .

Hani remembers the dark curiosity lurking underneath Somi's expression as she'd spoken about the art of killing. A slow smile spreads across her face.

She may not be able to eat any more livers, nor any more souls, but Somi . . .

Well. The young gumiho might be hungry for her first taste of human liver.

CHAPTER FIVE

SEOKGA

"PLEASE," THE MUL GWISIN RASPS, CLUTCHING AT THE wound within her chest, streaming blue blood so dark that it almost seems black. "Please, don't kill me." It almost sounds as if she is speaking underwater, her voice muted and muffled and *wet*.

Disgusting.

Seokga rolls his eyes, his sword leveled at her bloated neck, ready to bite into the mottled flesh and end the battle here. He is cold, and damp, and utterly irritable as he stands waist-deep in the Han River, trying not to shiver in the freezing water and wishing he was still asleep. His nap had been short as, unfortunately, tracking down this water ghost had been a priority. "Enough with the dramatics," he snaps. "You're already dead. I'm just getting rid of you. You can't be on Iseung any longer."

"No," the mul gwisin insists. "Please. Don't. I helped you, remember . . . all those years ago . . . I came to your aid, I journeyed to Okhwang from Gamangnara, I terrorized the gods at your side . . ."

The mul gwisin doesn't look even remotely familiar, except in the vague way that all water ghosts do. Either the mul gwisin truly was part of Seokga's twenty thousand from the Dark World, or she's lying. Unrulies often do, as if claiming comradery with Seokga the Fallen will somehow spare their pathetic little souls.

Which is ridiculous.

He could kill them all for fleeing from Okhwang when he needed them the most.

"I understand," Seokga continues icily, ignoring her previous claim, "that you've been having the time of your life—or, pardon me, *death*—drowning humans. Making them suffer like you did. Which sounds pitiful, but the bottom line is that you're an Unruly. So, the next river you'll find yourself in"—he tightens his grip on the sword—"will be the Seocheongang. Goodbye."

"No!" the mul gwisin sobs. "Please, my king!"

King. That word, that *title*, gives Seokga pause. Once, he'd desired nothing more than a crown. A throne. Unbeknownst to the rest of the pantheon, Seokga had taken the throne of the Dark World by assassinating its former dokkaebi king in a spectacular show of bloodshed and his own general superiority.

Seokga had then ruled over the creatures residing in that shadowy realm, training them until he'd (*very mistakenly*) thought that he had a glorious army at his disposal. Armed with nothing but his folly, he set out to claim the crown that truly mattered— and ended up losing both, along with an entire realm.

After his humiliating fall, the rest of the pantheon raided Gamangnara. That plane of chaos and trickery has been locked ever since, inaccessible to both the fallen Unrulies and Seokga.

Which is fine. The realm had always been too dark for his taste. He'd constantly been bumping into things. And it hadn't been Gamangnara's throne that he'd really wanted, anyway.

Derision curls Seokga's lips. "King?" the fallen god sneers, his insides twisting. "You're no subject of mine." Although he despises his brother just as much as the Unrulies do, he *also* despises the Unrulies just as much as his brother does. Betrayed by both sides.

The mul gwisin is hyperventilating, which is ridiculous, because mul gwisin do not breathe. "Please—please, send me back! If you unlock the realm, I'll leave! Anything but Jeoseung—"

The fallen god rolls his eyes. This plea is nothing new. It's pathetic, really, how many of the creatures believe that Seokga has the capacity to unlock an entire plane of existence when he cannot even shape-shift into a rabbit. A *rabbit*.

The ghost's appeal cuts off as Seokga flicks his sword across the mul gwisin's neck in a silver blur. He watches, dispassionately, as the mul gwisin turns to a blue ash that floats atop the river's surface before slowly dissolving.

He stands there for a moment longer, glowering with as much revulsion as he can muster (which is a truly impressive amount). Unrulies, the foul things, turn to that disgusting dust when they die—unlike their law-abiding counterparts.

"Ten thousand and fifty-three," he mutters bitterly before dunking his blade in a clean patch of water and trudging toward shore.

※

INSIDE THE HAETAE'S PRECINCT THE NEXT MORNING, Seokga folds his arms and warily eyes the jeoseung saja that stands above his cramped desk. Chief Shim stands next to him, sipping at a cup of coffee from the Creature Café. It is an effort not to scowl at that paper cup as the memories of his own experience at the café the day prior come flooding back. Seokga— still exhausted from the previous day's interrogation—would like nothing better than an iced coffee with one sugar and one cream, but he refuses to encounter that audacious gumiho again.

"Seokga," Chief Shim is saying, "this is Chang Hyun-tae. He is with Jeoseung's New Sinsi division."

Seokga regards the boy with very little interest. He is dressed like any other jeoseung saja, in the crisp black work suit, and clutching the standard black briefcase undoubtedly brimming with necessary paperwork. There is no telling his true age—jeoseung saja are as immortal as death itself, but he seems to be in his early twenties. Or perhaps even younger—he's fresh-faced and eager-looking. Seokga's attention is caught by the circular wire frames the boy wears. "The glasses," Seokga drawls. "Do you even need them?" It is rare that inhuman creatures do not possess perfect vision, most cases being only in elderly age. "You're clearly not as wrinkled and ancient as Shim," the god adds, unable to resist cutting his gaze to the bespectacled chief.

To his credit, Chief Shim chuckles wryly, unperturbed by the jab. "If I'm ancient, Seokga, I'd hate to wonder what *you* are."

"It's rather convenient that you remember my seniority only when it benefits you," Seokga drawls coldly.

The jeoseung saja blinks—clearly unsure what he should think of this entire exchange—and hesitantly takes off his hat to reveal shock-white hair. He bows. "Hello. It is nice to meet you."

Seokga sighs, turning his attention back to the reaper. Corporate workers.

So boring.

He turns his gaze to Chief Shim. "Why, exactly, is he here?"

Chief Shim rubs the bridge of his nose wearily, as if he wishes that Seokga could acquire some manners. Seokga frowns. His lack of manners is of no consequence to him. He is a god, after all. Being held to mortal standards is wearisome. "Hyun-tae collected two souls last night in downtown New Sinsi. You may be interested to know the circumstances."

A case. Seokga straightens and gestures impatiently for the jeoseung saja to begin. Almost mechanically, Hyun-tae does so.

"At eleven P.M. last night, in the downtown residential sector of New Sinsi, I was called to assist in the migration of souls from

Iseung to Jeoseung. Two mortal men, age twenty-one and twenty-two, had been found dead on the sidewalk by a passing pedestrian. There are no witnesses to the crime, but . . ."

"Was the cause an Unruly?"

"Possibly." Hyun-tae dips his head in a nod. "The bodies were both missing their livers."

Seokga flicks his brows upward. "Interesting." *An Unruly gumiho?*

"I spoke to the souls," Hyun-tae adds. "It was hard to communicate with them, though, because they were missing their tongues. It seems," he continues, oblivious to Chief Shim's cough of surprise, "that their attacker was a woman with claws."

Ah. Definitely a gumiho, then.

"What's even more interesting," Chief Shim chimes in, "is that at ten fifty-four last night, we received notice of an energy flare in the same location that the bodies were found. It was a fox bead flare. One of the most potent ones I've heard about since 1888."

"That date," Seokga muses. "It sounds familiar." In 1888, he'd been in Joseon, hunting down an elusive imoogi who'd been gorging himself on young children. But there'd been something else demanding his notice at that time, too . . . something in England . . . something Unruly . . .

"The Scarlet Fox was in London at that time," Chief Shim supplies. "Five hundred men, all missing both souls and livers. Five women, all brutalized in horrid ways. She'd been nicknamed Jack the Ripper by the humans—"

The Scarlet Fox.

The legendary Unruly of old, named such for her rumored mane of rich red hair. The gumiho that has killed more people than any other gumiho in existence. The gumiho that Seokga knew he should probably, at some point, try to stop.

He straightens in keen interest. London, 1888. It's coming

back to him now. That was the year that the consuming of souls and livers became taboo. Once, it had been done in moderation, but after the Scarlet Fox's little stint, it was banned entirely for drawing too much attention from the fearmongering mortals.

"No," Seokga replies slowly, "no. The murders of the men are separate from the murders of the women. Like all gumiho, the Scarlet Fox only touches men. The women were Jack's. The Scarlet Fox killed Jack the Ripper in November of 1888. He's thought to be her final kill." Because what followed has been more than a century of silence, the world's most notorious gumiho having seemingly dropped off the face of the planet. Until, quite possibly, last night.

How very, very interesting.

Seokga stands. "I want to see the bodies. The souls, too."

Hyun-tae shifts uncomfortably. "Each soul must be deposited in Jeoseung at most two hours after the incident of their death. Each man is currently awaiting judgment from King Yeomra. It is company procedure to bring them in on time." At Seokga's darkening visage, the jeoseung saja winces and averts his gaze.

Chief Shim sighs almost inaudibly. Although his face gives nothing away, it is clear by the cadence of his voice that he is miffed by this "company procedure," as well. "The bodies, Detective Seokga, are in the morgue. Lee Dok-hyun is currently examining them."

Seokga grabs his cane from where it leans against the side of his desk in the busy haetae workroom. "I will pay them a visit, then." If the Scarlet Fox is truly back . . . Well. It is Seokga's job to catch her, and catch her he shall. He stalks through the precinct, wasting no time as he heads toward the morgue.

The precinct's mortuary is silent and still as Seokga strides through the door, his shoes clacking on the tiled floor. The walls are white and washed out, spidery cracks running through the thick, bumpy paint. Overhead lights hum and buzz, illuminating the steel examination tables and the white sheets in a glaringly harsh light. He wrinkles his nose in distaste as his eyes flick to the steel vaults in which bodies are typically stored.

"Seokga." Lee Dok-hyun, the precinct's hired forensic pathologist, looks up from where he stands over one of the sheet-covered bodies. The doctor manages a tired smile, and Seokga cannot help but feel a prickling of respect. The mortal's job is not easy. Lee Dok-hyun is one of the few humans who is aware of the supernatural world around him—his family line had been chosen, long ago, to help serve the haetae in this way.

His father before him, Lee Dae-song, had been a skilled pathologist, as well. One of the precinct's best. Dae-song passed four months ago from a heart attack, but truly, Seokga doesn't feel his absence at all.

His son is basically a carbon-copy of him: Dok-hyun shares the same slightly crooked nose, lanky form, and notably bad eyesight (common, Seokga thinks in disdain, for mortals). Like his father, Dok-hyun wears a pair of tortoiseshell glasses that distort the sides of his face due to their heavy prescription, and the black lab coat with the golden embroidery of a haetae that signifies his position.

Like his sire, Dok-hyun is also a skilled worker. The precinct expected to be set back by Dae-song's death, going from two pathologists to one, but Dok-hyun has completely devoted himself to pulling twice his weight.

"Good morning," Dok-hyun says wearily.

"Debatable." Seokga makes his way so he stands beside the forensic pathologist, looking down at what he can make out of the body through the sheet. A hawk-like nose lifts the fabric a few inches from the dead man's face. He turns to Dok-hyun. "Have you begun examinations?"

"Not yet." Dok-hyun shakes his head. "The haetae brought

the bodies out for me, but I had a feeling that you'd be coming, so I waited." He rolls his shoulders and glances down at the sheet below. His hazel eyes are shrewd and dim in a way that suggests he has seen many, many deaths. Dok-hyun cannot be more than in his mid-thirties, but in these moments in the morgue, the man always appears much older. The illusion is only enhanced by the new, prominent streaks of gray in his dark hair, which appeared after Dae-song's sudden death. "I am aware, though, that both men are missing their livers."

"The work of a gumiho," Seokga mutters. "Undoubtedly."

"Well," says Dok-hyun with a sigh, "we shall see." He makes to pull the surgical mask hanging around his neck upward. "Kim Beom-seok," Dok-hyun declares, glancing down at his clipboard. "Age twenty-one. Undergraduate at New Sinsi University. Male."

"And dead," Seokga murmurs, his eyes drawn to the cavity underneath the right rib cage, splattered with gore. "Very, very dead."

"Yes. And dead." Dok-hyun makes his way over to the dead man's mouth, and Seokga watches as he gingerly examines the wound, both with his fingers and with a set of hemostats that he retrieves from a nearby metal cart. "The tongue is gone," Dok-hyun says slowly, examining the mouth. "It was pulled out by . . . fingers. Pulled out by fingers with very, *very* sharp nails." He glances toward Seokga, who tilts his head in catlike consideration, his sharp mind honing a theory.

"Not nails," he replies slowly. "Claws."

"Claws?" Dok-hyun frowns. "They were attacked by a gumiho in its fox form?"

"Gumiho in their human form can summon their claws at will," Seokga replies, staring at the dead man. Although his face is still in death, there is an underlying cruelness there, a predation that sends Seokga's lips tightening in aversion. "This one certainly did."

"An Unruly gumiho," Dok-hyun agrees, still examining the body.

Seokga frowns, a memory rising to the surface of his mind. A memory of fearful whispers of scarlet blades, ruby-red daggers flashing through the night, slicing into skin. Those knives had once been said to be the Scarlet Fox's weapon of choice. "Do you see any marks from a blade? Not from the claws, but from twin daggers?"

"Ah . . ." Dok-hyun frowns in concentration, moving from the mouth to the cavity on the right rib cage. "I'll need a few moments to examine this wound more thoroughly," he says slowly, eyes narrowed behind his glasses, "but it seems that it was a dagger that did this. The cut is more precise. More accurate. Cleaner, even."

Eyeing the gaping wound, Seokga swallows a dark laugh. If this truly is the work of the Scarlet Fox . . . Well. This shall be a much more interesting case to follow than that pathetic mul gwisin from last night.

The Scarlet Fox is back.

"I estimate the times of death around ten-fifty to eleven P.M." Dok-hyun glances at Seokga. "Would you like to see the other body?"

"There's no need," Seokga says, still looking down upon Kim Beom-seok, the beginnings of a dark smile tugging at the corners of his mouth. "I've seen enough."

CHAPTER SIX

HANI

"JUST TRY IT," HANI ENCOURAGES, WATCHING AS SOMI pokes gingerly at the bloodied livers on the plate before her. They sit in Somi's kitchen, Hani already dressed in her café uniform and Somi still in her pin-striped pajamas. "You'll like it. I promise." She ran over to Somi's small apartment first thing in the morning, carrying a Tupperware of human liver in an inconspicuous corduroy tote bag. It feels almost wrong to bring the bloodied organs into Somi's impeccably clean, unspoiled apartment with its pristine white floors, but it is no matter. Somi, Hani knows, will find the livers to be the perfect breakfast.

Eventually.

Once she stops thinking of it as taboo. Which, Hani supposes, is really her own fault in the first place.

"Are you insane?" Somi stares at Hani, the morning sunlight bathing her aghast face in a soft glow. "I can't believe that you *killed* them," she whispers hoarsely. "You actually killed them and brought me their livers. I literally don't know what to say."

"A simple thank-you would suffice. Would you rather have them prowling around the streets of New Sinsi?" Hani replies, cocking a brow. "Their kind is an infestation that I've taken it upon myself to get rid of."

"Do the haetae—"

"The haetae didn't see anything," Hani assures her. "Besides, these were bad men. And bad things happen to bad men all the time. You'll find, though, that their livers are scrumptious."

"Is this because . . . I asked what . . ."

"No," Hani replies, "it's because they attacked me. It was self-defense. Do you want them? Just a taste? Nobody will know. It's your lucky day."

Somi blinks, still evidently in a state of shock. "Do you know, Hani," she says slowly, "what this reminds me of?"

"What?" Hani asks curiously.

"When a cat trots up to its owner with a dead rat in its mouth and gives it to them as an unwanted present." Somi looks queasy.

Hani snorts. "If you don't want the livers just say so. I'll go bury them outside or something." She reaches for the plate, but Somi abruptly stops her, placing a slender hand on her wrist. Hunger flashes across her face, and Hani realizes that Somi has been acting disgusted because that's what she thinks she's *supposed* to do.

But in reality . . .

"Wait." The young gumiho fastens her eyes to the bloody organs, and Hani feels a surge of triumph as Somi licks her bottom lip. She knows that Somi is remembering the previous night, Hani's claim that a liver tastes better than bulgogi. "Nobody will know?" she whispers.

"Nobody at all."

"You promise?"

"I promise."

There is a split second where Hani watches Somi wrestle with her two conflicting sides—fox and human.

The fox wins.

With shaking hands, Somi raises the liver to her mouth and sinks her teeth into a blood-red lobe. Hani watches her chew, her lips stained with blood, and swallow.

"Do you like it?" she asks eagerly, leaning forward across the wooden table. "Isn't it delicious?"

Somi's smile of stained teeth and ruby red lips is the only answer that Hani requires.

⁕

"I FEEL LIKE I'VE DRUNK FORTY COFFEES," SOMI WHISPERS in Hani's ear as she flips the café's sign from CLOSED to OPEN. "I feel like I've drunk forty coffees and seven energy drinks. I can't keep still."

Hani smirks as she makes her way over to the counter. "I can tell." Somi hasn't stopped jittering since she polished off the second liver, licking her fingers with considerable satisfaction. "Try to calm down, though," she adds under her breath. "You never have this much energy in the mornings." It's true. Somi is usually bleary-eyed and groggy at eight A.M., but with her fox bead absorbing so much power, the girl is unable to contain herself.

"Nobody will know, right?" Somi follows Hani as she pours the (disgusting) coffee beans into the grinder. "I mean, with me being so energetic? They won't be able to tell by looking at me what I did, will they?" Fear seeps into her voice. "Oh, gods. Nobody will know, right?"

"I've told you," Hani says, shaking the last of the beans into the grinder. "You'll be perfectly fine." She grimaces as she switches the grinder on. GRRR. GRRR. GRRR. *Damned coffee,* she thinks bitterly.

"Do I have blood on my mouth?" Somi half-shouts over the grinding. "I don't, do I?"

Somi had washed her mouth out with water, and then soap, and then mouthwash and more soap. There is no chance she missed even a single spot of blood. Hani shakes her head, and plugs her ears. But Somi still looks nervous. *Do I?* she mouths, greatly exaggerating each syllable.

Hani shrugs, unplugging her ears and switching off the machine. She killed five hundred men in London and got away unscathed. This is nothing in comparison. "You're perfectly fine," she assures Somi, who doesn't look convinced. She sighs. "If you did, I would tell—"

The café's bell chimes, signaling the arrival of the morning's first customers. Somi hastily retreats to don her apron. Hani plasters a polite smile on her face as a young jeoseung saja with white hair and an elderly haetae in a black trench coat approach the counter. "Welcome to the Creature Café. What can I get for you this morning?"

The old haetae smiles, his golden eyes crinkling at the corners, where many laugh lines lay. "I'll have a small green tea," he says. "And a small iced coffee, one cream, one sugar."

"And for you?" Hani looks at his jeoseung saja companion—who, she realizes, is staring at Somi with what could best be described as *heart eyes.* Sensing his stare, Somi glances up from where she's shoveling ice into one small plastic cup and flushes a brilliant red. Not in admiration, but in discomfort at being subjected to a grim reaper's stare. "Hey." Hani snaps her fingers, drawing the boy's attention away from her friend. The haetae laughs under his breath, shaking his head ruefully. "Eyes up here."

"Oh." The jeoseung saja hastily straightens, juts his chin out, and fixes his circular wire glasses. "I . . . I will have a small black coffee. No milk, no sugar. Thank you very much."

Amused, Hani joins Somi to begin creating the drinks. "The jeoseung saja is looking at you," she murmurs as she stirs the iced coffee. The white-haired boy is again peering at Somi in clear admiration.

Somi frowns. Her skin is pallid. "Snap at him again, then. His kind creeps me out."

Hani smirks before carrying the beverages over to the two creatures. "Enjoy your drinks," she says as she hands the haetae his receipt. "But I have to warn you—drinking both the tea and the iced coffee will give you one hell of a caffeine rush."

The old man smiles. "The coffee isn't for me. But I'll take your advice to heart."

Warily, Hani's eyes narrow. *One iced coffee, one cream, one sugar.* She watches as the pair settle down at a nearby table. The haetae must work with Seokga in the city's precinct.

She deeply regrets not spitting in the god's coffee while she had the chance.

It is a slow day at the Creature Café. Only a few other customers trickle in throughout the course of the morning . . . a pair of gumiho followed by a trio of swooning haetae boys, a few more jeoseung saja, a handful of demigods, and a weary-looking dokkaebi who requests raisin tea for his blatant hangover. With no other customers to tend to, Somi shifts restlessly from foot to foot, and Hani busies herself with munching on another cherry tart.

Through her chomping, snippets of the elderly haetae's conversation with the jeoseung saja reach her ears. She listens halfheartedly, more focused on her breakfast than anything else.

". . . more on his plate at the precinct now than ever," the haetae is saying. "It would have helped, Hyun-tae, to be able to speak to the souls of last night's victims. If there are any strings that you can pull within your corporation, it would be much appreciated . . ."

Last night's victims. Hani pauses in her chewing. Next to her, Somi has gone rigid. "Unnie," she gasps under her breath, "do you think they mean—"

"*Shh,*" Hani retorts, setting down her tart. "I'm trying to listen."

Somi falls silent.

The jeoseung saja sips calmly at his coffee. "I am sorry, sir, but as I said, it is corporate procedure to deposit the souls into the hands of our CEO, King Yeomra, no more than two hours after their passing. It is likely that they are already being readied for reincarnation or prepared for their descent into hell. But," he adds, setting down his coffee, "Detective Seokga seems more than capable of handling the Scarlet Fox situation without their aid. As I said, they were missing their tongues. There is not much that they would have been able to tell him, anyways. If you would like to be put in contact with my higher-ups, Chief Shim, I can supply you with the necessary information . . ."

Next to Hani, Somi makes a tiny sound like a choke. "Hani," she whispers, "Hani, Hani, *Hani* . . ."

Hani swats at her, annoyance heating her blood to a boil. *Seokga. Seokga is handling the Scarlet Fox situation.*

Because apparently, there is *a Scarlet Fox situation.*

Fucking hell. That's just—that's great.

It seems that she has grossly underestimated the capabilities of New Sinsi's law enforcement. Quietly, she curses herself for not dumping the bodies into the Han River, weighed down by stones. It would have been the smart thing to do, but Hani is dreadfully out of practice, and now the consequences are staring her directly in the face.

"No, no." Chief Shim wearily waves a wrinkled hand. "That won't be necessary, Hyun-tae, thank you. We're working on a suspect list now. Thirty gumiho were in the area last night, judging by places of work and residence. We'll . . ."

"Hani," Somi whispers again, this time with a shrill cadence peeking through her hushed words. "Do you hear them? Oh, gods, oh, *gods* . . ."

Something thick and heavy has settled in Hani's stomach as Somi begins to hyperventilate.

The detectives will see, sooner or later, that both Somi and she were in the grocery shop close to the scene of the murder.

Hani misses the days where the closest thing to CCTV was a gossipy ajumma who didn't know when to hold her tongue. They'll both be pulled in for questioning, and while Hani can lie up a storm, Somi is *already* breaking into a nervous sweat next to her.

It doesn't matter that Somi's files say that she's only a baby—files can be forged. Hani's certainly was. With the way that Somi is already panting wildly and clutching tightly at her arm . . . this is not, Hani decides, looking very good.

Hani knows that she will do anything to shield herself from the haetae's suspicion. As much as she may love Somi, Hani's sense of self-preservation will far outweigh the possibility that Hani flat-out admits what she's done to take the scrutiny from her friend.

So that scrutiny will be redirected to the nervous, bumbling, sweaty gumiho that looks very, *very* guilty . . . and has a suddenly powerful fox bead rolling around within her. There are examinations, now, that can show that sort of thing. Hani curses modern technology vehemently in her mind.

"Hani," Somi whispers again. "Oh, my gods . . ." She's on the brink of tears. "They'll know what you did, what *I* did . . ." Her breathing is shallow and quick.

Hani doesn't bother to mention that technically, Somi isn't the real criminal here. A claim that Somi was cajoled into eating the livers *could* stand up in court, but it certainly wouldn't reflect very kindly on Hani. More accurately, it would most likely lead to the younger gumiho pushing Hani to confess that she was the one who killed the two men. And Hani does not want to confess.

"I'll fix it," she mutters to Somi out of the corner of her mouth, although she's not sure *how.* "You're acting suspicious. Go make coffee or something." She nudges Somi firmly with her hip and returns her attention to Chief Shim and Hyun-tae.

Chief Shim is sighing and taking another sip of his tea. He

taps the lid of the coffee that will likely be brought to the fallen god. "He's overworked, you know."

"Ah," says Hyun-tae, frowning. "I'm not surprised. His penance is . . . we have all heard of it."

The chief looks sad, Hani thinks curiously. So very, very sad. "I feel for him," he murmurs, more to himself than the jeoseung saja. "He is, in many ways, still a child. Petulant and hurt, abandoned and so alone. So, so alone." Shim sighs.

Hyun-tae clears his throat a bit awkwardly. "Have you considered finding him an assistant?"

"I certainly have. When I put in an ad for an assistant on the New Sinsi job search site," Chief Shim continues tiredly, "I expected to get a flood of applications from creatures willing to help out at the precinct. But there have been none so far. Likely due to Seokga's infamous, ah, disposition."

Hani blinks. *Interesting.*

"An assistant seems as if they would be able to greatly lessen the god's workload."

Hani cocks her head in acute interest as Chief Shim replies, "Precisely. Yet he won't admit that he needs the help. And I have a feeling that the Scarlet Fox situation will consume him whole. When he begins a case, he stops at nothing to close it."

"An assistant to Seokga," Hani murmurs to herself as her sly, cunning mind begins to whirl. *An assistant to Seokga . . .* this has fallen straight into her lap. Perhaps Gameunjang, goddess of luck, has decided to toy with Seokga by making today a very, very large payday for a certain Kim Hani.

"I would hope that you'll pay whoever is foolish enough to take that job a very large sum," Hyun-tae mumbles. "That god is irritable."

"Which is why I am willing to compensate."

Hmm. A smile tugs at Hani's lips as she eyes the chief. *Seokga needs an assistant. And the pay is high.*

Well, well, well.

This could be a very good opportunity for her indeed.

To work side by side with the insufferable god and steer him in the opposite direction of her and Somi. To fix the mess she's somehow landed Somi in. And, to protect herself.

Because although Hani has never been caught, she does not want to take any risks and be sent to Jeoseung for her past crimes. No, she wants the Scarlet Fox to remain buried, an urban legend, until she is once again hungry and can emerge from her fast with all the ferocity of a bear who has been hibernating during an exceptionally long winter. And if Seokga sticks his pointed nose in her business and uses his far-too-clever mind to somehow uncover the Scarlet Fox's true identity, to unravel the lies that she would spin under questioning . . . Hani is not taking any risks. Not when this opportunity lies in front of her, shining and golden, to lead Seokga on a wild goose chase as his assistant.

If anything, her proximity to him will most likely make him suspect her less. Only a fool would put herself so close to the one hunting her.

Get the job. Steer Seokga away from Somi. Play the game.

A foxy part of her mind revels at the thought of playing with Seokga the Fallen. It is revenge, in many ways, for his tendency to bring his shit-poor attitude to the Creature Café.

This is one case that Seokga will never solve.

And perhaps there will be more.

Hani, too, has heard of Seokga's price for penance. It would be quite unfortunate if he was prevented from paying it. If a new, clumsy assistant somehow botched all of his quests . . . if the Unrulies began escaping from Seokga's clutches.

I'm a genius, Hani decides. *I'm a fucking genius.*

It's almost as if Somi senses Hani's train of thought. She scampers back to her side, still sweating profusely. "Unnie—"

But Hani is already half-running, half-skipping over to the chief's table. "I'll do it," she declares. "I'll do it."

Chief Shim blinks up at her in confusion. "I beg your pardon?"

"The job," she explains hastily. "I . . . I overheard that Seokga the Fallen needs an assistant." Hani is acutely aware of Somi frantically shaking her head behind the counter and sends her a *calm down* gesture behind her back. "I'm willing to do it. To be the assistant, I mean. Sir," she adds as an afterthought.

The chief seems to be swallowing a laugh. "You're an eager one, aren't you?" His companion is watching Hani curiously.

"Truth be told," Hani continues, the words bubbling to her lips, "I hate this café. My boss is insane. She carries around this hideous purple purse and makes me buy her memil-muk. So, I'd love to work as Seokga's assistant." Hani smiles as brightly, as innocently, as she can manage. "I can provide you with a copy of my résumé—"

"That won't be necessary," Chief Shim cuts in with an almost grandfatherly twinkle in his eyes. "Just answer these three questions. Answer them correctly, and you got yourself a gig."

Hani nods her head, breathless.

"Are you squeamish around dead bodies?"

"No," Hani answers—a little too fast. Chief Shim arches a brow, and Hani fumbles for an explanation. "I mean, no, I don't think that I will be." She smiles winningly.

The haetae chief seems satisfied. "That's the sort of spirit we like to see in the precinct," he agrees jovially. "Next, then. Are you opposed to long hours?"

Yes. Beauty sleep is an essential part of Hani's nightly self-care routine. But she makes herself shake her head. There will be no beauty sleep for her if she is sent to Jeoseung. It is very unlikely that King Yeomra will allow her to reincarnate after her little stint in London. "Oh, no. Not at all."

"And last but not least . . ."

Hani holds her breath.

"Are you willing to make Seokga coffee?"

"Oh," Hani replies, a grin stretching her lips wide, "oh, you have *no* idea."

CHAPTER SEVEN

SEOKGA

SEOKGA FROWNS AS HE SCANS THE COMPUTER MONITOR displaying the CCTV footage from two nights ago, when the two young men had been brutally murdered by the Scarlet Fox. To his eternal suffering, there was no camera—none at all—stationed on Bomnal Street where the murder occurred. As a result, for the past three hours, he has been running through all available camera footage of the city that night, squinting for any sign of abnormal activity, any sign of a gumiho making her way to the street that would become the murder site.

So far, though, he has found nothing. All of the footage is fuzzy and blurred, and as for the camera stationed on the street just before his desired site, it was covered for a half hour by a particularly fat moth who had decided to use the lens as its resting spot for the night.

"Damned insect," Seokga mutters, rubbing his strained eyes wearily. He has been in the precinct since two A.M., determined to catch at least a glimpse of a possible suspect. But there is nothing, nothing at all, thanks to that *godsdamn moth*. To add to his woes, the DNA found on the corpses matches no DNA on file in either South Korea, China, Japan, Thailand, England, France, Spain, Italy, Australia, America, Mexico, or even Vatican City.

Files can be faked, Seokga reminds himself. He hadn't expected this case to be solved quickly thanks to easily accessed DNA files. He knows that he's in it for the long haul with this one.

But he has no leads at all, save for knowledge that the murder weapons used were gumiho claws and, possibly, the infamous daggers of the Scarlet Fox.

Seokga sighs thinly through his nose and shuts off the monitor. The precinct is still relatively silent in the early morning, with naught but the steady hum of the printer that is slowly spitting out the mound of paperwork that he'll need to complete later thanks to the four Unruly cheonyeo gwisin he'd dispatched the night before. The virgin ghosts had been erecting crude phallic statues all over the city . . . statues that *still* remain even after the four gwisin had been sent down to Jeoseung. He'll ask Chief Shim to dispatch some haetae to take them down, or wait for the city to take notice and eventually do it themselves.

Seokga rolls his neck and glances blearily around the precinct. In the early morning, the surrounding cubicles are still empty save for one weary-looking haetae who is practically chugging a large iced coffee. Seokga rubs his temples. What he wouldn't give for a coffee right now.

He begins the paperwork, barely glancing up as he hears the door of the precinct open, ushering in the muted hum and buzz of the city outside. That will be Chief Shim, no doubt, readying himself to scold Seokga for being at the precinct so early . . .

But it's a pair of heels that click against the grimy tiled floor, and oval, pink-polished nails that curl over the edge of his cubicle's divider. "Good morning," a female voice greets merrily— much too merrily.

That voice. Seokga is still glaring at the slender hands gripping the desk divider. It sounds awfully familiar . . .

Slowly, he raises his eyes to the woman peering down at him with what can best be described as a shark's smile. More specifically, the smile of a shark about to devour exceptionally delicious prey. *What the fuck?*

It takes him a moment to place her. It's not that he's never been good with faces, it's just that he doesn't particularly care to take note of any visage but his own.

She is small and slender, with ridiculously voluminous brown hair and angular eyes that glitter as they meet his own. Glossy red lips are stretched into that predatory smile, displaying two small, sharp white canines that just pierce her bottom lip. The woman waggles her fingers at him in greeting. *Remember me?* she seems to be asking.

Seokga imagines her wearing a brown apron, holding a cup of too-sweet coffee, and recognition sets his lips into a sneer. "You," he snaps icily, straightening indignantly and sending her a glower brimming with cold hatred. The coffee-thrower from the Creature Café. "What do *you* want?"

She pouts, even as it looks like she's holding back a snort of amusement. "You're not very nice, you know," she replies. "I even got up early to get here on time."

"On time?"

"Haven't you heard?" the woman asks sweetly. "I'm your brand-new assistant."

Seokga blinks.

The woman winks.

And then Seokga rises from his desk, irritation tightening his jaw and voice as he says, "I have no idea what you're talking about, mortal."

"Mortal?" She doesn't look remotely impressed as Seokga glares down at her, at least a foot taller than her. "I'm a gumiho, thank you. The correct phrase would be 'I have no idea what you're talking about, *immortal*.' But I'll let it slide. This time." Even though she's now using the correct honorifics to address him, they're blatantly mocking. The girl seems to notice his ire and her smile grows.

Seokga's teeth are grinding in pure, undiluted vexation. "Get out."

"No," she replies cheerfully. "I've been hired. As of today, I'm your trusty helper." And she sends him a thumbs-up. A *thumbs-up*. The audacity.

"Who hired you?" Because he knows, beyond a doubt, that he damn well hasn't.

"We-ell . . ." The gumiho's eyes move to the precinct's doors. "He did."

Seokga knows, without even looking, that Chief Shim has entered. "Shim," he calls out through clenched teeth as the older haetae tries to sneak into the room without him noticing. "I would like to speak with you."

With a sigh, the chief makes his way over to Seokga's desk. He sends the gumiho a small, almost apologetic smile, before turning his gaze to Seokga.

"Did you," Seokga demands, "hire me an assistant when I *explicitly* told you *not to*?"

Chief Shim grimaces. "Detective Seokga," he says, "this is Kim Hani. And yes, she'll be assisting you. I hired her yesterday."

The gumiho—Hani—grins. "See? I've been *hired*."

"I work alone," Seokga snaps at Shim, his chest stinging. He realizes, belatedly, that he feels *betrayed* by the chief. Betrayed. The realization boils his blood. "I have told you that, old man. Take her back to the café, let her go back to spilling coffee."

Shim, to his credit, does not waver. If anything, he only grows sterner. "Your manners are atrocious, Detective—"

Seokga sneers.

"—and I will not be firing Hani. From today on out, she *will* be your assistant. She will help you with paperwork, with cleaning up the Unruly messes you create, and she will make you coffee."

Hani's smile is much too sweet for his liking. His back goes rigid. "I do not," he grinds out, "want her making me coffee.

Ever." Not after that little *incident* involving a soaking wet suit. "I do not want her here. Get rid of her."

He watches in slight disbelief as Hani flinches, her eyes widening and a pale pink flush coloring her nose and cheeks. Tears swim in her angular wine-brown eyes, and her lower lip trembles. "You . . ."

"Detective Seokga," Chief Shim hisses. "How dare you? Young Hani here has volunteered to help you, and you're to treat her with the proper amount of respect." He rubs Hani's shoulder comfortingly. "Pay him no mind, dear. He's nothing but a bitter old man." He returns his glower to Seokga and does not see Hani's lips curl into a satisfied smirk as she sends the fallen god a smug little wink.

Sly fox. Seokga scowls and points at her with a stiff finger. "Did you not see—"

But Hani has reverted to her act, seeming as if she is barely holding back tears under Shim's confused glance.

"Enough, Seokga." Chief Shim's tone leaves no room for argument. "Hani is your assistant. Treat her kindly, or I'll put myself in contact with Emperor Hwanin. I'm sure he would love to know how his younger brother fares on Iseung." With a pointed glare, the chief departs, retreating to his own desk at the very back of the room.

Still feeling the chief's watchful glower on his back, Seokga closes his eyes and very slowly counts to ten in an attempt to get his temper on a leash. He doesn't, however, even make it to seven. Because Kim Hani has popped a piece of bubblegum in her mouth and is smacking on it in the most obnoxious manner possible. His eyes fly open. "Will you," he demands, "stop that."

She blows a large pink bubble that nearly conceals her entire face before exploding with a loud *pop*. "So," she says, ignoring his previous request, "Shim says that you're hunting the Scarlet Fox."

"Among others," Seokga mutters, slowly sitting back at his desk.

"Hmm." Hani smacks her gum and looks around at the precinct. "You know, I thought this place would have a little more . . . interior design involved. Is the disrepair part of your penance?"

He cuts his eyes back up to the insufferable fox and glowers.

She blows a very, very large bubble.

He watches as she smiles around it and pops it with a magnificent *crack*.

Seokga sighs, rubbing the bridge of his nose. "Go . . . Go do something useful," he mutters. *Go away. Please.*

"Like what?" Hani tilts her head. "Would you want a coffee?"

Yes. *"No."* Seokga sets down his pen, rummaging through his mind for a list of things for his *assistant* to do, away from his sight.

"Are we going hunting, then?" Hani looks interested. "For Unrulies, I mean? For the Scarlet Fox?"

"Once Chief Shim hands me a case," Seokga grits out, "then *I* will go hunting. You, however . . ." He smiles a slow, cold smile as he reaches into his pocket and withdraws a few crumpled bills. "*You* can go get me some breakfast."

CHAPTER EIGHT

HANI

"WHAT ARE YOU SUPPOSED TO BE DOING RIGHT NOW?" Somi demands as Hani approaches the counter of the Creature Café. "I thought you were working at the precinct, on the other side of the city, carrying out your insanely suicidal plan. Are you *trying* to make us suspects, by the way?" Beads of sweat have pooled above her upper lip and have soaked through the armpits of her shirt. She smells like terror and guilt with a potent undercurrent of shame. "I think we should hide. I think I'm going to hide. I don't want to go to jail. I don't want to be interrogated! Do you think they use torture?"

Hani narrows her eyes. "Keep your *voice down*," she hisses. There's a line behind her. She hopes it's not too much for Somi to handle—she was supposed to be on shift with her today, after all, and now on top of a constant crisis of guilt, Somi is also dealing with the morning rush of the café alone.

Somi wipes at her forehead and blinks rapidly. "I'm going to pass out," she says. "I'm going to pass out and then I'm going to wake up in *jail*. Oh, gods. How long is a sentence for eating somebody's liver? A century? A millennia?"

"You're not going to wake up in jail." Somi's panic has made Hani feel even more secure about her decision to take Shim's job. "I told you, I'm handling it, okay? They won't even look in your direction. I promise."

"I didn't sleep at all last night," Somi says and points to the dark bags under her eyes with a trembling finger. "Every time I heard a noise, I thought I was going to be *arrested* . . ."

"Somi," Hani snaps. "Voice. *Down.*"

Somi blinks meekly. And then clears her throat. "Are you here to order something?" she asks loudly, as if it will null anything the line behind Hani may have heard.

"Actually, yes." After being shooed away by Seokga with the request to be brought breakfast, Hani decided with malicious spite to keep the god waiting and hungry for as long as she can. Judging by his stack of paperwork, he won't be leaving his desk to go hunting anytime soon, anyway. So Hani has taken a taxi to her old café, where she plans to spend a very, very long time chatting with Somi. "Seokga wants breakfast."

Somi shakes her head and begins to gnaw on her nails. "I used to wonder how he liked his eggs in the mornings," she whispers in a thin, reedy voice. "Now I wonder if he's going to imprison me."

"*Somi.*"

She blinks rapidly. "I really can't believe that you left me here. What if they come for me while I'm working all alone?"

"Nobody's coming for you. And I'll return eventually," Hani promises quietly, mindful of the clusters of jeoseung saja and the handful of demigods fidgeting impatiently behind her, "once Seokga drops the Scarlet Fox case. But for now, I'll order two cherry tarts, one matcha latte, and one iced coffee with seven creams and seven sugars. Actually, make that eight of each."

Somi looks absolutely terrified. "*No.*"

"Yes." Hani smiles pleasantly.

"You're actually going to get me killed." Somi gulps down a deep breath and shakes her head, even as she punches in the order. "Fine. Fine, okay. Coming right up."

Hani grins and hands over Seokga's money. The cherry tarts

are both for her, as is the matcha latte. But the coffee ... Well, *that's* for him.

As she waits for Somi to produce her order, Hani eyes the ever-growing line with a guilty twinge. Without her, Somi is having to take on the jeoseung saja orders despite her fear of the reapers. She can only hope that a part-timer is hired soon ... Wait.

Hani narrows her eyes in interest.

There, at the very end of the line, is the white-haired jeoseung saja from the day before. Chang Hyun-tae. He's holding his hat in his hands, fiddling with the brim nervously as he watches Somi, a faint blush staining his cheeks. And though he looks wearier than she remembers—he probably needs a caffeine fix to help with the long hours of a jeoseung saja—Hyun-tae seems excited to see Nam Somi.

Hani tilts her head. Somebody, it seems, is smitten.

She continues to watch him as she snacks on her tarts at a nearby table. Somi, to her credit, is handling her interactions with the many jeoseung saja well. Although she does still avert her gaze from the grim reapers, her professionalism is something to admire. Hani slurps on her latte as Hyun-tae reaches the counter, nervously pushes up his glasses, and says in his oddly formal voice: "Hello."

If Somi recognizes him, she does not give any indication— mostly because her eyes are trained on a point well above Hyun-tae's head. "Welcome to the Creature Café—" Her voice wobbles, and she cuts off. She's sweating even more now, which Hani hadn't thought possible.

"I would like a small black coffee with no cream and no sugar," Hyun-tae replies promptly, as if he is answering a classroom question. "Thank you very much."

As Somi makes his coffee, Hyun-tae shifts from foot to foot.

And then . . . . "I saw the sign on the door," he says as Somi hands him the coffee. "You are looking for a part-timer?"

Somi's eyes snap to him, widen, and then immediately avert back to the point far above his white hair. "I . . . Don't you already have a job?"

"I do. Yes. I do." Hyun-tae clears his throat. "But my hours are not so bad. I would enjoy having another job. In the afternoon."

"You would enjoy having another job?" Somi sounds wary, dubious, amused, and terrified all at once. "Seriously?"

"I . . ." But Hyun-tae freezes as, within one of his coat pockets, his radio crackles. Hastily, he withdraws the walkie-talkie and presses a skull-shaped button. Hani tilts her head, her ears twitching as they curiously sort through the static crackle for the words on the other side.

"Chang Hyun-tae," a deep male voice says, *"we have a lost soul wandering around New Sinsi near the city park. Its body was uncovered just now in the residential sector. The haetae have already been alerted—it seems to have been an Unruly attack of some kind. Please dispatch immediately. Over."*

An Unruly attack. Hani lurches to her feet.

Seokga will undoubtedly be called to the scene of the crime. And as his assistant, she's meant to assist him in finding the perpetrator.

But as somebody who has a bone to pick with that god, she's meant to completely botch his entire attempt at finding that Unruly.

Hani is out the door and running with a very, very smug smile on her face as Somi makes a disbelieving noise behind her.

HANI BURSTS THROUGH THE DOORS OF THE HAETAE PREcinct and promptly collides with Seokga.

"Oof!" Hani stumbles backward, her forehead smarting from where it has banged against Seokga's (rather sharp) chin. She blinks the stars out of her vision while Seokga glowers down at her imperiously, those narrow green eyes flashing with no small amount of ire as he rubs at his reddened chin.

"I suggest that you watch where you're going," he cuts out, clutching that cane of his, the silver imoogi glowering at her with its beady black stone eyes.

Hani grits her teeth, still blinking spots of light out of her vision, and thrusts the iced coffee toward the fallen god. "Here," she snaps. "Breakfast."

Seokga casts one look at the drink and his scowl deepens. "No. Now move." He steps around her. "I have somewhere to be."

"The body?" Hani asks interestedly. She cannot help but be curious at the prospect of examining a crime scene that is the product of a crime she *didn't* commit.

Seokga whirls. "How do you know about that?" His eyes narrow. "And before you ask, no, you are not accompanying me."

"I didn't plan on *asking*," she replies sweetly, taking a sip of Seokga's coffee and immediately regretting it. Even with eight creams and eight sugars, coffee is still the worst beverage created by man. She tries not to gag. "And I overheard a message to a jeoseung saja at the café. I know that you're going, and I *am* coming with you. I'm your assistant, after all. Accompanying you is my sacred duty. Besides. If you leave me behind, I'll complain to Shim, who will complain to your brother." Hani's smile grows. "So yes, I am accompanying you, Seokga."

The fallen god closes his eyes, and Hani gets the distinct impression that he is attempting to count to ten, as she suspected this morning. She lets him again get to seven before saying, "Are you taking a cab? Or do you have a car?"

Seokga's eyes fly open. "I have a car."

She tilts her head in interest. "Can I drive?"

"No." The word is barely more than a very agitated and extremely murderous growl. "No. You cannot. You *can* sit in the backseat and keep your mouth shut." His eyes flash. "And if you interfere with my investigation, gumiho, I promise you that you will suffer."

She eyes him, unimpressed. "I won't interfere," she lies.

He scowls. "I mean it."

"Yes, I'm sure you do," she purrs, and watches in delight as Seokga stiffens in indignation and opens his mouth with a searing retort before abruptly snapping it shut, turning on his heel, and stalking out of the precinct.

With an immense amount of amusement, Hani follows.

CHAPTER NINE

SEOKGA

SEOKGA'S KNUCKLES ARE WHITE AROUND THE STEERING wheel as the gumiho props her feet up on the car's dashboard, dangles a hand out the open window, and grins at him in a way that suggests that yes, she *does* know precisely how much she is irritating him. She pointedly ignored his demand to sit in the backseat, instead hopping in next to him with a cheerful, "Your car is cool."

He sneered, even as a part of him had preened in pleasure. Yes, his car certainly is cool. A sleek black Jaguar XJS, his car is his second most prized possession (the first, of course, being his sword). Which is why he now hisses, out of the corner of his mouth, "Get your feet off the dash, fox."

Hani rolls her eyes as they weave through the city streets. Instead of doing as he's demanded, the gumiho opens the mirror before her seat and fluffs up her already insanely fluffy hair.

Seokga mutters an unsavory curse under his breath and slides his sunglasses back up his nose as the morning sun flares brighter upon the city. They are nearing the residential sector now. He wonders, warily, what sort of Unruly attack this was. Chief Shim was unusually pale as he gave Seokga the address and promised to meet him there. Perhaps the Scarlet Fox has struck again. The thought has him clenching his jaw as he pulls his car into the parking lot of an apartment complex, parking between Chief Shim's patrol car and the long black hearse that undoubtedly belongs to the jeoseung saja. Bright yellow police tape has blocked off the apartment's entrance, and the haetae and white-haired reaper are waiting for him there. The reaper, he notes with no small amount of smugness, has lost his fresh-faced enthusiasm. It's been replaced by a grim sort of weariness marked by the purple shadows underneath his eyes. He wonders how gruesome the murder was.

Seokga exits the car with Hani close behind, her heels crunching on the gravel pavement. The god sighs in bitter annoyance. Kim Hani is proving to be a persistent thorn in his side. *Perhaps,* he thinks as he approaches the chief, *the sight of dead bodies will scare her off and she'll leave.* Significantly comforted by the possibility, Seokga nods a coolly polite greeting to both men. "The victim?"

Hyun-tae gestures to the black hearse. "Her soul is waiting within the car," he says perfunctorily. "I collected her just now. She died last night. I am expected to drive the Hwangcheon Road to Jeoseung shortly, so if you would like to speak to her, now will be the time."

Chief Shim glances at Seokga. "The body was uncovered by a human neighbor a half hour ago. We intercepted their call to the police and redirected it to our channel. It seems to be an Unruly attack of some sort. The victim was a gumiho."

A gumiho. Seokga arches a brow. *Interesting.* He expected another set of human male bodies with the re-emergence of the Scarlet Fox, but the fact that the victim is a gumiho crumples up his expectations and throws them into the waste bin. Not knowing whether to be relieved or disappointed, Seokga nods, as beside him, Hani flinches. "Do you have the name yet? Age?"

"Ah. Yes." Chief Shim glances to Hyun-tae, who straightens and clears his throat.

"Cho Euna," he promptly rattles off. "Age in human form is

twenty-two. Total age, including time as a fox, is one thousand and twenty-two. Formerly employed at—"

"That's all I need." Seokga eyes the hearse. "She's in there?"

Hyun-tae nods.

"I'll be brief." Seokga starts toward the car, and to his annoyance, Hani joins at his side. He halts to glower at her. "Stay behind. I go alone."

"No." Her eyes are bright and her mouth is tight. With a finger, she jabs at his chest, and Seokga stiffens as the pad of her finger meets his crisp white shirt. Seokga feels a flare of rage—*how dare she*—and steps back with a cutting retort on his tongue. But Hani isn't done. "That's a baby gumiho in there. A dead. Baby. Gumiho." Hani has taken a step forward, and each word is punctuated by another jab on his chest. With a rush of anger, Seokga grabs her wrist, his eyes flashing. Hani doesn't even look fazed. "Who is probably scared and alone and *hurt*," she continues, yanking her arm away from his grasp. "I'm coming with you."

Seokga swallows the sharp syllables that cut his mouth, forcing down his bubbling rage at being touched with such a lack of reverence. Instead, he mulls over what Hani has said. *A baby gumiho.* Hani looks as if she's only in her early twenties, but it's impossible to tell her true age. "How old are—"

She cuts him off. "One thousand four hundred and fifty-two. I'm coming."

He grinds his teeth, feeling Chief Shim's stare on his neck. "Fine," he grits out irritably. "Fine." Seokga can still feel the touch of her finger, poking at him in a way that makes him contemplate the repercussions of shutting Hani into the hearse and having Hyun-tae deliver her to Jeoseung, as well.

Hani glares at him like she knows precisely what he's thinking.

The inside of the hearse smells of old wood and melted candle wax. The interior is more like a limousine than anything— the long seats lining the car's walls, the dark velvet carpet, the pristine tinted windows. Seokga ducks his head as he enters the car, sliding onto one of the black leather seats across from the soul. Hani takes a seat next to him, her eyes wide as she looks at the victim.

The gumiho is blurred around the edges and translucent, and seems to flicker with an aura of pale blue light. She looks up from her trembling hands as Hani shuts the door, revealing bloodshot eyes and a beautiful face that is marred by the black veins snaking underneath her skin. Seokga's blood runs cold at the sight. Something about those veins tugs on a distant strand of memory. He reaches for it, but it slips through his fingers. Unnerved, Seokga scowls.

"Who are you?" Euna asks, her voice quavering, eyes darting from Seokga to Hani and back. "What do you want?" Her eyes linger on Seokga for a moment and he thinks he sees recognition, but it's dwarfed by terror.

Next to him, Hani swallows hard. The older gumiho's face is pale. "Euna," she says quietly. "My name is Kim Hani, and this is my partner, Seokga."

Partner? Seokga bites down on his tongue to prevent himself from correcting Hani's absurd claim. "You're dead," he says bluntly instead. "So we need to ask you a few questions about how you were murdered."

Euna's trembling increases tenfold. "W-what?"

Hani's elbow digs deep into his side and he hisses. Touching him *again*. The fox's insolence never fails to astound him. "You dare—"

"*Shut up.*"

Dumbfounded, Seokga gapes. He cannot even find the words to respond. Never before has he been told to *shut up.*

She glowers at him for a moment longer, cheeks pink with anger, before turning back to Euna, and saying in a much gentler voice, "You've passed away, Euna. Soon, this car will take you to Jeoseung, and you'll go on to your next life. You'll be reincarnated."

"Or sent to one of the seven hells," Seokga adds, newly incensed as his shock fades. Shut up? Who, precisely, tells a *deity* to *shut up*? "There's the Hill of Knives, of course, if you committed murder. Imagine a toboggan ride down a mountain of blades—without the toboggan, of course. Not to mention the Tongue Field, where jeoseung saja stretch out your tongue until it's long enough to plant trees on. I helped design that one."

Euna whimpers, and Hani's elbow digs so deeply into Seokga's side that he can't help but to wheeze. With a violent motion, he shoves Hani off him and massages his ribs, contemplating the repercussions of murdering the gumiho with Euna as a witness, and a haetae chief waiting outside.

"Don't listen to him," Hani says, glaring. "You're not going to any hell, Euna."

"What's even better is the seventh hell—"

"Seokga," Hani warns, and the pink on her cheeks has turned to red, "shut up—"

"—where a giant saw—"

"*Stop it*—"

"—cuts fraudsters into pieces," Seokga finishes triumphantly, only to be met a second later with a sound like a high-pitched foghorn blaring across a bay.

Blinking hazily, Seokga realizes that the sound was in fact Hani, who had let out a screech of unintelligible rage. Ears ringing, he shakes his head to clear it of the stupefied fog (how is it even remotely possible for a *throat* to make *that noise*?) and is only vaguely aware of Hani murmuring reassurances to Euna, somehow already perfectly recomposed as if the last minute was in the distant past.

"But before you do that," he hears her conclude soothingly as his hearing slowly starts to come back, "we want to make sure that whoever hurt you is caught. You can help us with that, can't you?"

Euna swallows hard before rasping something unintelligible.

"Speak up," Seokga commands impatiently, earning another vicious glare from Hani. Slightly more wary of what invoking the gumiho's wrath can incur, he clenches his jaw, his fingers tightening around the cane. The sheer nerve . . .

"I said, I guess," she whispers. The younger gumiho can't even look at Seokga.

"Who hurt you, Euna?"

"I . . . I don't know." The soul shakes her head. "I . . . I don't remember."

Seokga sighs. "You do," he tells her peevishly. "Just think. What's the last thing that you recall seeing?" *How did those black veins emerge on your face? Who attacked you?*

What attacked you? Again, Seokga riffles through his memories. But he has centuries upon centuries upon centuries of memories in his head, and trying to sort through them is like trying to organize one of the precinct's filing cabinets.

Impossible and frustrating.

A long moment of silence passes. Finally, Euna whispers, "I remember . . . I'd gone out for drinks with my friends. We'd all passed an exam in physics. I'd passed, too, even though the last few nights had been rough. I . . . I'd been having nightmares. I hadn't been able to sleep much. But I passed, and we were celebrating."

"Where did you go?" Hani asks encouragingly.

"The Emerald Dragon," Euna replies slowly. "That creature club downtown. We all took the bus back to our apartments . . .

I got off here," she says, gesturing with a violently shaking finger to the window, "and . . . I went inside."

"What happened then?"

Seokga watches carefully as the gumiho shivers, pulling her black shirt closer around her body. "I felt cold," she whispers. "Really, really cold. And tired. I wanted to go to sleep . . . I had just closed the door to my apartment when I . . . I think I decided to lay down on my floor. I was tired. So very, very tired."

"And then?"

"And then . . ."

Euna jumps as there's a sharp knocking on one of the hearse's windows. Hyun-tae bends down, mouthing something that looks annoyingly like, *Time's up.* Seokga scowls, and even though the jeoseung saja can't see him through the tinted glass, motions for him to fuck off. Leaning forward, arms braced on his knees, Seokga takes in Euna's shaking fingers and wobbling bottom lip. Her eyes dart from him to Hyun-tae, who, behind Seokga, is continuing to rap on the glass.

He should really proceed carefully, but he is impatient. "And then you were brutally murdered. What did it?" Seokga's voice is sharp, and as Hani slaps her palm against her forehead, something shifts in the victim's eyes, clear comprehension replacing murky confusion as they meet Seokga's own. Stiffens as terror shines brightly within the brown depths—pure, undiluted terror.

He braces himself as Euna's hands fly to her head, as her eyes bulge out of their sockets in horror.

"Euna," Hani says in clear worry, leaning forward. "Euna, it's okay—"

But the soul begins to scream.

And scream.

And scream.

Her voice is hoarse and guttural as the screams tear from her lips, loud enough that Seokga flinches back, his teeth gritted. He fumbles for his power to calm her, to restrain her enough so that he can find his answers—but Hyun-tae yanks open the door of the hearse and gestures impatiently for Hani and Seokga to get out. "That's enough," he declares over the din. "If she stays on Iseung any longer, she'll miss her window for reincarnation."

Damn it. Seokga opens his lips to protest, but there's no use. He is out of time. Reluctantly, he and Hani step out. A moment later, Seokga watches, grim-faced, as the hearse speeds away with a squeal of tires. The sounds of Euna's screams still ring in his ears.

Hani is quiet next to him. He casts her a sideways glance. "If you want to quit," he says, "now's the time."

She sends him a vicious glare. "I'm not quitting."

Chief Shim comes up beside them. "Her body is in the apartment. We should take the investigation inside. I've contacted Lee Dok-hyun, and he's agreed to join us here before examining the body in the morgue." He sighs wearily. "The jeoseung saja will be contacting the family soon. They'll have questions for us, so let's find some answers before their visit.

"By the way," the old chief adds hesitantly as Hani starts toward the complex's entrance, "that sound from the car, that . . . shriek? The one that sounded almost like a *horn?*"

"Hani," Seokga seethes, "apparently has strong vocal cords."

EUNA'S BODY IS CRUMPLED ON THE CREAKY APARTMENT floor just a few paces from the flimsy door. She is curled into a ball, her eyes closed, one desperate hand outstretched in the direction of the nearby sofa, as if she'd been staggering to it before she'd fallen.

Seokga crouches above the dead gumiho, frowning as he takes in the bulging black veins that snake up her neck and cover her face in their spidery black web. Her arms are also covered in the veins, and he is sure that they also spread underneath the black T-shirt and blue jeans. Hani kneels beside him, her lips in a tight white line.

"She died scared," Hani says quietly.

So she did. The gumiho's face is forever frozen in an expression of horror, the eyes squeezed tightly shut, the brows drawn together, and pale lips parted in terror. Small curved claws protrude from her knuckles, yet it is impossible to tell what the gumiho had hoped to use them against.

"Her soul was disoriented," Chief Shim adds from where he is examining the door for any signs of a scuffle. "She was found wandering around the park. I'm not sure if she knew she was dead. Most souls remember their passing, but Euna didn't."

"Until she did," Seokga says, rising to his feet and glancing around the apartment. Aside from the body, there is no sign of a fight, no sign of forced entry. Chief Shim moves away from the doorway with a frown. "Check the surrounding rooms for clues. Maybe whatever did this was lying in wait in the kitchen, the bedroom, or the bathroom."

Hani nods and disappears around the corner, her brows set in clear determination.

"What do you think did this?" Chief Shim asks Seokga under his breath. "This is like nothing I've ever seen before. The veins . . ."

Seokga shakes his head, leaning on his cane in contemplation. Whatever memory that seeing the dark veins sparked is still reluctant to surface. "A demon, perhaps," he says slowly. "Some escaped creature of Yeomra's realm. But the veins aren't the only things that are bothering me." He taps his cane on the floor, the end of it hitting the wood just inches from Euna's face. "Euna died in her sleep."

Chief Shim gapes. "What?"

Seokga nods. "According to Euna, after a night out with friends, she returned home. Upon entering this apartment"—he gestures to the door—"she felt cold and overwhelmingly tired. She laid down on the floor, and from what I can guess, closed her eyes to sleep. But she never woke up." Seokga's mind whirs, connecting the fragments of testimony that he had managed to collect from the gumiho's soul.

We'd all passed an exam in physics. I'd passed, too, even though the past few nights had been rough. I . . . I'd been having nightmares. I hadn't been able to sleep much.

"For the nights leading up to her death," Seokga continues slowly, "Euna had been having nightmares."

"Nightmares," Chief Shim repeats.

"Yes. Nightmares." Seokga pauses as, finally, an *inkling* begins to blot the corner of his mind in dawning suspicion. "She'd been having nightmares." He turns to Chief Shim, his jaw tight. It's coming back to him now. Unfortunately. "When Dok-hyun examines the body, I want him to make an incision in one of these veins. I want to see what's inside." Because if it is what he thinks it is . . . "I want security camera footage for this apartment, too. For Euna's route home. I want to observe every stop she made, every person she passed. I want footage from the Emerald Dragon. I want to see who she danced with, who she flirted with. I want to see everything."

"Seokga." The chief's voice is grave. "Do you know what this is?"

"I have a suspicion," he replies quietly. "And if you love this city, Shim, you'd best wish that I am wrong."

CHAPTER TEN

HANI

"YOU'RE GOING TO CUT OPEN A VEIN? WHY?"

Seokga sighs a long-suffering sigh from where he stands next to the forensic pathologist, the weary-looking man in a black lab coat named Lee Dok-hyun who'd met them at the apartment and had accompanied them back to the morgue. "Because," he says very slowly, as if Hani possesses the mind of a snail, "I want to see what's inside."

Hani stares at the bulging black veins covering Euna's limp body. "Oh," she says in a small voice, feeling suddenly queasy. "I see."

"You can look away, if you want," Dok-hyun offers gently. "I understand that this must be an overwhelming first day for you."

"Better yet," Seokga purrs, "you can *quit*."

Irate, Hani straightens. "I'm not quitting," she snaps back. If anything, this new development has strengthened her desire to remain working as Seokga's assistant. Because that, lying prone on the metal table, is one of her little sisters. A gumiho just barely into her human form. She died alone. She died scared. And Hani will not walk away from her in death. Not until whatever did this is sent to the depths of the Seocheongang River. Whatever did this is an Unruly she *will* help Seokga catch. "So stop asking."

Seokga shrugs. "It was worth a shot," he drawls. "You can't blame me for trying."

Dok-hyun glances amusedly between the two creatures. "I see that you've finally made another friend, Seokga. Congratulations seem to be in order."

Emerald fire blazes in Seokga's gaze. "I was not aware that we are friends, Dok-hyun. And since when have you spoken to me in the informal?" He cocks a brow. "Remember your place."

Hani watches as Dok-hyun ducks his head and bows in apology. "I'm sorry."

Seokga's eyes flutter upward in obvious annoyance. "As you should be."

"You're a ray of sunshine, huh?" Hani says dryly, crossing her arms and staring at Seokga in disgust. "He's cutting open a vein for you. I would say that he warrants your respect."

Seokga pointedly ignores her.

"Aish," she mutters under her breath. Gods and their superiority complexes.

Dok-hyun clears his throat. "I'll make the incision now," he says, pulling up his face mask. "I'll cut this vein, here." He taps one of the black veins creeping up Euna's bare shoulder.

Hani holds her breath, watching as Dok-hyun pinches a thin silver scalpel in between his fingers, the sharp blade hovering just above the vein. The doctor narrows his eyes in concentration as he presses the scalpel onto the affliction, the blade piercing the tissue—

Inky shadow seeps from the cut, floating into the air and hovering, a small black cloud below the fluorescent lights.

Hani presses a hand to her mouth, unable to look away from that mist of darkness that continues to emerge from Euna's body. "What . . ." Her voice is barely more than a whisper. "What is that?"

Dok-hyun hastens to seal the cut. "Detective Seokga," he says, his voice frayed by confused panic. "Detective Seokga—"

But to Hani's immense suspicion, the god doesn't look even

remotely surprised. Instead, he eyes the shadows with no small amount of annoyance, his mouth a hard line. "Wonderful," Seokga the Fallen mutters. "How completely, absolutely, positively *wonderful*." He raises a hand to swat at the swirling darkness, and Hani gapes as it disappears, fading into nothingness and leaving only a few lingering wisps of smoke behind.

"What just happened?" Dok-hyun pants.

Seokga cuts him a glance. "You tell me, Doctor."

"I-I made the cut a-and a *shadow* came out." Dok-hyun grips the golden embroidery on the left side of his lab coat—the rendering of a haetae in its proud beast-form.

"Not a shadow," Seokga corrects, his tone hard. "Darkness."

"Darkness?" Hani repeats. "What do you mean, 'darkness'?"

"I mean," the god replies, turning his grim gaze toward Hani, "that this was done by no ordinary Unruly. This was done by something far more sinister." Seokga looks at Euna's body, limp and lifeless on the table, the morgue's harsh white light highlighting her colorless and graying skin. Hani follows his gaze with a lump in her throat.

"What is it?" she asks hoarsely. "What did this to her?"

When Seokga meets her eye, his gaze lacks the casual cruelty and malicious mischief that it so often possesses. Instead, weariness flickers there. An eternal sort of weariness that only an immortal god can possess.

"Eoduksini."

⁕

EODUKSINI.

The word is whispered all over the precinct that day in voices hushed with fear. *Eoduksini. Eoduksini. Eoduksini.*

"Eoduksini," Hani says slowly, rolling the word around in her own mouth as she sits at the desk next to Seokga, filling out Eu-na's paperwork. Seokga is scanning the city's security footage from the night prior beneath lowered brows. "I never thought one would enter New Sinsi." In fact, she never thought one of the darkness demons would crawl up to Iseung at all. The crea-tures used to frolic about in the Dark World, but ever since it was locked up, the demons are supposed to be confined to Jeo-seung. There, they torment souls far, far away from the living realm. Hani was prepared to meet one eventually . . . when she was *dead*. Not *alive*.

If an eoduksini is in New Sinsi, then the city is in very big trouble indeed. From what Hani has heard through her years on Iseung, the demons are creatures of death and darkness. They are a parasite, able to worm their way into the minds of others and produce horribly realistic visions—nightmares—that their host cannot escape from. Nightmares based on their host's most horrible fears, most terrible memories.

And once their victim is in their clutches, that is when they feed.

Usually, in Jeoseung, eoduksini feed on souls. The remnants of one's consciousness, one's energy. But it seems that on Iseung, eoduksini feed on life. On pure, undiluted life, on anything liv-ing. They eat humans and non-humans alike, adults, babies, haetae, dokkaebi . . . Nobody is safe from their hunger. Nobody.

Euna died during one of those nightmares.

And then she'd been fed upon.

The markings on her body, the black veins, are proof of what the poor girl endured. Euna's soul had been disoriented due to the way she'd died. Trapped in an alternate realm, a nightmare, with no sense of space and time.

But how in the world is an eoduksini on Iseung?

Hani risks a sidelong glance at Seokga. Sensing her attention, the god scowls. *"What?"* He's been acting shiftier than usual, if such a thing is possible.

"The eoduksini," she says slowly. "What else do you know about it?"

Seokga smiles unpleasantly. "That it would kill you if it got the chance."

Hani glares. "I'm serious," she snaps. "Why is it on Iseung? What does it want? I mean, other than snacking on university students."

The fallen god looks distinctly affronted. "How should I know?" he responds, and Hani's suspicions sharpen.

Hani waits. Seokga mutters something nasty, tips back in his chair, and pinches the bridge of his nose with two elegant fingers. "An Unruly eoduksini," he grinds out, "probably wants what most Unrulies want."

She considers this. Hani is currently a *very* Unruly gumiho (again), but her motives are relatively simple. When she attacked those men, she was following her nature, being what a gumiho was meant to be before she accidentally created a pesky stigma around the concept of gumiho mealtimes. When she gave Somi the livers, Hani was reminiscing about an easier time, when the nine-tailed foxes were free to chomp on livers whenever they liked.

This doesn't sound like it would apply to many other Unrulies, as inadvertently starting a taboo seems to be a singular experience that, so far, only Hani has been unlucky enough to have.

As if sensing her confusion, Seokga exhales thinly and mutters something under his breath.

"What?"

"I *said*," he drawls, "that most Unrulies are still a bit mad about the whole Dark World thing."

Hani snorts. "That's an understatement." Everybody knows about how Seokga single-handedly managed to get an entire plane of existence shut down and its denizens thrown out to Iseung. She never lived in Gamangnara (rumor has it that rent was *high*) but she's known many creatures who would have jumped at the chance to decapitate the god responsible for the locking-up of the Dark World. "You think this eoduksini is part of your fallen army? That it was dragged to Jeoseung when you completely fucked up your coup and now it's escaped?"

Seokga glares. Hani waits.

"All signs point to yes," he finally bites back, not looking too pleased at the thought. "Out of all the monsters, they were the most dangerous and the most capable of destruction. So my brother"—his face twists at the word—"decreed it a necessity to store them in the underworld, where there is high security. Although we can all see how that turned out," Seokga mutters.

"Hmm," muses Hani. "If that's the case, that means it's probably going to come after you. Retribution for the Dark World, and all that."

"Please. Nothing can kill a god."

"It's on a quest for revenge," Hani continues, narrating in a deep, documentary-esque voice. She speaks into her pen like it's a microphone. "It has reached its breaking point—"

"Ironic." Seokga gives her a coldly pointed look. "As I am growing closer to mine by the minute."

"Really." Exasperated, Hani clucks her tongue. "Do gods have no concept of humor?"

"Do gumiho have no concept of the fact that provoking a god is very, very dangerous?"

She sighs and sets down her pen. "I would be careful how you speak to me. One day, I might just poison your coffee."

"You think that you haven't already?" Seokga asks, turning back to his computer and clicking through another round of video footage, narrowing his eyes at the grainy records. "First with too much milk, and then with too much sugar."

"But never with bleach," she reminds him sweetly. "Not yet, anyways."

"It's better if you poison it with bleach," he replies icily, "than if you throw it all over me and wreck my favorite suit." He scowls, giving her a vicious side-eye. *What do you want?*

"I want to know what you're looking for on those tapes," Hani replies steadily. "Isn't the natural form of an eoduksini incorporeal?"

A muscle in Seokga's jaw pulses, as if he's debating whether or not he wishes to continue speaking to his unwanted assistant. Hani arches a brow and waits. *Spit it out,* she silently urges him.

He sneers. "Its natural form, yes. In Jeoseung, eoduksini are nothing but shadow. But the rules of hell are different from the rules of Iseung. However the eoduksini arrived here, I am assuming that it had a very limited amount of time to find itself a host. Without a body of flesh and blood, the eoduksini would not be able to remain in this realm for long."

"So you're saying that it possessed someone," Hani says slowly.

Seokga waves a hand at her in a clear *what else would I be saying* gesture. "Obviously." He drawls the word out, and Hani bristles at his condescending tone.

"And you're trying to find out who?" she pushes.

Another *what else would I be saying* gesture. "But the security cameras trained on Euna's apartment building all mysteriously blacked out last night," he mutters. "Much like the damned moth over the Scarlet Fox footage."

Hani straightens. "There's Scarlet Fox footage?" she asks, forcing her tone to be casual, only slightly interested. Up until now, she's been certain there were no security cameras trained on the actual street that night, but it seems as if she's been sloppy. Out of practice.

"No," Seokga snaps shortly. "The moth that covered the neighboring street's camera is to blame for that." He turns back to his screen, leaving Hani to silently and thoroughly thank whatever moth had decided to take a rest on the lens.

"Do you have any other evidence?" she asks, still doing her best to sound only remotely interested.

"No," he snaps again. "I only know the murder weapons must have been the infamous scarlet daggers."

Ah. Her beloved daggers. Hani has made sure to bury them deep, deep, deep within her underwear drawer. Satisfied, she turns back to the paperwork. "Maybe the Scarlet Fox and the eoduksini are working together," she suggests slowly. It's an outlandish proposition—she would *never* associate herself with such an unnatural demon—but steering Seokga in the wrong direction is one of her top priorities. "She reappears, and then a few days later . . . this."

"I doubt it." Seokga glares at her. "And last I checked, you weren't the detective here. Leave the creatures to me, and I'll leave the paperwork to you."

Hani huffs in annoyance. "You're insufferable," she snaps.

"You're intolerable."

"Likewise," she bites back.

"I'm nothing of the sort."

"I see why Hwanin threw you out of Okhwang," Hani replies in a faux-saccharine tone, abandoning jondaemal with gusto. "I would have done the same, I think."

The effects of her words are immediate. Seokga goes rigid in his seat, twisting toward her with a snarl so ferocious that for a moment, the entire precinct falls silent. His eyes flash with hatred—hatred and *pain.* "Say that again," he hisses, "and I'll hang your pelt in my living room, fox."

Rage heating her blood, Hani cocks her head and curls back

her lips. "Your god complex has gotten old," she sneers. "Seeing as you're not one anymore."

Seokga freezes, and his sudden silence is more chilling than any possible retort.

Hani refuses to balk under his fury.

"You," the god finally says, his breathing shallow as he reaches for his cane. "You. Get out. Get out of my sight."

Asshole. "I work here now." Hani smiles, even as she itches to stomp on his foot. Hard. Very, very hard. "Remember?"

"You are toeing a very dangerous line." Seokga smiles back, but it is an awful smile, a smile of cold, hard promises and death wishes. "A dog should not bark at a wolf."

"A wolf should not threaten a fox."

"Wolves are stronger," Seokga snaps.

"Foxes are cleverer."

"Is that why they're caught in fox traps so often?"

"Wolves," Hani fires back, "are just overgrown dogs."

Seokga opens and closes his mouth before finally spitting out, "Your argument makes no sense."

She smiles sweetly. "Doesn't it, though?"

"Enough! Both of you!" Chief Shim stalks to Seokga's desk, his cheeks stained red with irritation. "The entire precinct is listening to the pair of you fight like children, and I am *sick of it.*"

Hani holds Seokga's glare. She will not be the first to look away. *No,* she decides, *I will not even be the first to blink.* Her eyes water as she holds the green glower, but she grits her teeth and forces her eyes to stay open. *Bastard.*

Seokga's eyes narrow, like he knows what she's thinking.

Chief Shim makes a noise of exasperation. "What are you two doing?"

Hani leans forward, squinting as much as she can without blinking.

"Seokga. I am speaking to you. Look at me." The detective sounds almost like an insulted grandfather. *"Seokga."*

"Look away, fox," Seokga mutters under his breath. "Look away."

"Seokga. There is somebody coming to see you," Chief Shim snaps. "And if you give me your attention, I will tell you who it is. You will want to be prepared."

"You can tell me now," Seokga says, his stare still fixed on Hani. "I am listening."

Hani thinks that she sees one of Seokga's eyes twitch. *Ha. Good.* But wariness prickles her skin as she sees Seokga's gaze glitter with something that looks suspiciously like cruel mischief.

The god leans forward and puffs out a breath of air onto Hani's face.

Startled, she blinks—and then scowls. "You cheated." She's careful to use formal language again, seeing as Chief Shim is glaring daggers at both of them.

"I'm the god of deceit," Seokga replies smoothly, with a cold little smile. "Don't forget it." He turns to Chief Shim as Hani seethes, wishing very much that she hadn't overeaten in 1888. "Tell me, Shim. Who is visiting the precinct?"

"Not the precinct." The chief looks hesitant, almost scared, as he says, "Emperor Hwanin would like to meet with you tonight for dinner."

CHAPTER ELEVEN

SEOKGA

FUCK.

Seokga stares at the restaurant across the street.

Fuck, fuck, fuck, fuck, fuck.

Fuck.

It has been six hundred and twenty-eight years since Seokga has seen his only sibling, who just so happens to be the ruler of Okhwang and the leader of the gods.

Six hundred and twenty-eight years since Seokga tried to overthrow Hwanin and claim the throne for himself with his army of twenty thousand Dark World Unrulies.

He couldn't help it. As he's just told Hani, deceit is in his nature.

Six hundred and twenty-eight years since Seokga was hurled from the kingdom in the heavens, bloodied and battered from the beating he'd taken with Hwanin's final order ringing in his ears as he'd fallen, ripping the sky apart with his screams.

You will only be redeemed in my eyes once you have slaughtered twenty thousand monsters.

Only then will I allow you to return home.

Only then will you again be a god.

His silver tongue did not save him from Hwanin's wrath. If anything, it doubled it as he claimed that he had just been having a bit of fun trying to overtake Okhwang and depose Hwanin. *Just a bit of fun* had been his exact words.

It's likely his brother has come to blame him for this eoduk-sini problem. The darkness demons had once been in his army, their malevolent nature suiting the role of soldier well. This eoduksini must be one of the ones who served underneath him, therefore making this—*technically*—Seokga's fault. The demon probably never would have touched Iseung if the Dark World had remained open. Eoduksini had always been happy in that cesspool of chaos. Much happier than in Jeoseung, where they were stored after the coup and made to work as torturers.

Seokga adjusts the collar of his suit as he eyes the restaurant. It's not fancy—Hwanin, it seems, would hate nothing more than treating Seokga to a fine dinner. So instead his brother has chosen a mundane-looking restaurant wedged between a printing shop and a convenience store, a lopsided sign with flickering lights reading TASTY KITCHENS. The windows are grimy, the walls made of cracking concrete, and Seokga highly doubts that anything inside will be *tasty*.

Taking a deep breath and clenching his cane in his hand, Seokga crosses the street. He has prepared himself as much as he can for this dinner, donning a fine suit of silken black. He even went to his *barber,* a chatty bulgasari whose control over metal allowed him to perfectly trim Seokga's silky black hair back into its usual style: delicate sideburns, a "fluffy" (his barber's word, *not* his own) top with a clean middle part, and a tight taper on the nape of his neck. He looks polished, professional, but hair will do him little good against his elder brother.

Seokga desperately wishes that he could still be strong enough to attempt to murder Hwanin. Now, with his considerable lack of power, he does not stand the slightest chance.

He's grateful there are no *Godly Gossip* paparazzi in sight. He knows this reunion will be bad enough without it being immortalized in photographs and a headline like: BROTHERS BACK

TOGETHER? HOTTIE HWANIN AND SEXY SEOKGA SEEN SPLIT-
TING A MEAL!

Grimacing, Seokga pushes open the door. The restaurant smells of cooking rice and boiling broth. Its lighting is dim, but Seokga can easily make out square wooden tables with rickety chairs, wilted potted plants lining the concrete wall, and a large tank harboring a myriad of lethargic-looking fish that separates one half of the room from the other. Tasty Kitchens is empty save for two women picking at their plates of food near the fish tank and the hostess that sighs wearily upon Seokga's entrance.

"Welcome to Tasty Kitchens," she says. "Please follow me to your seat."

Seokga grinds his teeth as the hostess situates him at a table on the other side of the fish tank. So Hwanin is late, or simply not coming at all. The hostess plops down a greasy laminated menu in front of him. "Your waiter will be with you shortly," she mumbles before trudging away.

Seokga glances down at the menu in disgust. He will not be eating anything from this hovel. His tastes run far too dignified, too sophisticated, to stoop to such a level.

Where is Hwanin? Is this some sort of joke played on him by Chief Shim? Seokga shifts restlessly, crossing and uncrossing his legs, fidgeting with the jacket of his suit. *Ridiculous,* he seethes, glaring down at the empty seat in front of him. *This is ridiculous.*

Of course Hwanin isn't coming. Why would he? His brother has not bothered to contact him in centuries. He is a fool for coming here. Seokga shoves back his chair, the legs screeching on the floor, and begins to stand—

"Sit down."

Seokga freezes. That voice . . .

He watches in disbelief as the air surrounding the empty seat across from him ripples and undulates until Hwanin appears, sitting with his hands folded and eyebrows arched.

He has been there the entire time, Seokga realizes with rising incredulity that is quickly replaced by hatred. *He has been* sitting there *the entire time.*

For the first time in six hundred and twenty-eight years, Seokga stares at his brother.

Hwanin has always been everything that Seokga is not. While Seokga's hair is midnight dark, Hwanin's hair has become so pale a silver that it is almost white, falling to his chest in a sleek, icy curtain of long strands so different from Seokga's short ones. While Seokga's eyes are a deep emerald, Hwanin's are a depthless blue-black, swimming with stars and the secrets of the universe. Such a difference in color marks Hwanin's destiny to rule the blue heavens, while Seokga is destined to forever be lower than his brother—as the green realm of Iseung is to Okhwang. While Seokga is exiled, Hwanin keeps the throne. The only similarity the two brothers share is the color of their skin— a rich golden-beige flecked with the occasional freckle.

Hwanin is dressed like a human, lacking his usual kingly hanboks of silver and blue. Instead, his brother wears a gray knit turtleneck and a pair of black jeans, even going so far as to wear a watch on his wrist. "Hello, brother," Hwanin says quietly, tilting his head to the side and watching Seokga carefully.

Seokga gapes, his mind numb, the sharp blade of betrayal sliding between his ribs. After all this time, it still has not faded—the pain of plummeting through the sky, falling from grace, his brother watching from above with cold eyes. Slowly, Seokga sits back down and fumbles for his silver tongue. "Well," he replies as smoothly as he can through his complete and utter shock, "the last time I saw you, you were busy throwing me out of the sky."

Hwanin frowns. "And the last time that I saw you, you were leading an army of Dark World monsters in an attempt to steal my throne."

"For fuck's sake." Seokga forces his lips to curl upward into a cruel, cold smile. "You speak as if it's not a fond memory."

"I assume it is for you."

"Oh, I keep that particular recollection very close to my heart." Seokga's heart is in fact thundering in his chest, but he manages to drawl his words, leaning back in his seat—the very portrait of a bored god.

Former god, a dry little voice in his head corrects him.

Whatever.

"What brings you to New Sinsi, brother?" Seokga continues, arching a brow. "Don't tell me that you've come to lead me back to Okhwang."

Hwanin opens his mouth to reply—but is interrupted by a morose waiter, who shuffles over to their table with a notepad and mumbles, "What can I get for you today?"

"Away," Seokga snaps, waving a hand at him. "Your services are not needed."

"But . . ." The boy frowns. "This is a restaurant."

"And I do not want to eat your food." Seokga waves again in impatience. "Goodbye."

Hwanin slants a glare at Seokga. "I'll take a bowl of galbi-tang," he says in a gentle tone to the reddened boy. "Some soju, too. The same for him."

"Yes, sir," the boy mutters before scuttling away. Hwanin's glare returns to Seokga.

"I see that your temperament remains the same."

Seokga rolls his eyes. "Oh, please, brother. Have you expected me to magically change my entire nature? You're a fool if so."

"Perhaps it was wishful thinking." Hwanin inclines his head. "You resemble Father in more ways than mere appearance, Seokga."

He stiffens.

Hwanin and Seokga's father, Mireuk, ruled Okhwang before

Hwanin came into power. Mireuk created the kingdom in the sky, after all, along with the underwater realm of Yongwangguk, the underworld realm of Jeoseung, the wily realm of Gamang-nara, and the mortal plane of Iseung—sharing rule with Seokga and Hwanin's mother, Mago. But that was all before the god of creation went mad and unleashed torrents of suffering upon the worlds. He created plagues and with them the disease gods, including Manura, the smallpox goddess with a tendency to target children. Starvation, poverty, depression, droughts, floods. Mireuk dreamed all of it up in his delirium.

Seokga and Hwanin deposed the old god as neatly as they could, imprisoning him deep within Yeomra's realm, where he rots to this day. As bad as Seokga is, as evil and as wicked . . . he is nothing like their father.

Nothing.

"Do not," Seokga says, barely able to breathe around his fury, "compare me to Father."

"I will do as I please. And you're certainly not like our slumbering mother, Mago, delicate and kind." Hwanin shrugs. "I'm glad she sleeps underneath the mountains of this realm, if only to spare her from your misdeeds."

Seokga bites the inside of his cheek.

Yes, Mago would certainly be angry with her youngest son should she wake from her nap and find that he tried to overthrow her eldest son from the throne. *Of course you've engaged in more testosterone-fueled battle. I'm not even surprised,* she'd snip, and then most likely would cuff him on the ear.

Hwanin smiles blandly. "Just out of curiosity, Seokga, how much of a dent have you made in your assignment?"

"My *assignment?*" Seokga repeats incredulously. "My *punishment,* you mean. And I'm doing fine enough," he snaps, "thank you very much."

Hwanin doesn't so much as blink at the acid dripping from Seokga's tone. "Have you reached twenty thousand?"

"What," Seokga grits out, "do you *think?*" He would not be sitting in this grimy restaurant if he had.

"Ah." Hwanin settles back in his chair, his expression unreadable.

"Answer my former question. What brings you to New Sinsi?"

"I come on behalf of Yeomra."

"Yeomra?" Seokga blinks. The god of the dead cannot leave Jeoseung, but if he has sent Hwanin . . . *Ah.* "You mean because of the eoduksini."

His brother inclines his head in a slight nod. "One of the demons escaped his realm a night ago."

Seokga tries not to look too guilty.

Hwanin's (also silver) brows slant somewhat downward. "Why are you making that face? You look ill."

Seokga is spared a response as the waiter returns and slides the bowls of beef stew before the two gods, along with two small glasses and two bottles of soju. Seokga doesn't touch the food, even as Hwanin takes a bite.

"Never mind," his brother amends as he swallows and dabs his lips with a napkin. "I don't want to know what general unpleasantness is going on in your head." Hwanin sets down the cloth. "I understand that you've been attempting to hunt the eoduksini down."

"That's correct, yes," Seokga says warily.

"And have you gotten very far?"

"The eoduksini has taken a physical body," Seokga replies. "I am trying to uncover who it has possessed. There is a considerable lack of evidence."

"I see." Hwanin pours some soju into a glass. The clear alcoholic beverage burbles as it streams from the bottle. As he sets it back down, he meets Seokga's gaze evenly. "I come here, Seokga, to offer you a bargain."

Time seems to still. "A bargain?"

Hwanin sips casually at his drink. "Yes, brother. A bargain."

Seokga swallows, suddenly feeling incredibly light-headed. "I am listening," he says, careful to control his voice and hide any sign of eagerness that might slip through. Yet Hwanin doesn't look fooled, and seems as if he's hiding a bitter smile.

"The eoduksini cannot remain in New Sinsi," Hwanin says, setting down his glass. "It is hungry for life, and this place teems with it. We imprisoned this breed of demon far away from here for a reason. The victims will begin to pile up soon enough. The eoduksini will not stop until it has eaten its way through the entire city. I expect that there will be at least one more murder tonight."

Seokga waits.

"I do not know if you are aware, brother, but it is very easy for an eoduksini to kill a god. Permanently." Hwanin meets his gaze. "They feed on life, and we brim with it. We would satisfy a large portion of their appetites. And I assume that it will want to punish you for the part you played in Gamangnara's shutdown. You are, I think, in some danger."

It is very easy for an eoduksini to kill a god.

Permanently.

Impossible.

Gods can be severely hurt, yes, but they cannot be *killed*. Not for good, at any rate. Although their bodies can grow old, or occasionally even succumb to grievous injury, members of the pantheon do not suffer as others do. Instead, they simply undergo godly reincarnation and continue to exist in the realms above the underworld, perfectly fine (all things considered). Their injured or elderly bodies will disintegrate, to be promptly replaced by a younger, healthier body in which the same soul—with the same memories and same divine powers—nests. This is no normal reincarnation; this is deity reincarnation. For gods cannot die, not really. To claim that an eoduksini can truly murder a deity—to dispatch them into Jeoseung, *forever*—is blasphemous.

"No," Seokga cuts back, mouth dry. For if what Hwanin has said is true, then that means . . .

Hwanin studies him closely. "The eoduksini were in your army, brother. You mean to say that you didn't know what they could do? To me? To the pantheon? Even to you?"

The trickster god's lips tighten and he stares, fixedly, at his bowl of galbi-tang. It does not look particularly appealing in the least, with bits of grayish fat floating at the top along with limp scallions, but he takes a hesitant spoonful anyway—if only to have an excuse to delay his response.

It is disgusting.

He swallows with difficulty.

"Seokga." His brother is studying him suspiciously.

With a tight jaw, Seokga sets down his spoon and chooses his response carefully. "I didn't know the demons could *kill* you," he snaps. "I thought they would just . . . hurt you to the point of incapacitation."

Hwanin seems to have come to some sort of conclusion. His face softens for a brief moment as he ceases his antagonizing scrutiny and sips his soju. A flare of intense agitation shoves words to Seokga's mouth.

"Mind you," the trickster bites out, voice as sharp as a blade lest Hwanin should get the wrong sort of idea, "I wouldn't have been beside myself with grief if it murdered you."

"Of course not." His insufferable sibling seems to be trying, very hard, to hide a smirk.

"I would have been pleased." Seokga frowns. "But that's as-suming that you're even right. The eoduksini is a lesser creature in comparison to the gods—"

"You'll find, brother, that those whom you deem 'lesser' possess a hunger to become greater. A hunger that killing a god can sate." Hwanin stirs his galbi-tang as Seokga glowers. "Yeomra, unfortunately, has had the short stick for many years. Living with constant threats under his roof, fearing what will happen if his security measures were breached. I do not envy him."

"What are you trying to say?"

"I'm saying that the New Sinsi eoduksini is not a problem that I particularly want to deal with myself," Hwanin replies, calmly sipping his soup. "Nor does the rest of the pantheon. And now that I've told you this piece of information, I doubt that you do, either. But I'm afraid you have no choice."

"I'm no coward." But it's true. Seokga does not want to die. Perhaps if he relocates to Seoul . . . *Hmm.*

"The eoduksini will gorge itself on every Iseung country if it is not stopped," Hwanin retorts, evidently understanding Seokga's train of thought. "It is in their nature to destroy, and destroy, and destroy. Eoduksini are gluttonous. It's what makes them such capable torturers in hell. Tell me, Seokga, have you given any thought to the demon's motive?"

"It just escaped Jeoseung. It's hungry," Seokga mutters. "And it wants to be a pain in my ass."

"Yes, but there's more. Gamangnara is locked. It's inaccessible." Hwanin's eyes darken. "But Gamangnara wasn't always a Dark World. Before you or I were born, it was a realm much like Iseung. But then Father created the eoduksini and gave to them Gamangnara. They turned it into what we know it as: a place of darkness and destruction. If the eoduksini cannot go back to Gamangnara, brother, it will re-create it. The more victims it takes, the stronger it grows. Once it's capable, it will not hesitate to create another Dark World here."

Sweat slides down Seokga's temples. Why is it, he thinks, that his actions always have to have such big fucking consequences? "So reopen Gamangnara."

Hwanin scoffs. "You know that's impossible. Once the pantheon locks a realm, it's final."

"You have to *try*," he presses, hating that he is practically begging this of Hwanin. "If you manage to unlock Gamangnara, Iseung is saved. The eoduksini can go there, and the Unrulies, too. Everybody is happy." Except him. Seokga hasn't been happy since he discovered coffee for the first time, and even that was a fleeting burst of joy. Happiness just doesn't seem to be in the cards for him anymore.

"I wouldn't have come here," Hwanin replies quietly, "if we hadn't already tried. Besides, Seokga, we locked that realm for a reason." The heavenly emperor fixes the trickster with a look that's almost wry. "Even if we could, I'm not sure that unlocking Gamangnara would be the best idea."

Seokga groans as Hwanin continues. "There is no choice for South Korea but to rid itself of the eoduksini. To send it back to Yeomra's realm."

"And you want *me* to do that." Seokga sneers. "It's very typical of you, Hwanin."

"I am willing to offer you something in exchange."

He arches a brow, trying to hide his sudden flare of interest. "What?"

Hwanin hesitates before leaning forward, the stars burning brighter in his eyes. "I have heard things while in Okhwang," he says in a low voice. "I have heard of the eoduksini; I have also heard of the Scarlet Fox's return. It was she who terrorized Goryeo all those years ago, no? I distinctly remember receiving a suspiciously large number of prayers relating to the need for protection from a certain gumiho."

"Goryeo," Seokga agrees, "and Joseon. Among others." All of Korea once lived in fear of the voracious gumiho.

"Ah. Two monsters prowl the streets of Iseung, terrorizing those I wish to protect. So. Let me offer you this, brother."

Seokga holds his breath, rigid and pale in his seat as he waits for the bargain.

"Kill the Scarlet Fox. Kill the eoduksini. And in return, Seokga, I will lessen your sentence on Iseung."

"What," Seokga breathes hoarsely, "do you mean, exactly, by 'lessen'?"

"I mean that . . ." Hwanin offers a tight smile. "I mean that you will be reinstated to your former position. Effective immediately."

Reinstated to your former position.

Seokga hides his trembling hands underneath the table.

Effective immediately.

Hwanin watches him carefully, those tapered eyes not missing a single movement. "Of course, there will be restrictions. You'll be on house arrest in your old palace for a decade or two, and required to attend mandatory counseling to ensure that you don't . . . ah . . . *snap* again."

His old palace. The sprawling dark palace of ebony and glossy black roof tiles, stretching out across the cloud-covered hills of Okhwang. The bamboo gardens, the bubbling koi pond, the halls of polished stone and looming ceilings. Seokga's breath catches in his throat. Home. For the first time in centuries upon centuries upon centuries, he has the chance to go *home.* To leave these sniveling mortals to their own devices, to once again drink fine wines underneath the star-dappled skies, to once again be Seokga the God. Seokga the Powerful. Seokga the . . . Seokga. He will be Seokga again.

He swallows, his mouth dry, his tongue heavy. A hot sweat trickles down the nape of his neck as his heart pounds frantically against his rib cage. "How do I know," he manages to whisper, "that this isn't some cruel joke, brother?"

Too good to be true. Too good to be true.

"Because," Hwanin replies quietly, "I am willing to swear it on Hwanung."

Seokga lurches back as if he's been struck. To make a vow on the god of law is to make an *unbreakable* vow. When one makes a vow on Hwanung, the son of Hwanin will forever hold the promising parties accountable to their oaths. "On Hwanung," he repeats hoarsely. "You will swear it on Hwanung."

Hwanin inclines his head. "Yes."

Seokga's head is spinning. *Reinstated to your former position. Effective immediately. Reinstated to your former position. Effective . . .* "It's a deal," he rasps. "I agree. I agree to the terms." Find and kill the Scarlet Fox. Find and kill the eoduksini.

Become a full-strength god again.

His brother, Emperor of Okhwang, extends a slender hand.

Seokga hesitates. The last time he touched his brother, he was trying to hurt him very, *very* badly.

Hwanin waits, his expression patient. Serene. If there is any hint of a grudge still held, Seokga does not see it. His older brother has always been more mature than him.

Seokga extends a violently shaking hand. Hwanin clearly pretends not to notice the tremors wracking Seokga's fingers as he clasps his hand in his own.

For a moment, it's almost as if they're children again. Before the jealousy. Before the favoritism, the endless competitions. For a moment, the two brothers are shaking on a bet, helping the other off the ground, passing hidden notes from palm to palm. Hwanin's hand feels the same, even after all these centuries: calloused despite its smooth appearance. Warm. Firm. Steady. Like Mago's.

But then Hwanin's hand heats to a searing degree, and Seokga fights back a flinch.

"I swear on my son, Hwanung, god of laws and kept promises, that should you—Seokga the Fallen, Seokga the Silver-Tongued—kill both the eoduksini and the Scarlet Fox, you shall be reinstated to your former positions as god of mischief, god of deceit, god of chaos, and god of treachery, et cetera, et cetera." The heat of his hand cuts into Seokga's own, as hot as a crackling wildfire. "This is my bargain, my oath to you. May Hwanung hold me accountable."

Seokga hisses between his teeth as smoke steams from their interlocked hands. Hwanin finally withdraws, and as the burning sensation disappears, Seokga looks down at his right palm. There is a small crater of burnt skin in the center, a mark of the promise made. It fades quickly, for visible markings of a promise never linger long. It is on the individual to keep to the oath without blatant reminder, but the memory of it still burns into his skin, binding him to the oath.

Hwanin's stare bores into him. "You have until the Spring Solstice. If you fail to stop the eoduksini by then, the rest of our pantheon will have no choice but to intervene. And if we have to intervene, we won't be very happy with you."

The Spring Solstice. Chunbun. March 20.

Seokga has sixteen days.

He looks to his brother, but Hwanin is already flickering around the edges, preparing to teleport back to Okhwang. "Wait." The word flies out of his mouth before he can stop it. Hwanin lifts a brow, and Seokga can't stop the question that rips through his lips, a suspicious demand. "Why tell me of the risk hunting an eoduksini brings? I was already working on the case, unaware of the danger." *Why warn me? Why not let me die?*

Hwanin's answering stare is almost sad. Seokga does not quite know what to make of it. "Maybe," he replies, his form now barely visible, "because I do not want you to die, little brother."

Seokga gapes.

A moment later, Hwanin disappears into nothingness, returning to his kingdom in the sky.

CHAPTER TWELVE

HANI

WELL. *THIS* IS CERTAINLY AN INTERESTING TURN OF events.

"Kill the Scarlet Fox," Hwanin is saying. "Kill the eoduksini. And in return, Seokga, I will lessen your sentence on Iseung."

Inside Tasty Kitchens, Hani clenches her chopsticks tightly enough that one of them breaks with a soft *snap*. Across from her, picking at her plate of questionable-looking fish, Somi's bloodshot eyes widen. The young gumiho looks as if she doesn't quite know if she should be fangirling over Hwanin's appearance, or if she should be fleeing in utter terror. The end result is that Somi appears extremely constipated.

After committing the time and location of Seokga's reunion with the god-king to her memory, Hani promptly took it upon herself to accompany the fallen god to his meeting without his knowledge. She dragged Somi with her, as well, and the two gumiho slunk into the decrepit restaurant thirty minutes before Seokga was due to arrive, determined to know the cause of the family reunion. Hani donned a rather clever disguise before entering—a cheap blond wig from a costume shop, along with a pair of thick black spectacles. Seokga did not notice her upon his entry, and he does not notice her now as she stares at him through the fish tank, her eyes bulging out of their sockets in pure *annoyance*.

Kill the Scarlet Fox. As if. Hani sneers as she waits for Seokga's reply.

"What," he breathes hoarsely, "do you mean, exactly, by 'lessen'?" The god sounds as if he's about to keel over right then and there.

"Hani," Somi whispers across the table. The poor thing looks as if she's on the verge of losing it completely. The circles underneath her eyes are even more pronounced, and her skin is noticeably clammy. Hani can smell the horror on her. "Unnie, we need to—to leave the city. This is insane." She grabs Hani's hand, forcing her attention away from the two gods. Her fingers are sticky with cold sweat. "We're going to be *killed.* This world is going to be turned into a Dark World. And they think that you're the Scarlet Fox. Oh, gods. Oh, *gods.* We need to *run.*"

"*Shh,*" Hani hisses. "Quiet. We need to listen."

". . . You'll be on house arrest in your old palace for a decade or two, and required to attend mandatory counseling to ensure that you don't . . . ah . . . *snap* again," she hears Hwanin explain. She sneaks a glance at Seokga, who is completely shell-shocked, his face drained of all color. Foolish god to think that he can kill the Scarlet Fox. Oh, Hani will have a very, very fun time leading him on a wild-goose chase . . .

She watches in a mixture of amusement and annoyance as the two gods join hands, the deal sealed by Hwanin's words of promise. The plot, it seems, has thickened considerably.

Seokga will kill the eoduksini—she'll see to that. A creature of darkness has no place in New Sinsi. Hani loves this world, this mortal realm, where things as wondrous as cherry tarts and hot chocolate exist. She loves the roasted sweet potatoes that students sell on the streets during autumn and winter, loves the feeling of driving down a highway with music blasting through the speakers, and truly doesn't think she can live without those delicious American romance books with gorgeous, half-naked men on the covers. While Iseung certainly has its problems (and there are many problems, most of which are the same problems from hundreds of years ago that were never resolved because humans simply refuse to learn from history), it's her home. And Hani is not against fighting for it, nor is she against helping avenge Euna's death.

But Seokga will never be a god again.

Because he will never kill the Scarlet Fox.

Hani smiles as Hwanin disappears and Seokga slumps in his seat, covered in a sheen of sweat, his eyes wild, his chest rising and falling unevenly.

Foolish, foolish god.

"WE COULD GO TO SEOUL," SOMI PANTS AS SHE FLIES around her apartment in a flurry of fear, grabbing clothes from her closet and stuffing them into her suitcase. "Or—or Tokyo. I speak a little Japanese, not lots but—"

Hani sighs from where she leans against the doorway of Somi's room. The bedroom, usually pristine and tidy, looks as if a tornado swooped through. Blankets slump off the bed, well-worn *Godly Gossip* issues riddle the floor, and cosmetics wobble precariously on the dresser as Somi runs back and forth between closet and suitcase. Her bedroom walls have been stripped bare of posters of the pantheon. Hani realizes that Seokga's poster (which was a blown-up photo of the scowling god walking down a New Sinsi street, probably taken by a suicidal paparazzo) has been torn up into shreds and stuffed into the trash can near her bed.

"—or England! England would work, you speak English, don't you, Hani? I remember you told me—you lived in England for a little while—" Somi pants as she tries to zip up her bulging suitcase. "Hani?" When the older gumiho doesn't respond, Somi turns to her with wide, beseeching eyes. "Unnie?"

"We're not going anywhere," Hani says simply and watches as Somi pulls at her own hair.

"Are you crazy? There's an eoduksini running around, and it wants to turn this world into a Dark World! Plus, Seokga thinks you're the Scarlet Fox—he's going to try and *kill you*—here I was, thinking that going to jail was the worst they could do . . ."

"If we run, we look suspicious. From what I've heard in the precinct, Seokga is monitoring what gumiho have entered and left the city. The best thing we can do is stay here, and the best thing that you can do, Somi, is to trust me. Okay?" She nudges a stray sock away with her foot. "Trust me. Seokga isn't going to get me, or you, in any trouble. And I'm going to help stop the darkness demon, too."

Somi is still breathing heavily. "I—"

"Somi, calm *down*," Hani presses. "You're practically walking around and *screaming* that you ate their livers. It's going to get us into trouble."

Her face screws up like she's about to cry. Hani braces herself for the incoming waterworks. "I'm j-just so *scared*," Somi wails. "What if Seokga comes for me? I mean, I always hoped he would, but *not in that way!*" Her wails grow louder.

Hani is beginning to develop a migraine. "He won't," she says firmly. "I said I'm taking care of it, and I mean it."

"But what if he *does*?"

"Then you defend yourself."

"W-with these?" Somi draws her claws and stares at them in derision. "They're so—so small—"

"No. Not with those." Hani crosses the room and sits down on Somi's bed, tucking her legs underneath her. She's sitting on a *Godly Gossip* issue, and her butt is squashing Yongwang's printed face as he grins at the camera while lounging on a Jeju beach, but she couldn't give any damns about that. Somi wavers, furiously scrubbing away her tears with the back of her hand. "You're a gumiho, Somi. And what do gumiho do? What is in our *nature* to do?"

Somi shakes her head, tears spilling from her eyes.

"If you need a better defense than your claws, siphon power from your fox bead, or steal their soul."

"Steal their—no. *No*." She's still pulling at her hair. *"No, no, no."*

"It wasn't always taboo to steal a soul," Hani replies quietly, patting the mattress. Somi sits down shakily and stares at her, with her lower lip quivering violently. "Or to eat a man's liver. It was the most normal thing in the world, darling." Until she went a bit too far, and the world overreacted.

The younger gumiho sniffles. "Really?"

"Really. Back then . . ." Hani closes her eyes, remembering the thrill of the hunt, the slap of her feet against the cobblestoned roads of Joseon and London, the taste of souls and blood. "It was different."

"How?" Somi whispers. She's beginning to calm down now, although she's twisting her cream sweater tightly in her hands. "How did you . . . What was it like?"

"It was the best feeling in the world," Hani replies, and Somi falls into hushed silence, her red-rimmed eyes widening to discs.

"Really?" Somi sounds curious, despite herself.

Hani smiles. "The greatest part of it all is the seduction."

"The seduction?" Somi whispers.

Hani nods. "You steal a man's soul through a kiss. And you can't steal a soul if you force yourself onto him, so . . ." She winks. "Seduction. You find a target, and you pull him closer. It'll come naturally to you—it does to all gumiho. And when you've lured him into your trap, you summon your fox bead to your mouth. Here—you can try it now." Hani closes her eyes, letting herself reach for that orb of power that rests in her heart, hot and burning, rippling with one thousand and seven hundred years of accumulated power. "Find your fox bead," she murmurs, aware that Somi has fallen completely silent, undoubtedly following her lead. "And let it rise up from your heart, into your throat, and then . . . into your mouth."

Hani smiles as she tastes her bead—crushed sugar and syruped cherries, rich chocolate and spiced cinnamon, clover honey and sweet vanilla. Her tongue heats as the pearl rolls atop it, the size of a large marble. Her voice is slightly muffled as she says around the bead, "When you kiss your target, you'll let your bead roll into their mouth. It'll collect their soul and return to your heart." Opening her eyes, Hani lets her bead retreat back into her chest. "And that's how it's done."

Somi swallows her bead—which is undoubtedly little more than the size of a tiny pebble. There is a spark in her eyes that had not been there before, all terror and guilt gone, replaced by . . . awe? Amusement? Hani cannot tell, but she feels a rush of warm satisfaction all the same. "It's as easy as that."

"What if they swallow my bead?" Somi inquires breathlessly. "What would happen?"

"Ah." Hani winces. A mortal man once almost swallowed her bead, nearly giving her a heart attack. "If a man swallows your bead, he'll absorb its power, which will convert itself from energy to knowledge. He'll possess knowledge of the heavens, and your fox bead will be gone. You'll die. So you need to be quick about it, and make sure that your bead returns to you."

"I see." Somi hesitates. "And do . . . Do the souls taste good?" She leans forward, her voice hushed. "As good as . . . the livers?" There's something behind her eyes that pokes at Hani in a way that she doesn't entirely enjoy. She quickly shoves aside her concern. Perhaps she is a bad influence, but it is her belief that gumiho shouldn't deprive themselves of a good male snack every once in a while.

She winks. "Better."

CHAPTER THIRTEEN

HANI

"HERE YOU GO," HANI CROONS THE NEXT MORNING, setting a cup of very sweet iced coffee from a nearby Coffee Star on Seokga's desk. "Bon appétit, mon ami."

Seokga glares up at her, looking away from his computer screen. "You're back," he mutters, looking exceptionally *not* pleased.

"You could at least try to act a *little* nicer," she huffs in irritation.

"Why would I do that?" With a sneer, Seokga rises to his feet. "I'll be gone for the rest of the day. I'm giving you it off. You're welcome."

"What? No." Hani scowls and folds her arms. He's not going anywhere without her. "Wherever you're going, I'm coming with you. Do you have a lead on the Scarlet Fox? On the eoduksini?"

Seokga says nothing, pushing past her and striding to the precinct's exit. Hani is hot on his heels as she spits, "You could at least admit that you need my help. You only have fifteen more days to catch them both, you know—"

Seokga slams to a halt right before the door and whirls around. "My bargain," he snaps. "How in *Jeoseung* do you know about my bargain with Hwanin?"

Caught, Hani fumbles for an excuse. "Chief Shim told me."

The god's eyes narrow. "Chief Shim told you?" he repeats

slowly, and Hani blinks. Did Seokga not tell Chief Shim about his bargain? Has she miscalculated?

There's no time to try to figure it out. Hani needs to stick by her lie as resolutely as possible.

"That's what I said," she replies as smoothly as she is able to manage. "He said he got a message from Hwanin detailing your plan regarding the eoduksini and the Scarlet Fox. Oh, and the little tidbit about Iseung potentially becoming a Dark World. See, I'm your assistant," she adds, straightening indignantly, "so I have a right to know these things. And even though you will never admit it," she says firmly, stepping forward so there is only a foot of space in between them, "you *need* my help." To emphasize the word *need,* Hani pokes Seokga in the chest. The god scowls in outrage, but Hani pushes onward. "You only have fifteen days to catch two notorious creatures. That's only a day over two weeks. And if you insist on working alone, you'll *never* be reinstated as a god. So wherever it is that you're going, I am going with you."

Seokga's jaw works as he eyes her in a way that makes her suspect he is deeply considering the ramifications of murdering her on the spot. "Well," he snaps, "that's the last time I tell Shim anything about my personal life. It seems like he's a gossip."

"I don't think that the possibility of a demon devouring the mortal world counts as an element of your *personal life,*" Hani points out. "Besides, Chunbun is fast approaching. You need my help." She crosses her arms. "So," she says when he is broodingly silent, "where are we going?"

"*I'm* going," he grinds out slowly, "to speak to Chang Hyuntae. The jeoseung saja. Another body was uncovered a few minutes ago. I need to examine it and speak with the soul. I need evidence."

"I'm coming with you." Seokga opens his mouth, but she cuts him off. "Don't even try to stop me. Was it another gumiho?"

"No. A haetae." Scowling, Seokga exits the precinct, pushing open the grimy glass door, Hani close on his heels. "He died the night before, like the gumiho, but his body wasn't found until now. He was in an alleyway."

The early morning air does little to dissuade Hani's rising nausea. "And he's the only other victim?"

"That we know of," Seokga says grimly, striding to his car. "Backseat," he demands out of the corner of his mouth as Hani makes her way to the passenger seat. She ignores him.

"And does the body have the veins? Like Euna's?"

"I'm assuming so." Seokga sends her a withering look as he starts the engine. "Hyun-tae is already at the location with the soul. It'll be like last time. A questioning before the investigation."

"What will the haetae be able to tell you that Euna couldn't? If the eoduksini really did kill him, isn't it likely that he only remembers what Euna remembers? His soul is probably disoriented, too."

"Euna remembered the rest eventually." Seokga is driving fast, weaving in and out of traffic with lightning speed, a stream of outraged honking blaring in his wake. "And it can't hurt to try."

"Hmm." Hani settles back in her seat, frowning. It's true that Euna did remember the rest—but had been moved to screams. "And what do you plan to do about the Scarlet Fox?"

"I've been waiting for her next move, but none's come." Seokga runs a red with a notable lack of concern. "We're going to instead gather a list of all gumiho registered to live in New Sinsi. Specifically, the gumiho that have residences near the place of attack or are registered as workers in the area. I also want CCTV footage pulled from nearby shops and streets to look for entrances and exits around the time of the murder."

Damned CCTV. Although she knows Bomnal Street, where

the murder occurred, has no camera, there is likely one in the Yum Mart—the supermarket that Hani and Somi exited before parting ways. Hani is confident that she should leave her and Somi's names on the list, as leaving them out might actually increase suspicion, but the video footage is another matter entirely. It'll show Hani walking over to Bomnal Street. It needs to be dealt with. "That sounds tedious," Hani mutters.

"Which is why you'll be doing it, fox." Seokga smirks. "I also want the names of all the gumiho within the city past a certain age compiled in a separate list. The Scarlet Fox is rumored to have been in her human form for more than five hundred years. So I want the names of all gumiho over the age of one thousand five hundred by tomorrow morning. See that it gets done."

Hani sneers. "Fine." She'll be able to leave her and Somi's names off that list, at least. "And then what?"

"And then I find the Scarlet Fox and kill her."

"That's hardly a plan."

Seokga slants her a withering glare.

She winks.

"By the way, Hani, how old are *you*, again?" Seokga's smile is a wolf's smile, all cold predation. But Hani isn't fazed.

"One thousand four hundred fifty-two," she replies evenly. "But I do dearly wish that I was the Scarlet Fox. If only to torment you."

"I wish you were the Scarlet Fox, as well," Seokga retorts with a razor-sharp smirk, "if only to kill you."

Hani props her feet up on the dash. "Oh, come *on*—"

Seokga makes an abrupt turn into the parking lot of a café and slams the brakes. Hani yelps as she bangs her head against her knees. Forehead smarting, she glowers up at Seokga, but he's already exiting the car. Muttering an abundance of curses under her breath, Hani follows.

The hearse from the day prior is parked a few spaces away.

Hyun-tae leans against the car, looking weary as he sips at a cup of coffee with the label reading CREATURE CAFÉ. He straightens as Seokga and Hani approach. "Good morning," he says promptly. "I've collected the soul. You're able to have four minutes with him exactly before I must take him to Jeoseung. The body can be found over there." He points to the crack of an alleyway in between the café and the neighboring bookstore. Hani can just make out trash cans, and a crumpled heap on the cement . . . a heap far too large, and too bulky, to be human. Hyun-tae follows her gaze. "He was in his beast form when he died," he explains. "I'm the one who found the body. You'll need to move it quickly, before the humans spot it."

Seokga looks grim. "Hani," he says, "go inspect the body and make sure that no humans approach it. I'll speak to the soul inside the hearse."

Hani frowns. "I want to talk—"

Seokga turns his icy gaze onto her. "I said *go*."

Fine. Sending him a vulgar gesture, Hani stomps off to the alleyway, ignoring Seokga's insulted hiss behind her. Her eyes widen as she steps into the shadowed alleyway, her gaze falling upon the prone body of the guardian creature. The enormous, horned beast is limp upon the cracked cement, the brilliant golden eyes forever shut. Bulging black veins wind along the haetae's entire body, snaking through the golden scales and wrapping around the once-strong limbs. Hani swallows hard as she traces the haetae's mouth with her gaze—the muzzle is pulled back, revealing sharp white canines the size of her hand, and a tongue that is limp as it hangs out of the haetae's maw. Silently, Hani kneels on the cold, hard ground next to the dead creature. It is not right that he died like this—an inhumane death in both nature and form.

It is not right at all.

There is no question that the haetae suffered. No question

that the eoduksini drained the life out of him, leaving only its darkness behind. No question that the haetae was dragged through nightmare after nightmare while lying in this alleyway, dying.

Tears prick at Hani's eyes and she reaches out a hand to stroke the beast's cold, golden scales. "I'm sorry," she murmurs. "May you find peace."

Footsteps behind her alert her to Seokga's presence, and she hears the rumble of the hearse as Hyun-tae takes the haetae's soul. But she doesn't move, even as Seokga stands behind her, silent and watchful.

Like Euna, this haetae died alone.

Alone and scared.

"I spoke to him," Seokga says stiltedly after a long moment, leaning on his cane. "The haetae."

"What did he say?" Hani asks, her eyes tracing the slight pinch between the haetae's brow, the way one giant paw stretches out as if in protest, or seeking some nonexistent savior.

"The same as the last one. Nightmares leading up to his death. Feeling cold. Tired. But . . ." Seokga hesitates, as if wrestling with himself about whether or not he would like to share the next piece of information with Hani. With much difficulty, she tears her gaze away from the haetae and shoots him a demanding glare.

"What did he say?"

Seokga's mouth tightens. "He'd been cleaning up the café, and went into this alleyway to throw out the trash. From what I was able to glean before he began screaming, he was exhausted and laid down on the ground. The rest is identical to Euna's story." Seokga wrinkles his nose in clear disdain. "But what's different, this time, is that there was a witness."

A *witness.* Hani jumps to her feet. "Really?" Even to her own ears, her voice is desperate, hopeful, and skeptical all at once. "Who is it?"

Seokga inclines his head. "The haetae wasn't working the night shift alone," he says as he gestures to the brick wall on their right, the wall of the café. "There was a girl working with him as well. Specifically, a human girl by the name of Choi Ji-ah. The haetae claims that the girl was supposed to follow him out with the recycling, but she never came—at least not to his knowledge. My guess is that whatever attacked the haetae made it into the alleyway before Ji-ah. When Ji-ah finally emerged, she saw the eoduksini in the act of feeding and fled. I've contacted Chief Shim. He has officers scouring the city for her. It's possible—no, probable—that she is our witness."

"And they can find her?"

"She may have left the city entirely. I don't know." Seokga shakes his head. "But as far as I know, she's still alive. Alive, and with answers."

"Unless the eoduksini is looking for her, too," Hani says slowly, something awful occurring to her, seeping across her mind with a terrible sort of coldness. "How easily can an eoduksini change forms on Iseung?"

"Not easily. It must have been difficult to obtain a human form in the first place." Seokga frowns. "What are you suspecting?"

"If the eoduksini knows that Ji-ah is a witness, then it could be tracking her, as well. To silence her, because she alone knows what it looks like." Hani chews on her bottom lip, panic and concern quickening her heart. "We need to be the ones to find her first."

The fallen god's jade eyes are hard. "We'll find her." He gestures to the haetae's body. "We need to bring him to Dok-hyun. To confirm how he died."

"I think it's pretty obvious how he died."

Seokga sneers. "Yes, well, if you would like to avoid another mound of paperwork, fox, we need to have an autopsy done." He pulls out his cellphone, an expensive Nokia 121 that *he* probably didn't have to steal, and punches in a few numbers. The phone starts to ring. "I'll have a group of haetae collect the corpse while we head back to the precinct. When we get there, run up the names of all gumiho over the age of one thousand five hundred. You can meet me in the precinct morgue in around an hour. Or not," he adds pointedly. "Feel free to leave the investigation entirely."

Hani sticks out her tongue. "No," she says as cheerfully as she can manage with the haetae's corpse lying only a few feet away, "I think I'll stay."

He rolls his eyes. "Get the names to me within an hour," he snaps before the other end of the line crackles.

"Within an hour?" Hani watches in disbelief as Seokga presses the phone to his ear, his eyes lingering on the corpse. "It will take me longer than that to pull all of that information—"

"Then tomorrow morning, at the *latest*. I need a stretcher and transport," he says grimly into the phone. "And get here before *Godly Gossip*."

LEE AH-IN. AGE ONE THOUSAND, SIX HUNDRED AND ONE.

Hani stares at Ah-in's name, printed on the white piece of paper, and raises a brow. "Who knows?" she muses. "*You* could be the Scarlet Fox." Sighing, she taps the precinct's printer impatiently as it takes its sweet, sweet time spitting out the names, addresses, and contact information for New Sinsi's gumiho. It's taken her nearly an hour of clicking through the city's residential database, muttering foul curses as the internet does its very best to slug through her requests. Eventually, though, she'd been able to find a collection of gumiho who all fit Seokga's criteria—forty in total. As the tenth and final piece of paper prints out, Hani snatches it from the printer's mouth, grabs a nearby stapler, and stomps over to the precinct's computer lab.

The haetae in charge of pulling the CCTV footage looks up from his desk as she arrives. "Here," he says, standing up from the computer as Hani enters, then holding out a cardboard box of VHS tapes. There must be around ten. "All tapes from around the area and time of attack. It took me a while to get all of them—had to drive around town to collect these bad boys, so I didn't get a chance to look through any. But I understand that Detective Seokga assigned the task to you." He gives her a cheeky smile that suggests he doesn't envy her. "The VCR in the conference room can play these, or you can choose a computer here if you want me to digitalize them for you. Might take some time, but I can get it done for Detective Seokga. Names of each establishment, and what street they're located on, are taped on the sides of each VHS. You can throw out what you don't need and keep what you do. Got it?"

"Thanks," Hani says, taking the box and making a mental note to throw the VHS from Yum Mart into a blender. She dumps the tapes into her tote bag and sighs.

She'll take the footage home, play the tapes on her own TV. It's too risky to do it here. Hani rubs her eyes wearily and sets off to the precinct's morgue, clutching the list of gumiho names in her hand.

The haetae's autopsy will be happening now.

When word of the eoduksini's latest victim had reached the ears of New Sinsi's haetae precinct, officers quickly fell into a state of quiet mourning. So the precinct is unnaturally silent as

Hani makes her way to the morgue, passing a few somber guardian creatures with small nods of respect.

Lee Dok-hyun has already finished examining the body. He tugs off his mask and jumps slightly as Hani enters, before shaking his head to Seokga. The god stands at his side with an inscrutable expression. "It was the eoduksini," he confirms. "You can write that in the official report. Yang Chan-yeol, twenty-three, killed by eoduksini."

"Shit," Hani mutters, attempting to force some levity into her voice. "That thing is really getting around. I'm going to start carrying a metal bat with me everywhere I go. I'll give it a big old *whack* if it tries anything." She avoids looking at the haetae's corpse as she joins Dok-hyun's side.

Seokga's eyes flutter up toward the ceiling and he mutters something that sounds suspiciously like, *You are insufferable.* Hani opens her mouth to shoot back a biting reply, but Dok-hyun gets there first.

"Actually," the forensic pathologist says hesitantly, "the eoduksini doesn't necessarily need to be physically close to its victims to torture them with nightmares. He just needs to be on the same realm."

"That's great," groans Hani, but pauses when she catches sight of Seokga's face. He's frowning more than usual, and the fact that Hani now knows how to distinguish one of his frowns from another speaks to how much she's succeeded in annoying him lately.

"How do you know that?" Seokga asks. "You only just learned what an eoduksini is."

Dok-hyun shrugs, glancing away. "I read up on it," he replies. "After the last autopsy, I was frightened. The New Sinsi Library has a stack of eoduksini literature. I figured it would be helpful. I could send Chief Shim a list of the best references I found if you think that would be . . ."

"Perhaps," Seokga drawls, voice frigid. "Perhaps."

Hani doesn't know what to make of the sudden tension, and stares intently at Seokga, hoping that if she looks hard enough, a peephole into his strange god-brain will appear. Seokga bristles, as if the feeling of her eyes on him is offensive.

She smiles sweetly, continuing to stare at his forehead.

"What are you doing?" he snaps. "Stop that."

A moment later, Dok-hyun clears his throat and turns away from the corpse.

"We'll have a family member come in to identify the body," he says. "It'll shift into their custody at a different morgue." He peels off his surgical gloves and then pushes up his glasses. "I really hope, Detective, that you're one step closer to finding the one who is doing this. I don't want to see another body in this"—he swallows, looking slightly green—"manner."

"We have a witness," Seokga replies. "This will be over and done with soon."

"A—witness?" Dok-hyun blinks, fingering the golden embroidery on his black lab coat. "Really?"

Seokga nods in confirmation before his attention shifts to Hani and the stack of papers in her hands. "Those are the names?"

She nods, holding them out to him. "Yes."

Something that might be grudging respect—or, alternatively, a minor case of gas (as it looks so uncomfortable and out of place on his icy visage)—crosses the god's face.

Hani smiles and inclines her head smugly. "I didn't need until tomorrow," she informs him, quite proud of herself. "Just longer than an *hour*."

"Names?" Dok-hyun asks, looking slightly confused. "Of witnesses?"

"No. Possible Scarlet Fox suspects." Curious expression gone, Seokga snatches the files and tilts his lips upward in a hard smile. "Well. It seems like you're good for something, after all."

She smiles sweetly. *Oh, he has no idea.*

"The witness, though," Dok-hyun presses. "What . . . What have they said?"

Seokga, frown deepening, riffles through the papers as he starts toward the door. "We need to find her first. But I expect she'll be able to point us in the direction of our little demon friend. Fox," he snaps, glancing over his shoulder, "stop loitering around. There's work to be done."

With an apologetic smile to Dok-hyun, Hani stalks off in the direction Seokga has vanished, considering how screwed she would be if one day she finally punched his teeth in.

CHAPTER FOURTEEN

SEOKGA

A T ELEVEN P.M., THE PRECINCT IS UTTERLY SILENT SAVE for the keyboard clicking underneath Seokga's fingers, and Hani's obnoxiously loud munching as she makes her way through a carton of japchae at a nearby desk. A few on-duty haetae are slumped over at their desks, twiddling their thumbs and waiting for a call. Chief Shim has retired for the night, having left only a few minutes earlier.

As Hani emits an impossibly loud *slurp,* Seokga tears his gaze away from the computer and homes in on his assistant. "Would you," he demands, "stop that?"

She frowns, chewing on the glass noodles and pointing at him with a wooden chopstick. "I offered to buy you some. You said no."

"I'm trying to concentrate," he sneers, but his heart isn't in it.

Seokga is exhausted.

Utterly exhausted.

He has been working for hours in this damned precinct, scouring records and footage, desperate for any indication that one of the gumiho on the list provided by Hani is indeed the Scarlet Fox, desperate for any indication of Choi Ji-ah's location. But none have come. He has even gone so far as to make three separate trips to the café where Ji-ah worked, hoping to find coworkers with some knowledge of her whereabouts. Yet on both missions, he has hit dead ends. The only thing still fueling him is his desire to fulfill his end of Hwanin's bargain. His desire to once again be a god with earthshaking power at his fingertips.

Hani peers at him curiously. Despite the late hour, the gumiho is as full of energy as ever. "You don't look too good."

He bristles. "Of course I look good," he cuts back. He is Seokga. Even fatigued, he is far above the mortal beauty standard.

The gumiho seems amused. "Do gods sleep?"

"Why wouldn't we sleep?" Seokga glares at her. Isn't she supposed to be locating Ji-ah's residence, family members, and other contacts? It's quick work, *easy* work, but Hani has yet to inform him of any developments. "Have you found anything on Choi Ji-ah? Like I told you to?"

She frowns at him. "I told you two hours ago when I got back from visiting her old high school. I have everything on her." She points to a manila folder by his arm. "I put it right there and said, 'Here it is.' And you said, quote, 'Get out of my sight, fox. I'm busy,' unquote. Ring a bell? I've been waiting for you to look through it for two hours now."

Seokga grimaces. He didn't even know she went to the school—an oversight on his part. Still scowling, he flips open the folder and skims the black-lettered writing.

Choi Ji-ah. Age eighteen. Brown eyes, black hair, five foot four. There's a printed picture, there—a round-faced girl clad in a high school uniform. He flips the page, still skimming. Graduated from New Sinsi High School. Currently enrolled at New Sinsi University as a medicine major, second-year. Family contacts . . . Seokga narrows his eyes.

"She's an orphan," Hani explains, setting down her takeout. "No family to speak of."

Great. He rubs his forehead. That will impede the investigation greatly. Seokga does not think that his ego can handle it if

Iseung becomes a Dark World because of his failed coup. He can only be embarrassed so many times.

"She does have one friend. When I swung by her old school, I got a copy of her high school graduation's VHS footage and played it in the conference room. One girl cheered when her name was called, and they later left together." Hani swings her feet off the desk and strides over so she stands just behind him. He stiffens as she leans over his shoulder, her hair tickling his neck. She smells of citrus and vanilla, of crackling fires and—

Seokga scowls.

Why does he care what she smells like?

He doesn't.

"Look." Her breath is warm against his skin as she flips to a different page, her finger tapping a grainy image of a lanky girl walking side by side with Ji-ah. "This is her. I rewound the graduation footage to hear her name being called. Kim Sora. So if we go back here . . ." She flips back to Ji-ah's file and points to the bolded words: EMERGENCY CONTACT. "Boom. Kim Sora. This is her home phone number"—Hani taps the eleven digits with a manicured nail—"and this is her current address. Her apartment on the NSU campus." He can feel her grin. "You can thank me now."

"Wait." Seokga grabs her wrist and twists up to meet her wine-brown stare, half-impressed, half-skeptical. "How did you convince the school to give you the footage?" She has no badge, no credentials.

Her returning smile is pure fox. "I stole it." Undiluted mischief dances in her eyes—playful mischief that stirs something deep within him, something that answers to the troublemaking glint in her gaze. He can't help but to smile back—a crafty smile that seems to momentarily confuse her. He can appreciate a good theft, after all.

"Nicely done, fox," he purrs. "Perhaps you're not entirely useless. What a welcome surprise."

Her grin returns. "I'll take that as a compliment," she croons back.

Seokga is suddenly aware of their proximity. The feeling of her hair against his neck as she leans over him, the heat radiating from her body, his hand around her wrist. For a brief moment, god and gumiho stare at each other with matching expressions of stubborn dislike that seem to mask, on both sides, a flickering of respect.

But then Hani reaches down and flicks his nose—and just like that, the moment is ruined.

The gumiho's audacity never fails to astound him.

Swallowing his hiss of agitation, he releases his grip on her and she steps back as he rises, grabbing his cane. "Get your things," he says shortly. "We have a visit to pay."

Seokga can feel Hani gaping at him. "You don't mean to visit Sora *now*, do you?" she asks, reaching for her corduroy tote bag.

Exasperated, he sends a *what do you think* look over his shoulder. Of course he means to pay Kim Sora a visit now.

"It's eleven—"

"It's March. The first semester of college. She'll be awake. And we don't have a moment to lose." Because Seokga wants nothing more than to leave this miserable, miserable realm behind in exchange for Okhwang. "She may know where Ji-ah is." He doesn't wait for her response before striding out of the precinct and starting his car. Hani joins him a moment later, slipping into the passenger seat and shutting the door with too much force for his precious vehicle.

"Gentle," he snaps out of the corner of his mouth.

"Sorry," she says, not sounding very sorry at all.

✦

NEW SINSI UNIVERSITY IS A SPRAWLING CAMPUS OF WHITE brick buildings and cherry blossom trees already in full bloom illuminated by various wrought-iron streetlights and the ambient glow of the city. As Seokga and Hani make their way through a passage of sidewalk lined by at least one dozen of the damn trees, Seokga fights back a particularly violent sneeze. Hani is watching him with an amused side-eye.

"Are you allergic to cherry blossoms?" she asks curiously.

"No."

"I could have sworn that you were holding back a sneeze."

"I wasn't."

"Mm," she hums, not sounding convinced in the slightest. "So—what's your plan to get Sora to talk? She's a human. You can't really tell her that her friend is the sole witness to an eoduksini draining the life out of somebody, and you *definitely* can't tell her that you're a fallen god. We need a cover story," she muses. "A good cover story that can get us answers. Let's see . . . Oh!" She turns to him excitedly, now walking backward in order to grin wickedly at him. "What about good cop, bad cop? We can be undercover officers from the human precinct. I'll be good cop, of course, and you—"

Speak of the devil. Seokga opens his mouth to hiss a warning but it's too late.

"Oomph!" He can only watch as Hani collides with a stern-looking campus policeman, her back hitting his chest.

"Watch where you're going," the policeman snaps, shoving Hani off him. She bows in apology, even as Seokga can see that her expression is anything but remorseful—it's annoyed. He pushes down amusement as the chubby officer frowns at the pair of them. "Are you two students?"

Seokga inclines his head in a nod. "Yes." He makes to step around him, but the officer blocks him, seeming dubious.

"I'm going to have to ask to see your IDs," he says and crosses his arms. "Two students were found dead a couple of nights ago. You two shouldn't be out this late." He waits with a hand outstretched, anticipating their student identification cards. "I'm sure you know that punishment for breaching this curfew is a fine."

Well, then. It seems as if he has no choice. Seokga sighs and reaches for his remaining threads of power. It's ironic that most people in power—even common cops—have always possessed enough malice and deceit for Seokga to control. He hopes that is also the case for this particular policeman. He'll exhaust himself for nothing if it isn't.

Have him forget that he saw us, Seokga commands them as the emerald tendrils of mist wrap around the officer, whose eyes unfocus. Thankfully, his magic is able to take hold of the cop—for a price. Seokga cannot imagine anything more humiliating than swooning in front of Hani, but with the way his head is swimming in fatigue, he worries it's not an impossibility. *Have him forget that he . . .*

"What are you doing?" Hani asks, staring at the bands of power tightening around the officer, invisible to the mortal's eyes.

"What I planned to do to Sora." He'd been hoping to compel the answers out of her in this way—but after this, he knows that he'll be far too tired to summon his power again. When the officer closes his eyes, Seokga coils the magic back into himself and clutches his cane tightly. Between this compulsion today, and the compulsion of the drowning witness on the first, it is a struggle for Seokga to keep himself sharp and alert. He closes his eyes and tries to compose himself.

"Seokga?" Hani is asking, and Seokga feels her inquisitive stare like spiders scuttling down his back. He will *not* faint in front of her. He knows that if he does, he will never hear the end of it.

"Are you about to faint?"

Seokga's eyes snap open and he glowers at her. "No."

"Because it looks like you are," she continues with a smug little smile. "I'm not sure I'll catch you. I think watching you drop to the ground could be fun."

The nerve. "I just," he grits out, "need some caffeine. Get me some." Now. Before he amuses Hani by hitting the pavement like a stone.

Hani's smirk grows. "We have places to be, Seokga. Maybe, if you speak *nicely* to Sora, I'll get you a coffee afterward. And I won't even put too much extra sugar in it."

Seokga flattens his lips into a thin line, irritation swarming in his chest. But because the universe hates him, he is simply too tired to argue with her. "Fine," he mutters, attempting valiantly to keep his eyes open. "Let's go."

"Wait." The fox is staring at the officer with a crafty little smirk that has Seokga tilting his head in curiosity. The glitter in her gaze is dangerous, suggesting a shrewd mind whirling with a clever idea. "Wait," she repeats. Her voice is low, conspiratorial, and sends a small thrill through him. "I have an idea."

"THIS DOES NOT *FIT*," SEOKGA GRUMBLES IN ONE OF THE university's bathrooms, immensely peeved at the turn of events. He glares haggardly at himself in the mirror, clad in the officer's uniform, which is much too baggy on him. The black pants are at least twice his size, but only fall to his calves, and the stiff, navy-blue collared shirt smells of body odor and cheap cologne. The pins and badges make the shirt feel heavy against his skin, and he does not like having a gun at his waist—he has hated guns since their invention. They have always felt like cheating to him.

And the *hat*.

The navy-blue hat with the symbol of the human police department—the golden bird with outstretched wings—is far too big for his head. It slumps over his eyes. Seokga bites down on his rage as he shoves it back up. He is too tired to cope with looking this ridiculous.

Hani is waiting on the other side of the bathroom door. "It doesn't need to look perfect," she calls through the wood. "You just need to look like a policeman. A human policeman."

Seokga casts a glance at the unconscious officer lying in his underwear on the cold tiles of the bathroom floor. There is a rather large red welt on his head, courtesy of Seokga's cane. "I look nothing like that pathetic worm."

"Say what you will," comes Hani's muffled response, "but this way, Sora will be obligated to tell us the answers we're looking for. You're a campus policeman, and Choi Ji-ah is a missing university student." She knocks on the door, her raps quick, impatient, and grating on his already-frayed nerves. "Are you done yet?"

His mood significantly darkening with each passing moment, Seokga slowly pulls open the door and shoves his own clothes, folded neatly in a pile, into Hani's arms. "Put them in your bag," he orders, adjusting the hat once again. "And don't look at me like that." Her gaze is shining with gleeful mockery.

"Fine," she hums, folding the clothes into her tote. "Fine, fine, fine." But laughter is still audible in her tone as she steps aside to let Seokga enter the silent hallway.

It had been a struggle smuggling the officer's unconscious form into the admissions building, especially since they'd had to keep to the bushes and shadows to avoid the security cameras stationed outside the entrance. Hani, in an act of what she called "genius," had decided to, with a hefty rock and a violent pitch, break a lower-level window located just outside a camera's range. Seokga had wanted to throttle her. She was only spared from his wrath by his inability to fight in one-on-one combat while exhausted, and by the fact that nobody came running.

The following ordeal of throwing the man inside and climbing in after him has tired Seokga even further. That policeman is *heavy*.

Sora's dormitory is not far from here. "We should get going," Hani says, casting a glance about the hallway. "It's nearing twelve."

Seokga scowls as he once again shoves up the rim of the hat and follows Hani out of the quiet, darkened admissions building and onto the campus outside. The night air is cold and crisp as the pair keep to the shadows, creeping toward the large dormitory building in which their contact lays. Their footsteps echo on the pavement, accompanied by the soft clicking of Seokga's cane as he reluctantly trudges along, desperate for his coffee.

"Locked," Hani mutters, testing the glass door.

There is an ID card in the policeman's pocket. "Let me," Seokga says impatiently, gesturing for Hani to move aside, the card in between his fingers. *Lee Byung-ho,* the ID card reads underneath a small, square image of the heavyset policeman. *Campus Officer.* He holds it against the black ID scanner. The door unlocks with a click. Triumphant, Seokga wraps his fingers around the cool metal handle and tugs the door open. Hani immediately tries to enter first; he cuts her off and slips into the building before her. She mutters a foul word behind him, and it's an effort to stop his lips from tilting upward.

"Sora is on the seventh floor," he says under his breath, nodding a stiff greeting to the weary-looking woman at the front desk. "Room 42G."

Hani is already making her way to the elevator door and pushing the UP button with her thumb. The metal doors slide open with a muted *ding* and Hani steps inside, followed closely by Seokga, who wrinkles his nose against the elevator's musty smell. As Hani presses the grimy 7 button, the doors shut, and with a slight whir the elevator begins its ascent.

Hani leans against the wall opposite him and grins. "You really do look striking."

Insufferable fox. "Not another word," Seokga mutters, fantasizing about the coffee she has promised him. Icy. Cold. Caffeine. He needs it *now*.

She winks, toying with a silky strand of brown hair. "I've always loved a man in uniform," she replies with another one of those wicked smiles. "And you fit the look quite well, Seokga."

"Be quiet." The elevator doors cannot open quickly enough.

Hani pouts as she holds out her hands, pressing her wrists together. He watches incredulously as she bats her eyes. "Arrest me, Officer—"

The elevator doors slide open with a cheerful *ding!*

Finally.

Seokga sends Hani a final scowl before exiting, cursing his father violently for creating the world and, subsequently, creating annoying gumiho who do not know when to keep silent. Lost in his brooding thoughts, Seokga barely notices the glossy linoleum floors, smooth white walls, or bright overhead lights. With a small noise of exasperation, Hani catches his sleeve and yanks him to a halt. He nearly missed Sora's door.

"Here." She gestures to the plain wooden door with the chipped, bronze number 42 atop the brown surface. "Knock," she says under her breath. "Say that you're with the campus police. Rap your fist against the door and—"

"I know how to knock."

Hani shrugs. "Just checking."

Seokga takes a moment to push up his hat before striking the door thrice with his imoogi hilt, each thud reverberating through the otherwise silent corridor. Hani jumps and sends him a glare of disbelief.

"Seriously?" she demands. "You didn't have to do it that loud. You'll probably scare the poor girl to death."

"We need answers," he bites back shortly. "And if she's sleeping, I'll knock down—"

The door opens.

An unimpressed-looking girl stares back at Hani and Seokga with dark-rimmed eyes. Her hair is limp and lanky, her skin gaunt and pale under the hallway's harsh lights. "Yes?" she asks, frowning as she takes them in. In her hands she holds a bowl of still-steaming instant tteokbokki and there are faint red stains of gochujang around her thin lips. "Who are you?"

"You're Kim Sora, correct?" Seokga asks, shoving up the damned hat again.

"That's correct, yes," Sora replies warily. "And you are?"

"Officer Lee," he replies, guiding his voice to a flat, professional cadence that's not cold enough for Hani to deny him his coffee. "And this is my assistant. An Noying."

Hani chokes in outrage; Seokga presses on.

"We have a few questions for you regarding your friend Choi Ji-ah."

Sora's mouth tightens. "I see."

"We hate to take up your time," Hani adds, "and we apologize for a visit this late. But Ji-ah has gone missing, and we worry that she is in danger—"

"Ji-ah hasn't been kidnapped," Sora replies thinly. "You're wasting your time. She's run away. Again."

Seokga cocks his head. Sora's voice is irritated—but not at them. At Ji-ah. "What do you mean," he asks, "'again'?" Next to him, Hani is frowning in contemplation.

"I mean," Sora mutters, "that she's always been like this. I get that she has a hard life—I do. I get it, okay? But she does this all the time. Whenever something even remotely upsets her, she runs away. She's done it since we were kids, only as we got older, the distance she ran increased." Sora stirs her tteokbokki and takes a bite, leaning against the door. Just past her shoulder, Seokga can make out an unmade bed, a floor littered with laundry, and a desk groaning under the weight of a dozen textbooks. He stares at her bed. What he wouldn't give to collapse on a soft mattress, pull the covers over his head, and pass out. He blinks slowly, fighting back a yawn. "Anyway, you're wasting your time. She'll come back eventually."

"When was the last time you saw her?" Seokga asks, returning his stare to the university student with difficulty.

Sora shrugs. "Early yesterday morning. She ran over here, blubbering about something that had happened at work. She said: 'I'm in danger, Sora. I gotta go.'" She rolls her eyes in clear disdain. "I could barely even tell what she was saying, she was so hysterical. Aish. The drama queen. And then she was off as quickly as she'd come."

Seokga frowns. Even frowning is an effort at the moment, but he does it anyway. "And you didn't follow?"

Sora glares at him. "Why would I? This has happened four times in the past semester. I swear, being friends with her is the stupidest decision I ever made. She's an emotional leech, do you know that? Write *that* in your report." She points to Seokga's uniform with a scowl.

He raises his brows, slightly amused, slightly disgusted, and extremely tired. "Do you know, at least, where she went?"

Sora scoffs. "Well, after begging me for money—my money, mind you, like she doesn't have some of her own from that café—I assumed she went to her new favorite hiding spot. Geoje Island," she adds in answer to Seokga's demanding stare. "There's an abandoned village there where she's liked to hide recently. It's a ghost town, deep in the forest, and isn't even on most maps. I'm assuming she went there once with her archeology class last year." Sora takes another bite of tteokbokki, glaring at the noodles as she continues, "If you take a bus to Busan, you can catch another bus going from the Busan Seobu terminal over the bridge to Okpo, the main city there on Geoje. That's what I think she did." Sora stabs at a rice noodle with notable vehemence. "I wouldn't bother going," she mumbles. "She likes being alone. She'll come back eventually before leaving all over again once something else sets her off."

"What's the name of the village?" Hani's eyes are wide. "Do you know?"

Sora shakes her head. "It doesn't have a name. Ji-ah said it's in a bamboo forest on Geoje. Maengjongjuk Forest. It's open to everybody, as long as you stay on the trail. To get to the village, you have to go off the path. Way, way off the path." She hesitates. "Do you think she's really in danger?"

"Maybe," says Seokga, staring again at her bed. If he doesn't get some coffee in him soon, he will be out like a light.

"Oh." Sora hesitates, looking querulous for the first time. "Are you guys . . . going to go find her?"

"If we're in the mood." Seokga turns away. "Thank you for your time."

"Wait." Sora's voice is suddenly small. Timid. He turns back impatiently. Busan is already two hours and forty-five minutes away from New Sinsi—and Okpo even farther.

Not to mention that blissful unconsciousness is also looming before him. He needs coffee and a nap—and he has no time to waste.

"If you find Ji-ah . . . Will you be able to make sure she doesn't go off like this again?" Unshed tears swim in her eyes. "Please?"

Seokga fights down annoyance. Humans and their emotions. *Why didn't you stop her from going?* he wants to snap. *Our one witness is all the way on Geoje Island, thanks to you.* Biting his tongue, he turns away again, and Hani is the one to answer instead, murmuring reassuring promises that Seokga doubts will be fulfilled.

If the eoduksini is also looking for Ji-ah—if the eoduksini gets to her first—Kim Sora will never see her friend again.

With a muttered curse, Seokga sets off down the dormitory hall.

If he weren't a god himself, he might have muttered a prayer.

CHAPTER FIFTEEN

HANI

Seokga is asleep on Hani's couch.

An empty Styrofoam coffee cup is held close to his chest as he slumbers, scowling even in his sleep. Because Hani is nothing if not good, charitable, and altogether an extremely nice person, she kept true to her word and bought the exhausted god coffee at the twenty-four-hour campus café. She only dumped in three extra packs of sugar, too.

If Hani liked Seokga, she would have felt empathy for him. Such a high cost for using so little power.

But Hani does not like Seokga, so she is more amused than anything.

The energy boost lasted him long enough to drive to her apartment (which he so kindly deemed a disgusting hovel), stagger out of the car, into her building, and collapse on her ratty couch.

She suspects his exhaustion is the only reason why he is allowing her to accompany him to Geoje. Hani prattled on about it endlessly in the car until he gave in. She doubts, though, that he really heard any of her motivational speech about how she will defend Iseung to the death before it turns into a Dark World. He seemed to have been mainly focused on keeping his eyes open.

Now, Hani is supposed to be packing for their trip to Geoje, and *not* figuring out how to destroy the VHS tapes she snuck home in her tote bag, but Hani rarely does as she's told. In her small bedroom, Hani quietly shuts the door on the sleeping Seokga, and wonders what the repercussions of destroying all ten tapes would be.

It would be a brilliant plan, except for the fact that she's on file as the last person to have the tapes. Chewing on her bottom lip, Hani runs through the possibilities in her mind. She could hide them, of course, and pretend she lost them. But Seokga is an inherently suspicious person, and Hani was slightly unnerved when he asked for her age in the car. He was making a barbed joke, of course, but still. Hani wasn't even supposed to bring the tapes home in the first place, and it was tricky enough keeping her tote bag closed and herself quiet throughout their trip to the university. She has to be careful.

Sighing, Hani rummages through the tapes until she finds the one labeled YUM MART, as well as three others from establishments near Bonmal Street. Whatever the case, she can't allow these to go back to the precinct.

Aware that the trickster god is sleeping in the next room over, Hani quickly takes the tapes containing pesky evidence, and considers their fate with grim determination. The haetae at the precinct had said to keep the ones they need and toss the ones they don't. She'll certainly be tossing these, but they'll expect her to have found *something* on the other VHS tapes. If she comes back empty-handed, it will look suspicious.

There's a tiny television in the corner of her room. Hani reluctantly loads one of the other tapes into it—one from a street she and Somi didn't take—and plays it back, scouring for footage she could claim to be "suspicious." There are hours' worth of footage, but she fast-forwards, eyes glued to the screen. Maybe she can claim that the old woman hobbling down the sidewalk with a bag of what looks like carrots is suspicious. Who eats vegetables?

"Hani?"

Shit. Hani jumps almost a foot in the air as Seokga's voice, sharp and slightly husky, comes through the door. She curses whoever designed this apartment—there's no lock on the bedroom door. Foolishly, she'd thought he'd be out for at least another hour. "Don't come in!" she screeches, leaping to her feet and staring down at the collection of tapes on the floor in panic. "I'm naked!"

There's a long silence on the other end. Quickly, Hani pops the tape out of her TV and shuts it off. She gathers the four incriminating tapes and, in a moment of frazzled folly, shoves them underneath her bed.

"Why," Seokga asks slowly, "are you naked?"

"Trust me," she pants, gathering the other six and cramming them back into her tote bag, "it has nothing to do with you."

"I would hope not," he snaps back, sounding affronted at the very thought.

Hani pauses from her frantic cleaning to be completely and thoroughly offended.

"We're leaving as soon as you're not naked," Seokga continues frostily. "We've wasted enough time."

"You mean that *you* have wasted enough time," Hani retorts, stuffing the tote bag in her closet. "I wasn't the one who needed a nap." The tapes somewhat dealt with, Hani hastens to stuff spare clothes into a duffel bag. She also strips down—truly, this time—to swap her clothes out for new ones, in case Seokga continues to ask why she was naked. Nosy, bossy god.

There's a *thud* from the other side of the door, and Hani glares as the battered wood reverberates. "Did you just kick my door?" she snaps, glad that the chair is in place to prevent it from swinging open and revealing Hani in nothing but her underwear. There's another long pause, leaving her time to pull on a soft sweater and jeans.

"No," Seokga very clearly lies.

Muttering curses about fallen gods under her breath, Hani smooths down her hair, grabs her duffel, kicks aside the chair, and opens the door. Seokga leans against the doorframe, eyes puffy from sleeping, and she's pleased to see that his usually perfect hair is slightly mussed. "I don't like you," she informs him with a deep, soul-baring honesty.

"I'll get over it." His sharp green eyes try to slide past her into the bedroom, and she moves to block his vision. But it's too late. She opened the door too wide, and he's seen something.

"Why are there tapes under your bed?"

Hwanin's tits. Hani is momentarily stunned by her own stupidity as Seokga, taking advantage of her shock, elbows his way into her room and points accusatorily to the four pieces of incriminating evidence under her twin-sized bed. In her haste, she didn't shove them back far enough or pull the blankets down to conceal them, and the rectangular edges peek out through the shadows.

Seokga is scowling. "Are those precinct tapes?"

Shit. Okay. She has to play this cool. Use her gumiho wiles. Hani blinks at Seokga's finger and then smiles sheepishly. "You caught me," she says.

He stares at her in thinly concealed suspicion. She needs to wipe that suspicion away immediately. And she also needs to make sure he doesn't open her underwear drawer, where her scarlet daggers are hidden. She'd like to take them to Geoje, but with the hunt going on, she is perfectly fine with them being nestled underneath her lacy thongs. She'll rely on her sharp wit and sharp claws on Geoje, though she'll have to refrain from utilizing her fox bead again, in fear of the háetae locating the potent energy flare and tracing it to her.

Hani fixes her best approximation of a silly assistant on her face. "I didn't have time to go through all of them today at the precinct. I mean, you were working me like a dog. A list of names in an *hour*. Really? And I know I shouldn't have, but I brought them home." Heart beating fast against her chest, Hani walks over to the bed and stoops down to gather the evidence. "I've gone through these, but the six others in there"—she points to the tote bag, where the harmless tapes are—"are still unwatched. I was going to go through some before we left for Geoje." The temptation to throw the incriminating videos she holds in her hands out the window before Seokga can demand to see them is oh-so tempting. She tries not to hold them tight enough that her knuckles shine, but she's gripping them with a hard determination. He won't take them from her. He won't.

Seokga's eyes are fixed on her face. His mouth is a thin line, and his brows are pinched together.

"I didn't want to tell you in case you didn't let me go to Geoje. I want to stop the eoduksini from making this place into a Dark World." She grits her teeth, and then forces out the most difficult word she has ever said to this great, insufferable ass. "Sorry," she mutters.

"What was that?"

Hani glares. "You know what I said."

Seokga is smirking, and although it's *infuriating*, at least the suspicion hardening his face has mostly disappeared. "I don't, actually."

"Oh, fuck off," Hani grumbles before she can stop herself, and just like that, the last remnants of Seokga's visible suspicion drains away. As casually as she can, she places the four tapes on her desk, stacking them in a neat pile. She waits for him to reach toward them, but he doesn't.

Instead, the god eyes the rest of her room, taking in the uneven floorboards, the desk that she uses as a vanity cluttered with various cosmetics, the pile of dirty laundry in one corner (her empty basket was mysteriously stolen from the laundry room two weeks ago), and the box of Choco Pies situated on one of her pillows.

Hani tries not to flush as he walks to her bookshelf, which groans underneath the weight of hundreds of battered romance books. Seokga pinches one—*Kidnapped by the Time-Traveling Highland Pirate-King*—between his fingers and glances to her in dismay. She glares back, refusing to be ashamed of enjoying both the raunchy, cliché cover and its deliciously smutty content. Who knew she had a thing for pirates who wore kilts, time-traveled, and rolled their r's?

"Would you like to borrow it?" she offers sweetly.

"I would rather die. This place is a mess," he adds, nose wrinkled as he tosses the book back, "and I'm embarrassed to even be seen in it. I'll be waiting in the car."

SEOKGA SIGHS AS HE BACKS THE JAGUAR OUT OF ITS PARKing spot. "You know—"

Hani cuts him off. "Yes, Seokga," she croons, "I know that you'd much rather have me stay behind. I'm choosing to ignore that little fact."

She can almost swear that he smirks at that.

"Have you ever been on a ferry before?" Hani asks, twirling a strand of hair around a finger. "Some of them have gift shops with candies—"

"We're not taking the ferry," Seokga says. "There's a bridge between Busan and Geoje that we'll take."

"A bridge?" Hani furrows her brow. She hasn't heard of any bridge that spans the expanse of water separating the two cities.

"They're calling it the Busan-Geoje Fixed Link. It's been glamoured by a shaman. Humans don't know about it yet, but I

assume they'll somehow manage to infiltrate it eventually, and
meddle in its design." Mortals. Sticking their hands where
they're not needed. Seokga turns them onto the city street. "But
it's not for them. Bulgasari architects created it for the fairies.
Geoje has a large yojeong population, and their wings are too
delicate to handle long-distance flights. I memorized the route
to the bridge. We'll reach it in around three and a half hours."

Hani arches a brow, resting her head against the window.
"That's quicker than I expected," she says suspiciously.

"I plan to speed," is the smooth retort.

"Clever," Hani mumbles, her eyelids growing heavy as she
nestles back into the leather seat. "Do you want to alternate
drivers?" she asks, stifling a yawn. If she's exhausted, she can only
imagine how tired Seokga is, even after his nap. Seokga scoffs.

"You're not driving my car."

She rolls her eyes. "If we crash because—"

Hani is cut off by a shrill, high-pitched ringing. Seokga makes
a small noise of agitation, reaching for his cellphone and pressing it to his ear. "What," he snaps, and Hani rolls her eyes again.
Seokga clearly has much to learn in the way of manners.

"Seokga," the voice on the other side of the line says. "It's Officer
Park. Three more bodies have been uncovered—all within the past half-hour.
We don't have a lead on the eoduksini, but . . ."

"But what," he demands sharply, his fists tightening around
the wheel.

"All three victims are . . . brutalized in a way that the last two weren't.
We're conducting a questioning with the souls before they ride to Jeoseung, but
no new information is coming to light. If you want to come down to the sta-
tion, see the bodies for yourself . . . I think that it's imperative you do so before
chasing any new leads."

Three more victims. Hani swallows bile. The eoduksini is
still in New Sinsi—still feasting. She watches as Seokga's jaw
flexes, his brows lowering.

"I'll be there in ten." He tucks away the phone and glances to Hani with narrowed eyes. "I assume, fox, that you heard all of that."

"Three more bodies," she replies slowly. "Brutalized bodies. How can they be any more brutalized than Euna and the haetae were?"

"That," he says tightly, "is what we're going to go see. We can spare twenty minutes at the precinct, no more, no less." The Jaguar growls as he hits the gas, speeding through the city at a breakneck speed. "Damn it," he snarls under his breath. "Damn it."

Five minutes later, the Jaguar skids to a halt before the haetae precinct, the wheels screeching on the pavement. Hani jumps out of the car as Seokga slams his door hard enough that his entire beloved vehicle shakes. She struggles to keep up with him across the parking lot, his cane clenched so tightly in his hand that even from a few feet away, Hani can see the white shine of his knuckles.

Snap. Snap. Snap. There is a dokkaebi paparazzo lurking near the precinct's door and taking rapid-fire shots of Seokga and Hani, probably for *Godly Gossip*. Hani grimaces. The last thing she wants is dating rumors with *Seokga*.

Snap. Snap. Sna—

Seokga wrestles the camera from his grip, crushes it under his foot, and storms into the precinct.

"Hey—" the dokkaebi hollers, but the doors slam on him. Grim-faced haetae officers hastily clear out of the way as Seokga storms through the precinct and bursts into the morgue with what is almost a snarl. As Hani slips through the wildly swinging doors, Dok-hyun startles from where he is standing over a body, examining it with an array of metal tools.

Hani freezes in horror as her eyes fall upon the motionless victim.

He lies on the cold metal table, his eyes shut and forever un-seeing, his skin splattered with red and marred by those horrible black veins. There is a gaping red cavity in his chest, gore burst-ing from the wound, as if . . .

As if his heart has been ripped from his body.

The victim's sallow cheeks are sunken and scratched, vicious red cuts dragging from his brow to his chin, jagged and deep. Both of his ears are missing, only empty holes left behind, dried blood trickling down his broken neck. And his left arm . . . It dangles uselessly, only half attached to his shoulder, holding on just barely by a few nearly frayed cords of muscle.

Hani presses a hand to her mouth, horror tightening her chest, blocking her airway. "Fuck," she breathes, her stomach churning. "Oh, fuck."

Seokga's back is stiff and straight, his face pale. "Details, Dok-hyun. Now."

Dok-hyun removes his surgical mask with a grimace. "Pak Jonghoon. Human. Age forty-three. Found outside of a conve-nience store in the shopping district."

"And the others?"

Hani follows Seokga's gaze to the steel vaults lining the walls of the morgue. Her neck feels hot, damp and clammy with sweat, and it's an effort to look back to Pak Jonghoon's mutilated body. She holds the sleeve of her black sweater to her nose and mouth. Blood's coppery tang is overwhelming. She hasn't seen a corpse this badly mutilated since her heyday as the Scarlet Fox, when she was hunting down Jack the Ripper.

I'm going to be sick, she thinks. *I'm going to be sick.*

"One bulgasari and another human. All mutilated in the same manner. The bulgasari was found by a security guard in the city junkyard, where it had been eating metals. The other human was discovered in an alleyway on the city's edge. If you would like to see—"

A small noise escapes Hani's lips. No. No, she doesn't want to see them. Not at all.

"No," Seokga says quickly, his eyes snapping to Hani in what almost—*almost*—looks like apologetic concern. "No. We've seen enough."

"I see," Dok-hyun replies, bowing his head before covering Jonghoon's body with a sheet of white fabric, which is stained and spotted with blood. "The bodies," he says a moment later, "hold considerably more evidence of violence than the other two victims. It's clear from the veins that the eoduksini is behind the attacks. The eoduksini," he says, looking up and meeting Seokga's eye with a dark grimness, "is very angry."

"Angry?" Hani manages to whisper. "What do you mean?"

Seokga is tilting his head, expression inscrutable.

Dok-hyun gestures to the sheet-covered corpse. "It's more than evident that the eoduksini used significantly more violence on this trio than it did on the gumiho and the haetae. I would assume that the monster was angry. Furious, even." He hesitates. "It took all three hearts. I'd guess that . . . it's eating them."

"*Eating* them?" Seokga asks sharply. "What signifies that?"

The pathologist frowns. "You don't know? It's in the literature. Eoduksini will sometimes eat the hearts of their victims. It doesn't necessarily help them grow stronger, but it . . . well, it likely tastes good." He licks his lips nervously.

"I hadn't known that," Seokga admits slowly as Hani looks back to the victim and bites down on her lip hard enough to taste blood. It is disconcerting to see this carnage. She's killed, yes, ripped out livers—but this is . . . different.

"And the murder weapon?" the trickster god asks, his voice slightly more hoarse than usual. "What do you think it was?"

"Brute strength," Dok-hyun replies haggardly. "Sheer, brute strength."

"It must not have found Ji-ah," Hani realizes before she can stop herself, her mouth dry. "The eoduksini is looking for her, trying to silence her, but it doesn't know where she is. It can't find her. Dok-hyun is right; it's angry."

"Ji-ah?" Dok-hyun looks confused. "Who is Ji-ah?"

"Our witness," Seokga replies. "She alone knows the eoduksini's form. We located her an hour ago."

Dok-hyun stiffens. "You can find her?" the forensic pathologist asks. Nervously, his eyes dart back and forth between Seokga and Hani. Something very much like suspicion pools in the bottom of Hani's stomach as she watches him straighten in acute interest.

Too acute.

Something about this entire exchange is . . . off, somehow. The hairs on the back of her neck prickle, as if the primal fox instinct to sense a predator is seeping through to her human form.

Her eyes dart questioningly to Seokga's. The brief glance they share, Hani feels, conveys much, much more than either of their expressions do. She is careful to keep her face neutral, blank.

But how is it that Dok-hyun knew something about the eoduksini that even a god did not? She recalls his sharp interest in the eoduksini case's witness, beginning after that second autopsy, with some discomfort. How he licked his lips after suggesting that the hearts taste good. When she looks back at Dok-hyun, she sees him in a new light. A light that is not altogether pleasant.

"She fled." Seokga turns to Hani, his expression dark. "We need to move before it finds her. Come."

As they stride out of the morgue, Seokga's cane clicking on the tile floor, Hani glances over her shoulder to make sure Dok-hyun isn't following them. "Do you think . . ."

"Dok-hyun?" Seokga shakes his head, but his eyes are narrowed. "I'm not sure. I've known his family for centuries. They're annoying, but only to the extent that all humans are."

"But if the eoduksini's taken over his body, that's not Dok-hyun. You can't judge based on what you think you know about him and his family." Hani runs a hand through her hair. "I mean, did you see how he licked his lips? That was just—I mean, that was just *disgusting*."

"Yes. But that's not enough to move against him," the god replies curtly, pulling Hani around a hallway corner and into a grimy alcove. She folds her arms, glaring up at him. They are too close for Hani's liking, with less than a few inches between them.

"He knows more than he should."

"He said he found books in the library."

"Why are you defending him?" Hani asks curiously. "You don't even like him." She recalls his acerbic refutation that he and Dok-hyun are friends.

Seokga scowls. "He isn't squeamish about sticking his hands in dead bodies and gets the work done quickly. That's all. And unlike others"—he shoots a sideways glare as a haetae passes them in the corridor, whistling under her breath—"he doesn't ask me to introduce him to Hwanin, or where he gets his hair done, or whether he's single. As if I know. And I could ask for much less."

Hani leans against the wall. "Seokga," she says, "we have no other suspects right now. Even if all we have is a little suspicion against him, we should act. Iseung could be turned into a Dark World if we don't. I have an idea—"

"I don't trust your *ideas*," Seokga says, exhaling thinly through his nose.

Hani ignores him. "We detain Dok-hyun until we find Ji-ah. If she gives us a description that doesn't match him, we let him go with no hard feelings. If she describes him, then *bam*. Case closed, the mortal realm is saved, and you're halfway to reaching divinity again." She waits expectantly, arching an eyebrow.

It's clear that his strange god-brain is working hard. He narrows his eyes, and taps his cane on the ground, head cocked.

Finally, he sighs. "Fine. I'll tell Shim to put him under guard in a holding cell. Just until we get back from Geoje."

Chief Shim is waiting outside of the precinct, his eyes bloodshot and exhausted as he stands next to Hyun-tae and the sleek black hearse. "Seokga," he calls, voice cracking in the night air. "Where are you going?"

"Geoje," Seokga replies shortly. "We've located our witness. By the way, you might want to put Dok-hyun in a holding cell, and under heavy guard."

Shim blinks. "I— What was that, Seokga?"

"I *said*—"

"We think the eoduksini might have possessed Dok-hyun," Hani says quickly before Seokga can reply something truly nasty. "He knows too much about the eoduksini, and he's been asking about our witness. It's not a lot to go on, but we can't take any risks. Iseung is in danger."

"Lee Dok-hyun? Surely not." The old haetae looks alarmed. "Besides, precinct procedure requires more than just circumstantial evidence before detainment. You know that, Detective."

"Do you want this realm to be turned into a Dark World? You wouldn't last very long at all," Seokga snaps. "Detain him. That's an order. Even fallen, I outrank you."

"Seokga, that's just not how it works." Hani notes with amusement that the chief sounds like a harabeoji lecturing his grandson. "But Emperor Hwanin trusts you to solve this case, so this time—only this *one* time, Seokga—I'll bend the rules." He shakes his head and pulls out his walkie-talkie, turning away to issue the command into the microphone. Shim looks back at Seokga. "He'll be confined within minutes. I hope you know what you're doing. Dok-hyun is a good man."

Hani does not hear what Seokga replies in return; she is pulling out her cellphone (nabbed a while ago from a deliciously low-security tech store, along with one for Somi) with trembling fingers and punching in Somi's number. Turning away from the bleak conversation between the two men, she holds the ringing phone to her ear, gnawing on a nail until Somi picks up. Her voice is thick and sleepy—Hani woke her up.

"Hello?"

"Somi."

"Hani? Why are you calling so late?" She hears the rustling of sheets as Somi sits up, undoubtedly rubbing her eyes. "Is something wrong?" A familiar edge of panic seeps into her voice. "Oh, no. Oh, no—is—is Seokga—should I go to—does he know?"

"No. It's not about . . . that. I'm going to Geoje with Seokga, chasing a lead. You need to be careful while I'm gone. Don't go out at night." She knows that the odds are slim of Dok-hyun truly being the eoduksini's host, and Hani cannot abide the thought of anything happening to Somi while she's not there to protect her.

"Hani . . ." Somi sounds scared. "Hani, what's happened?"

"Three more bodies were found just now. I thought I should tell you."

"Three?" Somi's voice wavers. "You should be careful, too, unnie. You're already in enough danger."

"I'm fine." Hani is acutely aware of the fact that Seokga has gotten into his car, and that the engine is now running. She does not put it past him to drive off without her. "Look, I have to go now. But be safe, okay?"

"Wait. I-I have a question. I've been feeling odd . . . Hani?"

The Jaguar is pulling out of the parking space now. Seokga

smiles nastily at her, probably planning to gun it before she can reach the car. "Somi, I have to go. Call me later, okay?" Hanging up, Hani glares at Seokga's car and starts to hurry over to the door of the passenger seat. But a hand on her shoulder stops her. She turns impatiently to meet Hyun-tae. The jeoseung saja's eyes are dark with concern behind his spectacles.

"Was that . . . your friend? From the café?"

Somi. Hani smirks in amusement as Hyun-tae's cheeks flush pink. "It was." She pauses, cocking her head as an idea slowly forms in her mind. "You're fond of her, aren't you? Of Somi?"

"Somi," Hyun-tae repeats almost wondrously, a smile tugging at his lips. "Her name is Somi," he whispers to himself.

Hani frowns at a still-smirking Seokga, conveying exactly what she will do to him if he speeds off without her. Hyun-tae balks, evidently mistaking her frown as meant for him.

"I-I mean," he clarifies, clearing his throat, "that I find her very . . . That is . . . She is a pleasant—"

His stuttering is answer enough.

He does care. Good.

"I'm leaving town," she says to the grim reaper, closing her hand around the car door's handle as Seokga honks, the noise shattering the otherwise silent night. Asshole. "I can't watch over her, and with the eoduksini in the city—"

Seokga honks again. Hani grits her teeth.

"If you care about her, look after her until I'm back. Get that part-time job at the café. Make sure she's safe. Somi—she's a bit innocent, naïve to the world—*I'm coming*," she snaps as Seokga honks once again. Hani glares at him through the tinted window before twisting back to Hyun-tae. "Make sure nothing happens to her."

Hyun-tae straightens as this order reaches his ears. "I will protect Ms. Somi with my life," he replies dutifully. "No harm will come to her. I promise."

"Good," Hani sighs in relief, yanking open the car door. "By the way—if you fail, I'll kill you."

"Oh." Hyun-tae flinches. "Yes, ma'am."

With a sweet smile, Hani shuts the car door and nestles back in her seat. Outside, Hyun-tae bows in farewell and promise as the Jaguar pulls onto the awaiting street and disappears into the night.

"We're making one more quick stop," Seokga says as Hani buckles her seatbelt. She does not usually use seatbelts, but due to the breakneck speed at which Seokga is driving, it seems to be a good idea.

A very good idea.

Hani lifts a brow in curiosity. "Where are we going?"

"A weapons shop." The car narrowly avoids hitting the curb as Seokga executes a dangerously sharp turn.

"A weapons shop?" Hani repeats, not sure if she's misheard him or not.

"We need to be prepared for a fight. If the eoduksini isn't Dok-hyun, if it finds Ji-ah, blood will certainly be shed, and I'd like to make sure that it's not ours." Seokga blasts through an intersection, not paying any heed to the long line of cars now behind them. "I have a sword. You need something other than your claws."

"A sword? Where is it?" Hani asks curiously, twisting around to look at the backseat. There's nothing but two duffel bags and an empty water bottle.

Seokga taps the silver imoogi curled around his cane, which he's leaned against the door of the driver's side.

"That's a cane, not a sword." Her imagination births a vision of Seokga using his cane as a weapon, and she snorts. In her mind's eye, he resembles a grumpy old man chasing children from his lawn. She can't stifle the laugh that rips from her lips. "You don't mean that you wield *that* in a fight, do you?"

Seokga slides her one of those *are you stupid* looks. "The cane transforms into a sword," he drawls. "A very, very sharp sword that I will wield on you if you don't stop laughing."

How intriguing. Hani perks up in interest. "Am I getting a cane-sword, too, then?"

"No." Seokga slams on the brakes and Hani nearly topples forward, stopped only by the seatbelt. "No, you are most certainly not."

Seething, Hani takes in their surroundings. They're on the same street that the Creature Café is located on, parked before a small store with a sign reading WEAPONS, WAR ARMOR, AND OTHER WANTS. "They're open?" she asks skeptically as she joins Seokga at the wooden door, arching a brow.

"A dokkaebi named Jae-jin runs it," he replies, rapping his cane-sword's handle against the wood. "Jae-jin has no friends. So unlike other dokkaebi, he spends his nights working rather than partying. He's most certainly inside." He raps against the wood again. "Jae-jin," he calls through the door, his voice sharp and irritable. "I know that you're in here."

Hani doesn't know whether to laugh in amusement or cringe in sympathy for the creature inside.

A moment later, the door swings open, revealing a chubby dokkaebi with a pronounced underbite, wearing a pair of large, clear goggles and leather gloves. His eyes are distorted behind the goggles, bulging and fishlike. "Seokga! Sir!" he says eagerly, scampering aside to allow them entry. "What are you doing here?"

Seokga enters the shop, Hani close behind. Her eyes widen as she takes in the walls teeming with glittering swords and shining knives. This place is nothing short of heaven.

"I was working on some stuff in the back," Jae-jin stammers, hastily tugging off the gloves and the goggles. "I swear I don't usually walk around like this. Sir."

Seokga waves a hand impatiently. "Yes, I have enough common sense to figure that out myself, Jae-jin." He nods to Hani, who smiles in greeting. "This is my . . . assistant, Kim Hani," he says through his teeth, spitting out that one word—*assistant*—with no small amount of reluctance. "She's here to buy a weapon."

"It's nice to meet you," Jae-jin says with a hasty nod. "What sort of weapon are you looking for?"

Hani runs her eyes over the armed walls in admiration. "Do you make all of these?"

"Yes, ma'am." Jae-jin bobs his head eagerly. "And if you want something you don't see on these walls here, I can custom-make one for you—"

"We don't have that sort of time," Seokga cuts in. He jerks his head at Hani. "Choose something, fox, and let's go."

Hani's gaze lingers on a set of small silver twin daggers with plain white hilts. They're certainly not as beautiful as her scarlet ones, nor as deadly, but she can tell they'll do the job in a pinch. She approaches the wall on which they hang, and carefully retrieves them from their holsters. "These," she murmurs, holding their weight in her hands. They're heavier than her red knives, and thicker, too, but she'll certainly be able to inflict a vast amount of pain upon an opponent with them. She looks up to Seokga. "I'll get these."

The fallen god is silent for a moment, watching her—and Hani realizes her mistake.

The Scarlet Fox is known to fight with twin daggers.

Seokga's eyes narrow slightly, and he tilts his head, brows furrowing together in clear suspicion as he observes her, agonizingly silent. Heart in her throat, Hani stares right back at him, jutting out her chin in what she hopes appears as annoyed exasperation.

Hani has always been good at acting. She took classes from Shakespeare himself once in the sixteenth century. She uses those skills now. "Why are you looking at me?" she demands, holding up the knives and leveling the blades at his chest, careful to hold them slightly incorrectly even though it feels like an affront to her dignity. "Do you need proof that I can use them? If so"—she smiles—"take a step forward and I'll show you."

Seokga blinks at the awkward form of her hands around the hilts, enough to signify some talent with them, but not mastery, and the moment of suspicion is gone. Twin daggers are a common enough weapon, and there are more gumiho acquainted with them than one might think, inspired—maybe subconsciously— by the legendary Scarlet Fox, the most famous gumiho to have ever existed. Seokga probably thinks she picked up the knives for a similar reason. He glowers. "Hurry and buy them. We have somewhere to be."

"What?" Hani demands. "I thought *you* were buying them for me."

"You're truly unbelievable, fox. Why on Iseung would you think that?"

Hani grimaces. That's a good question. But she just assumed . . . Sighing, she turns to Jae-jin. "How much?"

The dokkaebi looks apologetic, shifting his weight from foot to foot. "Ah . . . Since they're handmade . . ."

That's enough of an answer for Hani. Wincing, she hangs them back on the wall's holster, and turns to Seokga. "I'll use my claws, thanks. Or if we stop at a restaurant, maybe I can grab a steak knife."

"A steak knife," Seokga repeats dubiously. "You'll fight off an eoduksini with a steak knife."

"If you'd rather have me fight with those knives," Hani retorts sweetly, "you could buy them for me. I'll pay you back." A blatant lie, and she's sure that Seokga knows it. But she holds up her right hand and crosses her index and middle finger with a wink. "I swear it."

Seokga does not look convinced at all.

But Hani still walks out of Weapons, War Armor, and Other Wants with a pair of shiny new daggers.

CHAPTER SIXTEEN
SEOKGA

THE GUMIHO IS SNORING.

And she is snoring very, very, *very* loudly.

Hani fell asleep an hour ago and has been snoring ever since, each snore rising exponentially in volume as Seokga's wish to throw himself out of the car rises exponentially to match. "Please," he begs. "*Please* be quiet."

Almost in answer, Hani utters a snore that leaves his eardrums shriveling in protest.

He has been driving for two hours now, following the route to Busan as the barest tinges of morning light begin to brush against the deep, velvet-black sky. Seokga has done his best to ignore the strain in his eyes which grow heavier and heavier with each passing moment, the cramps of hunger twisting his stomach, and the fog of exhaustion clouding his mind. But there's no denying he's completely drained. The coffee and the nap have helped him recover from using his magic earlier, but he's still pushing his limits.

Once they reach Busan, they'll continue on to the Busan-Geoje bridge, which will take another hour. Crossing the bridge itself will take forty minutes. He may have no other choice but to wake Hani and allow her to drive his car. Damn it. He is not pleased at the thought, but he's not pleased at the thought of falling asleep at the wheel, either.

He sighs and sneaks a glance at his . . . assistant.

She is slumped against the window with her mouth partially open, her usually flawless, wavy mane of hair rumpled and tangled. She cradles her two new daggers in her arms like they're (much more murderous) teddy bears, both tucked away in their respective sheaths. Seokga's eyes linger on those daggers. In the store, for a moment he'd wondered . . .

Hani's eyes snap open and Seokga hastily jerks his head away. "You were snoring," he says, unsure why his cheeks have heated slightly under her bleary glare. *In annoyance,* he assures himself. *Annoyance.* "You were snoring very, very loudly."

"Snoring?" Hani mumbles, sitting up and rolling her shoulders. "I don't snore."

Seokga bites back a laugh of derision. She cannot be serious. "Yes, you do."

"No," she insists, "I don't." Hani cracks her neck once, twice. "How close are we to Busan? I'm hungry."

"Forty-five minutes away."

"Mm." Hani yawns. "We should stop for breakfast once we reach the city. It shouldn't take long." He feels her scrutinizing him and scowls as that heat licks his cheeks again underneath her inspection. "You look tired."

"I am," he admits in a sour mutter.

"Pull over," Hani urges, gesturing to the space at the side of the highway. "Let me take over."

The thought is tempting. But he shakes his head. "No."

"Seokga," Hani says, "if you fall asleep at the wheel and you perish in a car crash, you'll never be reinstated as a god. Especially since when you gods go through your 'divine reincarnation' you first take the form of—well—baby you. Can an infant stop an eoduksini?" She examines her nails, still watching him out of the corner of her eye. Her gaze feels wry. Calculating. As if even though they've only known each other for a (mercifully) short time, she seems to know exactly what words to choose next. "And, Seokga, if you wind up as an infant version of your-self . . . Well." Hani grins. "I'm sure Hwanin would pay your babysitter well, and I'm never one to turn down a little extra cash . . ."

Seething, Seokga pulls over.

SEOKGA WAKES TO THE SMELL OF HOT CHOCOLATE.

The rich, chocolatey aroma brimming with sugary cream fills his car as he cracks open his eyes, blinking away the remnants of fatigue that still linger in his vision. His mouth is stale and his eyes feel gummy and swollen with sleep as they search out Hani, who sends him a wry little grin as she sips at a paper cup, from which tendrils of steam swirl. "Good morning," she says, rays of sunlight bathing her face with a pale-yellow aura. Her eyes are molten in the light, a warm, depthless brown tinged with red as they crinkle in the corners, the effect of her smile. She cheerfully waggles her fingers at him.

Seokga realizes that he is still hazily gazing at her and blinks, quickly looking away. "Please," he grumbles, rubbing his eyes and glancing out the window, "tell me that you are not eating in my car." They are parked outside of a Coffee Star, in which a few early risers sip at beverages and nibble on pastries. They've made it to Busan.

"I am not eating in your car," says Hani as she rummages around in a large paper bag and pulls out a breakfast sandwich. "Here. I got this for you. An egg bun with strawberry jam." She tosses him the wax-paper-wrapped food and he just barely man-ages to catch it. He sniffs it suspiciously.

"Egg with strawberry jam?" he asks in disdain, even as his stomach rumbles grumpily in hunger. The strawberry egg bun doesn't smell *bad,* but the concept is enough to have him glaring at the large Coffee Star bag in Hani's lap. "Is there anything actually edible in there?"

Wordlessly, Hani pulls out three more of the same breakfast sandwiches. At his glower of disbelief, she laughs. The sound is as bright and sparkling as the morning sunshine. And like the morning sunshine, it annoys him. "They're for me. But try yours," she urges. "It's good, I swear. I also got you this." There is a cardboard cup carrier resting on the dashboard; Hani grabs the remaining cup and hands it to him.

"Coffee?" Seokga asks hopefully—but he should have known better than to believe Hani has gotten him his favorite beverage. She smiles again.

"Hot chocolate."

"Hot chocolate," Seokga repeats in disbelief, staring down at the breakfast that Hani has arranged for him with an immense amount of wariness. "I want coffee. I need caffeine."

Hani wrinkles her nose. "Coffee is disgusting," she counters. "Hot chocolate is the perfect morning drink—sweet and loaded with chocolate. Whipped cream, too. Plus, chocolate does have some caffeine. And the sugar will give you a boost, too."

Seokga blinks. "You hate coffee." Impossible. Coffee is the only bit of good on this worthless realm. But the gumiho nods and takes a large bite of her own sandwich.

"You should eat," she says around a mouthful. "Once we reach Geoje, I think it's safe to say that we won't have time to snack. Finding Ji-ah will be our priority." She swallows and licks her fingers. "We should head out soon. Ten minutes, maybe less. I'll drive again," she adds, cozying back into his seat—which, he realizes, she has scooched up to the steering wheel and pumped higher.

Frowning, he opens his mouth to protest, but Hani cuts him

off. "Eat," she repeats. "I can hear your stomach growling from here."

He doesn't doubt it. His stomach is tight with hunger, desperate for sustenance. Sighing, Seokga raises the sandwich to his mouth and takes a tiny nibble. The egg is fluffy and slightly salty. The strawberry is jam sweet and sticky. The bun is the right amount of soft and chewy. Despite himself, he takes another bite—this one larger, grudgingly admitting that the gumiho is right. The sandwich is delicious. He sips at the hot chocolate and makes a face. Far too sugary for his liking. But, paired with the filling egg bun, it does its job. Seokga feels his energy slowly seeping back.

They eat in silence, Hani working her way through the other two sandwiches with an unbridled hunger, and Seokga slowly, thoughtfully consuming his one, careful to wipe his mouth as needed. When they're finished, Hani sends him a look of triumph and backs the car out of its parking space. "It was good, wasn't it?"

Seokga does not tend to admit that he was wrong. "No," he says frostily, even as he wishes Hani had bought him two more buns.

Hani laughs under her breath, and Seokga almost chuckles ruefully along with her.

Almost.

He stops just in time. Disgusted with himself, he scowls instead and digs out his cellphone. "I'm going to call Shim. Check on Dok-hyun." Despite the early hour, it's only a few seconds before Shim picks up on the other line.

"Seokga," the chief says pleasantly. "Good morning."

"Update on Dok-hyun?"

A sigh crackles from his phone, and he can just imagine Shim shaking his head. "Would it take too much out of you to say 'good morning' back?"

"Yes."

There's a long silence.

Scowling, Seokga takes a deep breath. "Fine. Good morning. Update on Dok-hyun?"

"That's better," Shim replies dryly. "As for Dok-hyun, he's doing as fine as one can be doing when they're in the precinct holding cell, swarmed by haetae, and not sure what they're doing in there."

"Has he said anything?"

"Well," the chief says, "he's said a few things. One, that he can't believe you would do this to him. He thought you and him were becoming friends."

Seokga rolls his eyes. Hani gives him a questioning glance and reaches for the phone. He jerks back, and she sticks out her tongue at him. There's whipped cream on the tip.

"Two, that after all his family has done for this precinct, he can't believe we would repay him like this. Which I really do have to agree with."

"Is that all?"

"Oh, no. Three is that he is not the eoduksini, that he's never killed anybody in his life, and after we release him, he wants to quit. You lost us the Lee family, Seokga." Shim's voice rarely turns hard when he speaks to Seokga, but it does now. "Lee Dae-song died just four months ago. It's been hard on Dok-hyun, and then you turn around and do this. The Lees have been integral to New Sinsi's haetae since its founding. If you're not right about this, I'm going to be very disappointed in you."

"He's being dramatic," Seokga snaps back. "We're nearly to Geoje, and we'll likely be back within a day or two. If you really want to clear his name, take a trip to the New Sinsi Library and see if there's really a stack of books on eoduksini. In the meantime, tell him he's basically on vacation. Give him something to amuse himself with. A coloring book or some toy cars."

"He's not a child, Detective Seokga—"

Seokga hangs up with a dramatic press of the button and tries to ignore the uncomfortable feeling buzzing around in his chest. It's not guilt. It can't be guilt, because Seokga the Fallen doesn't care about obnoxious humans and their feelings. But still, as he recounts the phone call to Hani, the inane feeling persists.

It's another hour to the bridge. Seokga watches Busan speed by the windows, the looming mountains in the distance passing by in a blur of deep browns and vibrant greens. Sansin, minor mountain gods, watch over Busan. He wonders if they watch Hani and him speed by, what they think of catching a glimpse of the infamous fallen god sitting next to a gumiho currently attempting to keep one hand on the wheel while taking a large gulp of now-cool chocolate.

The bridge finally emerges in the distance, crossing over a wide expanse of navy-blue sea toward rolling mountaintops of stone and forest. Seokga feels Hani glance at him, her gaze one of concern.

"Ji-ah is probably scared out of her mind," Hani murmurs as she urges the car onto the bridge, the tires rolling over the smooth cement road. "She saw the impossible."

Seokga watches the rippling blue waters below. "Once we get her back to New Sinsi, we can erase her memory. I can use my powers, or she can use the procedure available for human witnesses." A shaman could extract Ji-ah's memories of the eoduksini—and everything that followed. Shamans have become integral to New Sinsi for performing procedures like this, and for their skill weaving glamours over places such as the haetae precinct, the weapons shop, and the bridge. This magic allows the peaceful co-existence of creatures and humans. Seokga does not like to contemplate what the city would be like without the glamours.

Humans have a tendency to kill the things they don't understand.

"Should we erase it, though?" Hani frowns as she drives. "She'll need to know to be careful—of the eoduksini, I mean."

"We'll deal with it when the time comes."

"I wonder who she saw," Hani muses a few minutes later. "What form the eoduksini took. If it really is Dok-hyun."

Seokga sighs. "There's no telling until we speak with her." He gazes at the bridge's long expanse up ahead, at the first minuscule island the bridge passes through before continuing on toward the other two, then finally transitioning into an underwater tube leading to Geoje. Somewhere, on that larger island, is Ji-ah—their answer to the questions hounding them, and Seokga's ticket back to Okhwang.

Fifteen minutes of almost amicable silence pass, finally broken by Hani. Her eyes are still on the road ahead as she says, "What do you plan on doing? When you're a god again, I mean."

Seokga pauses, taken slightly aback by the question. There is no teasing cadence to her words, nothing but pure curiosity. "I . . ." He glances at her. "I wish to return to Okhwang. My home. My palace."

Her eyebrows lift as they exit the underwater tunnel, resurfacing as they pass through the first island, the bridge cutting through rich forestry. "You have a palace?"

He nods, his thoughts drifting toward his hopeful future. A future of power, of living in luxury once again as a god. A small smile plays on his lips as he confides, "Hwanin will have me, he says, on house arrest. I plan on breaking it immediately."

"Somehow, I'm not surprised." Hani snorts. "Any other plans? Another coup, perhaps?"

"In time . . ." Seokga sighs, a cruel smile twisting his lips. "In another millennia or so, it's very likely."

"Emperor Seokga," she hums. "It does have somewhat of a ring to it."

He cannot prevent his smile from growing. "Oh, I know."

"You know," Hani says, "I should get some sort of reward from Hwanin, too, for helping you with the eoduksini. And the Scarlet Fox. Compensation," she continues, "for dealing with your cranky old ass. Maybe some money. Or"—Hani straightens, turning to him with a grin—"a palace of my very own."

Seokga clicks his tongue in contempt. "You'll get nothing, fox."

"Except the pleasure of your company, of course," she replies with another sparkling laugh.

He frowns, not sure whether he is being mocked or complimented. Her laughter doubles, and he finally allows a small chuckle to escape his lips. She is . . . almost funny.

The revelation annoys him more than it pleases him.

As if surprised he laughed, Hani twists to him with wide eyes. Seokga immediately recomposes his face into its standard scowl. "What?"

Her eyes still dance. "Nothing."

Seokga rolls his eyes.

The next half hour is passed in pleasant, comfortable silence. When the bridge begins to transition back into the underwater tunnel, Seokga notes that Hani has gone slightly pale, and her fingers are tight around the steering wheel.

"What is it?" he asks—not in concern, he tells himself. Just curiosity.

"I don't like water," she says between clenched teeth. "Especially going under it."

The deep yellow light of the tunnel bathes the car in its glow, and Seokga watches as a bead of sweat trickles down Hani's forehead.

"Can you swim?" he asks, and she cuts him a venomous glance.

"None of your business."

Seokga smirks. "So you can't."

"I *can*," she fires back, "if—" Hani cuts herself off, snapping her mouth closed.

He leans toward her in interest. "What?"

"Don't laugh," she warns. "Because if you laugh, I will send in some very unfortunate tips to *Godly Gossip*."

"I won't laugh," Seokga replies, already planning on cackling and calling her bluff. Sending in those tips would give him legitimate grounds to fire her, and he has gotten the distinct impression that she's suctioned herself to this case like a leech.

"I can swim," she says, staring straight ahead at the barely visible end of the tunnel, "if I'm in my fox form. But I never learned how to swim in my human form. Satisfied?" Hani sends him a brief glower before turning back to the road.

Seokga waits one moment, one singular moment, before snickering himself hoarse with laughter.

Hani makes a strangled noise in the back of her throat. "You said you wouldn't laugh."

"And I don't ever keep my word. Relax," he says in response to her sneer. "It's not as if this tunnel is going to cave in. We certainly won't be crushed by the water and die."

"Not helping," she rasps. "Not helping at all, you buzzard."

Seokga just smirks.

When they finally emerge from the tunnel, Hani reaches over and drives her fist into his shoulder. He winces, pain flaring as her knuckles bash against his skin. "Was that," he grits out, "entirely necessary?"

"No," she replies sweetly. "No, it wasn't."

The pair is broodingly silent as the Jaguar struggles to climb the winding hills of Geoje, the tires crunching on the gravel road. The ocean surrounds the lush island in a glittering blue, green, and aquamarine halo receding farther and farther away as the car climbs higher and higher. Large, looming palm trees stretch their limbs up to the sky, their fronds scraping against the periwinkle expanse and sugar floss clouds. There are no buildings in sight, just pure, unadulterated nature save for the fishing ports hundreds of feet below them.

As they move deeper into Geoje, the first markers of civilization begin to appear. Street signs, neighborhoods and small towns, convenience stores and gas stops. Perhaps thirty minutes later, Okpo emerges all at once. Although it still surrounds them, the forest has receded, instead replaced by imposing towers, bustling sidewalks, honking cars, and rows of restaurants that fill the air with the delicious smells of grilled beef, spicy noodles, fried fish, and the unmistakably rich smell of budae jjigae. Seokga's stomach tightens in hunger once again, but he ignores it. They are here to retrieve Choi Ji-ah, not to explore the bustling city located in the heart of Geoje.

"Maengjongjuk Forest," he says to Hani. "It's going to be past Okpo, on the outskirts."

"Just tell me where and when to turn," she retorts sourly, clearly not yet over his laughing fit. For perhaps a split second, Seokga contemplates apologizing before stubbornly deciding against it. He has not once apologized for any of his actions, and he certainly will not start now.

Yet he finds that he much prefers the bright-eyed, laughing Hani who slurps at hot chocolate and smiles as brightly as the shining sun to the scowling Hani who not-so-subtly sneaks a vulgar gesture in his direction as he tells her to turn left.

CHAPTER SEVENTEEN

HANI

IF THE WORD *GREEN* HAD A PHOTOGRAPH NEXT TO IT IN the dictionary, Hani is certain that the photo would be of Maengjongjuk Forest.

The bamboo park is teeming with greenery: looming jade trees, thick emerald grass, shrubbery of the deepest olive, and a brilliant, bright green moss that creeps along the cobblestoned path leading toward the park's entrance—a humongous, faux-bamboo archway standing before the wooden building in which tickets can be bought. The real bamboo is not yet visible, undoubtedly located deeper within the park.

Hani hitches her tote bag higher up on her shoulder as she and Seokga pass through the archway. Her new daggers are safely hidden inside, ready to be whipped out at the first sign of an approaching demon.

The line for tickets is mercifully short. The woman at the desk looks bored as Seokga and Hani step forward—Hani with a polite smile, Seokga with an impatient frown. The woman gives Hani a cursory glance up and down before doing the same to Seokga.

"Two teenagers?" she asks, riffling through a stack of rectangular tickets. "That will be three thousand won each."

Seokga stiffens, clearly insulted at being mistaken for a teenager. But Hani jabs her elbow into his side, and mutters under her breath, "What she's supposed to say, tickets for two immortal beings? We look like young twenty-somethings who still get carded at bars. Don't pout," she croons as he seethes. "At least we'll never get wrinkles."

Reluctantly, Seokga hands the woman his credit card. A moment later, Hani and Seokga are showing the tickets to a cheerful security man guarding the path leading to a small outdoor plaza, in which are restrooms, signs displaying maps, and various entrances to paths leading into the towering bamboo forests.

Hani makes her way to one of the maps, Seokga close on her tail. "Do you think we should ask for directions to the hidden village?"

Seokga shakes his head. "They don't want people going off the tracks. They wouldn't tell us."

Hani sighs, eyeing the map with a fair amount of apprehension. There are at least four trails, all snaking their way through various points of the forest—north, south, east, and west. "Where do you think the village is?"

As Seokga leans over her shoulder to scan the map, Hani seriously considers ramming herself backward in order to send him stumbling, but decides against it. As miffed as she might be with the fallen god, they are a team now. A team with one goal: to find Choi Ji-ah.

Seokga traces the north trail with a slender finger, which eventually slides away onto a dense area of bamboo forest away from the path. "Here."

"How do you know?"

"I don't." Seokga shrugs, stepping away. "But it seems as good a place to start as any."

Hani starts to move, but her eye is caught on a small icon of a panda bear near the south trail. *Pandas!* Oh, Hani loves pandas. "Let's find Ji-ah quickly," Hani says over her shoulder, starting toward the north trail, "so I can go and see the bears."

✦

FOUR HOURS LATER AND DRENCHED IN SWEAT, CHOI JI-AH and the hidden village are still nowhere to be found, and Hani no longer has the desire to see the panda bears. She just wants to go *home*.

Slumped against a towering bamboo shoot's stalk, Hani glares at Seokga. North, west, east, south . . . They have traipsed through the entire forest to no avail. There is no village, none at all. Hani has decided that this village does not exist, that Kim Sora has sent them on a wild-goose chase.

Sweat sticks to the nape of her neck as the midday sun blazes in the sky above. She can barely feel her legs anymore after their four-hour hike through the unpathed forest. "You," Hani rasps to Seokga, who is leaning heavily against the bamboo shoot opposite her. His face shines with sweat and is streaked with dirt from when he tripped over a loose rock earlier. Hani laughed herself hoarse at the sight of the god hitting the ground, proclaiming something about karma. That event now seems like a lifetime ago—many, many lifetimes ago. "You," Hani repeats. "Give me the water." Seokga holds their last remaining bottle of water in his hands, bought two hours ago when they'd returned to the plaza, determined to once again analyze the map. There is only a sip or two left—and Hani plans to claim those two sips as her own.

He glowers at her. "I'm still drinking it."

"Seokga," Hani rasps, "give me the water. Please." Her mouth is on fire, her tongue made from sandpaper. Every breath is sharp against the back of her throat. "Please," she repeats, her head lolling back to rest on the stalk. She stares up at the towering bamboo shoots as they stretch toward the sky, her muscles aching with exhaustion.

Her vision is soon blocked by Seokga's frowning, dirtied face as it peers down at her. "Don't pass out, fox. We still need to find Ji-ah."

"I know," she grouses, snatching the bottle of water from his hand. The two sips of water trickle into her mouth, lukewarm and doing little to assuage the terrible parchedness. "Help me up," she demands, reaching out her hands.

Seokga stares at them in clear disgust. "Get up on your own."

Irritation heats Hani's blood, and her fox bead flares within her chest, sending a desire to hurt, to kill, through her body. Perhaps it's the heat, perhaps it's her exhaustion, perhaps it's the fact that they *still haven't found Ji-ah* . . . But whatever the case, Hani clambers to her feet, anger speeding her heartbeat to a horribly fast tempo. "Why," she demands, "do you need to be such a *dick* all the time?"

She watches through twitching eyes as Seokga blinks. As her words truly settle into him. As his face flushes a furious red, as he bares his teeth and growls, *"Do you not know to whom you speak, fox?"* That last word, *fox,* is spat with such hatred . . . such *superiority,* that Hani glowers back at him.

"Certainly not a god," she retorts, each word a bullet.

"You—" A vein bulges in Seokga's forehead. "You—"

"You're a *dick,* all the time," Hani pants, quivering in fatigue and anger. The words spill out of her, bursting past her lips like a torrent of bullets. "You are. And I'm so *fucking sick* of it—"

His eyes narrow to slits. *"I suggest that you stop talking,"* he hisses with a terrible coldness. But Hani plows on.

"Do you remember when you came to the Creature Café for the first time? You ordered an iced coffee with one cream and one sugar and I *gave it to you!* But then you announced that I'd added in *two sugars,* and when I disagreed, you asked me to call my boss and you told her I should be fired on account of being *inept at making coffee.*" Hani jabs a finger into his chest. *"Fucking fired.*" The memory heats her blood to a near boil. She doubts that he even remembers that day, even remembers how he smiled that cold, conceited smile down at her as he uttered those despicable words. How he managed to get a full refund for a drink that had been made in compliance to his exact order.

Seokga is silent, his expression inscrutable. But he's breathing heavily, his cane tight in his hand, his gaze sparking with sheer hatred.

"You treat the creatures of Iseung like they're nothing. Nobody. I've seen how you speak to Jae-jin. Dok-hyun, too, before we even suspected him! And Euna! Telling her about the seven hells right before she's sent down to Jeoseung? You can't use people as your personal punching bags just because your *miserable attempt at a coup failed*—"

Those words unleash him. Hani barely has time to blink before Seokga's hands are tight on her shoulders, his voice near guttural as he growls, *"Do not speak of my story."*

At his touch, something unleashes within Hani—something vicious and violent and feral. She snarls, grabbing *his* shoulders, and shoves him backward. He stumbles and she stalks forward, her body acting without her mind, her fist rearing back . . .

Seokga snarls and dives for her waist, aiming, no doubt, to tackle her to the ground. Hani curses in surprise and shifts as he gets close, but her feet stumble and—*shit.*

Hani's arms wrap around Seokga's back as he knocks her to the ground, his body hitting hers with enough force that she sees stars—but her slight stumble earlier has sent her moving, and Seokga's attack only propels her farther. Her arms clutching Seokga tight to her, Hani shrieks right into his ear in surprise and pain as they begin to roll, crashing through the foliage and shooting down a particularly large slope. Seokga is screaming, too—screaming in pure rage as they roll down, down, down, flying through bushes and hitting their backs on hard rocks, bouncing off bamboo shoots with heavy thuds. In a blur of speed, Seokga is on top of Hani, his cane flying out of his grip—and then Hani is on top of Seokga, a shriek bursting from her lips as the wind is knocked out of her, as they tumble over each other and crash through the forest.

It is only when the slope gives way to flat ground that they eventually roll to a stop. Seokga is limp atop of Hani, his head pressed against hers, his eyes closed. Hani glowers up at him, blood trickling from her mouth thanks to a particularly nasty whump from a very large rock. *Is he unconscious?*

"You fucking asshole," she croaks into his ear, just to check.

His eyes fly open and he stares down at her, panting. "You—"

"Get *off*," she moans, smacking his back. "Get off, get off, get *off*." Gods, he's heavy. Seokga rolls from her with a groan, lying on his back next to her and futilely reaching for his cane that lays a few feet away.

"I hate you," he whispers.

But Hani is already pulling herself up with difficulty, brushing off the dirt, twigs, and leaves riddling her body from their tumble. Tearing her glare away from the literally fallen god, she takes in their new surroundings—and freezes.

They are in the middle of a circle of seven traditional Korean chogajips, wooden houses with thatched roofs.

The village.

Hani and Seokga have found the abandoned village.

"Seokga," Hani says, glancing back down at the god who once again looks unconscious. "Seokga." She prods him with her foot. When he doesn't stir, she kicks him in the side. Hard. *"Seokga."*

Choi Ji-ah is here, somewhere. She's sure of it.

Groaning, Seokga sits up, massaging his head and collecting his cane. *"What?"*

"We found it. We found the village." Hani grins—not at Seokga, but at the homes in one of which she's sure Ji-ah hides. "We can find—"

An unnatural growl, wet and deep, resounds from a point just behind Hani . . . who goes very, very still, the hairs on the back of her neck rising in terror.

Seokga is staring at a spot just behind her shoulder. "Hani," he says under his breath, "don't move."

It's the eoduksini. Hani is sure of it. It's found them and she's going to die. It wasn't Dok-hyun, after all, it was somebody else, and it was one step ahead of them the whole time. A cold sweat trickles down her neck. She is going to rest lifeless on Dok-hyun's examination table, bulging with black veins, her heart ripped out.

Great. *Great.*

There's a soft *snap* as Seokga's cane transforms into a sword of pure silver, blinding and bright.

Hani can't take it anymore. Jaw clenched, she whips around, unsheathing her claws with sharp *snicks.*

Nothing meets her eye.

There is nothing there.

But then that awful growl sounds again, and Hani moves her gaze downward.

There, glowering up at her through black eyes, is a herd of fat, salivating children who are no taller than her knees—but twice as wide as both her legs combined.

For a moment, the forest is comedically silent save for the chirping of a single, faraway locust.

Hani chooses to break that silence. "What the *fuck?*"

The children smile, revealing pike's teeth and black, wizened tongues that drip with yellow saliva. Their skin is pallid, bulging from their bodies, as if they recently gorged themselves to the point of near-eruption. Their bare feet scuffle in the dirt as they form a circle around Hani and Seokga, those unnatural growls escaping from their chapped lips.

Hani looks to Seokga in a strange mixture of amusement, dismay, and terror.

Seokga flips his sword in his hand, scanning the circle of children. "Baegopeun gwisin," he mutters, slowly moving his way to Hani, so they stand back-to-back. He limps slightly without the help of his walking stick, but his eyes blaze with a self-assurance so potent that Hani is surprised that the children encircling them do not flee. They are doing little but growling, glowering at them through pouchy eyes. "Hungry ghosts. Gwisin. Unrulies. Ji-ah must have brought food with her this time. They've smelled it—and her." A baegopeun gwisin lunges for Hani's ankle, its teeth bared. She kicks it aside. The ring of baegopeun gwisin hiss in outrage and begin to close in on the god and the gumiho. Damn it. If the hungry ghosts have already gotten to Ji-ah, there's probably not much left of the girl to find.

"Do we kill them?" Hani asks, reaching into her tote bag and withdrawing the daggers, shaking off their sheaths. She doesn't want to dirty her treasured claws with the salivating children's flesh. "All of them?" Her plan of ruining Seokga's efforts to add more Unrulies to his ledger has crumbled before her eyes with the emergence of these . . . *things.*

"What do you think?" Seokga demands. "Of *course* we kill them."

"They look like children!"

"Trust me, they're not. Given the chance, they'll eat you, bones and all. Hair, too." Seokga scoffs in revulsion. "Just kill them and be done with it," he snaps over his shoulder.

Grimly, Hani twirls her daggers in her hands. "Fine."

"Fine," Seokga retorts icily.

"Fine," she snarls, and strikes.

Bending low in order to reach them, she slashes at the hungry ghosts, ripping through their pudgy bodies with her daggers and lurching out of the way of their gnashing teeth. She holds herself back, though, lest Seokga see she has mastered the daggers, after all. It's an effort to restrain herself, but she does.

As her blades tear through the gwisin, they crumble to ash, carried away into the depths of the forest by a stray wind. Hani is dimly aware of Seokga working his way through a cluster of snarling baegopeun gwisin with the lethal grace and deadly agility of a viper.

Hani yelps in pain as a baegopeun gwisin sinks its teeth into her left calf, biting deep. Holding herself back in combat has had an agonizing consequence, and she is unspeakably furious with herself for having sparked the hunt for the Scarlet Fox in the first place.

Seokga whirls toward her, sword raised, eyes going straight to her ankle. Hani is slashing at the gwisin desperately, but the damned Unruly holds tight and refuses to let go of her leg or crumble to ash. She shakes her leg frantically, but the fat ghost holds true. Her leg is on fire. *"Seokga."* Rivulets of blood run down her skin, thick and warm and red.

"He likes you." Seokga smirks, even as he kicks aside a growling ghost and drives his blade into another's chest. "It seems he's especially fond of your leg."

"Get it off," Hani pleads, panicking from pain. "Get it *off*."

"Magic word?" Seokga beheads three baegopeun gwisin in a singular stroke.

"Now," Hani shrieks, clumsily dispatching two more baegopeun gwisin as they attempt to jump onto her shoulders. They turn to ash mid-jump and disappear. To her surprise, there are no more baegopeun gwisin left—save for the one currently eating her leg.

And she's in agony. Its fangs are practically rows of small knives . . . small knives that are embedded in her flesh.

Ouch.

Ouch, ouch, *ouchouchouch*.

Seokga strolls over to Hani, a too-pleasant smile on his lips as he looks down at the state of her calf. "I'll get it off," he purrs, "once you apologize."

"Apologize?" she pants in disbelief. *"Apologize?"*

"Yes," he replies, a wicked glitter in his glare. "I'm sure you're familiar with the action. You apologized beautifully in your bedroom. What was that word you used? It begins with an 's' . . . "

This bastard. "I have nothing to say sorry for," she pants. "Nothing." He's the one who tackled her, after all. He's the one who started their entire feud, trying to get her fired.

Seokga sighs. "So be it."

And he turns away.

Grimacing, Hani slashes at the baegopeun gwisin again to no avail. Its teeth sink deeper, and a noise of strangled pain escapes Hani's lips.

At the noise, Seokga turns, his jaw set. With a swift, sharp motion, he beheads the baegopeun gwisin, his blade just nicking Hani's knee.

The last hungry ghost turns to ash in the wind.

Molten fire peels up Hani's leg, the deep bite marks burning relentlessly. She sucks in an agonized breath and stumbles to a nearby shoot of bamboo, leaning against it for support as her left leg threatens to give way, her entire body shaking with exhaustion.

Seokga's mouth is a hard line of what almost seems like concern as he strides to her side, his sword reverting back to a cane with another soft *snap*. "Hani."

"My leg," she gasps. "I need to bind it." Because blood is leaking out of those bite marks and dripping onto the soil below. Hani grabs the hem of her sweater, aiming to pull her top over her head to rip it up and use it as a bandage. Seokga makes a small noise of incredulity, and too late, Hani realizes that she's just flashed Seokga with a close-up view of her *incredibly* lacy black bra. She scowls, continuing to tug the sweater over her head. It's a rather large, knitted thing, and she's drowning in its fabric. "Don't tell me that in all of your immortal years, you've never seen a bra before." Cool air nips at her sweat-soaked skin as she finally breaks free.

Seokga mutters something in obvious vexation before placing a hand on Hani's arm, stopping her with her shirt halfway off. "You can't walk around like that." His green eyes bore into hers, as if he is trying very, *very* hard not to look down at her breasts.

"I can't walk around with an injured leg, either, *Seokga,*" she snaps back. "I really don't have much choice in the matter."

She watches as his jaw works back and forth. "Put your shirt back on," he grumbles before reaching for the buttons of his own tunic, a silken black long-sleeved shirt that looks as if it costs more than three months of Hani's rent combined. She watches in sheer disbelief as he unbuttons his shirt, revealing . . . *Oh.* Her mouth dries out slightly.

Although the fallen god is slender, Seokga's chest is tan and toned, muscles rippling as he shrugs off his tunic and bunches up the fabric before tossing it to her. "Use this," he says gruffly.

Hani gapes in grudging gratefulness.

And admiration.

Lots of admiration.

His abs are hard and chiseled, golden-beige skin covered in a thin sheen of sweat. At the waistband of his pants, a deep V-line appears and Hani swallows hard as her eyes snag on those two damned lines. She slowly becomes aware that her breathing has quickened—that her cheeks are suddenly warm and red, that no matter how hard she tries, she cannot look away from the fallen god.

And he's looking at her, too—looking at her in a way that is halfway between smug and annoyed and . . . something else as his gaze flickers from her face to her mouth. Hani realizes that she's biting her bottom lip, and quickly arranges her face into an exasperated, bored expression. And just like that, the moment is broken.

Thank fuck.

Seokga scowls, glancing away—but she can almost swear that his cheeks are tinged pink. "Bind your leg. I'll search the village for Ji-ah. If the baegopeun gwisin didn't eat her, she'll be here. Hopefully," he adds in a mutter, already stalking off, the corded muscles in his back rippling with every movement. Hani looks away, her own cheeks burning.

He's average, she tells herself as she rips up his tunic into thin strips. *Average. Not attractive at all. I hate him.*

Hani hisses through her teeth as she ties the strips of fabric around her calf with bloodied fingers. Seokga is nowhere to be seen, having ducked into a chogajip in search of their witness.

"Baegopeun gwisin," Hani grumbles to herself. "Damn them to Jeoseung." Finished binding, she unsteadily rises to her feet, and limps over to the circle of chogajips. "Choi Ji-ah?" she calls. "Are you here?"

Seokga ducks out of one of the homes and shakes his head. "Perhaps she's in—"

"Wait." Hani cocks her head, her ears picking up on a muffled sound. Quiet sobbing. "Over here," Hani whispers, following the noise. It takes her past the chogajips and back into the bamboo forest. Her leg screams in protest as she hobbles over to a small ridge in the ground, but she ignores it, peering over the crest of dirt and growth to find—"Ji-ah," she says kindly to the small figure curled up in the undergrowth. "It's okay. You're safe now."

Ji-ah lifts a tearstained face to Hani and Seokga and blanches in terror. "Who—who are you?" she wails, scrambling backward, clods of dirt flying upward in her wake. "What do you want?"

"We want to help you," Hani says as gently as she can. "We just want to help you, Ji-ah. We're not here to hurt you."

"Detective Seokga. This is my assistant, Kim Hani." Seokga inclines his head. "Kim Sora sent us."

"Sora?" Ji-ah's eyes widen. "You—you know Sora?"

"We do," Hani says, fighting to stay upright against the pain ravaging her leg. She feels Seokga's gaze snap to her, narrow with worry. To her surprise, he steps closer to her—just slightly. An offer, should she accept. Gritting her teeth, Hani leans against his bare shoulder. He tenses in what's either shock or disgust, but a moment later—to her surprise—she feels the god relax beneath her. "And we also know why you left New Sinsi. We promise that you're safe with us now. No harm will come to you."

"You know?" Ji-ah whispers in horror. "You know . . ."

"You're no safer in this forest than in the city," Seokga says grimly. "Those ghosts—the baegopeun gwisin—there may be more of them. We do not have time to loiter around. Come with us, Choi Ji-ah, or remain here. It's your choice."

Ji-ah's eyes dart from Seokga to Hani, and then back again. "You know Sora?" she asks again, her voice tremulous and ridden with tears. "Kim Sora?"

"We do." Hani reaches out her hand to the girl. "Take my hand, Ji-ah. You're safe now. I promise."

Ji-ah's face crumples in relief as her hand meets Hani's.

"You're safe now," Hani repeats, hoping desperately that she speaks the truth.

CHAPTER EIGHTEEN
SEOKGA

T HE GIRL EATS AS IF SHE HASN'T CONSUMED A MORSEL OF food since she fled New Sinsi—which might very well be the case if the baegopeun gwisin ate all the food she'd brought to the village. One of the ghost's breath had smelled suspiciously like dried-squid snacks.

Sitting in an Okpo restaurant, clad in one of his spare shirts, Seokga watches as Choi Ji-ah hunches over her bowl of bibimbap and shovels the rice into her mouth with an almost impressively inhuman speed. Next to her, Hani is staring into space. Her expression is one of exhaustion and pain. Seokga flexes his jaw. Those damned baegopeun gwisin.

Before stopping at the restaurant, Seokga tried to convince Hani to enter an urgent care hospital for treatment of her leg. The fox adamantly refused, stating that she didn't need a doctor despite the clear evidence of the opposite. So Seokga instead stalked into a pharmacy to buy bandages—real bandages—along with painkillers and a disinfectant cream. Hani has not yet used them, claiming that she'll heal soon enough thanks to her gumiho powers. But the bite marks are still deep in her leg with no sign of fading.

Stubborn fox.

It is late now, nearing evening. The walk out of Maengjongjuk Forest took nearly two hours, thanks to their utter lack of direction and Hani's badly wounded leg. Already, it's growing dark outside of the tiny diner. Okpo is slowly being covered by an inky darkness signaling the arrival of the night.

"We should find a hotel," Seokga says, meeting Hani's dazed eyes. The gumiho dips her head into a slight nod and winces.

"I saw one a few blocks away," she says wearily. "The Lotus Hotel. We can rest there for the night."

Seokga glances to Ji-ah, who is still shoveling food into her mouth. He arches a brow inquisitively at Hani. *Let's question her.*

Later. The gumiho shakes her head. *She's been through enough today.*

He sighs in irritation, settling back in his seat. He wants answers, damn it—and he wants them soon. Seokga called Shim a half hour earlier to check on Dok-hyun (still moping), and let him know they'd found the witness. Dok-hyun might be able to be released as soon as Ji-ah gives her statement, but he takes a closer look at the witness's haggard face and food-flecked mouth.

Perhaps the fox is right. All of them have had a particularly trying day. If Ji-ah gives her statement now, it might break her last grip on sanity. As for him, his limbs still ache from the little *tumble* that Hani and he took down that hill.

At the recollection, Seokga grimaces. Perhaps it will be a slightly amusing memory one day. But for now . . . He glowers at Hani as he recalls how the feeling of crashing through a bamboo forest was much less than pleasant.

She glowers right back.

"Thank you for the meal," Ji-ah mumbles as she sets down her spoon and wipes her mouth with the back of her hand. Has the girl never heard of napkins? "I appreciate it very much." She bows slightly as much as she can sitting at the small wooden table.

Hani smiles at her, although it's more of a grimace than anything. "Of course, Ji-ah," she replies as Seokga waves down the waiter for the check. "If you need anything else, just let us know."

The girl's eyes are dark and haunted as she turns to the

wood-latticed window next to her, staring out at the shadowed streets. Not for the first time, Seokga notes how terribly pale her skin is. As if she has been living in a constant state of shocked terror. "It's coming," she whispers. "I can feel it in my bones. It's coming for me; it's looking for me."

Seokga and Hani exchange wary glances.

"Unfortunately for it," Seokga drawls, placing cash within the leather folder, "it won't be finding you anytime soon, Ji-ah. Come." He leans heavily on his cane as he stands, his limbs heavy with fatigue. "The Lotus Hotel is not far away."

"What was it?" Ji-ah whispers, still looking at the street. "What was it? How is it possible that . . . these things exist?" She turns to Hani and Seokga with a trembling lower lip. "I've gone insane," she whispers before a slow smile spreads across her face, not reaching her haunted eyes. "Insane, insane, insane, *insane* . . ."

"You'll feel better after a night's sleep," Hani says, gesturing for Ji-ah to rise. "How long has it been since you slept?"

"Nights and days and nights," Ji-ah murmurs, rising unsteadily. "The ghosts were knocking on my door . . . knocking on my door . . . and every time I close my eyes . . . *nightmares* . . . it's coming for me; it's looking for me . . ."

Hani's teeth are clenched as they exit the diner onto the night-darkened street outside. "Cane," she demands, and Seokga sighs as he reluctantly hands her his staff. It does little to help her limp, and the absence of it in his hand brings out his own, but they manage to collect their duffel bags from his car and arrive at the hotel, a small building of white brick with a fluorescent sign reading WELCOME TO THE LOTUS HOTEL buzzing above the revolving glass doors. It looks like little more than a shabby inn, but Seokga finds that he doesn't quite care. As long as they have beds, he'll be more than satisfied.

The lobby smells of cheap candles and even cheaper air fresheners. Ratty sofas compose a makeshift waiting room, and a threadbare rug covers the creaking wooden floor. A woman sits at the front desk, lining her lips with a foul-smelling gloss and snacking on a bag of honey butter chips. She glances up over her glasses as they approach, arching a brow at Hani's pronounced gait, Ji-ah's nonsense mumblings, and Seokga's less-than-pleasant resting face. "Mm-hmm?" she asks, setting down her lipstick.

"Three rooms," Seokga says, reaching into his pocket for his wallet.

"Mm," the woman says again. "We-ell . . ." She looks as if she's about to say more, but abruptly cuts herself off, taking his card and swiping it. The woman hands it back, munching on a chip. "We only have two left," she says through a mouthful. "So I charged your card for the two remaining rooms. No refunds," she adds with an oily smile, sliding over two room keys.

Seokga is too exhausted to argue, even as annoyance tightens his chest. "How many beds in each?" *Please, please, let there be at least two.*

"One," the woman replies, crunching. "Mm . . . there are couches, though. One per room."

"It's fine." Hani sends Seokga a weary look. "I'll just share a room with Ji-ah."

The elevator is overwhelmingly heavy with the scent of gym socks as it creaks upward to the sixth floor, opening to a narrow corridor with a notably low ceiling and an uneven floor. Seokga hands Hani her room key. Room 603. Seokga is in room 610. They are directly across from each other. "I'll see you in the morning," he mutters. "Tend to your leg." He's stuffed the goods from the pharmacy into her tote bag despite her protests.

Hani rolls her eyes before handing him his cane and limping down the hallway, Ji-ah in tow. Seokga makes his way to his own room, unlocking the flimsy door and stepping inside to a cramped bedroom with an even smaller bathroom located just to the right of the entrance.

The bed is large enough for him, although the blankets are ratty and the pillows squashed. A flickering bedside lamp is the only source of light, illuminating a ratty sofa ridden with suspicious-looking stains. Seokga wrinkles his nose before peeling off his dirtied clothes and stepping into the bathroom's shower. The tiled floor is cracked, and the harsh soap smells of strong chemicals, but Seokga doesn't care. He only wants to be clean.

He has just stepped out of the shower when the door of his room shudders under the impact of three sharp knocks. Seokga frowns, reaching for a towel. "Who is it," he demands.

The answering voice is Hani's. "Me."

Seokga blinks. He hasn't expected to speak to Hani again tonight, not after their spat in the forest. "What do you want," he finally snaps, wrapping the towel around his waist and padding to the door.

"Ji-ah kicked me out," is the bitter retort on the other side of the door. "She also threw a lamp at my head."

Seokga stares at the door. *What?*

"She's hysterical," Hani says. "Her entire world has been turned upside down; it makes sense that she wants to be alone. But she didn't need to *throw a lamp* at my *head*." The door shakes again as she bangs her fist against it. "Let me in, Seokga."

"In a moment—" Seokga glances around for his clean clothes just as a suspicious clicking noise emerges from the door. He turns back to it, narrow-eyed. "Are you picking the lock?" He clenches the towel more firmly around himself.

In answer, the door swings open, revealing a very haggard, very angry Hani. "Yes," she says, stepping inside, seemingly not caring that he is clad only in a towel. She tucks a bobby pin back into her tangled hair and shuts the door. "It was worryingly easy."

Petulant, Seokga glares at her. "This is *my* room."

"It's our room now," she replies, and Seokga's breath hitches as her eyes run over him. His towel hangs low on his waist, and he grips the coarse fabric tightly in one fist, hating how his body suddenly feels hot all over. Her attention is like an itch upon his skin—an infuriating, annoying itch that he wants to scratch.

Seokga swallows hard. Narrows his eyes into a glare.

And notices that Hani's cheeks are the same color as the bubblegum she'd smacked at him that first day in the precinct.

An unexpected surge of satisfaction heats his blood as Hani quickly averts her gaze, limps over to the bed, and dumps her duffel next to Seokga's. "Is today National No-Shirt Day, or something?" she mutters, crossing her arms and staring at the wall behind him. "Put on some clothes."

"No," says Seokga, simply to annoy her.

"Yes." Hani scowls at him.

Exasperated, he stalks over to his bag. "You'll be sleeping on the couch," he mutters, grabbing a T-shirt and boxers.

Hani shrugs. "We'll see about that."

Not for the first time this week, Seokga wonders why his father bothered to create gumiho. Hani rummages around in her bag before pulling out a set of pink pin-striped pajamas. "I'm going to shower."

"Be careful of your leg," Seokga can't help adding. The harsh soap will certainly sting those bite marks. "You should clean and bind the wound before you shower."

Hani gives him a peculiar look as she limps to the bathroom. The echoes of their argument in the forest linger in his ears, and he swallows a twinge of remorse.

Why do you need to be such a dick *all the time?*

"I'll be fine."

"I TOLD YOU TO CLEAN AND BIND THE WOUND *BEFORE* YOUR shower," Seokga snaps, kneeling on the floor of the bathroom as Hani sits on the counter of the sink, her wounded leg dripping blood onto the ground where it mingles pink with the droplets of shower water. Her lips are tight with pain as she clutches the ratty gray bathrobe tighter around her body.

"The soap cleaned it out for me. While stinging like a little *bitch*," she adds under her breath in resentment.

Seokga looks up at her in exasperation. Hani was in the shower for approximately two minutes before her shrill, foghorn-esque yowl of pain shattered the quiet of the tiny hotel room. "I'm going to bind your leg with bandages," he grits out, deciding to do so if only to stop her incessant complaining. "Real bandages. And then you're going to take the painkillers." He reaches for the pharmacy bag he's carried with him into the bathroom, having run to the door as Hani's wails had begun to turn into animal-like screeches of agony.

"Fine," she says with a sigh, leaning her head against the mirror. "Do what you must."

Seokga shakes his head in annoyance and opens the box containing a tube of antibacterial ointment and the bag of cotton balls, eyeing the four deep punctures on Hani's bare calf. "This will sting, too," he cautions.

"Just get it over with," she grits out.

Seokga opens the ointment and wrinkles his nose at the acerbic smell. Carefully, he squeezes out a dollop onto a cotton ball. "I'm going to apply it now," he warns before gingerly dabbing the ointment onto one of the bite marks. Hani stiffens, but keeps still as Seokga cleans the first wound.

He tries to ignore how smooth Hani's skin is as his fingers curl around her toned calf in order to steady her as he cleans. Tries to ignore that Hani is dressed only in a ratty robe, that suds of soap still cling to the slopes of her neck and that droplets of water slide down the length of her leg. Tries very hard to ignore that the swell of her breasts is visible in between the folds of the bathrobe, pushing the image of her in the forest from his mind—that godsdamn lacy bra had affected him more than it should have. Seokga's mouth is suddenly dry and he twists it into a scowl, lest—gods forbid—Hani notices that he is hating her a little less than usual.

Hani tilts her head back against the mirror and makes a small noise of contemplation. "I think," she says slowly as Seokga begins to clean the second wound, "that when we get back to New Sinsi with Ji-ah, that we should do what you said and erase her memory. And maybe we can assign some haetae to look after her, to protect her from the eoduksini until we kill it."

Seokga glances up at her. "What changed your mind?"

"She's . . ." Hani shakes her head. "She's not doing so well. I think granting her amnesia would be best."

"I'm not surprised. The minds of mortals are fragile." Seokga dabs the fourth and final puncture, careful not to press down too hard. "This realm breeds nothing but weakness. It's an easy target for the eoduksini." It's surprising, he adds silently, that some of these weak mortals once grew into gods. Dalnim and Haemosu, the goddess of the moon and the god of the sun, were mere humans escaping from a bloodthirsty tiger before Mireuk transformed them into the divinities that they are now. Jacheongbi was once a human girl, as well. Seokga is quite proud to say that he, at least, has never been a mortal. He was born as he is now, a god—glorious and mighty, and altogether superior. Was born from two godly parents, Mireuk and Mago. The god of creation, and the goddess of the earth.

"You've lived on Iseung for six hundred and something years," Hani replies skeptically. "How is it that you still hate it so much? Is there seriously nothing that you like about it?"

Seokga stiffens at the fox's prying questions as he reaches for the roll of gauze.

"Ice cream?" Hani tries. "Amusement parks? Music? Thunderstorms?"

He does not answer.

"I knew it," Hani mutters. "Not even a single thing."

That's not true. The injustice of her scorn sets his shoulders squaring.

"I like coffee," Seokga bites out defensively. "No—I love coffee. It is the sole creation of this realm that pleases me."

Hani stares down at him from her seat on the sink, her eyes beginning to dance. "Oh?"

"It's delicious," he mutters, turning back to the gauze. She is deliberately provoking him, he knows, but cannot stop himself from defending coffee as he binds her leg.

Her lips are twitching. "I see."

"With one cream and one sugar."

"Of course."

He glares up at her, detecting thinly veiled glee in her tone. "Are you mocking me?"

The laugh that erupts from her lips is bright and beautiful, filling the small bathroom with chiming bells. Hani presses her hand to her mouth, but the laugh still squeezes through the cracks in her fingers, dancing through the hotel room with unconcealed delight.

Seokga stares at her, something in his chest quickening at the color in her cheeks, the life in her eyes, the joy bathing her face in a beautiful radiance. Hastily, he looks away, focusing on her wounded leg. Bind it. He needs to bind it.

He cups her calf in his hand, careful to keep his touch gentle. Above him, Hani falls silent. Seokga glances up at her, and as his eyes meet hers, something passes between them—something warm. Something . . . something friendly.

Hani smiles, and his heart stumbles. Just slightly. Probably in annoyance. Regardless, Seokga quickly chooses to ruin the moment, looking back to her calf and studiously wrapping it with the gauze. He feels Hani watching him in curiosity.

"You gave me your shirt," she says. "In the forest, I mean. Thank you. And your cane."

He continues wrapping her leg, trying to keep his face composed, his expression inscrutable. Seokga tried, in the bamboo forest, not to care when the baegopeun gwisin had sunk its teeth into Hani's calf. He was determined to leave her to her own devices, still enraged by the fall they'd taken together. Yet the strangled noise of pain that escaped her lips sent him acting without thinking, ridding her of the hungry ghost before his mind could catch up to his body. "Your leg was disgusting to look at," he manages to say, relieved to find his voice steady as he rips the gauze from the roll and ties it, securing the binding to Hani's leg. "I wanted to cover it up."

Hani rolls her eyes and flexes her foot. She tilts her head. "It feels better."

"Obviously. Here." Seokga gently lets go of her leg and stands, handing her a bottle of painkillers. "Take some."

She wrinkles her nose. "I hate medicine," she grumbles, even as she shakes out two pills and swallows them dry. Hani scooches to the edge of the counter and gingerly lowers herself to the floor. Seokga's face warms as she stares up at him with a wry smile. *Out of frustration,* he insists to himself. *Did I not tell her to bind her leg before showering?*

"I guess you're good for something, after all," she says, echoing the words that he once said to her.

Seokga allows a thin smirk to curl his lips upward. "Touché," he murmurs as he follows Hani out of the bedroom, noting with smug satisfaction that her limp is gone.

CHAPTER NINETEEN

HANI

"The bed," Hani declares, folding her arms as she eyes Seokga, "should be mine. Since I'm *wounded*."

"You can take the couch, fox," is the icy retort. "I paid for these rooms. I get the bed."

The god and the gumiho are glaring at each other, standing on opposite sides of the bed.

"*I*," Hani insists in extreme annoyance, "was bitten by the baegopeun gwisin."

"And *I*," Seokga replies coldly, "fell down a hill because of you."

"We both fell down the hill. And it was your fault, not mine." Hani straightens, shaking her head. "This is ridiculous. We sound like kids." It's almost comedic, save for the fact that she really, *really* wants the bed. The sofa is ridden with dark stains that look suspiciously like . . . Never mind. "Let's play rock, paper, scissors for the bed." That should be fair enough.

Seokga looks a little too pleased at this prospect, and Hani remembers with an immense amount of annoyance the result of their staring contest. "No cheating," she adds.

"I can't agree to that," Seokga says, placing a fist on an open hand.

Damned trickster gods. "Rock," Hani says, slamming her fist into her own hand with more force than is necessary, "paper, scissors—shoot!"

Hani draws scissors.

Seokga draws . . .

"A gun?" Hani demands, staring at the raised thumb and out-stretched pointer finger. "That doesn't count."

His tactics for cheating are remarkably cheap for a thousands-of-years-old trickster god. Hani doesn't know whether she should be disappointed or amused. In response, Seokga pretends to shoot her with a bit too much satisfaction for her liking. She cocks her head.

"You're immediately disqualified," Hani informs him triumphantly. "The game is rock, paper, scissors—not rock, paper, scissors, gun. You're disqualified," she continues smugly, "and I get the bed."

Five minutes later, Hani can't help but feel a surge of guilt as she lies in the bed, Seokga on the floor below her on a wad of bathroom towels, the grinding of his teeth audible. He refused the couch with vehement disgust. Hani rolls onto her side, peering down at him. His eyes are open and immediately flick to her face in visible infuriation. "Enjoying the bed?" he snaps.

Hani winces before rolling over onto her back, staring at the bumpy ceiling. Seokga has helped bind her leg, and she repays him like this. *No.* Hani frowns. Seokga deserves to sleep on the floor—perhaps it will humble him. And the fallen god can use some humbling.

She closes her eyes.

And opens them again.

The bed could be big enough for two.

Absolutely not.

Hani sighs, rubbing her forehead wearily.

But . . . both she and Seokga have had a trying day. The only difference is that she gets to end it in a bed, while Seokga suffers on the floor. And the bed *is* big enough for two.

Fine. Hani glances back down at Seokga and prods his head with a finger. He glowers at her. *"What?"*

"You get the left side," she says, "and I get the right side. Don't steal the blankets and don't kick me, or I won't claim responsibility for what happens next." Leaving it at that, she rolls away, facing the wall as she listens to Seokga's disbelieving huff. There is shuffling as he rises from the floor, and then the bed is groaning under his weight as he slides onto the left side, pulling the blankets up to his chin.

Hani stares determinedly at the wall as she feels Seokga's gaze on her back and the warmth that radiates from his body only a few inches away.

"Conscience caught up to you?" His breath tickles the back of her neck, where goosebumps rise.

"Unfortunately," she says with a sigh, turning around to face him for the sole purpose of sending him a frown. His emerald eyes glitter in the dimness of the room. He has propped his head up with a hand and is watching her in a way that alerts her to the fact that he is currently formulating another jibe. It comes a moment later.

"Try not to snore tonight."

"I don't snore," she murmurs, eyelids growing heavy. She tugs the blankets closer to her. She feels Seokga's sharp smile in the darkness.

"Yes, you do."

But Hani is too tired to answer him. Her breathing has slowed to a sluggish rhythm, deepening as her eyes flutter shut. She'll argue with him in the morning.

SHE IS NESTLED AGAINST SOMETHING WARM, TANGLED IN body-heated sheets, her head resting not on a pillow, but on something firm and hard. Blearily, Hani opens her eyes to midmorning sun filtering through the room's window, dust mites dancing in between the buttery yellow rays of light. She blinks. Her mind is still foggy with remnants of sleep, her thoughts slow and lethargic.

It takes a few moments for her to realize that her head is lying on Seokga's chest, one of her arms draped across his muscled, flat stomach. One of his arms encircles her waist, and the other dangles off the bed. The god is still asleep, his eyes shut, his breathing deep and even. His usually icy expression is soft and serene, the planes of his face illuminated by the pale-yellow light.

What . . . Hani stares at him in a state of disbelief and panic. *How . . . Why . . . Oh, no.*

She must untangle herself from him before he awakens. She grimaces as she carefully withdraws her arm, tucking it against her side and monitoring Seokga's expression. He sleeps, still, his lips slightly parted and puffing out drowsy breaths.

Hani pauses, something in her heart stirring as she takes in the dozing god. Asleep, there is an . . . innocence to him that she has never seen. He looks young, the constant downward tilting to his lips gone, the eternally furrowed brows smooth and clear. She swallows a smile, not yet removing her head from where it rests against his chest. Seeing him like this is—it's new. And she finds that she doesn't quite mind it.

If only he seemed as sweet awake as he does asleep.

As the events of the past night trickle back to her, Hani gazes up at Seokga. The memory of his feather-light touch against her wounded leg is fresh in her mind. He was so careful, so gentle when he applied that balm.

There was a look of true alarm in his eyes as he burst through the bathroom door, demanding to know what happened. Already clad in the ratty robe, Hani gestured to the punctures in her skin, and Seokga's eyes darkened to a forest green in concern.

He was kind. As much as he probably ever would be, anyway.

Perhaps he'd felt bad about trying to get her booted out of the Creature Café. Hani smirks, watching as the trickster god stirs slightly in his sleep. Her amusement turns to incredulity as he rolls to his side, his other arm wrapping around her back.

Seokga is holding her.

As if she's an overgrown stuffed animal of some sort.

Face now pressed in the crook of Seokga's neck, Hani wonders if the god sleeps with a teddy bear. If he's mistaken her for it.

The thought is hilarious and terrifying all at once.

But the truth of it all is that Seokga is holding her. *Holding* her, his assistant that he never asked for, the gumiho that he delighted in tormenting at the Creature Café.

Hani prepares to shove him, but something stops her. Slowly, her body relaxes into his. He smells of pine trees and soap and coffee, a strange combination that is . . . not altogether *unpleasant,* exactly.

It has been years since Hani has been held like this—with such gentle fondness, such warm content. Her long string of ex-boyfriends were never interested in *these* types of physical acts. Hani closes her eyes, lulled by the warmth of Seokga's body against her, by the sheer comfort of being in somebody's arms.

She'll rest within his embrace, just for a few moments.

And then she'll roll away.

CHAPTER TWENTY
SEOKGA

CITRUS AND VANILLA. CRACKLING FIRES AND SEA-SALT caramels.

Honey and . . . something else. Something sweet, familiar, and deeply satisfying.

Seokga breathes in the fragrances as he stirs awake, opening his eyes to a deep chocolate brown that smells of sweet shampoo. He blinks, confusion settling over the blanket of weariness already coating his mind. That color, that smell . . .

Hani's hair.

And then he realizes, with dawning horror, that he is *holding* the fox. Her back is pressed against his stomach, and her hands rest over his where they lay on her abdomen. She is asleep, her shoulders rising and falling to a slow tempo.

Seokga stares at the gumiho for a moment that feels like a small eternity. Her skin is warm, and she's snoring a little— shallow puffs of air that blow a stray hair strand away from her face. He swallows hard against a sudden, tender emotion that tightens his throat. Forces it down, pushes it away.

How long have I been holding her like this?

The god pulls away as if scalded, his eyes bulging out of his head in disbelief and horror.

No.

No no no no no.

He needs to get out of this hotel room immediately.

Seokga scrambles out of the bed, his cheeks burning with shame. He can only be grateful that he's awoken before she has. He can't imagine the questions she'd hurl at him if this had been the other way around, but he knows that they would be questions that he would not be able to answer for the life of him. To his immense relief, despite his panicked jostling, the gumiho is still fast asleep. Hani apparently sleeps like the dead.

Cuddling. The word nudges its way into Seokga's brain, an invasive thought bashing down the door to his mind. *You were cuddling her, you fool.*

Seokga runs a hand down his face in horror. He was cuddling her. Kim Hani. Seokga shakes his head, staring at the sleeping gumiho. Seokga has done many, many questionable things in his lifetime, but *this* . . .

This tops them all.

This is awful. Absolutely, irrefutably awful.

A noise of horror rumbles in his throat as he gapes at the bed. *How in Jeoseung has this happened?* Seokga has never . . . *cuddled* somebody before.

So lost is he in his horror that he barely notices Hani stirring until she's sitting upright in bed and gawking at him as if he's grown two heads. Belatedly, Seokga realizes that he has been staring down at his own two hands with an expression of complete betrayal.

"What," Hani demands, rubbing her eyes, "are you *doing?*"

He stiffens. "Nothing," he snaps hastily. "Absolutely nothing." Seokga thinks that he sees a spark of realization in Hani's bleary eyes, but it fades as fast as it appeared. She slides out of bed and busies herself with rummaging through her duffel for a fresh set of clothes.

"We should question Ji-ah today," she mumbles as Seokga stares at her. Does she know? No, she must not. She'd been sleeping. "We need to move, too. If Dok-hyun isn't the eoduksini—

if it's still out there—we're in danger. Especially if it realizes that Ji-ah is on Geoje. Like the other victims, she's been having nightmares. It's only a matter of time before the eoduksini tries to kill her."

Seokga turns his attention to his own duffel, pulling out his own clothing—a smart emerald sweater and sharp black pants. She doesn't seem to know that she'd been in his arms. Good. "We'll go back to New Sinsi. Wipe Ji-ah's memory and assign her guardians."

"Is it wise to bring her back to New Sinsi, though?" Hani scratches at her head. "Maybe we should put her in Seoul, Busan, or Incheon until we've gotten rid of the eoduksini. Maybe Thailand. Or even America."

"Let's get answers first," Seokga replies, forcing himself to meet her eye. *Cuddling.* He is appalled with himself. "And then we'll decide on the rest."

⁂

THE LOTUS HOTEL'S DINING ROOM IS NOTHING MORE THAN a cramped corner stuffed with mismatched plastic tables and chairs, and a spread of questionable-looking bagels, toast, and eggs. There is coffee, but to Seokga's eternal disappointment, it is warm, watery, and altogether disgusting. He forces himself to drink it, though; some caffeine has never hurt him—unless it is spilled all over his suit by a certain barista at the Creature Café, or poisoned with too much cream and sugar by that very same barista.

Hani and Seokga sit across from Ji-ah, who is morosely picking at a blueberry bagel with her fingernails. If Hani still holds a grudge for the lamp that was thrown at her head last night, she gives no indication as she leans forward and says, "We know that this must be hard for you to talk about."

Ji-ah stabs at the bagel with a yellow fingernail, broodingly silent. Her eyes are rid-rimmed and puffy, signaling a night of no sleep.

Seokga shifts impatiently in his seat. His answers are so close—and yet so very, very far away. He needs to know if it's truly Dok-hyun. Part of him hopes it is, so that this strange, prickling feeling whenever he thinks of Dok-hyun confined to the precinct goes away.

"But in order to stop the eoduksini—the demon you saw near your café—we need you to walk us through exactly what happened that night." Hani's jittering leg is the only sign of her waning patience. They have been sitting in the dining room for thirty minutes now, attempting to pull answers out of their witness. Shim is expecting Seokga's call this morning. "Okay? Can you do this for us, Ji-ah?"

No response.

Fine, then.

Seokga will get his answers another way.

His grip on his already-frayed patience snaps completely, and he leans forward, summoning the threads of his power. As much as he hates to admit it, last night was one of the best, rejuvenating sleeps of his life. Seokga doesn't know if it has anything to do with Hani's presence next to him, but hopes not, if only to preserve the dignity he has left. The gumiho frowns as the emerald strands, invisible to Ji-ah, begin to creep toward the morose witness.

"Seokga—"

"Do you want answers?" he demands from the corner of his tight mouth. "Or do you want to sit here watching her destroy her bagel all day? We gave her a whole night to recover. We can't waste another." Not when Chunbun is now only thirteen days away, and Dok-hyun—potentially innocent—wastes away in a New Sinsi holding cell.

Hani falls silent.

Tell us what happened, Seokga demands silently as the jade magic coils around Ji-ah's body. *Tell us what happened the night of the murder. The night that you fled out of New Sinsi. Tell us what happened.* He grits his teeth together in concentration. This is no small demand, and his weakened power recognizes that. Sweat pools at the nape of his neck. *Tell us what happened, Ji-ah. Tell us—*

The words wrench from Ji-ah's mouth all at once, and her eyes widen as they spill out uncontrollably, even as her skin whitens to a deathly pale. "I was working at the café," she says, clenching her bagel in her hands. "I was working at the café with a boy named Yang Chan-yeol. We had night shifts. Night shifts were the worst because that was when I was supposed to be studying for my classes, but I couldn't do morning shifts since there were no openings, and—"

"We get it," Seokga mutters. "You can skip ahead."

Ji-ah's bagel crumbles to bits. Her eyes are darting wildly between Hani and Seokga in fear as her mouth continues to move. "It was time to take out the trash and the recycling. Chan-yeol said that he could take out the trash and that I could do recycling. He took the bags and he went outside. I heard him throwing the bags into the garbage dump and I was going to go, too, but then Sora called me on the work phone. She wanted to know if I could come over later and watch a movie. We hadn't seen each other in a while, because of our schedules, but I said I couldn't because I was so tired. And then we had a fight, a small one, for maybe three minutes. Five minutes. I-I don't know. Sora was upset, and I was upset, too. She said that I was a slacker at being a friend, and I said that I wasn't. But then she hung up and I took the recycling outside and I saw . . ." Ji-ah gasps, attempting to press her traitorous lips together.

Tell us what you saw. Seokga struggles to maintain control over the emerald threads that have already begun to flicker. *Tell us. Now.*

Hani has leaned forward, her expression rapt.

"I saw . . . I saw a man who was not a man standing over the body of—of a beast. A big beast, almost like a lion with no mane or t-tail, but w-with horns and—and golden scales instead. He was crouched over the lion-beast, and there were . . . There were shadows in the alleyway, shadows that looked like they were flowing from the man. And the man was bent over the lion, who was snarling, and—and black veins started to run all through the lion's scales. It looked like he was *stealing* something from the lion—stealing something because the lion stopped moving. And I-I knew, I don't know how, but I knew that the lion was Chanyeol. And I knew that he was dead." Tears flow down Ji-ah's face as she continues. "And I-I dropped the bag of recycling and the noise had the man turning. H-he looked at me and the alleyway got so dark, so, so dark and I sc-screamed and I r-ran away. I ran," Ji-ah repeats in a whisper. "I ran to Sora . . ."

"The man. What did he look like?" Hani asks urgently. "Describe him."

Describe the man, Seokga commands, straining to deliver his order. *Do it now before I lose my patience.*

"His hair was graying," Ji-ah whispers hoarsely. "He was w-wearing glasses, and some sort of b-black coat. I think it had a golden symbol on it. The symbol looked like the l-lion thing that he k-killed . . ."

Seokga's eyes flare wide, and it's an effort not to drop his hold on Ji-ah. "A lab coat?" he demands, one hand fumbling for his cellphone.

"I g-guess . . ."

"Hwanin's *tits*," Hani chokes out, eyes darting to Seokga's. "We were right. We were *right*."

Seokga is inclined to agree. Heart pounding, he begins to punch in Shim's number. Ji-ah just described Lee Dok-hyun, down to the custom coat worn by all members of the Lee family throughout the years. The black lab coat with the golden haetae embroidery—the one that Dok-hyun has worn every single day at the precinct.

Ji-ah is still speaking as Seokga presses the CALL button. The phone rings once, twice.

"I th-think he was going to chase me, but he wanted to finish whatever he was doing to the h-horned lion first." Ji-ah presses a hand over her mouth as Seokga's grip over his power slackens and disappears, leaving him in need of some more coffee. "Wh-what . . . How did you . . ." Her eyes are round with terror as she abruptly shoves back her chair, clenching fistfuls of her bagel. "You're one of them," she breathes. "A monster. *You're a monster!*"

"Ji-ah—" Hani stands in concern. "We're not—"

Shim hasn't picked up.

Something is wrong. Something is very, very wrong.

The girl is stumbling backward, emitting a low keening noise as she trembles. "Monsters," she mumbles to herself. "Monsters here, monsters there, monsters everywhere . . ."

"Ji-ah," Hani repeats gently, making her way toward the girl. "Let's—"

It happens in an instant.

As Hani approaches the upset girl, her hands raised in supplication, Ji-ah stumbles into the spread of breakfast foods and closes her fist around a knife originally meant for cutting the bagels in half.

Seokga barely has time to shout a warning before Ji-ah hurls the knife toward Hani and makes her escape, sprinting out of the room and into the hotel beyond.

With an inhuman swiftness, Hani dodges the blade, leaving it to embed itself on the wall behind her with a *thud,* quivering in the cracked plaster.

Seokga has shot to his feet. "Are you—"

"I'm fine." Hani's face is flushed with agitation and worry. "We need to go after her. She can't have gone far, and we can't afford to lose her again."

"I know." Seokga tightens his grip around the cane. "I'll go up and check to see if she's gone back into her room. You go to the street outside, search the surrounding area. Call me immediately if you find anything." He's already dialing Shim again. *Pick up,* he thinks desperately. *Come on, old man.*

Hani nods and tenses as if to run—but pauses, panting. "I need your number. I don't have it."

Impatient, Seokga rattles off his number, hoping that the fox has a good memory. She nods, breathless, before turning on her heel and sprinting through the door. If Hani's injured leg pains her, she doesn't let on, and the fallen god feels a surge of respect for the gumiho.

Seokga turns his attention back to the still-ringing phone, his mouth tight. Shim always picks up immediately. Always. He has never answered later than the fifth ring, not once in all the years he's known him. Panic begins to rise in Seokga's throat. The old haetae could be dead, in a pool of his own blood . . .

"Shit!" Seokga curses, running a hand through his hair and imagining the horrors that could have happened at the precinct. It could be a massacre. His fingers itch to grip the steering wheel of his car, to hear the bestial roar of its engine as he closes the extra miles between him and whatever the fuck has happened.

And although it's necessary to check, he doubts that Ji-ah will be anywhere within the Lotus Hotel. Damn it.

His mouth tightens. They'll have to let her go. There are larger matters at hand. Shim isn't picking up. Seokga can't take it; he needs to know what's happened, and the drive back is too long. If he doesn't get answers soon, he'll go mad.

An idea creeps into his mind, nothing more than a whisper against the crevices of his consciousness, a whisper that he wants to ignore—but knows that he must not.

Call upon the yojeong, the voice whispers. *Follow the fairies.*

CHAPTER TWENTY-ONE

HANI

"SHE'S GONE," HANI PANTS INTO HER PHONE, BRACING her hands on her knees as she stands in the middle of an Okpo sidewalk, barely able to breathe. She's scoured every possible place where Ji-ah could have run, to no avail. The girl has vanished. "I can't find her—not anywhere. She's disappeared." Her gray sweater is soaked in sweat, and her black combat boots are thoroughly dirtied with grime. Her jacket hasn't fared much better. "She wasn't in her room, was she?"

Seokga's voice crackles back to her through the cellphone. "No. She's not anywhere in the hotel. But we have a bigger problem. The precinct isn't answering my calls. Something has happened."

Somehow, that's not surprising at all. Hani wipes her brow, her hand coming away damp with sweat. "Great. That's just great," she wheezes.

There is a long pause on the other end. "Hani," Seokga finally says, and she's surprised to find that his usually cool tone is somewhat . . . awkward.

Perhaps it has something to do with this morning.

Despite her better instincts, Hani fell asleep once again in Seokga's arms . . . and awoke to find him standing on the opposite end of the room, staring at his hands with a look of abject horror.

Which is certainly not a boost for her confidence.

Hani hasn't been able to prevent herself from wondering what Seokga's embrace meant. Whether his unconscious mind had been channeling his emotions through his body. Whether he is . . . fond of her.

But no.

It is more likely that Seokga mistook her for a teddy bear.

And she's fine with that.

Truly.

Right?

"What?" Hani asks, arching a brow.

"I . . ." The god sounds hesitant, and Hani frowns, tapping her foot impatiently. It is unlike Seokga to be so cautious. The pause this time is longer, and Hani's frown deepens. She wonders whether he knows she awoke in his arms and instead of rolling away, did the very opposite. Yet he can't possibly know—he was asleep.

Wasn't he?

"I think something may have happened to Shim," he finishes raggedly.

Hani blinks. That is . . . not where she expected the conversation to go. Nor did she ever expect to hear Seokga sound so . . . so *sad*. She honestly didn't think he was capable of such an emotion, or that he even cared about the haetae chief.

"He's not picking up," Seokga continues. "We need to leave Ji-ah. I need to know what happened, and what we should do now."

"Wait. Leave Ji-ah?" Hani shakes her head. "Seokga, we can't just leave her here. If the eoduksini is hunting for her . . ."

"If the eoduksini is hunting for her, it will find and kill her." Seokga now sounds irascible. It's almost a relief. "Yes, Hani. I know. But we cannot waste time—valuable time—scouring Okpo for a girl who already gave us all the information she has and is not willing to be found. The way that I see it, we can either twiddle our thumbs here and hope that Ji-ah turns up again, or we can visit the yojeong to learn what happened at the precinct, and what our next steps should be. For me, the choice is obvious."

The yojeong.

Hani blinks.

The gossamer-winged creatures are notoriously elusive, many preferring to dwell here, far away from large cities such as New Sinsi, Seoul, and Busan—far, far, far away. While creatures such as haetae, dokkaebi, gumiho, and even the bulgasari have adapted to modern life, many yojeong prefer keeping to the old ways. Prefer living in the wilderness to living in the bustling cities, prefer surrounding themselves with other fairies rather than joining a melting pot of human and creature alike. Hani tightens her grip on her phone. Although the yojeong are famous for their unnatural wisdom, they're equally notorious for their inability to speak in anything but vague, wily riddles. She does not quite see how the yojeong can help their case, and informs Seokga as such.

"Seokga," she says, "where would we even *find* a yojeong?" Geoje has a large yojeong population, certainly, but Hani highly doubts their ability to locate one of the elusive fairies. They're sly, clever things.

But Seokga makes a noise that is partially a sigh, partially a mumbled curse. "I may know of one's whereabouts. And they may have . . . scrying abilities."

Scrying abilities. Those could be incredibly useful. Hani's brows rise in interest. "Oh? How do you know of them?"

"Unimportant. The point is," Seokga continues before Hani can fully question him, "that she resides here. On Geoje. There's a mountain here. Daegeumsan. It's an hour away from Okpo. If we depart now, we can reach the yojeong just after noon."

"But Ji-ah—"

"I'm not taking *no* for an answer," he snaps back. "Something's happened in New Sinsi. Nobody is picking up my calls. Shim—" There's a strangled sound, as if the god is swallowing hard. "This could change the course of our investigation and determine our next steps. This information is valuable."

She sighs. Seokga has a point.

Foolish girl. She can only hope Choi Ji-ah is capable of fending for herself.

The knife that the girl threw at her head certainly insinuates so.

Seokga evidently hears her sigh. The choice has been made. "Where are you?" he asks urgently. "I'll bring the Jaguar around."

THE DRIVE TO DAEGEUMSAN IS HEAVY WITH SUFFOCATingly awkward silence, layered with Seokga's clear pain at the thought of losing Shim.

Hani tried to talk about it with him, and he quickly shut it down. But his knuckles are white around the steering wheel and his breathing is almost labored as he breaks every traffic law in existence. He's had Hani dial Shim every five minutes, but the haetae still hasn't picked up. The precinct general line has been silent, as well, along with the numbers of other haetae officers.

She calls Somi—but judging from the background chatter, she's working, and can't speak long.

"I'm sorry, unnie, I don't know. I haven't heard anything . . ."

"What about Hyun-tae?" Hani asks desperately. "Is he there? Working part-time?"

"Not right now," Somi replied tremulously. "He—he was called into his . . . other job early."

That's not a good sign. If the jeoseung saja are busy today, that means there have been many deaths.

"I could go by later if you want?"

"No, darling," Hani says quickly. "Don't. Stay far away from there. Go straight home after your shift." She's put Somi in enough danger already. "I'll let you get back to work now."

"Wait, Hani, I—"

But she can hear a voice impatiently ordering an iced Americano, and can't let Somi risk Minji's wrath. She hangs up and glances over at Seokga. He doesn't look too good, and his clear anxiety pulls on something in her chest.

"So," she finally says, staring straight ahead at the winding road bringing them out of Okpo.

"So," Seokga repeats, stiffening almost imperceptibly.

"At least we know who the eoduksini has possessed."

"We didn't act when we had the chance. Now, Dok-hyun's probably murdered everybody at the precinct. He could be anywhere by now."

Hani swallows hard. "Right."

"But the yojeong will have answers," he says, pressing down on the gas even harder, "for a price."

"A price?" Hani cocks her head warily. "How much, exactly?"

"The yojeong like to trade in bargains. There's no telling what this one will ask for."

"You said that the yojeong we're visiting is a she," Hani says slowly, suspicion scratching at the door of her mind. Suspicion and . . . jealousy? She scowls. Surely not. "What's her name? How do you know her?" Her voice, thankfully, comes out light and curious.

"Her name is Suk Aeri," Seokga mutters. "I . . . *encountered* her, once, some years after my fall."

Interesting. Hani narrows her eyes. "By 'encountered,' do you mean—"

"I mean that—" Seokga sighs through his nose and glares at her out of the corner of his eye. "I mean," he repeats tightly, "that Suk Aeri and I had a brief romantic encounter once, many, many, many years ago."

"I see," Hani replies slowly, a smile of amusement stretching her lips wide, even as traitorous envy tugs at her chest. "You slept with her."

Seokga seethes in silence.

"You slept with her," Hani repeats, and can't help asking, "Have you spoken to her since?"

His lack of response is answer enough.

"And now you're asking her for a favor?" Hani clucks her tongue. "Wow. You really do lack manners, huh?"

"Not," he snaps, "a favor. A bargain. There is a difference."

"Did you at least cook her breakfast before leaving?"

"Kim Hani," Seokga says thinly, "stop talking."

She does not. "Do you have *kids*? Demigod kids?" Hani watches with interest as the trickster god chokes on his own spit.

"The other members of the pantheon have a whole gaggle of them running around," she adds as Seokga continues to sputter. "Especially Hasegyeong. I see them all the time at the Creature Café. The cattle god has a whole herd of them." She snorts at her own joke as Seokga clears his throat, seemingly beginning to collect himself. "I think it's a valid question," she concludes as he glares at her from the corner of his eye. "You have dalliances, chances are you have kids, as well."

"I," Seokga replies, "am considering throwing you out of my car."

Hani waits. Seokga sighs.

"How many?" she presses.

"Two hundred since my exile," he slowly replies through his teeth. "Give or take. They're terrifying and most of them end up in jail for thievery, arson, forgery, and murder. Most of them also break out of jail." There's a note of triumph to his voice, underneath his exasperation.

"Would I recognize any names?"

"Likely."

Hani waits, wagering that Seokga's pride in his undoubtedly diabolical children will loosen his lips. It does. And she's relieved to see that there's a touch of amusement on his face, even amongst the clear worry for Shim.

"There was Yi Hang-bok," Seokga says, his tone *almost* nonchalant—save for the faint undercurrent of smug satisfaction as Hani's brows raise.

"The lord of Oseong?" Hani asks skeptically. The man was infamous for his pranks. Hani had often heard his stories told in jumaks over bowls of makgeolli and through peals of laughter. "Didn't he . . ."

"Win a riddle contest against a dokkaebi? Yes."

"I was going to say, didn't he spread a rumor about his friend's wife?" It's coming back to her now, and she crinkles her nose in disgust. "He said she was unfaithful, so in retribution, she tricked him into eating rice cakes stuffed with po—"

"Hani," snaps Seokga, "if you really believe that—"

She smirks. "Is it true?"

A long pause, punctuated only by Seokga's exasperated sigh. "Yes."

"You must be a proud father."

"Stop annoying me." But the corners of his lips twitch. "Do you have . . . any?"

"Any children?" Hani asks, and when he nods, she cackles. "Gods, no. Can you imagine me as a mother?"

Seokga is silent for a moment, and she thinks he's about to say something halfway nice, but then— "Call Shim again."

Again, the haetae doesn't pick up. The Jaguar screeches to a stop on the side of a rural road, next to which is a thick expanse of forest leading toward a distant mountain peak. Daegeumsan. Wearily, Hani walks to the forest's edge alongside Seokga. Another day, another hike.

Gods, she is so sick of hikes. "Please tell me that there aren't any baegopeun gwisin in here."

"One can never be sure," Seokga replies with a razor-sharp smirk bordering on the edge of malice.

Godsdamn it.

They quickly make their way into the forest, shoes crunching on fallen branches and clumps of weeds. In March it's not the middle of wintertime, but it's not quite spring, either—near the mountain, the air is still the dry sort of cold so native to Korean winters. It's also thick with the smell of wet wood, and frosty dew glistens on the tall grass that tickles Hani's hands as she walks. Birds sing in the looming trees above, fluttering their wings as their sweet song soars through the afternoon air. Eventually a small trail, partially obscured by the forest's undergrowth, emerges—a trail leading upward, toward the mist-shrouded mountain of Daegeumsan.

Her bitten leg only slightly protests in pain as their hike continues on. Seokga has tended to her wounds well. She glances at him out of the corner of her eye. The early orange afternoon sunlight bathes him in a golden glow, illuminating his handsome profile and deep green eyes. He cuts a striking figure as he strides through the forest, his eyes scanning the lush foliage. Hani tears her gaze away, even as something in her heart stumbles.

Perhaps a half hour later, when the elevation has risen considerably, Seokga turns to Hani. "We'll go off the path now," he says, gesturing to the deep forestry lining their trail. "Nothing here has changed much in the past centuries. If I remember it right, Suk Aeri is not far away."

"No," a sweet, ethereal voice murmurs just behind Hani. "No, she is not."

Startled, Hani whirls.

And for the first time in her immortal life, Kim Hani meets the eye of a yojeong.

The fairy is hovering a few feet off the ground, her gossamer, large rosy wings fluttering as she smiles down at Seokga and Hani with full lips. They are almost butterfly wings, lovely and sparkling under the spring sunlight. She is clad in a traditional hanbok, the jeogori a petal pink, the chima a flawless white. The gorum ribbon is a shimmering lavender, matching the color of the daenggi knotted at her glossy black braid's base. Her eyes, a hazel so light that it is almost golden, rove over Hani first before moving to Seokga, whose face has contorted itself into an exceptionally impressive grimace.

"Hello, Seokga," the yojeong croons, slowly lowering her slipper to the ground and tilting her head with a smile that appears, at first, sweet—until one notices the cruel glint in those hazel eyes. "It has been a while." She bows, but it is a mocking one, filled with spite.

"You startled me." Seokga's voice is tight with irritation as he bows back stiffly. "Hello, Suk Aeri," he says in the formal tongue—and that is when Hani realizes, with a slight start, that Seokga and she have both been speaking in banmal, the informal. Not to mock, not to deride—just *casually*.

But for how long? When did she make that shift? When did she stop speaking in the informal only to mock him and start speaking to him as a friend?

When did he begin to *allow* that?

Was it before or after she woke in his arms?

Not important.

Hani has much larger things to worry about.

But—how long has it been since she spoke to him in the formal?

Aeri is eyeing Seokga with a vast amount of dislike only

somewhat hidden behind that sweet smile. "You fled from this mountain as quickly as a scalded cat," she murmurs, "and you return centuries later, with another woman." She flicks her eyes to Hani, who is surprised to see that the cold cruelty is immediately replaced by genuine kindness. "You should run while you still can," she warns.

"Oh, I plan on it," Hani replies, instantly warming to the yojeong.

The two creatures exchange matching smiles before Aeri turns back to Seokga, who looks as if he's started to get a very, very large headache. "What is it, exactly, that you want? Certainly not pleasure, since you're here with her. Unless . . ." The yojeong tilts her head and sends another smile in Hani's direction. Hani fights back a laugh.

Seokga scowls. "How long were you following us?"

"A while," the fairy admits, shrugging her slender shoulders. "I was curious to see why you came to my mountain."

"Your mountain? I thought that Daegeumsan belonged to a mountain god."

"It did," Aeri replies saccharinely, "until I kicked him off. This mountain is mine, now. I own it." She taps a delicate ear with a finger. "The trees whisper things to me. They say that you have come for a bargain. That you wish to use my scrying ability."

Hani glances around at the trees with wary curiosity. Their leaves rustle in the wind, sounding much like hushed whispers.

"The trees speak the truth."

"Ah." Aeri arches a brow. "Why do you seek my gift?"

It is Hani's turn to speak up. "There is an eoduksini ravaging my city. New Sinsi." She watches as Aeri takes this in, her lips parting slightly. "We had it contained; we think it escaped and attacked the precinct. We need to know where it is, and what we should do next."

"A demon of darkness from King Yeomra's realm," she muses.

"In your city, you say? And you're trying to stop it. I see, Seokga, that you have not yet fulfilled your debt to Hwanin." She chuckles. "Very well. I will find this eoduksini for you—for a price."

"What do you want?" Hani asks curiously.

Aeri tilts her head, tapping her chin in contemplation. "Hmm."

"We do not have the luxury of time, Aeri," Seokga says irritably. "Do hurry up."

"Hmm," Aeri says again, and Hani suspects that she does so only to annoy Seokga. *"Hmm."*

Seokga scowls. "You dawdle."

Hani's ears prick as the trees begin rustling again, whispering to Aeri, whose eyes widen in . . . delight? Curiosity? She looks between Seokga and Hani once more, cocking her head as her lips curl into a half-moon. "As you wish," she replies. "I have decided on my price. I shall give you what you seek . . ."

Hani holds her breath. Seokga seems to be doing the same.

". . . if you share a kiss with the wine-eyed," Aeri finishes with a smug little smirk.

It takes Hani a too-long moment to realize that *she* is the wine-eyed.

Oh. *Oh.*

Aeri winks at her almost encouragingly before Hani slowly, very slowly, moves her eyes to Seokga—who has gone an alarming shade of white. "Aeri," he grinds out through a clenched jaw, "don't be ridiculous. What's next? You have us fornicate before you? Voyeurism is a perversion."

She straightens and crosses her arms. "I am *not* being ridiculous, or perverted." Her wings seem to quiver in rage—but then she composes herself. "A kiss for a clue. That is my bargain."

Hani swallows hard, hating how her heart has begun to pound against her chest. *In dread,* she tells herself. *My heart has begun to pound in dread. Lots and lots and lots of dread.*

Seokga runs a hand through his hair. "Hani," he says, his voice quiet, "if you don't want to . . ."

"It's fine," she says—a little too quickly. Her face heats. "For the clue."

"For the clue," he agrees.

Aeri is watching all of this in visible amusement. "For the clue," she echoes. The branches above rustle, as if laughing in agreement.

Hani swallows her nerves, taking a step closer to Seokga and peering up into his green eyes that seem much darker than usual. The scowl on his face has softened, and his expression is gentle as he brushes a stray piece of hair out of her eyes.

The surrounding trees quiet in anticipation.

As she stands on her tiptoes to reach Seokga's lips, his hand slides around her waist.

"Are you sure?" Seokga asks softly.

In answer, Hani slants her lips against his.

His lips are warm and silken against her own, his hand firm and steady on her waist. Hani's breath hitches in her throat as Seokga runs a hand through her hair, his palm pausing so he cups her cheek and their kiss deepens—as something that sounds suspiciously like a purr rumbles deep in his throat. He tastes like ferns and fire and coffee—and to her shock, she finds she doesn't quite mind it.

This, a small voice whispers in the back of her mind, *why does this feel so right?*

Because it is right, she answers slowly. *Because despite everything, despite it all . . . Somehow, this is* right.

Seokga's lips are soft, the kiss gentle and slow and deep . . . almost lazy, as if the pair of them have all the time in the world. Her mouth melds deeper into his, and another noise vibrates in Seokga's throat—hoarse and hungry all at once. Her blood warms, and Hani runs her hands up his chest, marveling at the way it's rising and falling in an uneven rhythm, marveling at the hard muscle underneath the fabric, marveling at the sheer existence of *him*. She gasps slightly as his hands rove down to her waist, pressing her closer to him.

This is right.

But there is a time and place for everything, and Hani is very aware of Aeri's voracious stare. Shakily, she pulls away, gazing at Seokga. The god is staring at her as if he's never seen her before, shocked. "Hani," he whispers, his voice more guttural than ever. She watches as he raises a trembling hand to his lips. His eyes are wide and dark. *"Hani."*

She swallows hard, breathing heavily, not daring to look away from him—

"Well," Aeri's voice cuts in, "that certainly was fascinating." The yojeong looks impossibly entertained as she claps her hands together in a smattering of applause. "Bravo, bravo. In return . . . I will give you what you wish know." With that, she closes her eyes, and the trees begin to whisper once again, growing in cadence until the trio is surrounded by an ocean of murmurs, rising and falling like waves in the sea.

"Hani," Seokga whispers as Aeri doesn't stir, still scrying. "Hani, I—"

But he cuts off as Aeri's eyes flare open, burning a brilliant shade of gold. Aeri opens her mouth, allowing an unfamiliar voice to swirl through the forest. It is deep and vibrating, so at odds with her previously merry tone. *"The precinct has fallen. Within its walls, darkness abounds. Yet the haetae you hound is alive and well."*

"Shim," Seokga breathes in relief, closing his eyes and staggering back. "Oh, thank fuck—"

But Aeri isn't done. Wind begins to whip through the forest and the trees shake frantically. Aeri rises even higher in the air, her arms spreading. *"The ones you seek are closer than you imagine . . ."*

The ones.

Hani stiffens.

If Aeri reveals her identity as the Scarlet Fox . . . if all her efforts to spare herself and Somi are thwarted . . .

"*. . . but you are alone, god, in a sea of deception. Let your mind not be fooled by surface perceptions. Look to the one with the eyes of the weary. Look to the one with the eyes of the teary. There, you will find verity, hidden beneath insincerity.*"

The forest, once again, falls abruptly silent.

Aeri falls silent, as well.

But a moment later, her eyes fly open. They have returned to a pale, glittering hazel. "Well," she says, her voice back to its normal pitch, glowering at Seokga, "now that we're done with that . . . Get off my mountain."

CHAPTER TWENTY-TWO

SEOKGA

DAMN SUK AERI AND HER CHEAP TRICKS.

Seokga pointedly avoids Hani's eyes as they sit in the same Okpo restaurant they'd visited the night before, focusing instead on the tendrils of steam curling upward from the miyeok-guk that the pair of them ordered. As much as they are in a hurry to return to New Sinsi, he needs to eat. To recuperate before rushing headlong into what will surely become a whirlwind of chaos. Using his magic on Ji-ah, combined with the stress of thinking he had lost Shim, has drained him. Seokga eats as quickly as he can, shoveling the soup into his mouth, trying not to choke on the slick pieces of savory seaweed.

"Slow down," Hani says in concern. "You're going to give yourself a stomachache. Shim's alive, and if we head out in an hour, we'll still reach New Sinsi by tonight. You have time." The gumiho is dialing Shim's number over and over again. Seokga trusts Aeri's scrying—it's served him well in the past—and trusts her when she says Shim is alive. But he needs to hear it for himself, Shim's voice.

"He's not picking up," Hani says with a sigh, and he raises his gaze to see her biting her lips. Lips that he has kissed.

It was a kiss that damn near weakened his knees if he's being honest about it. A kiss that felt so . . . good.

Seokga has been alive for thousands upon thousands of years, but never before has he shared a kiss crackling with such . . .

heat. It was brief, yes, but he cannot deny that in those moments, he wanted her. Wanted Kim Hani with every fiber of his being.

And he still wants her.

Something has gone wrong.

He is supposed to despise Kim Hani—the gumiho who threw coffee in his face, the gumiho who is infuriatingly obnoxious—but between this morning's cuddling and the afternoon's kissing, something has gone incredibly, unbelievably wrong.

He does not hate Kim Hani.

Does not hate her sunny laughter or her sharp, witty tongue. Does not hate the way that her nose crinkles when she laughs or sneers, does not hate the way that her eyes widen in amusement whenever he says something that is not at all intended to be amusing.

Seokga does not hate Kim Hani.

And it has not escaped his notice that for some time today, they have *both* been speaking in banmal. As . . . friends.

As friends, even though the day prior they were attacking each other in a bamboo forest.

Friendship appears in strange ways, sometimes.

Seokga is not amused. Scowling, he shovels a mouthful of too-hot soup past his lips. It nearly blisters his tongue, but he doesn't care.

Seokga the Fallen does not have *friends*. Seokga the Fallen does not use the informal except to insult others or address those younger than him—never in friendship. But with Hani, it is clear that he is using banmal because . . . because she is his friend.

He squeezes his eyes shut, hoping that when he opens them, this truth will disappear.

"Do you want to talk about it?" Hani inquires, as if reading his mind. Seokga tries not to jump.

Absolutely not. "Talk about what?" he asks, hoping that he sounds even the slightest bit innocent.

"You know." Hani shrugs, avoiding his gaze. "The—well, the kiss. And that . . . other thing."

Seokga straightens. *That other thing.* "What?" he demands, and Hani winces.

"I mean—we should talk about Aeri's scrying. And Ji-ah. And the eoduksini . . ."

"What," Seokga says, his voice strangled, "do you mean by 'that other thing'?" It is odd, he thinks dimly, that he is more appalled by the cuddling than the kiss.

"I . . ." The color of Hani's face matches the color of the kimchi bokkeumbap a couple is eating a few tables over. "It doesn't matter."

He glowers. "Spit it out."

She knows.

But how does she know?

She was *sleeping* . . .

"Fine," she snaps back, her eyes bright with embarrassment. "I know that you—I know that you used me as some oversized teddy bear last night. I woke up and you were holding on to me. *Cuddling* me. Happy?"

Something in her story doesn't quite fit. Seokga tilts his head. "When did you wake up?" he asks, frowning.

"Early morning."

Comprehension dawns on him. "And then you went back to sleep?" *In my arms?*

Hani glowers down at her bowl of soup, half-looking as if she would like nothing better than to drown in it. "That's beside the point. But if you really want to know—" She meets his gaze, her cheeks still burning ruby red. "Yes. I did go back to sleep."

Seokga gapes at her, unsure whether he should frown, laugh, or stand up and walk out of the restaurant.

Or possibly slam his forehead down onto the surface of the table.

But Hani is on a roll now, and she's showing no signs of stopping. "But only because I was so cozy," she insists, glowering. "If you know anything about foxes, you know that they like to be warm. And you were very, very warm. I think that your body temperature might run higher than what's even remotely healthy. You were using me as a teddy bear; I was using you as an overgrown heating pad. The way that I see it, it's a fair deal. You get to hold a makeshift stuffed animal, and I get to be warm. So it's really not a big deal. Okay?" She finishes, gasping for air. All of this had been said very quickly, each word blurring together.

Hani rambles when she is nervous.

Something in Seokga's chest warms at the realization. Something that has been encased in ice for six hundred and twenty-eight years. Something that is cold and dead, and yet beats for this peculiar gumiho.

"It amuses me how you think you can out-deceive the god of deception."

Hani blinks. "What do you mean?" Her tone is wary. Cautious.

"You awoke in my arms," Seokga says, feeling as smug as a cat after devouring a particularly juicy mouse, "and you liked it. So you stayed there."

"*Semantics,*" she snaps back.

The notion that this is simply semantics brings a scoff to his lips. He cocks his head, biting back another snicker. "What if I told you," he asks, hardly believing that he is allowing the words to pass his lips, "that I liked it, too?"

Immediately after he says it, he wonders what has made his sharp tongue so loose. Perhaps he hit his head harder than he realized during their tumble down the hill.

A moment of silence stretches between them, like a droplet

of water suspended precariously between the eave of a roof and the pavement below, unsure of whether it should tumble to the ground or not.

"Seokga, I—"

The phone rings.

Seokga jumps, then lunges across the table to yank the cellphone from Hani, who splutters at his sudden motion. He grips it with a slightly shaking hand.

"Shim?" He's too exhausted to care that his voice wavers with hope and fear.

"Seokga." Chief Shim's voice crackles through the phone in all its warm, grandfatherly glory. Seokga presses a fist to his mouth, breathing hard. It's him. "You were . . . You were right about Dok-hyun."

Shim is alive. Shim is fine. Seokga struggles to contain himself. What is *happening* to him? Why—why does he care about these snarky gumiho and tired haetae chiefs?

"What happened?" he manages to ask, putting the chief on speakerphone as Hani leans in, eyes wide.

A long sigh from the other end. "It happened early this morning. Around one A.M. I wasn't at the precinct—the nightshift officers were, and the guards watching Dok-hyun. What happened next is unclear. The cameras didn't pick anything up. Their lenses were suddenly blocked with shadow. By the time I made it to the precinct, my night-watch officers were dead— hearts ripped out—and Dok-hyun was gone. It was a bloodbath."

"Fuck," groans Seokga.

"Language," reprimands Shim, although there's no force behind it at all. "We're scouring New Sinsi for Dok-hyun. I've initiated stakeouts at various locations he might return to or pass by. I'm assuming you're still on Geoje?"

"We'll be leaving soon."

"The witness?"

"Confirmed that it was Dok-hyun, as did a yojeong we vis-
ited." *The eyes of the weary. Alone in a sea of deception. Verity, hidden beneath insincerity.* Godsdamn Lee Dok-hyun. "Not that it matters
now. He's clearly revealed his hand in the most dramatic way
possible," Seokga adds in disdain as he stands, flinging down
some cash on the table. "This whole thing was a waste of time.
Choi Ji-ah has gone missing. If you have officers to spare in the
coming days, send some out here to find her and bring her back
to New Sinsi. Have them take her to a shaman and wipe her
memory. We're heading back now. Are you . . ." He awkwardly
clears his throat. "Are you . . . okay?"

Seokga can almost hear his sad smile. "I'm fine, Seokga.
Thank you for asking. I'll see you when you return and we can
plan our next move."

"Right," Seokga says, and hits the END CALL button before he
can begin showcasing any more embarrassing displays of emotion.

CHAPTER TWENTY-THREE

HANI

NEITHER OF THEM DARES TO CLOSE THEIR EYES THAT night as they speed through Busan, determined to make the journey back to New Sinsi as quickly as possible. Dok-hyun still hasn't been found, but Hani has the suspicion that he'll turn up eventually—probably at the most inconvenient time possible.

Especially when Seokga re-enters the city.

"Have you been having nightmares?" Hani asks as Seokga flies through an intersection with grim determination, one hand on the steering wheel and the other holding a large coffee from a Coffee Star.

"Not yet," he replies, glancing at her. "But I'm sure they'll come. The demon in Dok-hyun's body hasn't forgotten about me. If I had to guess, he's biding his time. He's probably had great fun dragging us all over South Korea for nothing."

Hani nods, but bites her bottom lip.

An eoduksini can kill a god. And Seokga doesn't have access to his full powers, and thanks to her, he never will.

The ones you seek are closer than you imagine, the yojeong had said in that deep, otherworldly voice. *But you are alone, god, in a sea of deception. Let your mind not be fooled by surface perceptions. Look to the one with the eyes of the weary. Look to the one with the eyes of the teary. There you will find verity, hidden beneath insincerity.*

Sighing, Hani drags a hand through her hair. Although the

part about *weary eyes* was certainly about the haggard forensic pathologist, everything else had to be referring to the other half of Seokga's mission: the Scarlet Fox. And as vague as Aeri's declaration is, it's true. Hani is certainly deceiving Seokga. He will never catch the notorious gumiho.

And because of that, Seokga the Fallen will never reclaim his power.

Teary eyes. Perhaps Hani will cry for him, one day. She grimaces and shoves down a rising tide of guilt. Seokga cannot truly expect her to trade her life for the restoration of his former position, especially when he brought his fall upon himself with that attempt at a coup. That is an unfair deal, an unfair trade.

He won't have to know, Hani tells herself, watching as the highway speeds past the window in a blur of gray. *He won't ever have to know.*

So she is deceiving him, yes. Deceiving the god of deceit quite well, despite his claim that trickster gods cannot be tricked.

It is both a blessing and a curse that the fairies always speak in fickle riddles. Seokga mulled over Aeri's words and came to the conclusion she'd hoped he would: Weary-eyed Dok-hyun had deceived him from the start. Despite outward appearances, they cannot afford the belief that Dok-hyun is still human—his body has been possessed by something great and terrible.

If Seokga had heard that little plurality in *the ones you seek,* he has not mentioned the Scarlet Fox. Perhaps he is too tired to stretch his mind past the case of the eoduksini. Perhaps he simply didn't hear it over the whispering of the trees and his panic over Shim and his probable shock over kissing her. Whatever the case, Hani is relieved. She drags her hand down her face.

She feels Seokga slide her a sideways glance. "What are you doing?"

"Thinking," she admits. "About this godsdamned investigation." She peeks over at him through her fingers. His brows are drawn in concern. Worry. "And you are, too."

"Inaction breeds restlessness," the god mutters. "Call Shim. Tell him we want a shift on one of the stakeouts he's running tonight. We'll be within the city limits by eight." He hands her the phone, and she does as he says. Shim picks up with the first ring.

"Of course you can help," the chief says after she's explained what they want. "I can put both of you down for watching his house."

"His house?" Hani asks dubiously, frowning. "You think he'd go back?"

"After escaping custody, it's what most criminals do. To grab weapons or other resources. I don't want to write it off entirely. The eoduksini might be feeling cocky."

"Have you looked inside?"

"As much as we were able to without disturbing it. There are lots of, ah, ropes and gags. A good number of whips, too. We're unsure if this signifies a hostage plan."

"Ask for the address," Seokga says. Shim, hearing him, rattles off an address in a suburban section of New Sinsi.

"Park a few blocks away. We'll switch you into an undercover vehicle. Seokga's is rather conspicuous. You'll be on shift from nine to ten."

"Got it." Hani hesitates. "But . . ."

"What is it?" Shim asks.

"It's just—I don't think he'll go back to the house. Wouldn't it be quicker to lure him out somehow?" Hani thoughtfully picks at the hem of her sweater as Seokga cocks his head, listening to her. "It's definitely going to go after Seokga soon. Since he, you know, got the Dark World locked and all."

Seokga mutters something distasteful under his breath and runs a red light.

"So what if we set a kind of trap for it? We could end this sooner. Seokga could be cheese in a mousetrap."

The trickster seems to choke at being referred to as *cheese*.

Shim hesitates. "In light of recent events, it's best for the precinct to follow procedure. If the stakeouts yield nothing, we can regroup. But for tonight, we're following protocol. I'll see both of you at nine." He hangs up.

"Surprisingly," Seokga says, "it wasn't a bad idea."

Hani draws her knees up to her chest, peering at him in curiosity. Peering at the god who held her in his arms that morning, at the god she's shared a kiss with. At the god who is . . . the god who is becoming her friend, despite his perpetual grouchiness and inability to remember his manners.

This could be slightly problematic.

"If we don't find anything tonight . . ." Seokga shrugs. "We could try your strategy."

"Shim wouldn't approve."

Seokga snorts. "Shim wouldn't need to know. Until we succeed, that is. He's held back by protocol. We aren't."

Hani stares at him. "You want to spend even *more* time with me?" she demands incredulously.

He rolls his eyes. "Don't sound so shocked."

What if I told you I liked it, too? Hani can't stop the heat from rising to her cheeks. "We don't make a terrible team, you know," she says. "We can be the new Sherlock and Watson."

"Sherlock and Watson," Seokga says dubiously. "Those are strange names."

"They're British names." Hani eyes him. "You've never read the books?"

"No." Seokga wrinkles his nose. "I prefer Seokga and Hani."

"Hani and Seokga."

"Fine." A small smile tugs at his lips, and Hani cannot stop the sudden quickening of her heart. "Hani and Seokga."

CHAPTER TWENTY-FOUR

SEOKGA

WHO BRINGS *SNACKS TO A STAKEOUT?*

Kim Hani, that's who. When she demanded he stop outside of a Yum Mart for an emergency, he had assumed her leg was bothering her again despite the fact she'd been walking on it fine all day. That was his first mistake. Because ten minutes later, Hani had practically waltzed out of the grocery store with a large bag of junk food and a smug, satisfied smile.

Now, as they sit in the undercover car in front of Dok-hyun's empty home—a modest two-story sandwiched in between two other homes with the same gray paint and nondescript black shutters—Hani crunches loudly on shrimp chips, her legs propped up on the dashboard of the passenger seat, and her eyes glittering in the semi-darkness as she stares at Seokga. He shifts uncomfortably in the driver's seat.

"What?"

"I really think you'd like them," she says, nudging the box of Choco Pies even closer to him from where they rest on the car's console.

Seokga pinches one of the chocolate-coated atrocities in between two fingers and scowls. "No," he says, dropping it back into the box, and focusing again on Dok-hyun's house. It has been fifteen minutes, and nothing on the street has even so much as moved. Inaction breeds restlessness, he'd said, and even now it holds true. He can already predict that this stakeout will

yield nothing. Unlike Shim, Seokga doesn't think that Dok-
hyun will go back for his weapons. They can be easily replaced.

The ropes and gags, though, do seem to indicate some sort of
propensity for kidnappings. Perhaps they are meant for Seokga.
The thought is not comforting.

Hani polishes off the bag of shrimp chips, licks her fingers,
and dives back into the Yum Mart bag. She surfaces with a lollipop.

"Your stomach is a bottomless pit," Seokga says in amaze-
ment.

"Thank you," she replies around the bright red candy, tossing
the wrapper on the floor.

Seokga's mouth dries as he watches her suck on the lollipop
with a cheeky glitter in her eyes that lets him know she is perfectly aware of what she's doing. He clears his throat and looks
back, fixedly, at the house. Hani sighs.

"I'm bored. Let's play a game."

"We're on a *stakeout,* Hani," he says, still staring at the house
and trying very hard not to think about her now bright red lips.
"We don't have time for games."

"Truth or dare?" she asks, ignoring him, and damn him if he
can't ignore *her*. Seokga can't help but to look back over at her
and feel a flutter of . . . something . . . at her mischievous expression.

"Truth," he says after a long pause. He is extremely suspicious of what Kim Hani will dare him to do.

Hani pauses, considering. "Why did you tackle me? In the
forest?"

Shit. Seokga winces and reflects that he does not like this
game very much.

The gumiho smirks, but there's something almost like hurt
hiding behind her eyes. Seokga swallows, hating that he's the
one who has made her feel that way. "I'm serious," Hani contin-

ues around her candy. It clicks against her teeth as she speaks. "Why? I'm going to assume that you no longer hate me very much, seeing as you like to cuddle me. And maybe even kiss me. Right?" She peers at him expectantly.

Seokga can't even deny it. He nods, heat rising on his neck, and triumph flits across Hani's face.

"Ha!" she crows. "You *like* me!"

"Hani—".

"Seokga the Fallen likes me!" Tears of mirth brim in her eyes, and she brushes them away. "Hwanin's tits. Oh, this is good. I bet it pains you to admit that."

"Actually," he finds himself saying quietly, hoping she will not ridicule him for this, "it doesn't."

Hani's eyes widen, and something in her expression softens. Her lips, glossy from the lollipop, begin to curve into a smile that is as sweet as any of the candies in the gumiho's bag.

Seokga hesitates, glancing out to the street. Still no movement, but it'll be easier to say what he has to say if he isn't facing her. "I tackled you because—I was angry. I didn't hate you, though. I don't think I have for a while. It's just . . ." He grits his teeth. "A touchy subject."

"Your fall?" she asks.

"Yes," he mutters. "It is embarrassing."

"I can understand that. But you didn't need to knock us down a giant hill—"

"I didn't . . . I wasn't thinking. We were hot, and tired, and—and you called me a dick." The words spill out before he can stop them. Embarrassed, Seokga leans his forehead against the cool glass window.

Hani is quiet for a moment. "You were hurt."

He thinks back to how his chest tightened when she'd spat that word at him, how he'd felt—bizarrely—shame when she accused him of treating the creatures of Iseung poorly. Maybe it was true. Fine. *Definitely* it was true. But for some reason, Seokga hadn't liked hearing it from Hani. "Maybe," he grumbles. "I reacted . . . poorly. I shouldn't have tackled you."

"It's not a big deal," she replies softly. "I mean, it helped us find Ji-ah."

Seokga finally cuts her a glance. She's looking at him with gentle eyes. "You got your leg gnawed on by a hungry ghost."

Hani shrugs. "It healed. In all fairness, maybe I shouldn't have called you a dick."

"I've been called worse," he admits reluctantly. "I don't understand why I . . ." He rubs the nape of his neck. "Why I care so much," Seokga finishes hoarsely, and his voice sounds bewildered, even to himself. "I don't know why I care so much."

In the semi-darkness, Hani is all glittering eyes and glossy lips. The angles of her face are soft, blurred by shadow. Staring at her, Seokga *wants*. He wants to kiss her again, he wants to wake up with her again. He wants *her*. His fingers twitch, and he fights the urge to pull her toward him and meld his lips against hers. What if she doesn't want him as much as he wants her? What if . . .

"I have another one for you," Hani says, and is he wrong in thinking perhaps her voice is a bit husky, too? "Truth or dare?"

Seokga is hardly able to breathe. "Dare," he whispers.

She grins, pointing her lollipop at him. "Good choice."

And then she's closing the distance between them, tossing her lollipop onto the floor of the car. Shim will have a fit about that later, but right now, all Seokga cares about is how she's slinking a hand around his neck, tugging him closer to her. Their noses bump awkwardly together and her smile grows in that split second before her lips are fitted against his, warm and soft and slightly sticky from that godsdamn candy. Crushed sugar and cherries. That's what she tastes like.

Seokga's heart pounds wildly in his chest as he tries to tug

Hani closer, but the Choco Pies and the car's console get in the way, and he groans low in frustration. Hani laughs, and the sound is so clear, so bright as she breaks away. Seokga feels the bite of disappointment as the distance between them once again widens, and he's overcome with anxiety that this was all a joke, a cruel sort of ruse—but then Hani is impatiently shoving her beloved Choco Pies back into the bag, clambering over the console, and fitting herself neatly on his lap. Two surges of relief overtake him: One, that there's enough room for her between him and the steering wheel. Two, that she's again nestled against him, hips bracketing his own, bending her head down and surrounding them with a curtain of her lush brown hair that smells heavenly and tickles the sides of his face. As her lips crush against his, he runs his hands over her waist, marveling at the soft curves, and then the smooth feeling of her back as his hands slip underneath her sweater. How, Seokga thinks, is it possible for anybody to be this beautiful?

He could get drunk on kissing Hani. Could get drunk on the way her teeth tug impatiently on his lower lip, just enough for him to feel her canines, but not enough to truly hurt. To his complete and utter mortification, he is trembling as she rolls her hips atop him, atop the straining evidence of his arousal, sending waves of delicious heat through his body and up his spine— and then her hands are unbuttoning the top of his pants. "Is this okay?" she asks, and Seokga closes his eyes, thinking, *Yes, yes, it's more than okay, it's perfect,* the feeling of her fingers toying with the waistband of his briefs. "Seokga?"

Seokga pants, nodding, and then her hand is slipping inside, cupping the length of him, and he groans, low in his throat. The trickster's breathing grows husky, hot desire seeping down his spine as Hani's slender fingers wrap around him, stroking upward—

Two brisk knocks on the car's window. His eyes flare open in alarm. Shit. They're on a *stakeout,* and they've been doing anything but staking out the house. Is it Dok-hyun? Seokga is ready to grab his cane and transform it into a sword, but . . .

"Hwanin's tits!" Hani screeches as Chief Shim—out of uniform, incognito in a nondescript hoodie and, bizarrely, a giant pair of sunglasses—peers through the window. She yanks her hand away and practically dives back to her seat. Seokga, having the inane feeling that he's been caught fooling around with a girl like a teenage boy, quickly rebuttons his pants, smooths down his hair, and tries to calm his breathing.

"It's okay," he says hoarsely. "It's fine. The windows are tinted."

"Seokga?" Shim asks through the glass, glancing around the street. "Hour's up. The two officers on the back of the house didn't see anything, either. We'll let you go now."

Seokga closes his eyes and reflects that he has never been so thankful for tinted windows before in his life.

CHAPTER TWENTY-FIVE

HANI

SUITCASE ROLLING BEHIND HER AND DUFFEL BAG SLUNG over her shoulder, Hani follows Seokga through his apartment's ebony doors, trying not to let her eyes widen in awe as she takes in the god's residence. The floor is an expertly polished glossy black marble, which is partially covered by a plush white rug that stretches out underneath a large beige-colored couch adorned with various throw pillows and situated before an elegant coffee table.

Around the corner of a set of twisting wrought-iron stairs leading to another level, a large kitchen is visible, complete with an island in the same black stone as the floor and mahogany cabinets undoubtedly brimming with gourmet foods. The skyline of New Sinsi shines through the large glass panels of the back window wall, colorful lights twinkling and flashing against the inky night. Seokga's apartment is nothing short of luxurious; Hani closes her dropped jaw with notable difficulty, aware that Seokga is watching her reaction carefully. Curiously. Hopefully. As if he wants her to like his home. Something tugs on her heartstrings.

"Well," she says, turning to face him. "You certainly have an affinity for interior design."

Before coming here, Seokga drove to her apartment. While he waited outside her "hovel," she stuffed some more clean clothes and a few of her favorite romance books into a new suitcase. And something else. Something that she definitely shouldn't have grabbed, something that had been hidden deep within the bowels of her underwear drawer, concealed by lacy thongs.

Seokga shrugs, a lazy, cool gesture—but there's no masking the glitter of pleased self-satisfaction in his gaze. He's had the air of a very pleased god ever since they left the stakeout. Hani doesn't quite know what to make of it, although she suspects that *she* has the air of a very pleased gumiho.

The stakeout yielded nothing—well, that's not true. The stakeout yielded something *very* pleasurable, but nothing in terms of the eoduksini case. So they've moved on to their next plan: Drawing the eoduksini out. Making it come to *them*.

Shim would never approve. He's too reliant on protocol, on precinct procedure. Which is why they're not going to tell him until they succeed in taking down Dok-hyun.

But first, rest. She can tell Seokga is still drained from the events on Geoje. He needs to recuperate. When he suggested that they stay together to plan their trap, Hani was both surprised and pleased.

And guilty.

Seokga, for all their bickering, *likes* her. The gumiho he's meant to kill. Hani tries not to dwell on it. The focus is on the eoduksini, on saving Iseung from being turned into a Dark World. Hani has always been somewhat of a procrastinator, and she is all too happy to procrastinate dwelling on her and Seokga's potential fallout.

"Our room is upstairs," he says, gesturing to the curving black staircase. "Down the corridor and to the right."

"I'm sorry," Hani says, quirking her lips, "did you say, *our* room?"

She's amazed to see a slight flush darken Seokga's cheeks. He clears his throat once, and then twice. "No," he grumbles, and Hani snorts.

"You did."

Seokga's eyes narrow. "Do you enjoy torturing me?"

Hani runs her tongue along her teeth. "Yes."

The trickster god points at her. "Just for that," he says, "you're taking the guest room." It doesn't escape Hani's notice, though, that the acidity in his voice is less, well, *acidic* than usual. Maybe it has something to do with the fact that she stuck her hand down his pants and kissed the shit out of him.

Hani shrugs. In all truth, she doesn't think they'll sleep a wink if they share a bed tonight, and Seokga needs to rest. And besides, this new . . . reluctant friendship/enthusiastic hookup thing . . . she has with Seokga feels dangerous. She knows she'll get burned if she plays with fire, and what she felt with Seokga in the car is like a flame—precarious, dangerous, and hot. Hani stares at him, admiring his emerald eyes, his silky black hair, the way his mouth is usually a tight line but has begun to soften around her. Yes—very, *very* hot.

"Hani?" The god is frowning. "Hani?"

She snaps out of it with a jolt. "What?" Hani asks, embarrassed at being caught.

Seokga smirks. "I said, 'Be careful.' I suspect that the eoduksini will eventually haunt my dreams, and I wouldn't put it past it to target you, as well. You've been integral to the case, and it might hurt you just to fuck with me."

Hani grins despite herself. For some reason, Seokga's admission that she's become important enough to him to warrant the eoduksini's wrath feels . . . well, less frightening than it ought to. "Integral?" she purrs.

"Don't let it go to your head," he warns.

"Too late," she replies, rolling her suitcase over to the stairwell.

"Down the hall and to the right?" she calls over her shoulder as she mounts the stairs, the rungs chiming slightly underneath her feet.

"The *left*," Seokga corrects. "The one on the right is mine."

"Mm." Hani tosses him a smile.

As he rolls his eyes, the ludicrousness of it all slowly sinks in to Hani. She is in Seokga's apartment, preparing to settle in as his *roommate*. This is absurd. Utterly insane.

Roommates.

Hani makes her way up the stairs and down the corridor, eyeing the various paintings in ornate frames hung on the wall. Seokga lives in luxury—she supposes that *he* was wise with the concept of credit when it first emerged. *We can't all be perfect,* she reminds herself.

She follows his directions, pausing at the door to the left. But she eyes Seokga's door across from hers curiously, wondering what lays behind it.

A tiny peek won't hurt.

Hani turns the doorknob of Seokga's bedroom, peeping inside through the sliver of open door. The room is dark, but she can just vaguely make out a large bed, a teeming bookshelf, a—

"What are you doing?" Seokga's voice demands (rather huskily, she thinks) from behind her, and Hani whirls around with an innocent smile. The god frowns, but he doesn't look too upset at the thought of her in his bedroom. "I said last door to the left."

"Oopsies," Hani replies brightly, quickly sidestepping him and opening the door to the guest room.

The bedroom is large and expansive, a gloriously huge bed situated with a terrific view through another window wall overlooking the sprawl of New Sinsi. A polished black dresser sits just below a gilded mirror, a vase of flowers set on the dark wood. There is an adjoining bathroom, complete with a large,

claw-foot bathtub as well as a shower. Hani's brows raise. Perhaps Seokga will allow her to live here forever.

"Try not to break anything," says Seokga wryly, leaning in the
doorway. "I'll charge it to your tab if you do."

Hani rolls her eyes, plops her suitcase onto the edge of her
bed, and unzips it. It's followed by the duffel. "Isn't it past your
bedtime?" she asks as she begins to unpack the duffel. From it,
Hani takes out the sensible clothes she had brought with her to
Geoje before reaching for the suitcase and the slightly *less* sensible clothes she'd nabbed from her apartment. Lingerie and
skimpy dresses included.

Seokga's eyes narrow, but he steps into the hall. "Scream if
you're being murdered by the eoduksini."

"I have no doubt that I will." Hani watches in amusement as
Seokga's lips twitch. "Good night."

"Good night," Seokga replies—softer than she's ever heard
him—and gently shuts her door.

Hani sighs as she places her clothes in the dresser.

Judging from their escapade in the car, it is safe to say that
she and Seokga are no longer sworn enemies. But *what* are they?
Friends? Friends who sometimes stick their hands down each
other's pants? Are they just a casual hookup? Are they . . . Could
they be something more? Are they going to kiss again? Hani
hopes they kiss again. Seokga is deliciously good at kissing. She
knew it on the mountain, but the kiss tonight stunned her. If
Shim hadn't interrupted them, Hani suspects they would have
gone much, much further than they did.

She shakes her head as she riffles through her mound of
socks. In a matter of days, her life has become significantly more
complicated.

Her fingers brush against sharp metal, and Hani straightens.
Right. The daggers.

It is probably *beyond* foolish of her to have brought her scarlet daggers to Seokga's apartment, considering that he is set upon killing the Scarlet Fox, but . . . if the eoduksini attacks her here, the scarlet daggers are her most trusted weapons. She has no doubt that with them in hand, she can make the kill. She doesn't trust the silver ones as she does her scarlet blades. But where to hide them? Hani's eyes land on the dresser. Perfect. She'll hide them in an underwear drawer again.

Hani shoves the knives under a pile of lingerie and shuts the drawer quickly, her heart beating rapidly. But Seokga's room is silent—perhaps the god has indeed already gone to bed. Old men, after all, do tend to go to sleep early. She can only hope that the eoduksini does not take advantage of that little fact.

She climbs into bed, nestling deep within the soft blankets and staring at New Sinsi through the glass windows sparkling with multicolored lights. This bed is much more comfortable than the one at the Lotus Hotel, but . . . Hani sighs, wishing for the comfort of Seokga's warmth.

She wonders if he, across the hall, is wishing the same.

CHAPTER TWENTY-SIX

SEOKGA

SEOKGA WAKES, NOT TO THE SMELL OF CITRUS AND CIN-namon, but to a shrill ringing.

His brief sleep was dreamless, but he is not grateful. This, he knows, is the calm before the storm. Nightmares will come soon enough—and with them, the eoduksini. He has the uncomfortable, prickling feeling that it knows he's returned to New Sinsi.

Seokga blearily reaches for his cellphone and fumbles to answer. "What," he mutters as he sits up in his bed and pushes away the silken black sheets.

"Detective Seokga."

"Chief Shim," Seokga says, annoyance draining considerably. He glances at the digital clock on his bedside table. Four A.M. "Is everything all right? Did you find Dok-hyun?"

"No. But you'll want to know that three more bodies were uncovered last night, all at NSU. We have officers on the scene now." The old chief sounds like he is utterly done with the world. "I'd hoped you and your assistant would join us."

Three bodies. Seokga stiffens. "The eoduksini?"

"No." On the other end of the line, Chief Shim sighs. "The Scarlet Fox."

THE EARLY MORNING AIR IS FRIGID AND SHARP AS HANI and Seokga stand underneath the cherry blossom trees, staring down at the three bodies limp on the white cobblestones below. For the sake of appearances, the surrounding haetae officers are clad in the standard human police uniforms, waving off wide-eyed students as they approach the taped-off area that spans the entire underpass of trees. Although it is still dark, barely yet dawn, the red and blue lights of the surrounding precinct cars illuminate the white sheets covering the bodies.

He is acutely aware of the dokkaebi paparazzo standing just outside of the yellow tape, zooming in on Seokga and Hani, snapping away with his bulky camera. No doubt *Godly Gossip*'s next issue's title will read: FAMILY FEUD—SEXY SEOKGA STILL SEEKING FORGIVENESS FROM HOTTIE BROTHER HWANIN! (PLUS: WHO'S THIS MYSTERY BRUNETTE? IS SINGLE SEOKGA FINALLY *TAKEN*?)

If Seokga ever finds out who the inane magazine's editor in chief is, they will suffer.

He grits his teeth and tries to concentrate on what Shim is saying underneath the wailing of sirens, but it is becoming increasingly hard to do.

"They were found an hour ago by a janitor. We're already collecting as much footage as we can." Shim rubs at his forehead wearily. Chang Hyun-tae stands beside him, his expression dark underneath his black hat. "Hyun-tae has confirmed there are no souls to collect. They are gone. The amount of paperwork," Shim adds to himself as he shakes his head, "will be obscene."

Hyun-tae nods, his expression incredibly fatigued. "I looked everywhere," he confirms. "Sometimes, there are errors with this sort of thing. Souls can't be found because they're hiding, or scared. This isn't the case here. They're just gone. And I called my superiors, too: Jeoseung's internal database confirms that no souls from this area were predicted to be collected this morning."

Seokga drags a hand through his hair. The souls of the dead boys are gone, along with their livers. The Scarlet Fox has struck again. "Great," he mutters.

And the Spring Solstice, Chunbun, is only eleven days away. With both the eoduksini and the gumiho still on the loose, Seokga's chances of returning to Okhwang are looking slimmer and slimmer. "Souls and livers," he repeats coldly. "It seems like she was hungry."

"It does." Next to him, Hani is staring at the three dead boys, her face slack with . . . horror? Shock? It seems to be a combination of both. Odd. She wasn't so pale when examining the other two dead boys.

"Did you pick up on another power flare?" Seokga asks Chief Shim. The old haetae shakes his head.

"It's probable that the Scarlet Fox didn't use an energy blast to subdue her victims. Logic tells us that this is still clearly her handiwork." Chief Shim rubs his temples with a wrinkled hand. "Without Dok-hyun, we haven't been able to have an autopsy yet. I believe a human coroner is on his way; he can handle the rest. Until we get the footage, there's not much that we can do. I'll call you, Seokga, when we've collected the security camera recordings of both the campus and the city. Hani, have you been able to go through the tapes from the first murders?"

"I've been able to go through some," she replies quickly. "There was nothing on them. There are six others, though, that I wasn't able to look through before going to Geoje. If you want, I can return those to the precinct—"

Shim frowns. "Why were they taken off precinct grounds in the first place?"

Hani falters. "It was so busy, and—"

"It's my fault," Seokga interrupts. "Out of necessity, we've been focusing mainly on the eoduksini case. I didn't give her enough time to watch all of them, so she took some home. She didn't do anything wrong." Hani, he sees, is blinking in what looks like surprise. He tries not to feel offended. They're ... well, friends, aren't they? Of course he'll defend her.

The haetae raises his brows, now looking slightly amused. Seokga scowls. "What?"

"Nothing, nothing," says Chief Shim, still looking somewhat pleased despite the crime scene around them. "Nothing at all." He sighs, turning back to the sheet-covered bodies. "Return the unwatched tapes at your earliest convenience. We'll go through them when we can. But to be honest, I doubt that there is anything of use on any of them. We've been interrogating all of the gumiho supplied to us on the list you made of those old enough to be our fox, but so far, all alibis have checked out. Whoever she is, she's adept at hiding. And between her and the darkness demon, this city doesn't stand a chance."

"We'll find her," Seokga assures Shim.

Without a goodbye, Shim departs, tiredly making his way over to the other officers. The remaining trio stands in silence, all eyeing the bodies. Hyun-tae is the first to break the quiet, turning to Hani.

"I did what you asked of me in your absence," he says dutifully. Seokga only half-hears him, still glaring at the corpses. Damn the Scarlet Fox to the depths of Jeoseung. "I now work part-time at the Creature Café from three to five."

"Good job," Hani replies, her voice vague, as if addressing an eager puppy. But then her voice stiffens, straining as she says, "Seokga."

He turns to her. "What?"

Hani's face is still ashen, but the fox gives him a small smile. "I'm going to go grab some chocolate at the Creature Café. I'll be back soon."

Seokga nods. "I'll come with you," he says. A cup of cold, bittersweet coffee and the subsequent caffeine buzz may calm his rising temper, soothe his fraying nerves.

And breakfast with Hani may have a similar effect. Being around her has become . . . very enjoyable, to say the least. Putting her in the guest room last night had been a reluctant decision on his part, and he's eager to be with her again. Perhaps they can also talk about what they are. Seokga feels—lost, out of his depth. Was the car a one-time thing? Seokga has had many one-time things, but he doesn't want Hani's name on that list. He wants her in his bed, perfuming his sheets with her citrus and cinnamon scent, his name on her lips.

"I will go, as well," the jeoseung saja chimes in promptly, adjusting his hat and glancing at Hani.

Seokga scowls.

A peculiar expression crosses Hani's face, and his stomach drops as he wonders if she'd rather Seokga not accompany her. If she has gotten sick of him already. Was their kiss in the car a mistake? Does she regret it?

It has been a while since Seokga has felt wounded.

He does not enjoy it.

At all.

But then Hani is cheerfully smiling and nudging Seokga with her elbow. "I have a feeling that I know your order," she says with a snort. "Coffee," she rattles off, deepening her voice, "with one cream and one sugar, or *fear my wrath*."

He bristles, offended even as relief settles over his shoulders. "I don't sound like that."

"Oh?" Hani winks, looping her arm through his with a comforting casualness. An intimacy that is new, yet entirely welcome. He fights back an involuntary smile as she gazes up at him, her nose crinkled in a way that suggests she finds what she's about to say very, very amusing. Seokga loves the feeling of Hani being by his side. "I think that my impression was pretty accurate. Perhaps we should ask Hyun-tae's opinion."

"Do not."

"Hyun-tae," Hani says as the three of them start to walk away from the crime scene, "on a scale of one to ten, ten being the most accurate, how would you rate my Seokga impression?"

"I would rate it a ten," the grim reaper replies dutifully before meeting Seokga's glare and clearing his throat abruptly. "A five, I mean. A middle ground."

Hani snorts, tightening her grip around Seokga's arm. Before he can stop himself, he leans into her touch.

And she leans back.

CHAPTER TWENTY-SEVEN

HANI

TWO GUMIHO, A JEOSEUNG SAJA, AND A FALLEN GOD ALL sit around a table in an empty café.

One gumiho is glaring at the other.

One gumiho is studiously stirring her iced coffee and avoiding the older gumiho's suspicious stare while also sweating profusely and flinching every time the god moves.

One gumiho is wondering who the *fuck* killed three NSU boys because it damn sure wasn't her.

The god and the jeoseung saja are sitting in awkward silence, eyeing the two gumiho with equally wary expressions.

Moments tick by.

Minutes.

"Hani," Somi says tremulously, looking up from her swirling coffee as the ice rattles against the glass cup, "how . . . was Geoje?" She is flushed, her cheeks a bright, bright pink and her eyes sparkling in a way that is almost feverish. Her short curly hair is wild and untamed, and her Creature Café apron is stained with hot chocolate. Her hands are shaking. They were trembling violently when they made Hani's drink.

Hani clears her throat. If her suspicion is correct—and she hopes that it is not—their two other companions cannot be alerted to the . . . possibility. "It was a mess," she admits honestly. "While we were gone, the eoduksini attacked the precinct."

"R-right," says Somi. "I heard about that."

"And then a fairy made Seokga and me kiss." She darts a glance over to the god. Seokga looks incredibly pleased with himself.

Somi's eyes bulge out of her head in surprise. *"What?"* She had been in the process of raising her drink to her lips, but at Hani's words, her hand seems to have a spasm. Coffee spills all over her lap, and Hani winces.

The young gumiho has the Jitters.

Seokga is watching Somi coolly, sipping at his own coffee. Unsurprisingly, the fallen god does not bother to help. But Hyun-tae leaps to his feet.

"Ms. Somi," Hyun-tae says in alarm. "Do you need napkins?" His cheeks flush as Somi spares him a glance. "Of course you do. I will go and get them for you. Stay there!" He scampers off, hasty in his desire to help.

If Somi is still unnerved by the jeoseung saja's presence, she gives no indication. "The part-timer is very useful," she says to Hani, those feverish eyes laughing while still wide with fear. "He does all of my work for me, did you know that, unnie? All I have to do is point, and he takes out the trash, cleans the floors, wipes the tables . . . And all for part-time pay!"

"It's clear that he's smitten with you," Hani replies, careful to keep her voice smooth and level, even as she watches those shaking hands. "You have him wrapped around your little finger, Somi."

"Don't I?" Somi gives a wavering little smile. Hani's eyes flick to her too-red lips. Somi hardly ever wears lipstick. "Minji loves him." Having sensed Hani's scrutiny, Somi presses her lips together and stares at the floor.

"I bet she does." The jeoseung saja is just Minji's type for a model employee. Eager to work, professional, polite. Everything that Hani is not.

Hani finds that she does not quite miss working at the Creature Café.

She watches as Hyun-tae returns with a roll of paper towels and hands them to Somi with a deference usually reserved for the occasions where waiters serve royalty.

"Why are you here so early, though?" Somi asks, mopping her jeans with a wad of paper towels. "Did something happen this morning with . . . the eoduksini?"

Hani watches her reaction carefully, even as she phrases the answer in a way that won't startle Somi enough to slip up. "There was a situation at New Sinsi University—similar to the situation I told you about a few nights ago."

Somi is silent, suddenly intensely interested in scrubbing her pants. To her credit, her expression is almost nonchalant.

Almost.

"Three men missing souls and livers." Seokga has looked up from his coffee, an expression of great annoyance crossing his face. Somi has turned a concerning shade of green and gray all at once. "The Scarlet Fox," he says to Hani, who has begun to wonder how suspicious it would be if she were to grab Somi and run, "may have to be lured out like the eoduksini. If the new footage Shim recovers is useless, we'll . . ." He continues speaking, his tone clipped and cold—furious at their lack of leads—but Hani doesn't hear. She is watching Somi very, very carefully.

Kim Hani did not kill those men last night.

Kim Hani was lying in Seokga's apartment, claws unsheathed, half-expecting an eoduksini to leap out of the shadows for the entirety of the night and possibly also fantasizing about a certain trickster god.

But Somi . . .

Somi has the Jitters.

It is something that happens to baby gumiho when they eat too much, too quickly. And is it a coincidence that Hani gave Somi her first taste of liver days before last night's murder? Is it a coincidence that their souls were stolen days after Hani explained to Somi how it is done? She hopes, desperately, that it is so. Because Seokga believes that the Scarlet Fox is behind all five murders. And if the footage reveals Somi as the perpetrator of last night's events . . . Fuck. *Fuck.*

This is Hani's fault. She has corrupted Somi—naïve, innocent Somi. And she has led the wolves right to her door. At the university, she was plagued by a suspicion, but a rational part of her whispered that Somi couldn't possibly have killed the three boys. Somi, who had been a nervous wreck after consuming those livers. Somi, who'd never killed a human in her life.

But now, taking in Somi's glazed eyes, her pink skin, her trembling fingers . . .

Hani remembers the dark curiosity lurking underneath Somi's otherwise innocent visage. She should have known better. Should have been wiser in her influence. Although she has gotten away with murder for centuries, Somi has not. And that is on her. The fact that devouring souls and eating livers is now illegal is also on her.

Guilt twists Hani's stomach into hundreds of tight knots.

The footage will show Somi as the perpetrator of the crime. She will be marked as the Scarlet Fox, hunted down, and killed.

Unless Hani intervenes.

Unless she finds a way to delete the footage.

Sweat dribbles down Hani's neck as Somi meets her eyes. The baby gumiho is pale, the blood drained from her face even. Her words, when they come out, are quiet and carried on only a little thread of a voice. "Hani," Somi says, standing abruptly, "I've been meaning to ask. There's a . . . problem with the ice machine in the back. I know you don't work here anymore, but . . ."

"I'll check it out with you," says Hani as she stands. She casts a quick glance at Seokga, who is drinking his iced coffee at an alarming speed. "I'll be back."

He waves her off, still deep in his own musings.

Hani follows Somi into the back kitchen, hidden behind the café's counter, and shuts the steel door behind her. She presses her back against the door, just to be sure, and stares at Somi, who is trembling near the café's large freezer.

"It was you, wasn't it?" Hani asks softly. Gently. "Somi-ah, did you kill those men?"

Somi's eyes swim with tears, and her bottom lip trembles rapidly. "I-I didn't mean to, Hani," she rasps. "But I . . . Ever since I tried the livers, I've been . . . I've been craving it. The rush. And I-I tried to tell you, but you were heading out to Geoje, and I didn't want to call again and bother you . . . And then the last time we talked, I was g-going to tell you, but you hung up . . ."

Guilt slices into Hani's heart as she remembers the discussion that she had with Somi before climbing into Seokga's car. *"Wait. I-I have a question . . ."* Somi had whispered into the phone. *". . . I've been feeling odd . . ."*

But Hani hadn't been listening.

"I tried to ignore it," Somi continues, blinking back tears even as a stray one trickles down her cheek. "I came to work from morning to evening, and did my very best. I even got along with the jeoseung saja part-timer. I made the coffees, I wiped the counters, I was a good worker. I was fine for . . . for a while. Even though I was c-craving it so bad that I couldn't even see straight, I was fine. But then, last night . . ."

"The Cravings got worse," Hani guessed. Gods. This is—this is all on Hani.

The Cravings occur when a gumiho has a hypersensitivity to the rush of power that comes with consuming livers, consuming souls. Not all gumiho have this hypersensitivity, but it's not extraordinarily uncommon. The Cravings can be sated—by consuming more livers, more souls—but the urge will come back eventually, clouding the gumiho's mind with bloodlust until they kill and eat again, starting the cycle all over. That day after Somi consumed those two livers, she was bouncing off the walls. Hani chalked it up to the fact that she had never had liver before, but Somi's trembling hands tell a different story. Somi is hypersensitive to power. And she is still Craving.

Somi nods, and the dam finally breaks. She dissolves into tears. "I killed those men," she sobs. "I killed them, and I liked it."

"Somi," Hani murmurs, peeling herself from the door and enveloping her friend in a comforting embrace. "You have nothing to feel bad about, Somi. Gumiho are meant, genetically, to kill. You haven't done anything wrong, not in my eyes."

"But they think we're the Scarlet Fox," Somi whispers into her shoulder. "They're going to kill me. Hani, I'm scared."

"No," Hani says firmly, "no. They're not going to touch you." She pulls away, holding Somi by the shoulders. "I won't let that happen."

"What are you going to do?" asks Somi waveringly.

"I'm going to teach you all the tricks in the book. So you can feed and never get caught. But for now . . ." She leans in to whisper in Somi's ear. "I need you to listen very, very closely."

Hani has made the ingenious realization that Somi will not be on camera if there *are* no cameras.

She leaves Somi with the god and the jeoseung saja, giving her clear instructions to state that Hani is in the washroom and to keep them busy. She has no doubt that Seokga will stay satisfied if he is given another ginormous iced coffee on the house and knows that Hyun-tae will remain in the café solely for the purpose of spending time with "Ms. Somi."

Hani has at most fifteen minutes to make it to the university and back. Fifteen minutes to destroy the cameras trained on the spot of the crime and the nearby areas, fifteen minutes to leave undetected. Fifteen minutes. With the beginning of morning traffic, stealing Seokga's Jaguar and speeding off won't get her anywhere. But changing into her fox form just might.

In the alleyway of the Creature Café, Hani takes a deep breath and lets the change wash over her. Lets herself transform into a sleek, scarlet fox with nine tails that wave slightly in the wind. Lets herself flex her muscles, reacquainting herself to the fox form, reacquainting herself to the sudden rush of her doubling senses. In her fox form, she is able to hear every whisper of the city within a two-mile radius, smell every scent, see everything with unnatural clarity.

And in her fox form, Hani is very, very fast.

She can only hope that the footage has not yet been reviewed by the haetae. Hani tilts her head, stretches her joints.

Ready, set, go.

Nobody notices the scarlet blur that speeds through the city a moment later, nothing more than a flash of ruby wind. Nobody notices the pounding of paws against the pavement as the nine-tailed fox weaves through pedestrians on the sidewalk, muzzle pulled back in determination.

Nobody notices as Kim Hani runs like she's never run before, set upon fixing her mistake.

I'm sorry, Somi, she thinks as she runs. *I'm so sorry.*

CHAPTER TWENTY-EIGHT

SEOKGA

SEOKGA IS WATCHING THE INTERACTIONS BETWEEN THE young gumiho and the awkward jeoseung saja with a fair bit of amusement.

The jeoseung saja is clearly in love. The gumiho is arguably not. They sit side by side across from him as he drinks his second coffee of the morning. The gumiho—Somi—is clearly a youngster. A nervous youngster, at that. She is studiously avoiding both Seokga's and Hyun-tae's gazes, bouncing her knee up and down as Hyun-tae gazes at her with what can best be described as a dreamy expression. Somi goes red when she accidentally meets Seokga's gaze. By the blush staining her cheeks, he tags her as the type to read *Godly Gossip* and mull over which brother— Hottie Hwanin or Sexy Seokga—is hotter. *Ridiculous.*

He snorts under his breath. Somi jumps and again averts her gaze. Hyun-tae's lovesick stare doesn't falter. Jeoseung saja are strange creatures, so detached from the world of the living that when they fall, they fall quickly—and they fall hard. It's probable that despite his lovesick expression, Hyun-tae has only known Somi for a week, or two, at most.

He is growing bored without Hani. There is no conversation, nothing but the sipping of his coffee and mulling over the morning's events. No eoduksini attacks yet, but the Scarlet Fox, on the other hand . . .

Chunbun is coming soon. Seokga ignores the twist of anxiety

within his stomach as he sets down his coffee. If he has not succeeded in fulfilling Hwanin's orders by then... He does not
want to even think of it.

"Ms. Somi," Hyun-tae is saying eagerly. "Yesterday we spoke
of possibly asking Minji for more stylish aprons. You will be
pleased to know that I have drawn up various sketches of ideas
in between collecting souls. If you would like to see them, I have
them here, in my briefcase." He taps his black briefcase briskly,
his expression alert and keen to please.

Somi blinks at him. "You did?"

"I did. Yes." Hyun-tae nods. "Four variations, all different in
color. I recall that you said in passing you like the color pink..."

Somi gapes at him, still jittering her leg. The table has begun
to shake. Seokga scowls in annoyance as Hyun-tae continues.

"...so I took that into mind while preparing these designs
for you."

The table is practically vibrating at this point.

Seokga has had quite enough. Leaning forward, narrowing
his eyes to slits, he snaps, "You're shaking the table."

Somi flinches back as if struck; her eyes are wide and teary,
her lips tremble. Immediately, Hyun-tae whips around to
Seokga. The grim reaper looks appalled, as if he cannot believe
that Seokga has dared speak to Somi in this way. "Apologize," he
demands, and Seokga laughs quietly. It's impressive, the nerve
that one possesses while in love.

"No," he replies coldly. Somi has gone white.

Hyun-tae straightens in clear offense. "You—"

But then the door to the washroom around the corner opens,
and Hani is striding out, her hair disheveled as she hurries over
to the table, a strange gleam in her eyes as she takes her seat next
to Seokga's. "What did I miss?" She is slightly out of breath, and
before Seokga can stop her, she snatches his coffee and takes a
long sip.

She's back. Seokga fights down a smile as his mood brightens considerably. "I thought you didn't like coffee."

Hani makes a face as she sets down the cup and wipes her mouth with the back of her wrist. "I don't." She glances at Somi. "You'll be fine here for the rest of the day?" It is phrased like a question, but something in her tone dips, and it sounds more like a statement than anything. Seokga tilts his head as Somi nods her head.

"I-I will. Thank you, Hani."

Hani smiles, and Seokga watches as her eyes go to Hyun-tae. "Hey. Part-timer."

Hyun-tae straightens. "Yes?"

"Still keep to your promise." Hani's gaze moves back to Somi, who seems visibly confused. "Protect this one here—from the dangers of broken ice machines." She rises to her feet and tugs Seokga upward with her. "The café will open soon. We should head out."

Seokga drains the rest of his iced coffee and tosses it in the waste bin before following Hani into the early morning outside. She waits for him to catch up before they begin the walk to his Jaguar, side by side. "What's the plan for today?"

In the sunlight, her eyes are molten pools of chocolate and wine. Seokga's heart stutters—and not from the caffeine. He mentally slaps himself across the face.

He is no better than Hyun-tae.

As he opens the door to the Jaguar's passenger seat, allowing Hani to duck inside, he says, "We'll head to the precinct. We'll start the hunt for the Scarlet Fox and plan our next move with the eoduksini." Seokga gently shuts the car door before sliding into his own seat. "The footage," he says, starting the engine, "should give us a lead on the Unruly gumiho. DNA evidence on the body may, as well." All creatures living in New

Sinsi have their DNA in the haetae database. "We may kill her today."

"Mm," says Hani, smoothing down her hair. "That would be—" She is cut off by Seokga's phone ringing shrilly in his pocket. Seokga sighs, not bothering to hide the haggard exhalation as he answers. Shim's voice reaches his ears.

"Seokga." The old haetae sounds panicked. "Where are you?"

"What happened?" Seokga demands, hand tightening around the wheel and heart beginning to pound in his chest. "I'm driving. I can get to you right now—"

"I'm fine, I'm fine. It's the footage from last night," the chief pants. "The cameras, the computers . . . They're all destroyed."

Seokga's mind empties out until there is nothing but roaring silence. "And the bodies?"

"Gone," Chief Shim rasps. "The bodies are gone."

"How," Seokga demands furiously, standing before Shim's desk with his arms folded, "did this happen? How did you *lose* the *bodies*?"

The precinct is entirely silent save for his cold, commanding voice. All other officers filed out of the room once Seokga had entered, his cane thudding against the tile floor as he'd stalked over to Shim. Before driving to the precinct, they'd stopped by Hani's apartment to grab the tapes she hadn't yet gone through from the first attack, leaving behind the ones she said yielded nothing. Hani sets them quietly on the chief's desk, but the haetae doesn't even seem to notice.

Besides the aura of grief hovering in the precinct's air, there is no sign of the eoduksini's attack. The bodies of the night-watch haetae have been given to their families for burial, and the bloodstains have been scrubbed from the floor. Yet there is a smell in the air, something sour and bitter all at once. Terror. Seokga tries to breathe in only through his mouth.

"I don't know," Chief Shim whispers. He is slumped at his chair, dark purple circles underneath his eyes, his face haggard and beyond exhausted. He does not look like the city's most powerful haetae in these moments—he looks like a very upset old man on the brink of collapsing. Seokga blinks and bites his tongue.

Once, perhaps, he wouldn't have cared. But now, looking at the old chief, he's careful to gentle his voice as he continues to speak to the haetae. He even uncrosses his arms. "I just don't understand how the bodies, camera, and footage could have disappeared."

"I have officers scouring the city for them," Shim says hoarsely. "I'll contact you when something comes up. I'm sorry, Seokga. I know what this investigation means to you."

Seokga swallows an acerbic retort. It's not Shim's fault. "Let me know if you find the bodies," he manages to say, before giving a hasty farewell and striding out of the precinct with Hani on his heels, frustration thrumming in his blood.

CHAPTER TWENTY-NINE

HANI

CONSOLING SEOKGA IS A LOT LIKE COMFORTING A MOrose child prone to throwing tantrums.

In his apartment, Hani taps the notebook held in her hand, where she's written out Aeri's clue in her looping handwriting as Seokga asked her to. It was with a bitter jolt of disappointment that she realized Seokga had heard that little *s* sound in the fairy's clue, after all. Yet Seokga has been vocal about the clue's "*vexing uselessness*" in terms of identifying the Scarlet Fox.

She's curled up on the overstuffed couch, clad in sweatpants and a ratty gray sweater, Seokga slumped next to her, eyes shut and face pale. Hani sighs. He has been like this ever since they left the precinct. "Seokga," she says for the fiftieth time. "We need to plan our trap for the eoduksini."

Seokga mumbles something in return that sounds suspiciously close to "*No.*"

Hani winces.

It would be a lie to claim that her guilt has not caught up to her. It would be a lie to claim that she doesn't feel the slightest pinch of remorse for breaking the cameras, smashing the computers, and then dumping the bodies in the Han River—all within a matter of nine minutes and forty-seven seconds.

It would be a lie to claim that this game of deception that she is playing has not begun to . . . hurt her heart, somehow.

Because of her, Seokga is pursuing a fruitless goal.

But the circumstances are not changeable, Hani reminds herself. There is no point in dwelling on it. Instead, she must focus on what Seokga and she can do.

They will never catch the Scarlet Fox, but together they *can* catch the eoduksini. They won't be signing up for another stakeout—they'll be plotting something more effective. As soon as Seokga is shaken out of this morose trance.

"Seokga," she repeats, nudging his shoulder. "Come on. Quit moping."

He grumbles and, in an oddly childlike gesture, turns so that he sits facing away from her.

"Seokga. For the love of gods." She pulls at his shoulders. "Stop acting like a baby. You've been alive for thousands of years." She tugs him backward, and to her surprise, he lets her. Something in Hani's chest breaks a little as Seokga's head lowers to her lap, and as he stares up at her with those eyes that are usually so cruel and cold but are now almost vulnerable.

"Hani," he says in that eternally hoarse voice. "If I am not reinstated as a god, I will burn Iseung to the ground."

Hani runs her fingers through his inky black hair. "I believe you," she says dryly. She watches as his eyes flutter closed again as she plays with his hair. Her throat tightens.

You are alone, god, in a sea of deception.

"Listen," Hani says, reaching for her notebook even though she knows she shouldn't. "We can go over Suk Aeri's hint again—" Seokga's hand covers hers, stopping her from grabbing the pad.

"I've gone over it hundreds of times in my head," Seokga says resignedly. "It's exactly the sort of watery, half-baked, entirely useless prophecy that I should have known to expect from one of the yojeong. I don't know if any part of it is even in reference to the Scarlet Fox. I am alone in a sea of deception. That was about Dok-hyun. I should not be fooled by surface perceptions. Also Dok-hyun. I should look for those with weary eyes. Dok-hyun. The part about the teary eyes is the only part that hasn't been met by him." He gazes up at her. "Bend closer," he says. "Show me your eyes."

Hani's heart lurches, but she bends over him all the same, her nose nearly touching his.

"Well," Seokga mutters petulantly, "your eyes aren't teary."

"Only weary," Hani grumbles, even as she is overcome by a mixture of relief and guilt. She wonders again if Aeri's clue signifies that one day, she will weep for Seokga. "I didn't sleep a wink last night."

He smirks but it's half-hearted. "Scared, fox?"

"Not at all," Hani lies smoothly. "The bed is just obscenely uncomfortable." She frowns down at him, still only inches away. "Why are you grinning?"

The god is staring up at her with a small, lopsided smile that is so *unlike* the Seokga that she knows. Whereas his leers are cold and calculated, this smile is almost subconscious.

Seokga's eyes widen slightly in confusion, his smile faltering. "I . . . I don't know," he snaps, but Hani recognizes that his frustration is not with her. It is with himself. "I don't know," he says again, this time quieter. And she swears that his voice wavers with hesitancy. "Hani," Seokga asks, "what are we?"

"I have no idea," she whispers. And it's the truth. She knows what she wants them to be, but with the scarlet daggers stashed upstairs and secrets hidden in her heart, it's something that she shouldn't chase.

But Hani has never been very good at ignoring temptation, and there is a fallen god on her lap, gazing up at her with an unusually naked expression of hope and what might even be the same anxiousness that she feels. He's infuriating and snarky and grumpy and cold—but he's also sharp-tongued enough to keep up with her banter, to return it in full. He gives her his own shirt and binds her leg, he buys medicine and daggers for her when she needs them.

And gods, he's beautiful. Nothing, in all her one thousand and seven hundred years, has matched the exact shade of his evergreen eyes, nor the midnight locks of his hair.

She begins to ramble, losing all of her usual confidence with one fell swoop. "I mean, are we—are we friends? With benefits? I know you liked it when we—when I—in the car. Kissing. Hand. In pants. And if you'd want to do that again, sometime, I wouldn't say no." She needs to stop talking. Hani really needs to stop talking. But she can't. It's all spilling out. "I would say yes. Very loudly, probably. I like kissing you. More than I should. But I don't know what to call that. I don't know if I *want* to be your friend."

His brows have inched together; he looks hurt. Hwanin's tits. She really didn't phrase that right.

"That's not what I meant," she says, suddenly overcome with the urge to hurl herself out the window. "I want to be more than a friend. More than your makeshift teddy bear. I want to keep kissing you, and—"

Seokga is laughing. It's not mocking laughter, though. It's soft. Almost tender. "Hani," he says, "I want to keep kissing you, too."

Warmth blossoms in her heart. "Oh," she murmurs. "Good. That's—that's good."

The trickster smiles. "And I think I know what we are, after all," he adds. "We already decided."

"We did?" she whispers.

"Coming back from Geoje. Remember?"

Hani's lips quirk upward. She does. "We're Hani and Seokga."

Seokga reaches a hand upward and tucks one of her loose strands of hair behind her ear. And the tenderness with which he does so, the uncharacteristic gentleness, the kindness that is so unlike him . . . That simple act answers all her questions.

Hani leans down and kisses him.

CHAPTER THIRTY
SEKGA

SEOKGA SWALLOWS A SOUND OF DELIGHTED SURPRISE AS Hani's lips meet his, warm and sweet, and tasting of hot chocolate.

What are you doing? A voice in his head demands, a voice that is cold and crotchety, a voice that has been his source of guidance since his fall and the entirety of his very long, cranky immortal life since. *This is foolishness. Pull away. Push her away. They all betray you eventually.*

Seokga ignores that voice.

Instead, he reaches up and tugs her head down farther. And damn it, the way that her soft hair tickles his face, the way their kiss is a little awkward and fumbling due to his position, the way her pert nose bumps against his . . . it's all enough for him to want to unravel completely, to shred the boundaries between them into nothing.

He loves the way her breath hitches in her throat, loves the way her hair smells like some ridiculous, fancy shampoo. Seokga wonders at the warmth of her, the softness of her skin, the sweetness of her lips. Seokga wonders at *her.*

When Hani's hands cup the sides of his face he can feel his heart stutter—actually fucking stutter—at the way her fingers feel against his skin. He wants to hold those hands in his, wants to knit his fingers with hers, wants to trace the lines of her palms.

Hani pulls away, but only slightly, and Seokga makes a petulant noise of discontent that he would be embarrassed about if he weren't so—so godsdamn . . . obsessed. Hani laughs and her lips slant against his again, her tongue tracing his, one hand lazily toying with strands of his hair. Something blooms within the barren plains of his heart, something that is green and small and smells of spring. A seed of happiness, nurtured by Hani's kisses, just beginning to grow.

It has been so long since he has felt this stirring of life, of joy, within him.

Seokga allows himself to smile against her lips as they slowly break the kiss. He gazes up at her—this gumiho who he has somehow become head over heels smitten with.

"Hani," he whispers, longing to pull her closer, to crush her against him, to hold her and never let go. "Hani." He loves the way that her name tastes on his lips—like citrus and cinnamon and hot chocolate and home.

Home.

It has been so long since Seokga has had one.

"Hani," he whispers again, reaching for her.

And for the first time in six hundred and twenty-eight years, Seokga feels as if there is somewhere he finally belongs.

CHAPTER THIRTY-ONE

HANI

Lips swollen and hair messy, Hani stares up at the ceiling of Seokga's living room with an immense amount of satisfaction. The fallen god is asleep on top of her. His arms are circled around her back, his head buried in the crook of her neck as he breathes deep and slow and even. He's heavy—crushingly so—but Hani does not mind.

No, she does not mind at all.

She runs her fingers over her tender lips, marveling at the sheer hunger that consumed Seokga during the last hour. At the hunger that consumed *her.*

Hani once thought of Seokga as a bewildering puzzle. But now . . . now, she sees that Seokga and she are one and the same. Two jigsaw puzzles that fit together perfectly, despite their difference in natures, their ridges and edges.

They spent the hour doing nothing but kissing, but the mere act of it set Hani on fire in a way she's never known before. And he burned along with her until the embers of passion smoldered to something more comfortable, something sleepy and content. Hani running her fingers gently through Seokga's hair until he'd fallen asleep.

Hani sighs softly, still playing with the silken black waves. *So odd,* she muses to herself. Less than a week ago she'd been dumping far too much sugar and cream into Seokga's coffee and handing it to him with a scowl. And while she still plans on continuing

to do the same, it is entirely possible that she will hand the coffee to him with a smile instead of a sneer. Yet the absurdity of
the situation quickly fades. She knew it on the mountain, in the
car, and she knows it now. Seokga and her just make *sense*.

She sighs again, this time in contentment.

This moment. She wishes to freeze time as it is and stay
within this moment forever.

But Kim Hani has never been so lucky.

Goosebumps rise, slowly, on her arms, prickling with discomfort. Hani moves her gaze from the ceiling to the room before her as her sharp senses hiss for her to *look*.

Hani's muscles tauten as the shadows of the room grow
darker, stretching out across the black marble floor like spilled
ink and seeping toward the couch on which Hani and Seokga lie.
The air drops in temperature until Hani's breath clouds before
her face and hangs suspended in a fog of pale white.

Her eyelids are suddenly heavy, every part of her body murmuring sleepily as her limbs slowly loosen, relaxing. *Let's sleep,* her
mind mumbles. *Let's go to sleep.*

But . . .

One word slithers through her mind—a singular, awful word
carrying with it tendrils of shadow. *Eoduksini.*

No, Hani thinks, struggling to keep her eyes open. *No.*

She fights back the debilitating exhaustion and shoves Seokga
from her, shaking his shoulders in an attempt to wake him. To
her immense relief, his jade eyes fly open, clear and alert.
"What—"

Hani presses a finger to her lips, standing from the couch
and unsheathing her claws with a slight *snick*.

They appear to be alone in the room.

Yet Hani is no fool, and appearances can be deceiving. She
scans the room's deepest shadows, searching for the figure of
Dok-hyun, heart pounding in her chest.

Silently, Seokga stands as well, and curls his fingers around his cane's hilt where it leans against the sofa. With a flick, his cane transforms into his sword, razor-sharp and shining silver within the growing darkness. The shadows crawl along the glass panes of the window until they obscure the late morning sun, preventing any trickle of light from entering the apartment. Hani watches as the room's lamps flicker off.

Drowning in darkness, Hani barely dares to move, instead urging her eyes to adjust.

Her entire body is stiff with anticipation. Something is going to lurch out of the shadows at any moment, something terrible and awful that will steal the life from Hani and her god . . .

But moments, heavy with tension, tick by and nothing comes.

Seokga's voice rips through the silence, as sharp and as frozen as she has ever heard it. *"Show yourself."*

Only silence, thick and suffocating, answers him.

Hani swallows hard. Her daggers, her trustworthy red daggers that have never failed her, are just upstairs. Is it worth it to run for them? Is it worth it to wield them in front of Seokga? She takes a deep breath, reaching for her fox bead, energy humming in her bloodstream, ready to be released in a blast of pure power if needed. The flare will surely capture the attention of the haetae precinct and reveal Hani's identity, but she has no other choice. Not when it is so entirely probable that a monster of Jeoseung is watching them, waiting.

A low, unfamiliar laugh creeps out from the shadows, echoing through the room, bouncing from wall to wall. It is impossible to determine its point of origin. Hani whips around, pressing her back to Seokga's, holding her fists in the air.

"Seokga," she breathes. "What do you—"

Hani is cut off by the smell. The smell of rotting flesh. She feels Seokga stiffen against her back.

The echoes of the laugh slowly fade into nothingness. Hani

tenses as the shadows writhe and undulate, rippling as something emerges from their darkened depths. Her eyes strain, trying to make out Dok-hyun . . .

Hani falters as a woman wearing a blood-red surgical mask steps into view.

She is long and lanky, glossy black hair falling to her narrow waist, dark eyes wide and framed by thick curtains of lashes. She wears a hospital robe and is barefoot, her toes painted a bubble-gum pink. Her fingers may be painted the same, but Hani cannot tell. The girl holds her hands behind her back.

The scent of rotted flesh strengthens.

"This isn't Dok-hyun," Hani whispers under her breath to Seokga, adjusting her position so that she faces the woman, poised to strike. The red-masked woman blinks at her, and Hani has the horrible impression that she is smiling underneath her mask.

"No," comes the reply, sharp with annoyance. "No. The eoduksini is toying with us. Sending cheap lackeys."

She blinks at him slowly. Uncomprehendingly.

Hani's brows inch together warily as the woman fails to respond. But then—

"Am . . . I . . . pretty?" Her voice is wet. As if she's speaking through a ruined, blood-filled mouth. Hani wonders, clenching her fists tighter, what is underneath that mask.

"No," Seokga says coldly. Cruelly. "No, I've heard of you, Slit Mouthed Woman." He steps fluidly around the coffee table that sits in front of the couch, twirling his sword in his hand. "So spare me the pleasantries."

Slit Mouthed Woman?

Hani tenses as the woman laughs, a horribly moist sound, and lifts one hand to her mask. In a jerky, violent motion, she rips it off, revealing a rotten mouth gashed open from ear to ear. Her gums are red and irritated, dripping with blood that coats a

tattered tongue. "Wrong . . . answer," she says wetly and pulls
her other hand out from behind her back. A scalpel shakes men-
acingly in her right one. Her nails, Hani notices, are not bubblegum pink as she'd suspected. They are yellowed and ragged,
crusted with blood.

The Slit Mouthed Woman launches herself forward, her scalpel slashing through the air as she makes for Seokga. Seokga easily sidesteps her attack, looking more bored than anything. Hani
leaps over the coffee table, knocking away a pile of magazines as
she launches herself at the Slit Mouthed Woman, her claws ex-
tended. She digs them into the woman's slim shoulders, ripping
them out as the woman shrieks. Blood splatters through the air,
wetting Hani's face, but she's already moving again—dodging the
slashing blade and sending the Slit Mouthed Woman crashing
back to the wall with a roundhouse kick.

Seokga moves next, striding toward the woman with a look
of exasperation. "You know," he sneers to the darkness, "your
games have only just started and already, I'm sick of them."

The Slit Mouthed Woman starts forward, but in a quick
movement, Seokga severs the hand holding the scalpel from her
body and slams her against the wall in a choke hold. "What did
he promise you?" he snarls over her wounded screams. When
she fails to do anything but shriek in agony, Hani watches as
Seokga levels the bloodied blade at her throat, the tip biting ever
so slightly into her neck. "Gamangnara, remade?"

The Slit Mouthed Woman shudders, shaking her head.

"*What,*" Seokga growls again, "*did he promise you?*" This time, the
blade draws blood.

The shadows of the room seem to darken in warning.

"A . . ." The Slit Mouthed Woman pants, eyes on the blade.
"A . . ."

"Spit. It. Out."

"A . . . world of . . . darkness," the Slit Mouthed Woman slurps. "The . . . Dark . . . World . . . born . . . here."

Chills run down Hani's spine.

The Slit Mouthed Woman strains to break free, but gives up as Seokga's sword cuts farther into the skin of her neck. "He will make . . . you suffer before . . . the end. . . . There is a . . . message for you . . ."

"What is it." Seokga's tone is brittle. Hard.

"He wants to . . . thank you . . ."

"Thank us?" Hani asks, dumbfounded. "Why?"

"He has not had . . . this much fun . . . in millennia . . . and he is so . . . hungry . . . The two of you . . . will be delicious. . . . Your combined power . . . your combined life . . . is satiating . . . and you are so fun to . . . scare."

"I've heard enough." Seokga glances to Hani. "Have you?"

"Wait." Hani takes a step closer to the Slit Mouthed Woman. "What is his next move? Who does he plan to kill? Is it random?"

Her gory smile grows. "Foolish fox. . . . Your futile investigation . . . will end with you. . . . There are no . . . happy endings . . . in your story. . . . The god and the gumiho . . . ends with . . . tragedy . . ."

She does not get the chance to finish her sentence.

Dark blood, mixed with ash, sprays through the air as Seokga beheads her and the shadows in the room slowly recede.

⁎

"THE EODUKSINI HAS FED ON ENOUGH LIFE THAT HIS POWER has begun to grow," Seokga says as he sits on the couch, staring at the heap of ashes and the discarded red surgical mask, "and with it, his influence."

"The Slit Mouthed Woman," Hani mutters, still standing, prepared for another attack. "What was she?"

"An Unruly. In more detailed terms," Seokga grumbles, thumbing his silver imoogi, "a specific sort of gwisin. There was only one of her—and now, thankfully, there are none." He scowls. "She'll take a while to clean up."

"Her mouth," Hani says, remembering that upturned gash spanning from ear to ear. "How did that . . . She died like that?"

"Plastic surgery gone wrong," Seokga answers. "I've been meaning to kill her for a while now. She tends to mutilate her victims in the same way. It's revolting."

Hani wrinkles her nose. "I don't suppose there's a key, is there? To unlock the Dark World?"

"I wish." The trickster god pokes at the ash heap with his cane. "It was nothing special," he adds with a scowl, "but with the way that they drone on about it, you'd think that it was some sort of paradise. The truth of it is that it was always dark, chaotic, and too noisy. You should hear how they plead," he adds, "when I kill them. Always asking to return to Gamangnara, as if I have the power to unlock an entire plane of existence. A key really would come in useful."

"You *were* the king," Hani points out, nudging him with her shoulder.

"Being the king of Gamangnara," the god retorts dryly, "was like being the homeowner of a dirty cave while living next to a mansion. The most glorious mansion in existence. With a pool." He shifts, leaning into her touch. Hani savors the slight press of his body against hers as he speaks, voice taking on a subdued— almost philosophizing—tone. "But the Unrulies don't view it like that. The ones that fell from it see it as their home. The ones born here, on Iseung, see it as a haven where laws don't apply. And I suppose they're right, in that regard. And it would make my job much easier if I could just ship off the entire Unruly population to Gamangnara."

For her own sake, Hani is obscenely grateful that such a thing isn't possible. The Dark World doesn't quite sound like her scene.

"But Hwanin," Seokga spits, voice growing cold, "likes to torment me. It's been so long even he cannot reopen Gamangnara. So the Dark World remains locked and *I* remain here."

Hani's stomach clenches as she gazes at Seokga, at the bitter set of his jaw, the way his brows are furrowed, his knifepoint nose slightly wrinkled in repulsion.

He will never return to Okhwang.

Never be a god.

Because of her.

She swallows hard, shifting uncomfortably—

But suddenly Seokga's eyes soften and meet hers. "Not," he says quietly, "that I loathe everything about this forsaken realm."

Her heart stumbles in a curious mix of surprise, pleasure, remorse, and self-hatred. "Coffee, of course—"

"—and you," Seokga finishes.

She blinks rapidly. "In that order?" she manages to say, hoping that he doesn't realize how thin her voice sounds.

"It has potential to change." He's begun playing with her hair tentatively, wrapping a dark brown strand around a long finger. Hani wonders if she's the wickedest of all for letting herself enjoy it. For savoring his attention even as she deceives him. She wonders whether she should atone in some way for her lies.

But she is long past being worthy of redemption.

CHAPTER THIRTY-TWO

SEOKGA

SEOKGA BUTTONS THE JACKET OF HIS SLEEK BLACK SUIT AS he waits for Hani near the apartment's front door. Perhaps he is overdressed for a night in New Sinsi's largest nightclub, but a good suit is equivalent to armor. And Seokga plans on entering this battle fully armed.

Tonight, they will lure out the eoduksini.

He tightens his grip on his cane as a noise sounds from the stairwell. Seokga turns, and his breath catches in his throat as Hani descends the flight of stairs, clad in a skintight black dress with a sultry glint in her eye.

A dark color is swept over her eyelids, enhancing the warmth of her gaze as she strides over to Seokga, her stilettos clacking on the floor below. Her hair, impossibly, is larger than ever as it bounces with every step she takes. Hani cocks her head under Seokga's gaze, her glossy lips curving into a smile.

And that smile.

Shit.

Seokga blinks before its radiance. The way that she smiles at him—it ignites something powerful within his chest. If sunshine were a feeling, he thinks, it would be the feeling he gets when Hani smiles like that.

You're ridiculous, that cranky voice snaps. *Absolutely ridiculous.*

He ignores it. "You look—nice," he says, his silver tongue

stumbling over the foreign words. Hani's smile grows and she steps closer to him, fixing his tie.

"You clean up well yourself," she replies, glancing up at him with those fox eyes.

Seokga allows himself a small, pleased smile. Yes. Yes, he certainly does. He offers Hani his arm. "Can you fight in those heels?" he asks curiously—not skeptically. He has a sneaking suspicion that the answer is *yes, of course.*

She gives him a look of amusement. "What do you think?"

That fact that he's right fills him with a stupid sort of pride.

A stupid, dangerous sort of pride.

THE EMERALD DRAGON IS A CREATURE OF POUNDING MUSIC and blazing strobe lights, shitty drinks and even shittier company. Standing in the middle of the dance floor, Seokga whacks more than a few people with his cane as they come far too close for his liking, gyrating in a way that makes him wonder whether the eoduksini's world of darkness would truly be such a bad thing, after all.

He knows he should try to act carefree. That is the plan, after all.

The eoduksini has been hiding cleverly. Shim still has no leads, but Seokga knows how the minds of demons work. That *thing* inside of Dok-hyun's body still hasn't crossed Seokga's name off his list. And what better way to draw a wrathful demon out than to pretend you have no clue it's coming? If the eoduksini sees Seokga and Hani having fun—not hunting it for once—it might choose to strike. Which is exactly what they want—for the eoduksini to show itself.

It's a gamble, of course. The demon might simply send another gwisin. But after the Slit Mouthed Woman incident, Seokga believes that Hani and he showed, simply put, that simple Unrulies do not quite faze them. So perhaps the eoduksini will try a different tactic.

In approximately an hour, Hani and Seokga will stumble out of the Emerald Dragon into a nearby alleyway, laughing and displaying typical *carefree* behavior as, hopefully, the eoduksini follows. Because it's watching—certainly watching. The Slit Mouthed Woman's little visit proved that.

Seokga scowls as a dokkaebi covered in glow-in-the-dark jewelry twirls toward him, her eyes sparkling with a lewd invitation. He jabs his cane in her direction with a cruel sneer.

A camera flashes. *Damn it.* Trust a paparazzo to be here— most of them are dokkaebi, after all, and he's in a nightclub. *Godly Gossip*'s next title will read: SEXY SEOKGA ATTACKS INNO- CENT DOKKAEBI! WHAT DOES HOTTIE HWANIN HAVE TO SAY ABOUT THIS? Undoubtedly some nosy reporter will shout up into the heavens until they convince Hwanin to agree to an exclusive interview regarding his estranged brother.

He always agrees to those.

"My little brother, Seokga," Hwanin once said, "has always been troubled. I assume it has to do with Mireuk dropping him on his head when he was young. He never did recover."

And then another: "Seokga was terribly jealous of me, even when we were small children. One time, he snuck into my room and shaved off my eyebrows while I was sleeping. Of course, soon after I was spotted sans eyebrows, that became the trend around Okhwang, and Seokga seethed for days. Then he shaved his own eyebrows off right when the trend was dying down, and he was mocked relentlessly."

"The moment Seokga emerged from Mago's womb, he tried to attack me. I swear it on my son. I was holding him, gazing down at my new baby brother, when he started punching me with his tiny fists. It's really not a surprise that he ended up trying to seize my throne."

"One time, for my birthday, Seokga left a beautifully wrapped box outside my door, complete with a red bow. I was excited to open it, to see what it was. Do you know what Seokga had put in the box? My brother had tracked down a chollima, one of those breathtaking winged horses who also happen to have monstrously large, ah, defecations. It was by far the worst gift I have ever received."

Seokga scowls, twisting around and trying to find that damned cameraman.

"Dance," Hani shouts over the bass, waving her hands in his face to capture his attention. "You look like a grumpy old man! We'll never pull this off if you don't dance!" She laughs, throwing her head back, and moving to the booming music with such ease. Seokga feels, admittedly, awkward next to her litheness and grace.

"I am trying," he shoots back, discomfort sharpening his tone. He immediately regrets it—but Hani tilts her head, eyes lighting with understanding.

"It's easy," she says encouragingly. "Just . . . dance to the beat. It's fun—I promise." She places her hands on his shoulders, trying to loosen him up as she moves to the music. Seokga, as still as a rock, tries to ignore the wave of heat that rushes to his groin with an immense amount of difficulty. He grits his teeth.

If the eoduksini is watching, it is probably also laughing.

Hani grins. "Let's get a drink," she hollers.

"Mortal alcohol," he retorts, "does not have an effect on me." It's true. Human alcohol—while pleasant to drink—is much too weak, much too watery. He has not gotten drunk in centuries. A pity, that.

But Hani is already dragging him over to the bar. He plasters on a scowl, but he enjoys the feeling of her hand around his wrist—it's almost possessive, in a way that he doesn't quite mind at all. And godsdamn it, maybe he does need a drink. Seokga's mouth dries out as Hani deposits him beside her at the bar and grins—such a happy, glowing grin that he suddenly feels faint.

"We need to stay sober. For the eoduksini." His voice comes out hoarse. Hani quirks a brow.

"I thought that mortal alcohol didn't have an effect on you?" She snaps her fingers at the bartender. "Shot of soju for me," she shouts over the music, "and the strongest shit you have for him!"

The bartender obliges. Hani downs her shot of soju as Seokga stares warily at the shot of what looks like vodka. He pinches it in between his fingers and makes a face of disdain, but swallows it down all the same—just to amuse Hani, who is cackling next to him.

"At the very least, maybe it'll loosen you up!" She's still laughing as she grabs his hand again. A rush of pleasure flows through him as she does so, even as she pulls him back onto the floor. "What do you drink in Okhwang?"

"Alcohol that would make mortals go blind."

Hani snorts, dancing again, her eyes sparkling. Seokga admires the way her bouncy hair flies through the air, the way the strobe lights catch on the angles of her face, the way that despite everything, the gumiho looks like she's enjoying herself. A sense of pride pricks at his heart again, pride that she's enjoying being here, with him, despite the murderous monster on their tail.

"Just let go," Hani suggests, tugging at his hands, urging him to dance. "Nobody's going to laugh at you, not when they've witnessed you smacking people on the head with your cane! We need to do this," she adds softly, barely audible as she pulls closer to him, close enough that he can see the tiny birthmark above her right eyebrow. "We need to pull this off."

She's right.

This music is impossible to dance to—but Seokga will try.

CHAPTER THIRTY-THREE

HANI

Hani laughs, drenched in sweat, each breath shallow and rasping against her throat—but she doesn't care, doesn't care at all as she throws her head back, eyes closed against the raging strobe lights while she dances and dances and *dances*. Her skin sparkles with sweat and glitter that rubbed off on her from a few giggling glitter-dusted dokkaebi, and now shimmers on Seokga as he moves with her.

Hani sways her hips, sliding her hands up her body until they run through her hair, laughing in delight as she watches Seokga dance. Earlier, it was awkward—his limbs stiff, his mouth arranged in an unamused scowl—but now he moves with the same lethal grace that he's displayed while fighting. They orbit each other, two lonely planets that are drawn together and then pulled apart, spinning and swaying. Everything else in the club seems to fade away until it is just them on the dance floor.

Behind her, Seokga's hands find her waist, and she rolls her hips to the booming beat. Even over the music, Hani hears Seokga's breath hitch—and then she's whirling around to face him with a rush of ecstasy as she runs her hands up his chest, cocking an eyebrow. "This is fun, isn't it?" She grins and turns once more, her arm around his neck, moving her body against his. She can feel him tense, but then his hands are back on her waist and they're dancing again, slick with sweat underneath the flashing lights. Hani has visited many nightclubs in her time, with many boys, and she knows precisely how to dance with them.

"It's . . . fine," Seokga breathes huskily, barely audible over the pounding bass.

"Just fine? How rude." Hani mock-pouts, pulling away from Seokga—but he catches her hand and holds on tight. She stares at their interlocked fingers for a moment before Seokga abruptly twirls her, spinning her so she lands nose to nose with him. Hani can't help but smile in surprise as her hair settles back around her shoulders. Seokga looks embarrassed and triumphant all at once.

Hani grins. "Again," she says. Seokga shakes his head, looking acutely reluctant, but grudgingly twirls her a second time. The lights of the club blur as she whirls, her hair flying in every direction, smacking a dokkaebi in the face. Hani throws her head back and laughs.

"Your turn," she says, but Seokga stands as still as a statue as she attempts to spin him. "You buzzkill, you," Hani grumbles, shoving against him. He doesn't move. "Don't you want to spin? Like a beautiful ballerina?"

"I do not *spin*."

Hani snorts. "You will once I'm done with you."

Seokga's mouth curves a little in return, but his eyes are somber. "Hour's almost up."

Hani ignores the twist in her stomach. These last few moments could very well be their last moments on Iseung. The fight with the eoduksini is approaching.

Even as guilt, dread, and anxiety clench her gut, she manages another grin. "Come with me," she shouts over the music, grabbing Seokga's hand and tugging him through the tight crowd of pleasure-seeking creatures. A few pause in awe and admiration, their eyes going straight to Seokga, hungrily devouring the fallen god. Hani can't blame them. In his sleek black suit with his emerald eyes blazing underneath the lights, Seokga cuts a striking figure.

There are a few plush black love seats circling various tables at the edges of the club. Hani slides into one and tugs Seokga in after her. She leans against the cushioned back, panting as she watches the ebb and flow of the dancers. Seokga is breathing unevenly next to her, and she can feel his hungry stare.

She is not surprised when his lips crash against hers— bruising and biting, yet gentle and sweet all at once. Hani drags her hands up his back as she deepens the kiss, hungering for *more*—more of him, more of Seokga.

More, more, more.

Hani curls her hands in Seokga's hair, gripping the soft black waves as he pulls her onto his lap. He nibbles at her bottom lip, a quick burst of sweet pain that sends an aching thrum of longing through her. His hands are roving up her dress, and one of the spaghetti straps has fallen away, baring her narrow shoulder. Gazing up at her with those heavy-lashed emerald eyes, Seokga plants a tender kiss on her bare skin.

And that does it.

When Hani is overcome with the sudden urge to strip naked then and there, in the middle of a packed nightclub, she realizes this has most definitely gone too far. Breathing unevenly, she pulls away from Seokga, sitting back on the love seat and pulling her dress down where it was rucked up. She chances a glance at him as she fixes her hair—the god's lips are full and red, the same color as his cheeks. His throat is bobbing, and locks of dark hair fall into his face in a way that makes Hani want to climb back onto his lap all over again. She nearly does it.

But suddenly Seokga's eyes narrow, all hints of lust disappearing. "Do you feel that?" he whispers, his face turning cold and cruel—but not at her.

Hani takes a moment to regain her senses.

And at once, she does.

The air of the Emerald Dragon has grown frigid. Hani's chest tightens in dread as she notes how the movements of the mass of dancers have slowed to a sluggish, sleepy rhythm. The colorful strobe lights of the club flare—and flicker out.

Darkness cradles the nightclub in its lethal embrace.

"It worked," Hani breathes, hastening from the love seat. "It's here." Here, where there are bystanders. Here, where there are civilians. They've planned for this, of course, but the reminder is still daunting. "We need to lure it to the alleyway," she says, fighting away the cloud of sleepiness fogging her mind. "Away from them."

"Go," Seokga says grimly. "I'm right behind you."

Hani's limbs feel leaden as she struggles toward the dance floor, toward the EXIT door that she knows is not far away. But . . . something is wrong. She is disoriented; she is dizzy.

And she is so, so tired.

Hani grits her teeth as her legs cross each other, sending her stumbling to the side. Seokga grabs her arm, his face tight and pale. "Hani," he says, but his voice is a slur. His eyes are bright with horror, and yet rapidly dulling with exhaustion.

Everything is moving so slowly. Every breath is deep and longing for slumber.

In the middle of the dance floor, Hani falls.

And she does not get up.

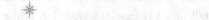

SHE FALLS THROUGH SHADOWS AND DARKNESS, A SCREAM ripping from her throat as she tumbles, dropping through nothingness.

The eoduksini, she thinks in a panic, staring up at the never-ending darkness rushing past. *I need to wake up. I need to wake up . . .*

But she cannot.

All she can do is fall.

And fall and fall and fall and fall . . .

Until she hits solid ground, groaning as her bones scream in pain, bruises already spreading along her skin, a dark and blackening blue. Blinking past the stars in her vision, Hani focuses on the ground before her. It is white, impeccably so. Not a stain to be found on it. Like the floor in Somi's apartment.

Horror twisting her stomach, Hani rises from the ground. She is indeed in Somi's apartment, standing in the small kitchen where she convinced Somi to eat the livers exactly one week before. That is the smooth wooden table, the mahogany counters, the kitchen island laden with a flower vase, cookie jars, and a stack of tattered thrift-store cookbooks. *Why,* Hani thinks slowly, *has it brought me here? This is no nightmare.*

Almost as if in answer, a soft sobbing reaches her ears.

Hani whirls around, her heart in her throat.

"Oh, gods," she tries to say—but her tongue is heavy in her mouth. Useless.

Somi is sobbing as she sits on the ground, leaning against the fridge. Her hands are slick with fresh blood, her white sweater stained red. Around her, droplets of blood shine on the floor that is usually kept so impeccably clean.

Her knees are drawn to her chest. Somi rocks back and forth, wailing, tears streaming down her face and into her mouth . . . her mouth that is red and bloodied. Hani stumbles over to her, crouching in front of her—but Somi cannot see her. All her attention is focused on what she holds within her hands.

A half-eaten human liver.

No, Hani thinks, staring at Somi. *This is a nightmare. Somi is fine—she's fine. Her Cravings shouldn't be back by now. Not now . . .*

Somi's cries are daggers through her heart. She watches as Somi raises the liver to her mouth, tearing off a bit and chewing as her sobs grow louder.

Not real, Hani reminds herself. *This isn't real. I need to wake up.* The eoduksini could be crouched over her, draining her of life. *I need to wake up . . .*

Hani freezes as the shadows of Somi's kitchen lengthen and darken, as the air grows brittle with icy cold. As she hears the front door open and close.

No. No.

Hani grabs Somi's shoulders and shakes. "Run," she tries to say, but the words are stuck in her throat. "Run—"

An invisible force slams Hani away from Somi, sending her crashing into the opposite wall. She pants, struggling to rise, but freezes as a distorted voice cleaves through the air. "Somi," it says, deep and vibrating at times, yet high-pitched and grating at others, "why do you cry?"

A figure steps into the kitchen.

Hani gapes. The figure is blurred, as if it is part of a censored video. She cannot make anything out save for its height and frame, which are infuriatingly average. But is it censored to Somi? It's not. She's certain of it. The eoduksini is blocking Hani, and only her, from witnessing his appearance.

Why? Hani frowns. The eoduksini knows his host, Dok-hyun, has been revealed. It's common knowledge throughout the precinct. What's the point of hiding himself? Something about this, she thinks, is very wrong.

And not just in terms of the censorship. This feels like a nightmare, certainly, but it doesn't feel like a *dream.*

This is real.

Hani tries once more to scramble to her feet, but the invisible force keeps her rooted. All she can do is watch as the blurred figure strides into the kitchen. All she can do is watch as Somi goes pale with fear, leaping to her feet and unsheathing her claws.

"*You,*" she gasps. "How did you get in? Get out. Get out or I will *kill you!*"

Run, Hani thinks desperately. *Oh, Somi. Just run.*

The eoduksini holds up his hands. "I am not here to hurt you, Nam Somi."

"You're *it,* aren't you?" Somi pants. "The eoduksini. You're here to kill me."

"No. No, I'm not." The eoduksini gestures to Somi's claws. "Why don't you put those away? I just want to talk."

"Get out," Somi growls.

The eoduksini pays her no heed. "You know," he says, "when I heard about the killings at the university, I was . . . impressed."

"Impressed?" Somi demands, even as she blanches. "That wasn't me, I—"

"I know," the eoduksini continues, "that you are not the Scarlet Fox."

"W-what?" Somi flinches. "I'm n-not—"

"Your friend," the eoduksini replies, and there is a terrible sort of laughter in its distorted voice, like flares of white noise on a struggling radio. "Kim Hani."

Hani closes her eyes. *No,* she thinks.

"Hani?" Somi's voice is tight and strangled, as if she is suffocating. "What about Hani?" Each syllable blurs together in a smudge of panic. "What about her?"

"Kim Hani," the eoduksini croons, clearly enjoying Somi's shock, "is the Scarlet Fox."

"No," Somi whispers hoarsely. "You're—lying. You bastard! Get out, get out, *get out!*" Hani's eyes fly open as Somi hurls the liver at the eoduksini, who dodges it nimbly and chuckles. The organ skids across the floor in a red smear and Somi breaks down into wet, gasping sobs. Hani's heart shatters in her chest. Somi knows that it's true. She just doesn't want to believe it. Hani watches as the younger gumiho clings to her denial like a child clutches a blanket.

"Tell me, Somi," the eoduksini says quietly. "Tell me, do you know that Kim Hani colors her hair brown? That her true hair is a deep, flaming red? Legend says that the Scarlet Fox had the very same color. Just look at the name the world has dubbed her."

Somi buries her face in her bloodstained hands. Hani swallows hard, guilt and fear turning her stomach over. She was always careful about upkeep on her chocolate brown, but that past December during the holiday rush at the café, she'd been so busy that she'd missed her appointment at the salon. Her ruby roots had been noticed by Somi, who hadn't thought much of it at the time . . . but now . . .

"And do you know any other gumiho who kill as nonchalantly as her?" The eoduksini sighs in pity. "Look at you, Somi. Wracked with guilt. The Scarlet Fox feels no such emotion. You, Nam Somi, I pity. I do."

Somi is trembling, tears running down her face as she stares fearfully at the demon through her wet, red fingers.

"Look at yourself," the eoduksini says cruelly. "Covered in blood, eating a man's liver. How many did you kill tonight, when the Cravings got so bad? One? Two? Three? Four? You know," he continues, "this never would have happened had the Scarlet Fox not corrupted you. Had she not brought those livers to your door. Clever, on her part, isn't it?"

"H-how do you know about that?"

"I have been watching." The eoduksini takes a step forward. "You were innocent, Nam Somi. So, so innocent. And now . . . look at yourself. You're a monster. Can you imagine what they'll do to you? Hani is not here to clean up your mess this time. She is with the god, at the Emerald Dragon, performing lewd acts on a love seat."

Hani swallows the taste of bile. Her eyes ache with unshed tears. *Somi. Somi-ah, I am so sorry.*

"They will name you the Scarlet Fox. And they will kill you. It's what Hani has planned for, after all."

"What do you mean—" Somi blanches. "What do you mean, 'it's what Hani has planned'?"

Hani stops breathing. And the eoduksini laughs.

It is a clever trick. The demon of darkness is no fool.

Very slowly, Hani begins to realize that she has underestimated it.

"I mean precisely what I said." The eoduksini clucks his tongue. "Kim Hani is very, very old. How do you think she has managed to remain uncaptured, unblamed for so long? There is always somebody else that she pushes off the ledge to take the fall for her. And this time, Nam Somi, it is you."

No. No. Somi, I wouldn't. Hani strains to break free. *Somi . . .*

But there's a horrible feeling in the pit of her stomach.

If Somi had been arrested, if it had been up to Hani to come clean to save her . . . Hani knows that she wouldn't have.

Her sense of self-preservation is too strong.

Her *selfishness* is too strong.

And that damning knowledge is why Hani took the job as Seokga's assistant, to steer him away from Somi in the first place, and to therefore ensure she was never put in the position where she had to come clean.

Because she would have pushed Somi off the ledge.

The eoduksini is right.

Somi's face has gone slack. "She wouldn't," she whispers again, but this time quieter. Uncertainly. "She's my friend."

"Friends don't turn friends into monsters," the darkness

demon counters. "How many times has Hani stopped you from leaving New Sinsi? She needs you here, to shoulder the blame for her. See the truth, Somi. See that she killed those two boys and immediately went in search of you, to feed you their livers, to ignite your Cravings and desire to kill, to place you in the investigation's crossfire. See that she has told you to trust her, while she leads the god closer and closer toward you with every step. See that she is the Scarlet Fox, but the world will never know that—they will see *you* as the Scarlet Fox when you're caught. And you will be caught, Somi. Hani has staked everything on it. Seokga the Fallen will kill you as Kim Hani watches. Oh, yes. She'll watch. Do you really think that Hani will step up to save you if it means revealing her secret?"

Somi is completely still. The sparkling light in her hazel eyes has dimmed. She is a statue, made of stone, cracks running up and down her marble length. She is broken.

"But imagine," the eoduksini purrs, "a world where you didn't need to feel this shame, Nam Somi. A world where *you* could live on, feasting as you desire. Feasting with *me*. A world where you live wrenched free from Kim Hani's clutches. I have big plans for Iseung. And I think that you would like them. Iseung is ripe for the devouring.

"Join me, Nam Somi. By my side, you can satisfy your Cravings without ever being caught. By my side, you will be untouchable. By my side, you will feel no guilt, no shame. This suffering, *your* suffering, will end." The eoduksini stretches out a hand. "Take my hand, Nam Somi. Take my hand and leave this pain, this betrayal, behind."

"*No,*" Hani tries to growl, but her voice is useless. *No. Somi . . . Somi . . .*

"A world where I don't feel this shame," Somi repeats in a whisper, a final tear slipping down her pale cheek. "A world where I don't feel this . . . this betrayal. Friends don't . . . turn friends into monsters." Hatred threads through her voice. It makes it strong. Somi raises her head. "I will not take the blame for Kim Hani."

The eoduksini might be smiling now. It is impossible to tell.

Hani's scream is silent and entirely useless as she watches Somi take the eoduksini's hand.

CHAPTER THIRTY-FOUR

SEKGA

HANDS SHACKLED BEHIND HIS BACK AND MOUTH gagged with a foul-tasting cloth, Seokga is roughly escorted from his holding cell in the dungeon by a squadron of scowling palace guards. His emerald hanbok is ripped and tattered, splattered with blood. His own blood from the beating that Hwanin ordered. Every step sends pain bursting through his body, and his vision dims. *No.* Seokga forces his eyes to remain open as he is shoved through the corridors of Cheonha Palace, through the ruined wooden archways, and across the cold stone-tiled floor that bites into his bare feet. Rubble from the battle of his traitorous army litters the ground. It smells like blood and shit and rage. Seokga gags. He will not faint. He will *never* show such weakness.

The doors of the throne room loom into view. Two guards shake their heads and haul open the battered doors as he approaches, revealing the cracked scarlet pillars and cratered black floor inside, and the impressive dais on which Hwanin's throne is situated—a throne of ruby red, embellished with golden designs of the moon, the sun, and the stars that are echoed on the redwood ceiling. Hwanin himself sits on the throne, so high up above the floor, with his strange blue eyes cold with hatred. His son, Hwanung, stands beside him, nearly identical to his father in both looks and clear abhorrence.

It's poetic, Seokga thinks bitterly, that Hwanin's damned throne survived the battle.

The other deities are gathered before the throne and part to allow Seokga entry, roughly shepherded by the Okhwang guards. There is Jacheongbi, goddess of love and agriculture, black hair woven with cherry blossoms that match the color of her elegant silken hanbok. Her eyes narrow in distaste as Seokga is shoved to the ground, his knees barking in pain. And there is Dalnim, goddess of the moon, her silver eyes bright with disgust as she inches away from Seokga and toward her brother Haemosu, god of the sun. Haemosu's mouth puckers in clear revulsion as Seokga glances toward him, his expression nearly as black as the crow-feather headdress he wears atop his head.

"Disgrace," Habaek the river god sneers down at him. "There has not been such a big disgrace since Mireuk. Shame on you, you miserable, loathsome bastard. You truly do take after your father. Mago would be ashamed."

Seokga breathes heavily from behind his gag. That mad old god. It is undoubtedly thanks to Mireuk and his creation of suffering that Seokga now suffers so. Perhaps he should pay a visit to his pitiful excuse for a father in his underworld prison and show him his thanks.

Or perhaps he suffers so because of Gameunjang. The goddess of luck has never been fond of Seokga. He glares at her where she stands with Samsin Halmoni, goddess of motherhood. As always, Samsin Halmoni is very, very pregnant. If there was such a thing as a sixth trimester, Seokga would estimate that Samsin Halmoni was a good halfway through it.

"Silence," Hwanin orders. His voice cleaves through the throne room. He rises from his throne, his flowing blue robes rustling with the movement. He glances to the guards. "Ungag him. His silver tongue will be of no use here, anyways."

The gag is ripped from his mouth with an incredible amount of violence. Seokga spits blood out onto the ground, glowering up at Hwanin.

"Really, brother," he says through the blood dripping down his chin, "aren't you overreacting? This was just a bit of fun."

"You tried to overthrow him," Jowangshin, goddess of the hearth, reminds him venomously. "You brought a legion of monsters from the Dark World into our heavenly realm. You ruined half of this palace. An Unruly yong almost bit me in half. You ought to be put down in Jeoseung with Mireuk."

"Silence," Hwanin repeats frostily, still glowering at Seokga.

Jowangshin gives Seokga one last sneer before turning away.

"Enlisting twenty thousand Unrulies from Gamangnara," Hwanin says softly, "is a coward's tool. But I suppose it makes sense. For you, Seokga, are a coward." He descends from the dais, his robes flowing behind him. "And an envious, power-hungry coward at that. You have always desired what you have not been able to have. When we first planned to dispose of Father, you knew that I would claim my birthright at the end of it, yet you still despised me when I did. And you still hold that grudge close to your heart. I have been anticipating an attempt at a coup for a while now—ever since I took the throne, I have known one was coming. I was not surprised when it failed. If anything, I was disappointed your try was so . . . sloppy."

Seokga rolls his eyes. "Oh, please," he says, fumbling for a way to utilize his silver tongue against whatever Hwanin has planned for him. "I am the god of deceit, brother. God of tricks. God of untrustworthiness in general. This little . . . attempt at a coup was merely in my nature, as giving birth daily is in Samsin Halmoni's. I can't be blamed for it, not really."

"Samsin Halmoni," Hwanin says, staring down at Seokga, "did not try to *kill* me."

Hwanin does have a point. But Seokga scoffs. "Listen,

brother. This was but one bump in a very long and ever-winding road. We are immortal, you and I. Let us make amends now, for we have an eternity to spend together in Okhwang."

"Well, that's the thing," Hwanin says very quietly. "We don't."

Oh, no. Seokga does not like the gleam in Hwanin's starry blue eyes. *Oh, no . . .*

"I have arranged a suitable punishment for you, brother. A punishment that will take you away from my sight for centuries." Hwanin tilts his head. "Hwanung, come forth."

The god of laws dutifully joins his father's side and smirks at Seokga.

"This, Seokga the Silver-Tongued, is your punishment. Your realm of Gamangnara will be locked for all eternity. And I swear on my son, Hwanung, god of laws and kept promises, that you will henceforth be cast from Okhwang to the mortal realm of Iseung with your demons. You will be stripped of your power. To earn your redemption, Seokga the Silver-Tongued, you will live as Seokga the Fallen in a state of disgrace until you have slaughtered twenty thousand Unruly monsters. You will only be redeemed in my eyes once you have done so. Only then will I allow you to return home. Only then will you again be a god."

Seokga chokes as Hwanin smiles down at him cruelly. *No. No. No.*

"No," he rasps as around him the other gods snigger. This isn't . . . Hwanin can't . . . *No.* "You cannot—"

Hwanin bends down to look him square in the eye. "I most certainly can," he says softly, "and I most certainly will."

Sharp, merciless betrayal pierces Seokga's chest as deeply as a finely honed dagger. "This," Seokga snarls, rage overtaking rationality, "is not fair. My nature—"

"Consider yourself lucky, *brother,* that I have not sent you to Jeoseung."

"Iseung," Seokga hisses, "with those sniveling mortals is far, far worse."

"Perhaps." Hwanin shrugs, turning his back on Seokga as he walks up the stairs toward his throne. Once, Hwanin would not have dared to show his back to his brother, lest Seokga plant a dagger in it. That he does so now is a purposeful barb, a reminder that the trickster god has utterly failed. "But you have no heart for anything, Seokga. For anyone. Iseung will do you a great service."

"You fucking bastard—"

Hwanin smoothly sits back on his throne. "Goodbye, Seokga," he says coolly. "I will see you again one day, perhaps one thousand or so years from now."

Seokga screams in utter rage, straining against his shackles. "You *dare*? You—"

Hwanin sighs, looking bored.

And then he snaps his fingers and it all goes white.

Seokga is falling, falling through the sky . . . and falling fast.

✧

Seokga awakens with a great gasp, drenched in a warm, sticky sweat. He sees nothing but darkness, and feels nothing but terror as he lays on something hard, tasting bile.

He . . . What was . . .

He has fallen. He is doomed to carry out this punishment for an eternity. *Damn* Hwanin. *Damn* the other gods. *Damn* Iseung—

But . . . No. No, that was six hundred and twenty-eight years ago. Seokga trembles, scrambling to sit up, events of the past centuries rushing back to him in a flood. The Unrulies. The Scarlet Fox. The bargain, *Hwanin's* bargain.

The eoduksini.

Hani.

Seokga sits up, his eyes slowly adapting to the darkness of the club. *Where is she?* He freezes as his eyes adjust to the shadows blanketing the room.

Bodies lay limp all around him, piled over one another, ridden with bulging black veins. Blood seeps across the dance floor, a pool of gleaming red, and Seokga realizes that he's not drenched in a thick layer of warm sweat, after all—he is drenched in blood. *Their* blood. The writhing, gyrating crowd of the Emerald Dragon is no more. The dancers are lifeless on the ground that had shaken with the booming of the bass and the stomping of feet just moments before, their faces contorted in terror, their eyes gone, nothing but empty sockets in their place. Their chests are in tatters, hearts gone. Bodies pile up over one another, forming towers of death and mutilation.

Seokga is drowning in a sea of gore as he struggles to his feet, a blinding, crippling terror overtaking him. He is alive—but where is Hani? *Where is Hani?*

If she has been fed on . . . If . . . If she has been taken . . .

A low, hoarse noise escapes his lips as he falls back down to his knees. He bows his head, struggling to remain conscious as a wave of dizziness pounds at his skull. "Hani," he groans, scanning the bodies for her. "Hani . . ." Seokga turns around, ignoring the way that the floor seems to spin beneath him as he catches sight of her—of Kim Hani, still, a hand reached out limply in his direction.

What if—what if— Seokga chokes out a sound that might be a whimper. But although Hani's still face is screwed shut in horror, she's alive. She's breathing. She's *breathing*.

Seokga staggers over to her. "Hani," he croaks, shaking her shoulder gently. "Wake up." Foolish—they have been so foolish to think that they could thwart the eoduksini. "Hani." But she doesn't stir, still caught up in the tide of a nightmare.

He can almost swear that the shadows of the Emerald Dragon tremble in laughter.

"*You*," he snarls into the darkness, even though he knows that the eoduksini won't reveal itself. No, it's having far too much fun. "You will fucking *pay*. I swear it on Hwanung." Muscles shaking from exhaustion, he hefts Hani into his arms. Her head lolls limply as he wades through the sea of corpses and blood, the weight in his arms not as heavy as the horror weighing down his heart.

CHAPTER THIRTY-FIVE

SEOKGA

"D O YOU *REALIZE*," SHIM DEMANDS, "THE ENORMITY OF what you've done?"

The raw anger and disappointment on the chief's face hurts Seokga more than it should. Shim, standing outside of his apartment door, quivers in anger. It has been three hours since the attack on the Emerald Dragon. Three hours, and already tendrils of unnatural darkness swirl through New Sinsi, coalescing with the deep shadows of alleyways and hidden crevices, growing larger and growing stronger. Seokga has watched it from the apartment's windows.

"Shim," Seokga says. "Come in." Perhaps he can offer him a cup of coffee, some food, and a place to sit down. Shim looks unsteady on his feet, and—

"No," snaps Shim. The lines on his face are deeper than usual, and Seokga sees that his hand is shaking as he lifts it up and points—*points*—at the fallen god. Once, Seokga would have felt the urge to smite him, then and there. But with Hani still asleep in his bed, and the eoduksini slowly devouring Iseung, he is incapable of feeling anything but tired remorse. "No. Precinct protocol, Seokga. That's all you had to follow. But instead, you deliberately concealed your plans and went rogue. Your actions cost lives. And what did you gain? Anything?"

Seokga swallows hard. "No. But, Shim, your stakeouts were never going to work."

"My stakeouts," the old chief bites back, "weren't going to kill civilians, either."

The god has no response to that.

"I am incredibly disappointed in you, Seokga," Shim whispers. It would be so much better if he yelled. If he hit him. This quiet rage is too much to bear. "All these years, I put up with your cruel sarcasm and your superiority complex. All these years, I respected you. I even liked you. You reminded me of my son—prickly only to hide a gentle heart. But *this*. This is the last time, Seokga, you will have anything to do with my precinct. You can find somewhere else. Go to Seoul's haetae, or Incheon's. Busan's. Daegu's. Anywhere but here. I cannot stand the sight of you any longer." He turns to leave, but Seokga cannot stop himself from flinching backward, as if he were physically struck, after all. Cannot stop himself from urgently grabbing Shim's shoulder.

"Wait," he finds himself saying gutturally, "wait. Please."

Shim tenses underneath Seokga's hand.

"I can fix this," Seokga says desperately. "Let me fix this." If he is not reinstated as a god, he doesn't want to leave New Sinsi. It is where Hani is, where coffee is. He doesn't want to leave its precinct, as grimy and cramped as it may be.

But most of all, he doesn't want Chief Shim to hate him.

There's a long stretch of thick silence before the haetae chief sighs and turns around. Seokga's hand slowly falls back to his side.

"Please," Seokga rasps.

Something softens behind Shim's hard, angry eyes. "I don't think you've ever said that word to me before," he says. "Not once, in all the years we've known each other. I came to the precinct at thirty-seven. I'm sixty-three now. And I've never heard you say 'please' until today."

"I've never fucked up this badly before," Seokga replies.

"Nobody has ever fucked up this badly before. Pardon my language."

"I'm going to fix it. I swear on Hwanung. I'll stop the eoduksini." Seokga swallows hard. "And if I do, you can't banish me. You can't." Is this his fate? To be exiled wherever he goes?

Shim shakes his head, dragging a wrinkled hand through his thinning hair. "I wasn't banishing you," he says gruffly. "I was firing you."

"Don't do that, either." Seokga wonders what he can bribe the chief with. Money? No. Too obvious. "I'll stop having a superiority complex."

"Seokga, I don't think that's possible." But there's a hint of a careworn smile on Shim's face. "I can't let you work with the precinct right now. If you do this, you're on your own. For better or for worse. If I get word that your actions have caused more innocent deaths, then that's the end of it. You won't be coming back."

"I understand."

Shim pulls something out of his pocket, presses it into Seokga's hand. It's a photograph. "Technically, I shouldn't give this to you since it's precinct evidence, and you're no longer officially on either of your cases. But you might want to see this." The chief meets his eye. "We identified the Scarlet Fox earlier tonight. Evidence on the scene indicates she's working with the eoduksini."

Seokga's eyes slowly travel down to the photograph he holds in his hands.

And his blood goes cold.

CHAPTER THIRTY-SIX

HANI

DARKNESS SLOWLY GIVES WAY TO LIGHT.
Hani awakes in a warm bed, strong arms wrapped around her waist. She blinks, blearily, uncomprehendingly. Her mind fumbles for memory of who she is—*where* she is—but fails to grab the strings of remembrance that dangle tauntingly out of reach. Panic overtakes her, hot and buzzing, and she jerks upward with a scream in her throat.

The room is unfamiliar. Black walls, a glossy black marble floor, a bookshelf teeming with novels upon novels upon novels. The windows are concealed by gray curtains, the only source of light an elegant bedside lamp. The room is heavy with the smells of pine trees and soap. It is familiar, somehow, that scent.

"You're awake," a hoarse voice rasps. She moves her gaze downward. On the bed next to her, in the black sheets, lays a man. A man with a cruel, hard mouth that she somehow knows is capable of the brightest smiles. A man with icy emerald eyes that soften as they look at her. A man who is . . . A man who is reaching for her in concern. A man who is not a man at all, but a god. Slowly, she lets him fold her into his embrace. A name is whispered through her mind with loving gentleness. *Seokga.*

"Seokga," Hani says slowly, rolling the name around her mouth. And as if that name is the magic key, everything comes rushing back to Hani with terrifying clarity. She stiffens in Seokga's arms, choked by panic. The club. The eoduksini. Somi.

The nightmare that felt far too real to be one.

The nightmare that, try as she might, keeps slipping out of her reach. There was something she knows is important to remember, something that was *wrong*. What was it? There was Somi, and there was . . . Dok-hyun. But it feels as if she's forgotten something important about the eoduksini. Something . . . pivotal.

Yet all she remembers is Somi, turning against her, believing Hani to be her enemy.

Hani scrambles out of Seokga's embrace. "Seokga," she chokes again. "*Seokga—*"

"You were asleep for a day," he says very quietly. "A night and a day. The eoduksini struck the Emerald Dragon. Other than us, there are no survivors. Shim is—" Seokga's throat bobs. "Shim is furious with us. We can't work with the precinct anymore."

No survivors. The mass of dancers, the glittering dokkaebi . . . All gone. She raises a trembling hand to her mouth. "No . . ."

They have failed.

They have *failed.*

"Hani," Seokga says gently, gathering her to him again, "you've been asleep for a very long time. Take a moment to—"

"Somi," Hani croaks. "I need to call Somi."

Seokga's arms stiffen around her. "I don't suggest it."

"I-I had a dream," she whispers. "A dream that the eoduksini came to her. And he said . . ."

Join me, Nam Somi. By my side, you can satisfy your Cravings without ever being caught. By my side, you will be untouchable. By my side, you will feel no guilt, no shame. This suffering, your suffering, it will end.

The words echo in her mind, distorted and horrible.

"You saw Dok-hyun?"

Hani doesn't understand why her first instinct is to say no. She did *see* him, didn't she? The eoduksini was irrefutably in that vision. Wasn't he? What is Hani forgetting? "Yes. He manipulated her, he told her . . . I-I need to call Somi."

"Hani," Seokga murmurs, stroking her hair, "there is something you should know."

Oh, gods. "What?" Hani rasps.

"You don't know Somi. Not really." She feels Seokga's voice rumble in his throat as she rests her head on his chest, hardly able to breathe. "I know you think that she is a baby gumiho, no more than twenty in human years. That's what her files say, as well. But she's been lying to you, Hani. Somi is old—very, very old."

No.

"Nam Somi," Seokga says quietly, "is the Scarlet Fox. She is working with the eoduksini as we speak. Suk Aeri's clue. The ones I seek are closer than I imagine. Teary eyes. In the Creature Café, I noticed her eyes were glassy. You were in the restroom at the time, so perhaps you didn't see. But it all makes sense. All this time, it was Somi. And since the nightclub, Hani, things have . . . escalated."

Hani closes her eyes, unable to breathe, unable to speak. Her worst nightmare has come true. *She's not the Scarlet Fox,* she wants to say. *It's me. It's me.* But . . . she can't.

Perhaps the eoduksini is right about her, after all.

Do you really think that Hani will step up to save you if it means revealing her secret?

"New Sinsi is in a state of emergency," Seokga says, still running his hands through her hair as if to comfort her. It does not do much. "The haetae are doing their best, but in the past day, there have been forty murders. Twenty by the eoduksini, and twenty . . ."

"Twenty by a gumiho," Hani whispers, tears pricking the backs of her eyes. This is all her fault. "Have you—" Her throat is so impossibly tight. "How do you know it's her?"

"CCTV footage. Photographs from civilians," Seokga says

quietly. "But even that isn't necessary. She's not making an effort to hide, Hani. People have seen her. Here." The god shifts, pulling something out of his pocket.

It's a grainy black-and-white photograph: Somi, standing over bodies in what looks to be a convenience store. Hani takes the photograph in her hands with trembling fingers and swallows hard. There's blood all over Somi's mouth.

"Shim says she's working with Dok-hyun."

Hani flinches as she remembers those words that she said in passing so long ago. *Maybe the Scarlet Fox and the eoduksini are working together.*

"Once we find one, we find the other. And . . ."

"And?" Hani whispers. "And what?"

Seokga is silent for a long moment before untangling himself from Hani and slowly walking toward the window. "The eoduksini has grown stronger," he says, lingering by the curtains. In the dim lighting, he is nothing but a silhouette. "The city is plagued by nightmares—nightmares and darkness." Slowly, Seokga pulls back the curtains to reveal a night sky so black, so impenetrable, that the blinking city lights are barely visible. "It looks like Gamangnara," he whispers.

Hani swallows hard. "That . . . that's the eoduksini?"

Seokga's gaze is somber. "It's mid-afternoon, Hani," he says. "At this point in the day, the sunlight should be golden. Gleaming. But the eoduksini has become too powerful. Unrulies are crawling the streets and it's only a matter of time before the humans become aware of their existence on a scale that we can't control. The shamans are working overtime. I haven't left your side since the nightclub, but the New Sinsi situation is all over the news. The mortals think that it's a chemical malfunction from a factory causing the darkness. But the darkness is spreading, and they'll soon see that's not true." Seokga grimaces.

"Hwanin sent a message while you were unconscious. If we don't contain this situation soon, he's going to have to get involved, Chunbun be damned."

Fuck. Hani's stomach twists as she rubs her face. That darkness outside . . . "Let me call Somi," she whispers. "Please. My cellphone . . . Let me try to call to her."

Seokga's eyes darken, but he still nods, leaves the room, and comes back a moment later with Hani's cellphone in his hand. He hands it to her gently before returning to stare out the window, his back straight and shoulders tense.

This is all my fault, Hani thinks as the line rings once. Twice. *I should tell Seokga the truth.*

But what will the truth change? Hani is not the one out on a killing spree. Somi will still be put to death. And so Hani keeps her mouth shut—and hates herself for it.

The line crackles to life, but it is not Somi's voice that answers. It is Hyun-tae's. "Kim Hani. This is Hyun-tae."

"Hyun-tae." Hani clenches the phone between trembling fingers. "Where are you? Are you with Somi?"

"No." His voice is ridden with remorse. "No. I have been informed of her . . . discrepancies. She left her phone at the café two nights ago, and I've had it ever since."

"Are you trying to find her? Do you have a lead? Do you have anything?"

"No." Hyun-tae sounds as if he's in a deep state of grieving as he mumbles, "I can't believe that Ms. Somi is evil."

"She's not," Hani snaps angrily. "She's just . . . a little misguided, that's all." Hani is not furious about the fact that Somi has begun to kill—no, that's fine. Hani has killed quite a few in her time. She feels, instead, a crippling guilt that she is the one who has given Somi the Cravings, not knowing her sensitivity to power.

Hani bites down on a blinding terror.

And the fact is, Somi is working with the eoduksini to devour the world. If she continues like this, aligning herself with a monster . . . Somi might really become one, after all.

Hani listens to Hyun-tae sigh at the end of the line. It is clear that the jeoseung saja, with his heart eyes and flushing cheeks, has Somi's best interests at heart. And that—that is exactly what she needs right now. Somebody who is on Somi's side. Who will give her the benefit of the doubt. Somebody who Hani can work with knowing that they will not hurt the young gumiho.

It is clear that Seokga plans to. But Hyun-tae . . .

"Hyun-tae," Hani says, "how quickly can you get over here?"

HANI SITS AT THE HEAD OF SEOKGA'S LONG DINING TABLE, with Hyun-tae to her right and Seokga to her left. Seokga is cradling a cup of coffee in his hands, staring down into the dark depths. The god looks his age in this moment—so very old, and so very tired.

Hani takes a small sip of the hot chocolate Seokga made for her before setting her teacup down and finally saying hoarsely, "We don't kill Somi." This is aimed toward Seokga, who flicks his gaze up from his coffee, fixates his attention on Hani, and frowns.

"She's the Scarlet Fox."

"No," Hani insists. "We don't know that. She's been manipulated. Until she is given a chance to explain, she remains untouched."

"There must be an explanation," Hyun-tae says mournfully, adjusting his glasses and blinking in fatigue. They've been sitting here for so long as the city outside the windows swirls and eddies in a sea of darkness. "There has to be."

Oh, there is. But Hani keeps her mouth shut as she pushes on. "Has the new coroner found any markings left by scarlet daggers on the recent bodies? The latest victims of the Unruly gumiho?"

"He hasn't," Hyun-tae says quickly, eyes widening. "You're right—he hasn't."

"But," Seokga replies after glowering in what looks like annoyance at the jeoseung saja, "he did on the first two."

"You should consider," Hani says, very carefully, "that there are two Unruly gumiho in New Sinsi. One is the Scarlet Fox. The other is Somi. I know," she insists as Seokga opens his mouth to argue, "what it looks like. But I also know, beyond a doubt, that Somi is too young to be the Scarlet Fox. She's only one thousand and twenty in total, in both fox and human form. Her records must show that."

Seokga's lips tighten. "I told you, Hani. Her records were masterfully forged. The Scarlet Fox has eluded capture for so long due to a reason. And Aeri's clue leads right to her."

"Regardless." Hani stares Seokga down and tightens her grip around her cup. "Until Somi has a chance to explain, she remains untouched." As Seokga fails to respond, she softens her voice. "Please. For me."

He mutters a curse, glaring back down at his coffee. "Fine."

Hani relaxes, but only slightly. It is still clear that Seokga is eager to kill Somi and be done with it, despite any promises made.

"We must find Ms. Somi," says Hyun-tae. "I fear for her."

"Hyun-tae," Hani says, turning to the jeoseung saja, "you're a grim reaper. When do you get notification of a death? Is it before or after it occurs?"

"We are given a number at the beginning of each shift," he replies promptly, straightening in his seat. "We don't get the specifics of who dies and where they die before the event, but we do get a number. And it's unpreventable—the haetae have tried, in the past, to utilize this knowledge to save lives, but it never worked. One way or another, the number will be met. This morning, I received the number three. One of them died in a car crash, the other in the hospital, and the last one fell from a roof. I knew to expect three deaths, but only received the walkie calls with the location moments after they passed."

Hani's mind whirs with blinding speed. "Do you have the numbers for tonight?"

"The night shift?" Hyun-tae shakes his head. "No. I work during the daytime. But I suppose," he says slowly, evidently catching Hani's drift, "that I could fill in for Pak Dong-wook tonight. He's been wanting to have a night off. I mean—I know that laziness is a sin," he adds quickly, "and I don't mean to perpetrate it. But—"

"If we get the numbers for tonight and if they're higher than usual, we can assume that Somi or the eoduksini will strike. If we get a call that sounds as if Somi has attacked," Seokga says, his eyes glinting, "we can make it to the bodies while a trail is still fresh. Find one, we find the other. Somi will lead us to the eoduksini. Two birds with one stone."

"*One* bird with one stone," Hani returns in warning. Seokga nods—but only slightly.

Hyun-tae pushes back his chair, standing abruptly. "I will travel to Jeoseung now and retrieve the numbers for the night shift from my superiors."

"Wait." Hani frowns. "We need to be ready to face the eoduksini again." It had been easy—so unbelievably easy—for the eoduksini to send her down into unconsciousness in the nightclub. "We need to go in prepared." She frowns at Seokga, something occurring to her. "Seokga," she says slowly, "did you dream at all? In the Emerald Dragon?" Had he even fallen asleep?

The god nods, his face darkening. "I did."

Hani nearly asks him what he dreamed of but decides against it. The planes of the fallen god's face are sharp and haunted. Whatever Seokga has seen, it is probable that he does not wish to speak of it. So instead, she inquires, "How long were you out for?"

"Two hours. Maybe three."

Only three hours. Whereas Hani had been out for a night and a day. "How . . . How did you wake up?"

"I just did. The nightmare ended, and I awoke." His gaze is dark with a painful memory. "It was . . . disorienting."

"Why did you wake up before me?" she muses, frowning deep enough that her head aches.

"I am a god," Seokga says, sounding quite self-important.

"You're a *fallen* god," Hani corrects, ignoring his offended scowl. "Your powers are equivalent to mine. Did the eoduksini let you go? Or . . . Or is there something else? Something you did in the dream? Something . . ."

Seokga rubs his temples wearily. "The eoduksini showed me a memory," he says, his voice stiff and cold in the way it becomes when he is displeased. There's no need to ask what memory he speaks of—the shadows under his eyes inform Hani of all she needs to know. He dreamed a memory that haunts him every day he remains on the realm of Iseung, so far below his home of Okhwang. That much is clear. "It played out how it did in real life. And then I woke." He shakes his head and raises his cup of coffee to his lips.

Hani blinks. Once, twice.

Coffee.

Surely not.

That is the easiest, most simple explanation, so it cannot be true. It simply *cannot*. No, Seokga must have done something within his memory to burst from the eoduksini's clutches. He must have regained some sort of godly strength, if only for a few moments . . .

But the morning before the attack, in the Creature Café, Seokga drank two extra-large coffees with one cream, one sugar. Had drained them to the bottom. That is no small amount of caffeine.

Is it coincidence? Or is it Gameunjang throwing her, for once in her life, a bone? Hani stifles an incredulous giggle as it pushes upward in her throat. Is *coffee* the solution? Is coffee—her most detested drink—the most powerful defense against a demon of darkness?

Both Hyun-tae and Seokga are staring at her. "What," Seokga demands, looking wary, "are you thinking?"

"I'm thinking," Hani says, a wicked smile stretching her lips, "that we should make some more coffee."

CHAPTER THIRTY-SEVEN

HANI

With Hyun-tae gone to Jeoseung for the numbers, there is not much else for Seokga and Hani to do but wait.

And waiting with Seokga is very, very satisfying.

It is the best sort of distraction—the only way her mind will stop running laps around Somi and the eoduksini and the streets of shadow outside.

Hani writhes in satisfaction as Seokga kisses the column of her neck, his lips burning her skin, lighting her on fire. She is swimming in a sea of black silk sheets, running her hands up his bare, corded, muscular back, in awe of the way she burns beneath him. She has never felt alive in the way that she does underneath his touch, even the whisper of his skin against hers sending a thrill through her body, desire distracting her from the messy tangle of guilt and horror knotting her insides. She sighs, running her hands through his hair as his lips once again meet hers. Hani can feel him suppressing a smile, and she wonders how it is that this fallen god—this pillar of ice and steel—melts so completely around her.

Her and nobody else.

"Hani," he murmurs against her lips, pulling away. And there is that look of soft vulnerability that she adores, that she first saw on his sleeping face in Geoje, highlighted by the morning sun. There is no sun now—only darkness covers the city of New

Sinsi—but somehow, this look remains. "Hani," he repeats, voice thick with desire.

"Seokga," she replies teasingly, toying with a strand of his hair.

"Do you . . ." He looks so uncertain, so shy, that it breaks her heart. "Do you want to . . . all of it?"

"Yes," she whispers back. "Yes, I do."

A burst of pure joy flashes across Seokga's face, and he suddenly looks young—so much younger than his thousands of years. Hani smiles up at him, tracing the sharp curvature of his face with a hand. He leans into her touch, his eyes fluttering closed.

"I still hate you," he says softly, a smug little smirk playing on his lips.

"I hate you, too," she whisper-laughs. Seokga's green eyes open and refocus on her, glittering.

"I guess we'll have to change that," he murmurs.

Hani grins up at him as he toys with her Henley shirt, slowly unbuttoning it until his cold knuckles can brush against the swell of her breasts. His gaze has gone dark as he stares at her bra.

"Take it off."

A smirk tugs her lips upward as she sits up and pulls off her shirt. The soft fabric pools on the ground as she brushes it from the bed. Seokga's cheeks are tinged pink as she drops her bra onto the ground and quirks an eyebrow at him.

She watches as Seokga swallows hard.

His cheeks are the shade of ripened cherries as she sheds the rest of her clothing with a particular gusto, loving the way he stares at her ravenously.

"Your turn," she says, and her grin widens as he hastily strips before leaning in and kissing her again—this time without that final barrier between them. His mouth is hot and heavy and hungry as he lays her back on the pillows, as he trails kisses down her neck, her chest, her stomach, and . . . lower. *Much* lower.

Hani gasps and fists the black sheets in her hands as Seokga takes his time, teasing her, relishing her building tension. She can tell by the wicked glint in his eyes that he's enjoying this. Hani's head falls back as he grips her waist in his hands, as she tumbles over the edge, his name on her tongue.

Seokga rises, smiling slightly. His lips are glossy, his eyes bright with mischief.

Quivering with pleasure, Hani reaches for him, drawing his body against hers. He kisses the crown of her head and slowly, steadily, joins her as one.

Seokga is not a selfish lover, Hani learns as he rolls his hips, his hands braced on either side of the pillow. No, Seokga is not selfish at all. He is tender and gentle, his breathing shallow, his eyes bright, hooded with pleasure, and perhaps even a little bit nervous. And Hani knows that this—this is different from all the other times, for her and for him. Their lovemaking has a rhythm to it, like the rhythm to a favorite song—sweet and slow.

When they dance toward that dangerous edge, they do so together—Seokga gasping softly, burying his face in the crook of Hani's neck, and Hani wrapping her legs around his narrow waist tightly and holding him close, never wanting to let go.

And so for a long time, she doesn't. They hold each other, sleepy and sated. Seokga toys with her hair, idly combing through the tangled locks. She falls half-asleep like that, with the fallen god's fingers in her hair and her heart in his hand.

SOMETIME LATER, HANI'S STOMACH GROWLS VERY, VERY loudly.

Seokga chuckles from where he lays behind her, his arms wrapped around her waist, his face buried in the crook of her neck. "Are you hungry, fox?"

"Perhaps," she admits, smiling against the pillows.

He lifts his head immediately, and she can practically feel the gears in his brain turning. "What would you like?"

"Seokga," she murmurs as she turns to face him, "do you know how to cook?"

For some inexplicable reason, she has a feeling that despite his impressive kitchen, Seokga has never made a meal for himself in his life. She's right—Hani watches as Seokga narrows his eyes at her and says in a much-too-indignant tone, "Of course I can cook."

"Mm." She snickers and flicks his nose. Seokga scowls, but it's only a half-hearted sort of scowl. "I'll have gimbap, then."

"Gimbap," Seokga repeats, hesitating. Hani is thoroughly amused.

"Gimbap," she repeats, fighting back a smile. "It's simple enough."

"I have made it before."

"Oh?"

"Ye-es."

"For the god of deceit," she murmurs, "you're not very good at lying."

"Just not around you, it appears," he grumbles. "I'm quite good at lying otherwise."

Even as Hani smiles, her chest tightens. She is very good at lying to Seokga. She has been lying to him since she met him. Hani tears her gaze away from him abruptly, sliding from the bed and collecting her clothes from the ground. As she tugs on her sweatpants, she lets herself imagine what his reaction would be if . . . if she told him the truth now. He wouldn't kill her, surely—or perhaps he would, if it meant reclaiming his power. If it meant that she had deceived him, wronged him. Which she has.

"What's wrong?" Seokga's eyes narrow in wary concern as he watches her.

"Nothing," Hani says quickly. "I'm just . . . I'm just worried about tonight."

"The caffeine is a clever trick," Seokga says as he also slides out of bed. Hani's face flushes at the sight of his bare skin, and she hastily resorts to buttoning up her shirt. "I think that you are right. The eoduksini relies on paralyzing its victims with nightmares in order to feed. But one cannot dream if they physically cannot fall asleep."

"But it seems too easy," Hani mumbles, smoothing down her hair. "Too simple."

"The best answers are often in front of our eyes," Seokga says with a lopsided smile that is so wholly unlike him that Hani blinks in surprise. "It's only that we don't see them . . . until we do." He stands in front of her, his hands sliding around her waist as he brushes a kiss against the top of her head. "I am glad that you decided to be my assistant," he murmurs into her hair. "As obnoxious and annoying as you might be."

"Thank you," Hani says, mock-graciously.

She feels Seokga grin. "You're welcome," he replies drolly. Hani laughs and sends him a lewd gesture as she pulls away and makes for the door.

"You're impossible."

"You're insufferable."

"You're intolerable," Hani counters, descending the stairs and making for the kitchen.

"You tolerate me," Seokga smirks and follows, leaning against one of the black-marble counters. "One could even make the compelling case that you *more* than tolerate me."

She rolls her eyes and then snorts, suddenly remembering

Somi's fan fiction. It had been nothing like the younger gumiho had fantasized about—there was no animalistic growling. But there had been, she reflects, a bulging—

Seokga is narrowing his eyes at her razor-sharp smirk. "Do I want to know?"

"No." Hani turns, her chest growing heavy at the thought of Somi. She wishes she could go back to those days, when her friend's only vice was writing smut. "What do you have?" she asks as she opens the pantries in search of sufficient nourishment. But the pantries she'd assumed harbored gourmet foods hold only . . . "Ramyeon?" Hani stares at the hundreds of packs of instant noodles as she swallows a laugh.

Seokga makes a sound suspiciously like a groan of pain behind her. She turns, laughing openly now. "Is all you consume ramyeon and coffee?"

"No," Seokga mutters, avoiding her gaze. "I usually eat out. But when I don't, I like ramyeon. It's decent. And easy."

Hani grins as she grabs two packs of the noodles. "Do you want the spicy one," she asks, holding them up in her hands, "or the shrimp-flavored one?"

Seokga's eyes are on the spicy one, but he shrugs. "Whatever one you don't want."

"We should mix them together," Hani suggests, already searching for a saucepan in which to boil water. "Spicy shrimp."

"No."

"Yes," Hani counters sweetly. "Spicy shrimp ramyeon." She locates the saucepan and sets it on the stove. "Get water," she orders over her shoulder as she twists the knob of the stove and the flame flares to life.

Seokga sighs but does as she says. As the water boils, Hani dumps in the two flavor packets with an odd sort of amusement.

The city is being devoured by darkness while she and Seokga are making noodles. *It makes us sound like terrible people,* she thinks, and feels an entirely inappropriate urge to both snicker and cry.

"Spicy shrimp is going to be disgusting," Seokga says as he unwraps the dried noodles and gently plops them into the water. "You're a barbarian."

Hani rolls her eyes as she presses the ramyeon down with a long soup spoon, letting them soften and break apart. "You'll like it."

And he does.

Seokga and Hani sit side by side on his sofa, eating their spicy shrimp ramyeon. Hani slurps at her noodles, savoring the mundanity of the situation. The normalcy. She can almost pretend that Somi is still sweet, innocent Somi, and that the eoduk-sini never escaped Jeoseung.

Almost.

Until Seokga swallows a bite of ramyeon and looks to her with a grim expression. "Nam Somi gets one—and only one—chance to explain herself," he says, setting down his chopsticks. Hani frowns. It's clear that this argument hasn't died despite their tumble in the sheets. "Even if she isn't the Scarlet Fox, she is still an Unruly. She's still killed twenty people in the last day." She can tell that he is trying his best to say it gently, but there is no mistaking the cold undertone to his words. He means it. One chance, and only one.

Hani swallows her own bite with difficulty, and with it, her rising irritation. "It is in a gumiho's nature to kill," she snaps back as calmly and as smoothly as she can. "She can't be blamed for following her most basic instincts."

Seokga is watching her carefully. "But there is a difference between you and her. You do not act on these feral instincts. She has chosen to. There is a choice in the matter."

"They're not feral," Hani retorts, clenching her chopsticks

between her hands. "They're natural. And perhaps she has the Cravings. It's what happens—"

"I'm familiar with the term."

Hani sighs, setting down her bowl. "What would you do," she asks, her heart quickening, "if it was me instead of Somi?"

"For fuck's sake." Seokga frowns and averts his gaze down to his bowl. "I'm not in the mood for these ridiculous hypotheticals, Hani."

"Would you kill me?" Sweat dribbles down her spine as she continues, "Or would you do as I've asked you to do for Somi and give me a chance to explain myself? Would you still believe that the instinct to kill is feral, or would you consider that for a gumiho—it's natural? Taboo, now, sure—but natural? Just like tigers eat elephant calves, gumiho eat men and steal their souls." She holds her breath as Seokga is silent, his stare shrewd. "So— what would you do?" she asks, her voice straining. "If it was me, not Somi?"

Seokga scowls at her, stabbing at his noodles with a notable amount of force. "Luckily," he says tightly, "we do not have to contemplate this situation. You are not the Scarlet Fox." Seokga holds her gaze for a too-long moment. Hani suddenly feels feverish and shaky, her head pounding with a dull ache as he holds her stare. Finally, he looks away, a muscle in his jaw jumping. "Fine. I swear on Hwanung, god of kept promises, that I will give Somi one chance. For you. And only one. But the moment she puts either you or me in jeopardy, I will do what is necessary. But I promise that her death will be quick. Clean."

Her death.

Somi's death.

The food in Hani's stomach suddenly threatens to rise to her throat. She pushes to her feet and presses a hand over her mouth. "Bathroom," she manages to rasp out before hurrying from the living room into the restroom, firmly locking the door behind her. Her cheek is hot on the cold tiled floor as she collapses, drawing her knees to her chest, struggling to breathe.

When she finally stands to splash water on her face, her eyes lift to the crown of her head. Immediately, she flinches. Because there it is. On the top of her scalp, peeking out from in between curtains of chocolate brown, is the tiniest hint of a rich, ruby red.

You can't hide your roots that easily, after all.

Hani closes her eyes and swallows hard.

What a mess this is, a little voice in her head whispers. *What a godsdamn mess.*

CHAPTER THIRTY-EIGHT

SEOKGA

SEVEN.

That is the number for tonight, from eight P.M. to ten P.M. Seven deaths in New Sinsi. It is not outrageously high, but it is not outrageously low for a two-hour time span, either. Seokga exchanges wary glances with Hani as Hyun-tae stands in the kitchen with them.

"It's possible that the seven will all be killed at the same time," Hyun-tae says before frowning in disapproval. "Dong-wook's hours are small. I never understand why he's so lazy when all he has is a two-hour shift," he adds under his breath before addressing Hani and Seokga again. "If they die by Ms. Somi's hand, it will be anywhere from eight to ten tonight."

It's currently six-thirty. Seokga rubs his temples wearily.

"Levels of caffeine peak in the bloodstream fifteen to forty-five minutes after consumption," Hyun-tae continues, as if re-citing a paragraph from a textbook. "So—if we want to be at peak caffeination by, say, eight…we should begin drinking around seven-fifteen."

"It takes ten hours for caffeine to leave your system," Hani murmurs next to him. "We should be loaded for the night with fifteen cups each." Fifteen cups of potent black coffee are the maximum amount that they've decided that they will be able to consume without going into cardiac arrest—or, in the immortal

Seokga's case, having non-deadly but very annoying and debilitating heart palpitations.

"My ringer is set to the loudest setting," Hyun-tae assures them. "When there is a call, we will hear it."

"If you're coming with us," Hani says, looking at the jeoseung saja, "you'll need weapons. I have a pair of silver daggers that you can borrow. Are you well-trained?"

"Yes." Hyun-tae nods. "I'm sure that I can use them should the need arise."

Seokga furrows his brows in confusion. He bought those daggers for *Hani,* not a lovesick reaper. "You cannot go into this weaponless, either, Hani." His heart feels tight, pinched in concern. His nerves are fraying, not in irritation but in fear.

He cares for her. Deeply. So, so deeply.

And after the time they spent in his bed . . . He would have damned this city, this world, to Jeoseung if it meant that he could spend an eternity with Hani atop those silky black sheets.

He needs her to be safe. He *needs* her to be okay. The very prospect of her being hurt—it sends a shard of glass into his chest, and he considers asking Hani if she would stay here, out of the fight, out of danger, but he knows it is impossible.

Her fire, her fierce courage . . . he adores it.

Adores *her.*

And he would never try to change her.

Seokga holds his breath, watching Hani with that awful pinching feeling in his chest. "I bought those daggers for *you,*" he says and shoots Hyun-tae a scathing look. The jeoseung saja blinks, caught off guard. "They're a gift. They're yours." Fear makes his voice stiffer than he wishes. "Yours, Hani," he says, softer this time. "Please, use them."

"I have something else to use," she mumbles in return—and it does not escape Seokga's notice that she does not meet his gaze.

But Hyun-tae is bustling around his kitchen, opening and closing cabinet doors. "Where's the coffee?" the jeoseung saja asks and Seokga feels a surge of irritation as he riffles through his things.

"It's in the other cabinet. No, not that one," he growls. "That one—your left. No, your *other* left—" Muttering a string of curses, Seokga shoulders past Hyun-tae to open the door to his impressive stash of caffeine . . .

And freezes.

The cabinet is empty.

Hani makes a startled, choking noise. "*You* don't have any coffee?" she demands. "*You?*"

Seokga winces in response, and Hani presses a hand to her mouth, mirth sparkling in her eyes. It seems that Seokga has been drinking much more coffee than he realized. Yet he could have sworn he'd still had at least a couple of bags . . .

"Hwanin's tits," Hani says, shaking her head. "I don't know whether to laugh or to cry. The one time I need you to have coffee—"

"I'll go to the store," Seokga says grimly, tightening his hold on his cane. It's risky to venture out into New Sinsi, especially with the eoduksini fantasizing about all the ways it can get back at him for locking Gamangnara, but they don't have a choice. Besides, it's not as if New Sinsi has closed down. While creatures have been alerted to the eoduksini, the humans believe the darkness to be from a chemical malfunction, or some inane theory like that, and are going about their daily lives (with the increased risk of being murdered). The store will be open, and it will have coffee.

"I'm coming with you," Hani says, and looks to Hyun-tae expectantly, but the reaper cringes.

"I, uh, would rather not," he replies as he nervously pushes up his glasses. "If that's all right with you."

"It's more than fine," says Seokga, who does not like Hyun-tae and wants alone time with Hani, even if said alone time is in the middle of a shadow-covered city crawling with Unrulies. As if knowing precisely what he's thinking, Hani's gaze slides to him, and the corner of her mouth quirks up. There's a dimple there, and Seokga has the sudden urge to kiss it. Yet before he can reach for her, she's skipping for the door, tossing him a wry look over her shoulder.

"I want to drive."

HANI, IT TURNS OUT, IS TERRIBLE AT DRIVING IN THE DARK. Beads of sweat pool on Seokga's neck as Hani tears through the city, bumping his cherished Jaguar XJS against curbs, flickering streetlamps, and a phallic statue constructed by a cheonyeo gwi-sin in his absence.

"Perhaps you should slow down," he manages to suggest through gritted teeth.

"We can't afford to be out in the open like this for long," she replies and promptly runs over the virgin ghost who had leapt in front of their car, attempting to defend the statue, which was of considerable length and girth. "Oopsies."

Seokga closes his eyes and tries not to be sick. When she finally skids to a stop outside of the Yum Mart closest to Seokga's apartment, he fumbles to open the passenger door and practically falls onto the pavement. He takes a moment to cherish the pavement. It's still. Unmoving. Steady. Seokga presses his cheek to the cold ground and vows to never let Hani drive his car again, no matter how much he likes her. Some lines should never be crossed.

A foot prods his back. "Seokga," Hani said, laughing. "A fallen god sprawled on top of a parking space is a little sad to see."

Seokga groans and hauls himself to his feet. The world is still spinning.

Inside the Yum Mart, fluorescent lights provide a welcome contrast to the blackness outside. On the speakers, tinny music plays.

"Ooh, I love this song," Hani says as she grabs a cart, balances a foot on the lower bar, and pushes off as if the cart is a scooter. Seokga, cane clicking on the floor, hurries to keep up with her. "It's 'Good Bye' by Shin Hae Chul. Have you heard it?"

Yum Mart is mostly empty, save for the two bored-looking cashiers at the registers up front and a handful of NSU students stocking up on instant noodles, looking exhausted and dazed, as if running through flashcards in their heads.

"I hate music," he replies, still a bit grumpy, thanks to the car ride from hell. Hani gives him a *that's so bullshit* look as she pushes off toward the coffee aisle.

"Even TLC?" demands Hani, still looking back at him. When she rams into a cardboard display of Choco Pies, Seokga pinches the bridge of his nose in fond exasperation. Hani, he decides, should not be allowed to drive any sort of moving vehicle, even if the moving vehicle is a grocery cart.

Seokga would rather die than admit that he actually quite likes TLC. It just doesn't seem very trickster god of him to have their CD hidden somewhere deep inside his car. Instead, he shakes his head. "Here," he says gruffly, and steers Hani into the coffee aisle, lest she somehow destroy the entire store.

Yum Mart's coffee aisle is Seokga's happy place. He feels his irritation drain as he gazes up at the rows and rows and rows of coffee. He breathes deeply. How he loves coffee.

"This one looks good," Hani says, grabbing a bag of coffee

beans. "Well, as good as coffee can look, anyway. I like that it says 'intense bold.' It sounds promising." She tosses it into the cart, hesitates, and then sweeps four more bags into the cart. "Just in case," she says.

Seokga opens his mouth to reply, but words die on his tongue as the lights of the store flicker—once, twice—and then go out entirely.

"This can't be good," Hani mutters, and Seokga has to agree. The hair on the back of his neck is standing on end, and his ears strain to pick up on their suddenly silent surroundings. Shin Hae Chul's voice no longer streams from the speakers, and he hears nothing but a strange sort of whispering, as if many mouths in the store are moving, releasing hushed murmurs. The air suddenly smells stale, old, sickly. With no sun streaming in from the windows, the store is pitch-black.

For a moment.

The lights flare back on in a burst of blinding light, revealing a mottled face pressed inches away from Seokga's own. He shouts, stumbling back into the grocery cart with a rattle of metal, flicking his sword into existence as the demon before them drops back down to all fours and laughs. It is humanoid, but only vaguely. Disease has taken it, disfigured it.

"Hwanin's tits," Hani gags. "What is *that*?"

Seokga only has to take one look at the skin ruined by thousands of raised, pus-seeping bumps and the green-tinged saliva dripping from the blistered mouth to know. "Plague demon," he says as it grins, showcasing yellow teeth. "Unruly. Probably some bastard child of Manura, the smallpox goddess. It can't infect you unless it touches you."

"Fuck," Hani mutters. "Courtesy of the eoduksini, I'm guessing."

"Right," he says between his teeth moments before the demon lunges. The aisle is narrow, too narrow. Seokga moves to the side, but the demon comes too close for comfort and he grits his teeth, slashing his blade toward it while simultaneously dodging the swipes of its curled, black nails. It leers as it once again becomes bipedal, herding him so his back is pressed against a shelf, hand poised to rake down his cheek . . .

Something hits the demon, hard, in the head.

Growling, the plague demon jerks away to glower at Hani, who is hurling coffee bag after coffee bag toward the demon, and hitting with expert marksmanship each time.

"Disgusting!" she shouts, grabbing more bags off the shelf. "The least you could do is wear a mask!"

The demon snarls, a wet, sick sound, and drops back to its four limbs—leaving Seokga and prowling toward Hani, who swears. The aisle really is too narrow. Seokga meets her eye and mouths, *Run.*

Hani doesn't need to be told twice. The gumiho sprints out of the aisle, the plague demon scurrying after her, and Seokga chasing after it. The three of them run through the store, and Seokga barely has time to note that the other shoppers, and the cashiers, are lying limp on the floor, covered with boils. Shit.

Their feet pound on the linoleum floor as Hani takes them into the large space that's the fruit and vegetable section of Yum Mart. She leaps over the large stand of apples, the demon not far behind.

"SEOKGA!" Hani screeches. "DO SOMETHING! I don't know how to fight it if I can't risk *touching it*—"

Seokga tightens his grip on the sword as they run in circles around the giant bin of melons, arm rearing back. He has to be careful. He can't hit Hani.

"SEOKGA!" she howls.

He lets the sword fly through the air.

The blade buries itself in the fleshy neck. Panting, Seokga lurches away as green pus flies through the air, splattering the fresh produce—but thankfully not Hani, who dives behind a nearby display of persimmons. Groaning, the demon begins to dissolve into putrid-smelling ash.

When nothing but a puddle of pus and dust remains, Hani creeps out from behind her barricade. "Thank you," she says hoarsely. "That was unbelievably gross."

"Did it touch you?" Seokga asks, striding over to her, hands rising to her shoulders. He checks her frantically for any boils, any worrying discoloration. The demons are nasty things, their diseases even more so. He spins her around, lifting up her hair, checking the nape of her neck. There's nothing he can see, but—

"Seokga," she says gently, turning to cup his face in her hands, "I'm okay." Hani presses her lips to his, and he closes his eyes, relief washing over him. "But," she says mischievously as she pulls away, "if you want to check every single inch of me later, feel free."

He laughs. He can't help himself.

Hani smirks, looking pleased with herself, and then gestures to his pus-covered sword. "I'm guessing we need to clean that?"

She's right. "Plague demons," Seokga mutters. He can't pick up his sword until it's been disinfected. He hopes that there are antibacterial wipes and gloves around here, somewhere.

And there are. Hani goes to retrieve the coffee while Seokga painstakingly cleans his sword and returns it to its cane form. He calls the incident in to Shim, who passes the message along to an on-duty cleanup crew, and an ambulance for the demon's victims. The Magical Mishaps Unit of the New Sinsi Hospital, hidden away from mortal eyes by a glamour, should be able to treat them well enough before wiping their memories.

"The eoduksini knew where we were," Hani says as she dumps the bags of coffee beans into the car's trunk. Seokga scans the dark lot warily. "Dok-hyun is watching us."

"Let's go home," Seokga says quietly, and when Hani nods, he wonders when his house became their home. Something warm blooms in his chest.

Hani grins. "Can I drive?"

The warmth is overcome by fond annoyance. "Absolutely not," Seokga says, and is quick to claim the driver's seat.

CHAPTER THIRTY-NINE

HANI

ALONE IN HER ROOM, HANI PREPARES FOR A NIGHT OF violence.

Standing in front of the room's ornate, gilded mirror, Hani scrapes her hair into a tight twist, dragging her fingers across her skull and fighting back a wince as she knots the hair into an austere bun, trying not to look at her red roots. It has been long since she went into battle—very, very long. Her last skirmish was in, predictably, 1888, when Jack the Ripper was tearing his way through London's female population. Hani didn't let that slide for very long. She didn't steal his soul through a kiss, either.

She just killed the bastard.

Her fingers still remember the movements of battle preparation. She finishes knotting back her hair and moves on to tying her black combat shoes as tightly as she can manage, yanking the laces back before weaving them together in unbreakable ties.

She is clad in clothes that are easy to move in, black yoga leggings and a loose black sweatshirt. She would have chosen a tighter shirt, but she's hidden her scarlet daggers on her forearms, keeping them ready to be flicked out at a moment's notice. She does not wish to dwell on what will happen after the red blades capture Seokga's attention. A downfall of this strategy is that she must keep her arms straight, so as to not disturb the sheathed knives, but Hani can manage. Her fox bead is a fine weapon, and one that channels energy from her outstretched palms. She is not completely compromised.

Hani sighs as she stares into the mirror and runs her fingers across the little valley of red on either side of her hairline.

There is no telling how this night will end. None at all. At the end of it, Hani could be dead. Somi could be dead. Seokga could be dead.

The thought makes her chest ache with fear and guilt. It's premature, she thinks, to even realize such a thing, but Hani does not want to live in a world without Seokga. Without his cruel sneers that melt into soft smiles. Without his odd eating habits of coffee and ramyeon.

And if he is never reinstated as a god because of you? a bitter voice hisses into her mind. *Do you think he will want to live in a world with you then? This peace that you have found with him will shatter soon, either way. Look what your selfishness has caused. Somi, hunted. Seokga, doomed to wander Iseung for hundreds of years more. Stupid, foolish gumiho.*

Hani blinks rapidly, turning away from the mirror to avoid seeing her eyes gleaming bright with tears. Instead, she takes a deep breath in an effort to compose herself. *Let's kill the eoduksini first,* she tells herself, striding to the door. *The rest will be handled later.*

She finds Hyun-tae standing near the window wall of the downstairs living room, holding his hat in his hands, his white hair bright in the apartment's dimness. Hani silently joins his side, staring down at the inky darkness covering the city below. Seokga is nowhere to be seen. Good. Hani does not want him to hear this conversation.

"Hyun-tae," she says softly, "I need to ask you for something."

He turns to her wearily, shadows deepening the skin beneath his bespectacled eyes. "I will do anything for Ms. Somi," he says with a hint of his usual, scholar-like promptness. "I don't believe that she is . . . evil. Whatever it is that I can do to help her, I will do it to the very best of my abilities."

Hani nods, still staring at the world below. "I need you to take her away from this city," she says quietly, pressing a palm to the cold glass. "Somewhere far, far away. Take her to Tokyo or London. America. Mexico. Just take her to somewhere that Seokga cannot immediately follow. Hide her. Do as you have promised me and keep her safe."

"He plans on killing her." Hyun-tae's voice is flat. "Doesn't he?"

"There's no explanation that Somi can give to dissuade him," Hani murmurs. "Seokga knows this. I know this. Somi will die tonight if you do not act." She stares at her reflection in the mirror, and this time she does not turn away as her eyes fill with tears. "The only thing that Somi is guilty of is following her nature. She's been manipulated, approached in a moment of fragile vulnerability. And you're right, Hyun-tae. Nam Somi is not the Scarlet Fox." She presses her palm more harshly against the glass. The coldness bites into her skin. "She is hurting and she is scared. She is driven by her shame and her desire to cease feeling it. When you take her, tell her . . . that I am so sorry. That I'll come for her soon. That I'll teach her how to control them. Her Cravings." She swallows hard. "Once Somi leads us to the eo-duksini, I need you to do whatever you can to get her out of range. Her fox bead has grown in power, but you need to match her strength. Take her away. And keep her safe. Keep her fed until I arrive. Can you do this for me?" Hani finally looks to Hyun-tae. His skin is pale, his eyes drained and fatigued—yet his face sharpens with determination. "Can you do this for Somi?"

He bows his head. "I will keep to my promise," he says softly. "I will protect Ms. Somi until the end."

"Good." Hani feels faint with relief. Hyun-tae can be trusted to have Somi's best interests at heart. Of that she is certain. "And do not speak a word of this to Seokga the Fallen."

"I would not dare." Hyun-tae dons his hat once more, and turns to the window as well, his eyes scouring the streets below as if they can somehow pinpoint Somi in the shadows.

HANI RAISES HER FIFTEENTH AND FINAL CUP OF COFFEE into the air. "Cheers," she says to Hyun-tae and Seokga, her stomach churning. She *hates* this drink. Her mouth tastes foul, but the caffeine has begun to do its job. Hani is close to bursting with energy. She could not sleep now even if she tried. Her fingers spasm around the coffee cup, and she bounces her knee up and down to relieve some of the nervous energy from the disgusting beverage.

"Cheers," Hyun-tae echoes promptly before determinedly gulping his own cup down.

Seokga arches a brow. "Cheers," he says wryly.

Hani grimaces and drains the coffee to dregs. She wipes her mouth on the back of her wrist. Her heart is thundering against her chest from the caffeine and she hopes she doesn't go into cardiac arrest. She's relying rather heavily on her gumiho genetics to prevent exactly that.

"What next?" Hyun-tae asks.

"We find the bodies," she announces, "and we hope that they've been left by Somi. If they have, the trail will still be fresh. I'll track her."

"And you plan on doing that how?" Seokga asks warily. "I've been meaning to ask."

"Shifting." Hani rolls her shoulders, uncomfortable as the caffeine buzzes along her blood. "I know Somi's scent. In my fox form, my senses are doubled. I'll follow her, and the two of you will follow me to wherever she's retreated."

"The eoduksini will try to drag us into nightmares." Seokga sets down his mug. "If Hani's theory proves true, it won't work. We'll remain awake."

"We kill him. Working together as a unit. When he dies, the darkness around New Sinsi should be lifted."

"It's a strong plan." Hyun-tae nods, adjusting his hat. "It is nearing eight. I expect that a call will come soon. All we can do now," he says quietly, "is wait."

CHAPTER FORTY
SEOKGA

THE CALL COMES AT 8:46.

Seven bodies found near the Han River, in the city park. They waste no time at all.

Seokga speeds through the impenetrable night in Hyun-tae's hearse (which he commandeered from the boy with a pointed scowl), Hani and the jeoseung saja silent as the car screeches to a halt near the river. His breathing is shallow in anticipation as they sprint through the cherry blossom trees toward the sidewalk lining the river, their shoes beating against the pavement until the bodies come into view. A stray dog is howling as it runs around one of the corpses who still holds a leash in its bloodied hand.

"Well," Seokga mutters dryly and with some relief, "she didn't kill the dog. I'm sure that counts for *something*."

Hani cuts him a glare as she kneels next to one of the scattered corpses. "Livers missing," she mutters. "Hyun-tae?"

"Souls gone, as well," the jeoseung saja confirms grimly. Despite the caffeine, he looks impossibly tired, his gaze dull and empty.

"How is that *possible*?" Hani demands. She's staring down at the bodies, looking so thoroughly shaken that sweat beads on her brow. Or perhaps it's from the coffee. "She shouldn't be able to steal souls this quickly. It's unnatural. Gumiho steal souls through kisses. How did she have time to kiss everybody here?"

Seokga meets her eye as Hani whirls to him. "And the twenty others. How—how did she do this?"

"I don't know," Seokga replies grimly. He doesn't know whether it's the bodies or the caffeine, but he's restless, tapping his cane on the ground, shifting back and forth. "But you know what to do," he says, even as his chest twists in apprehension. They are in the eye of the storm. It's only a matter of time before the thunder and lightning and pounding rain overtake them.

Hani nods and opens her mouth as if there is something she wants to say—but she swallows her words and closes her eyes. Seokga watches in curiosity as the change ripples over her, as Hani transforms into a sleek fox, her nine tails alert as she raises her nose to the air, sniffing.

The fox glances toward him with wine-brown eyes—Hani's eyes. *Follow,* they seem to command before she takes off, a blur of red against the darkness.

"She's fast," Hyun-tae says stupidly next to him.

Seokga grips his cane tightly in his hand even as he feels a surge of pride. Hani *is* fast. "Keep up," he snaps irritably before he, too, is sprinting, following the red streak before him. His breath rattles in his throat as he pushes his muscles to their limit, every stride making them burn. But the caffeine fuels him, and he manages to follow Hani through the winding city, past closed restaurants and shuttered shops, through narrow alleyways and winding side roads. Hani is like a shooting star flying through the night, a shooting star that he wishes upon—wishes for the two of them to come out of this fight alive. Together.

Hani takes them through the city and toward the small warehouse district lining the Han River. Hyun-tae is breathing raggedly behind Seokga as Hani finally slows to a stop in front of a large, decrepit warehouse. The shingled roof is twisted and distorted, half caved in and rusted with deep orange stains. Seokga's eyes go to the door as Hani transforms back into her human form, spiraling upward until she is once again Kim Hani. The huge padlock on the entryway is laughable, protecting a large, rotted piece of wood which serves as the main door.

"She's here," Hani pants, wiping her brow. "I can smell her. But there are other scents, too." She glances at Seokga. "Other Unrulies are inside. I can't tell what sorts—but the scents coming from inside are unnatural."

"And the eoduksini?"

Hani shrugs, still breathing heavily. "The scent of the demon is impossible to discern. There was no smell in the nightclub when it attacked, and there wasn't one in the convenience store. If it does have an unnatural scent, it's somehow managed to mask it. But logic tells me that he's inside. He has to be."

"How many Unrulies?"

"Thirty. Maybe more. Thankfully, no more plague demons." Hani shakes her head. "The Unrulies we can handle. They're easy enough to kill. It's the eoduksini I worry about. Is it possible that he knows we're coming? That he prepared this army to meet us?"

Seokga's stomach drops, but he fights to remain calm. This is no place for panic. "It is," Seokga admits, "but a fight is still a fight. Between the three of us, we are ready. We know what to expect." *I hope.*

By the end of this, he can either be a god—or dead.

And what if Hani—no. He cannot think like that.

Hani will be okay. She'll be okay.

They'll be okay.

But . . .

Seokga takes a steadying breath in. This. *This* is why he has never allowed himself to—to care for anybody the way he does for Hani. Because caring makes everything more complicated. Caring sends jagged blades of anxiety dragging down his spine, thinking of the worst possible outcome and hoping that it never comes to fruition. Caring has his skin dampening with a cold sweat. He is teetering on the brink of horror, digging his heels in and hoping that he does not fall.

Seokga wonders if Hani is feeling the same terror.

He hopes that she isn't. He needs her mind to be clear, her heart hardened. He needs her to walk out of this uninjured. Okay.

He watches as Hani nods slowly, eyeing the padlock. "I don't think we should go in through there," she says, shaking her head. And her voice is even, all smooth strategy. Good. "We need to take him by surprise as much as we can at this point."

"What do you suggest?" Seokga asks, seeing the way she's cocking her head, beautiful eyes narrowed with careful thought.

Hani turns to him, seeming surprised—and pleased. "I do have one idea." She turns, and points to the caved-in roof of the warehouse, jabbing toward the gaping hole in the middle.

"Oh, no," Hyun-tae moans.

The gumiho grins. "We go in through *there*."

CHAPTER FORTY-ONE

HANI

HANI GRUNTS IN EXERTION AS SHE DIGS HER CLAWS into the crevices between the warehouse's gray concrete bricks, pulling herself up toward the roof, careful to avoid the cracked windows. Seokga is not far behind her, and Hyun-tae, to his credit, is keeping up remarkably well. An icy night gust whistles around her ears as she climbs, whispers on the wind taunting her. *Coward. Liar. Your fault. Somi's blood will soon be on your hands. Liar. Liar. Liar.*

Hani bites down on her lip hard as she pulls herself to the roof, pushing herself across the shingles on her stomach toward the cavernous hole leading down into the warehouse. A soft grunt alerts her to Seokga's presence—he lies beside her in a similar position, his eyes bright in the shadows as he glares at their point of entry. "Damned demon," he sneers as Hyun-tae joins them, panting. "When it's sent back to Jeoseung, I'll ensure that King Yeomra gives it a suitable punishment. Better yet—I'll inflict it myself."

"We should look down," Hyun-tae whispers. "It is wise to see what we are walking into."

Hani nods, and as silently as she can, creeps toward the void. Clenching the edge of the ruined shingles with her hands, she peers down into shadows and darkness, careful to keep her face hidden. Her eyes take moments to adjust, but when they do . . .

The inside of the warehouse is a dump. The stone ground is

littered with garbage, the walls are coated in sloppy graffiti, and there are more than a few overturned cars lying in heaps of crumpled metal atop seas of shattered glass. But these things are not what capture Hani's attention.

The warehouse is, as she predicted, teeming with Unrulies. She watches as clusters of Unruly bulgasari rip the cars apart, stuffing the metal into their mouths with greedy hands and cackling as they chew. Hani winces. It is more than likely that those cars were abducted with their drivers in them. And there are no signs of the drivers now.

Unruly bulgasari are not the only creatures within the warehouse. Hani bites back a curse as she catches sight of a crowd of fat baegopeun gwisin scampering through hordes of other Unrulies, stuffing something red and raw into their maws. *So that's where the drivers went.*

There are a few gumiho leaning against the crumbling cement pillars of the warehouse and Hani's eyes flicker between them as she searches. She clenches her jaw as she takes in a handful of dokkaebi, a few dripping-wet mul gwisin, but no Somi.

And no Dok-hyun, either.

Hani retreats, sitting on the shingled tiles and shaking her head at her two companions. "No Somi," she whispers. "No eoduksini."

Seokga's face tightens. "They must be somewhere inside. Somi's scent led here."

"It did." Hani chews on her bottom lip. "You're right. She must be here—she must be. She's just not visible." She frowns. "The eoduksini has amassed quite the following in a short time." She's pleased that there are no Unruly yong or imoogi—the powerful dragons and serpents would give a hard fight. There are no samjokgu, either. Hani feels a rush of tentative relief. The ferocious three-legged dog-shifters are frighteningly capable of ending a gumiho life.

"Its ideology is appealing," Hyun-tae offers grimly. "The Dark World reborn. Unbridled chaos. It's exactly the sort of thing that homesick Unrulies would flock to."

"What do we do?" Hani glances at their point of entry with trepidation. "Do we go in now? Or do we wait for Somi or the eoduksini to show themselves?"

"The eoduksini would expect us to wait," Hyun-tae replies, pulling the silver daggers from his pockets and clenching them in his hands. "And we cannot fall into its expectations. We should go now." It's clear he's itching to find Somi.

"Unless it's watching us," Hani replies warily.

"If that's the case," Seokga mutters darkly, "then either way, we don't have the element of surprise. But I suggest that we take our chances and hope that he hasn't been watching. We take him by surprise—or in the worst-case scenario, we get this battle over with sooner."

The worst-case scenario, Hani wants to bite back, *is that we die.* But she stays silent and lets her expression speak for her.

This battle is unlike anything she has ever faced before.

Chances of survival are low, to say the least.

Seokga's gaze softens. "We'll be all right," he says quietly. "We will see the morning light dawn over New Sinsi again, Hani. Together. I swear it on Hwanung." He takes her hand in his, and she flinches in surprise at the burning heat of it. "I swear on Hwanung, god of laws and kept promises, that the sun will shine on us both once again."

Hani's eyes widen. "You shouldn't make oaths you cannot keep." Hwanung will hold him to his oath, and if he can't fulfill it, there's no telling what Seokga's punishment will be.

"I will find a way to keep this one," Seokga replies, his thumb tracing circles on her skin. "I promise."

Her hand sears with heat from his, burning and blistering as the promise settles in. She fights back a wave of overwhelming emotion as she stares at Seokga. If they make it out of this fight alive, she'll find a way to . . . explain. She will.

Her throat aches from withheld tears as she kisses Seokga softly. Gently. It is a bittersweet kiss, light and hesitant.

It is worryingly close to a goodbye kiss.

You will lose him, she thinks, fighting back those tears. *Either way, after tonight, you will lose him.*

"We'll see the morning," Seokga whispers against her lips. "We'll see the dawn."

Hani barely has time to manage a smile—a sad, broken thing—before the roof shudders underneath them . . . and shatters completely.

CHAPTER FORTY-TWO

SEOKGA

WITH THE TERRIBLE SOUND OF SHEARING METAL, Seokga is falling from that precipice, tumbling down into horror.

And all he can do is hope the two of them come out okay.

Fuck.

CHAPTER FORTY-THREE

HANI

A SCREAM OF SHOCK LODGES IN HANI'S THROAT AS SHE tumbles through open air, cutting her skin on the debris that plummets with her as she falls. She barely has time to hold her arms out in front of her before she hits the concrete ground hard, only just managing to push herself forward into a roll to spread out the jarring impact.

Through the blinding pain, she is dimly aware of surprised screeches tearing from the maws of the pack of baegopeun gwi-sin, and the outraged shouts from the surrounding Unrulies. Groaning, spitting blood out of her mouth, and raising her clawed fists, Hani drags herself to her feet. Seokga is struggling to do the same next to her, his sword at the ready. Hyun-tae is nowhere to be seen—but Hani has no time to puzzle over that as Seokga presses his back to her as the two of them are slowly surrounded by thirty glaring Unrulies.

"What," Hani says through another mouthful of blood that she spits out onto the concrete floor in a scarlet splatter, "the hell just happened?" She readies her fox bead, letting her body hum with energy, with power. The caffeine rushing through her blood has her senses on high alert and sweat beading on the nape of her neck. "What the actual hell," she repeats in a vicious demand as the bulgasari approach with sharp shards of metal clenched in their hands, "just happened?"

They are surrounded. Completely surrounded by snarling Unrulies.

Gods*damn* it.

And neither Somi nor Dok-hyun are anywhere in sight. She can only hope that Hyun-tae will find Somi—find her and stun her, then take her to safety.

"I think," Seokga replies hoarsely, "that we just fell through the roof."

Hani sneers as a few dokkaebi step forward, the white-hot, blue-flamed dokkaebi fire dancing in the palms of their hands. "Stay the fuck back," she growls, letting her own palms heat with golden power from her fox bead. She has more than enough after her London binge. And with this many gumiho in the warehouse, a power flare won't be traced back to her.

But the circle of Unrulies surrounding them is growing tighter. Hani stiffens. "Seokga," she says under her breath, "we need to strike first." Otherwise, the horde of Unrulies will have the upper hand. "We strike now."

"Together," Seokga replies, and she can feel the hope and the desperation in his voice.

"Together," Hani agrees—and attacks.

She aims for the dokkaebi first, blasting them back with a surge of golden, searing power. They crash into a cement pillar, shrieking as they fire back blue flame that Hani easily dodges. She lobs another surge of power from her fox bead toward them, forever silencing their screams. The scent of burnt flesh fills the air as their skin sizzles.

But Hani is already moving toward the gumiho who are stalking forward, golden power of their own in their hands. She bites back a curse as one lands a blow, singeing the side of her waist with her power flare.

She doesn't want to kill them—but what choice does she

have? Hani swallows another surge of bitter guilt as she whips around, catching one in the stomach with a heavy combat boot and mauling another's face with her claws. Blood sprays through the air, splattering Hani's face. Nausea runs through her, only exacerbated by that disgusting drink sloshing around in her stomach.

The gumiho fire back, scrabbling with violence, their claws singing through the air—but they are no match for the Scarlet Fox's power. Another release of her energy has two of the seven Unruly gumiho flying upward impossibly high before dropping back down to the ground with sickening cracks, limbs bent at awkward angles and red blood pooling on the concrete. The other five hesitate, slowly retreating. Good. Clever foxes.

Hani nearly reaches for her daggers as a small horde of bae-gopeun gwisin rush for her but decides against it, instead letting the power of her fox bead warm her palms, filling her blood with a crackling energy.

As the fat, hungry ghosts rush for her, Hani burns them to a crisp. Flabby skin curls and burns before finally crumbling into foul-smelling ash.

"Oh, that's just nasty," she pants, heart pounding in her chest. The coffee has certainly taken full effect, and her fingers are shaking with tremors. Her mouth tastes foul, her tongue is dry, and her stomach seems to be tumbling over itself.

"Hani," Seokga shouts, and she whirls to see him fending off a bulgasari's sharp teeth as they attempt to pummel him with one of the metal scraps. "Don't burn yourself out—"

She shakes her head before summoning more power.

This won't burn her out. Her reservoir of power is nearly bottomless. It's not immune to drainage, but it'll take more than this to deplete her bead. And the caffeine is helping her stamina. She hopes it holds. Once it wears off, she'll be exhausted and likely fall down, dead to the world.

Another horde of baegopeun gwisin move forward, only to meet the same fate. But Hani chokes as strong arms wrap around her neck, squeezing until stars swim in her vision. She retches, slamming her fist backward, claws rupturing somebody's stomach like a pin popping a balloon. Hani breaks free from the choke hold and whirls around to meet the hateful eyes of a female haetae. She fights back surprise. Unruly haetae are rare, but not nonexistent.

With a snarl, the haetae leaps forward, shifting into the horned, scaled lion in midair. Hani barely has time to leap out of its path before she slams to the ground, emitting an earthshaking roar.

Hani is not impressed.

The haetae charges for her, and with a grunt, Hani leaps into the air, flips, and lands on the beast's back. She roars again, this time in outrage, as Hani balances atop her despite her wild bucking. A downward blast of power has the beast collapsing, dead.

She looks for Seokga as the haetae falls. He is slaying another group of baegopeun gwisin, unaware of the dokkaebi standing just feet behind him, blue fire rolling in its hands. Hani grits her teeth and sends her own power surging toward the bastard, feeling a rush of satisfaction as it falls, turning to ash.

The din of the battle is deafening. Hani dispatches four bulgasari with ease, scanning the warehouse for Somi. Still nothing. Hani dodges a mul gwisin's bloated, blue outstretched arms, and slaughters the water ghost with a scoff. There is no water in the warehouse. A mul gwisin is useless.

The number of Unrulies has dwindled considerably. Where there were once thirty, there are now only ten at the most. Hani grunts as one of the remaining gumiho who has not fled gashes her face with her claws. Staggering back, Hani glares. "Go home," she snaps to the gumiho, a short-haired girl with buglike eyes. "Get out of here while you can."

"No," the Unruly gumiho sneers, golden power flaring as she stretches out her hand. "I want a world of feasting. A world of—"

Hani sends her flying out of the warehouse with a singular burst of power.

"A world of what?" she mutters to nobody in particular, dispatching a stray baegopeun gwisin with another flare. "I didn't quite catch that."

Thanks to Hani and Seokga's combined efforts, there are only four Unrulies left now. Hani joins Seokga's side once more, glancing at the god, who shoots her a sidelong glare as he beheads another mul gwisin. "Your power," he pants. "How is it so limitless?"

Hani bites down on her tongue hard as she kills two dokkaebi with another fox bead flare. "It's a long story," she rasps, out of breath.

There is only one Unruly left—a fat baegopeun gwisin who is staring at Hani and Seokga with no small amount of terror. Hani watches as it turns around and begins sprinting for one of the holes in the warehouse walls, a courtesy of a stray power blast.

Hani kills the fat little demon before it can make it even four feet. It crumples into a heap of ash.

The warehouse is coated with an unnatural sort of silence, the only noises the god's and the gumiho's heavy breathing, and the whisper of ashes against concrete as the mounds coating the warehouse ground shift in a night wind. Neither Hani nor Seokga speak for a long moment, drenched in sweat and warily scouring the empty warehouse for another threat. But there is none—they are alone.

"Where is Hyun-tae?" Hani rasps. "Where the fuck did he go?"

"I don't know," Seokga replies tightly. "I don't know."

Hani struggles to even her breathing. "Where are—" She cuts off as goosebumps rise on her skin, as the air freezes to a brittle, biting cold, burning her eyes. The shadows of the warehouse thicken, swirling through the concrete pillars, dancing through the piles of ash littering the ground. Hani grabs Seokga's hand in hers as they are plunged into complete and total darkness. His hand, usually cold and smooth, is sweaty against her own. Like hers, his fingers are trembling. The god, it seems, isn't immune to the effects of fifteen coffee servings, either.

"Seokga," she whispers hoarsely, heart slamming against her ribs.

"I'm here." His voice is less steady than usual. "I'm here, Hani."

Hani trembles as the air grows colder still. It is icier than even the most wicked of winters. Frostbitten fire gnaws at her bones as she shakes. She summons the power of her fox bead to her palms, but even the golden energy does not show within the darkness.

The eoduksini has arrived.

"Show yourself," Hani demands, spitting the words with a rage so potent that it warms her frozen blood. "Show yourself, you fucking coward."

No response.

Hani snarls as a wave of exhaustion beats at her body, clearly sent by the underworld demon. "It won't work," she grits out as she fights off the wave and silently screams in relief that the coffee, the caffeine, has worked. Actually *worked*. "Not this time. Show yourself. Tonight it is a fair fight."

Seokga's hand tightens around her as a low, low laugh creeps out from the darkness. As the impenetrable shadows begin to recede, swirling away until they cluster around one of the overturned cars. Hani squints, but she cannot see who stands within it.

Slowly, so very slowly, the shadows quiver before falling to the ground like clothes shed from one's body. Like feathers falling from the body of a crow.

Hani bites down on her tongue hard enough that she tastes blood.

Hyun-tae stands atop the overturned car, his eyes cold and hard as he tilts his head in greeting. And next to him, hand in hand, stands Nam Somi.

CHAPTER FORTY-FOUR
SEOKGA

CHANG HYUN-TAE.

Seokga stares at the jeoseung saja standing atop the ruined car. Shock empties his mind. Hyun-tae is working for the eoduksini? For Dok-hyun?

Sharp applause fills the room as Hyun-tae claps, his smile cruel and cold. "Well," he says softly, "this is certainly amusing."

Next to Seokga, Hani is frozen, her eyes locked on Somi. The Scarlet Fox seems to be ignoring her.

"You should see the looks on your faces," Hyun-tae continues, taking off his glasses and tossing them onto the concrete below where they shatter upon impact. "Priceless. Truly priceless." The young, eager-to-please jeoseung saja is gone. In its place is a monster with hard eyes circled by haggard shadows and a dead smile. "Did you really think it was Dok-hyun? I mean, if you did, that means I did my job well. But, still. You two are such dolts."

"It's been you," Hani rasps. "All along, it's been you. How?"

"Me." Hyun-tae smiles dully. "Yes, it's been me. This body has been . . . useful. You should have seen how the poor boy fought. It was so opportune, you know. Chang Hyun-tae was checking in to his morning shift just as I was escaping. He'd just met this one, here"—Hyun-tae gestures to Somi—"and was so distracted by his love that it was simple enough to steal his form with nobody being any the wiser. His soul is in the afterlife now." He smirks. "There is no point in trying to recover this body for him."

Look to the one with eyes of the weary.

That first time Seokga had met the grim reaper in the precinct, he'd marked him as fresh-faced. Young-looking. But then, after that first murder, Hyun-tae's eyes were bordered by that purplish bruising underneath his spectacles. Yet Seokga hadn't thought that . . .

He's a fool. An immortal fool.

"The witness. She described Dok-hyun; he attacked the precinct—" Seokga loses any semblance of his silver tongue as he gapes at the eoduksini, who shrugs.

"That poor, awkward pathologist." Hyun-tae snorts. "Exhausted from his grief, plagued by constant anxieties, friendless and lost. So alone. All he wanted from life was a bit of respite, perhaps to go grab a coffee with you, Seokga. But you held him in such disdain, even before you started connecting the wrong dots. That was courtesy of me, of course. It was easy to turn you against him, to make him my perfect red herring. I took that black coat—the Lee family coat, with the haetae—from his house. He had an extra."

Seokga briefly closes his eyes. Hyun-tae took the late Dae-song's coat.

"Then it was easy enough to look like him." Hyun-tae waves a hand. Shadows swirl upward and cover his hair, graying the white strands. He points to his shattered glasses and snickers. "A simple trick, but an effective one nonetheless. And Dok-hyun certainly wasn't the one who attacked the precinct," Hyun-tae continues with a malicious smirk, "I was. I sent in the shadows and took Dok-hyun from his cell. In the darkness, nobody was any the wiser. They all blamed him, but what would you know?"

"The ropes," Hani says slowly. "The gags, inside his house—"

"It seems poor Dok-hyun took the death of his father rather

hard," the eoduksini said, snickering. "He took up some, ah, *kinky* pastimes in the aftermath. Tried to find companionship that way. But that's not a crime, you know," he adds. "Lee Dok-hyun was innocent."

"Was?" Seokga rasps, stomach plummeting.

"Oh. Did I forget to mention? I killed him."

His heart slams wildly in his chest. Seokga does not know if it's from the caffeine, or from the shock of losing Dok-hyun. Dok-hyun, who was innocent. Dok-hyun, who he blamed. "You fucking—"

Hyun-tae chuckles. "Choi Ji-ah saw a man who exactly matched Dok-hyun's description, and she did exactly what I hoped she'd do. Further confirmed your incorrect suspicions. That was fun. And it was even more fun escorting my victims here in New Sinsi into the afterlife with them being none the wiser." His expression suddenly twists in disgust and cold fury. "Except that one girl, my first victim. Euna. She recognized me. Started screaming her fucking head off."

The fallen god swallows hard, remembering how Euna had collapsed into hysterics after Hyun-tae had knocked on the hearse's window.

"I did get a thrill out of that—and watching the two of you. Oh, yes. I've been watching you for a while. I saw," he says, looking at Hani, "*you* immediately. I felt your power, your life. Absorbing it, I knew, would be delicious. Just as delicious as killing the god who got my home locked up. But what was even more fun was watching the two of you play your little game." His eyes move to Seokga, who tightens his grip on his sword. "Yes, your little game, god, is far more interesting than you'd ever even expect. Your gumiho has been hiding a dirty little secret from you—which is in fact a very, very *big* secret. Isn't that right, Hani?"

Seokga ignores him, even as Hani tenses. The eoduksini is

trying to distract them, that much is obvious. He doesn't care about his little monologues, his explanations, his gloatings. All he wants is to kill him and be done with it. But the trickster knows that the best thing he can do right now for himself and Hani is to keep the eoduksini and Somi talking as his mind whirs through various strategies—various sequences of attack— where Seokga and his gumiho emerge victorious. Alive and well. Because if his rashness costs Hani her life . . . he could never forgive himself. "So, you've been the one ravaging New Sinsi. And you," he snarls, looking to Somi, "have been working with him."

The girl's eyes are red-rimmed as they dart toward him. "Yes," she says quietly before straightening, drawing back her shoulders and jutting out her chin. "Yes, that's true."

Bastards. Bastards, the two of them.

"Somi." Hani's voice is raw and cracking with pain. The sheer agony in it sparks a fury that Seokga has never known. "This isn't the way to do things."

Somi is silent, but Seokga thinks that she may have flinched. "Tonight's numbers," he continues, glaring at the demon. "You planned that out, didn't you? You had Somi kill seven mortals to lead us here. Because you wanted to keep toying with us. Breaking the roof, landing us in this trap of Unrulies. You should have known," he snarls, "that these Unrulies posed no threat to us. I am a god, you miserable demon. Did you really think a few dokkaebi would harm me?" Seokga is still weighing his options in his mind. If he leaps forward, sword raised in the air, taking the demon by surprise . . . Not yet, Seokga thinks, noting how Hyun-tae's eyes narrow as if the eoduksini knows precisely how his muscles have tensed. So the trickster keeps talking, letting his silver tongue do what it does best. "Are you really so foolish?"

"I thought," the eoduksini replies lazily, although his eyes are still narrowed, "that it would be entertaining to watch you fight them off. And I was right. Think of it as the appetizer before the feast." He clucks his tongue. "It is true, Seokga the Fallen, that *they* cannot kill you, but *I* can. I have had my eye on you for a while. Ever since you sauntered into the Dark World and took the throne."

"Don't act as if you weren't complicit in that," Seokga sneers. "All of you insufferable monsters were *happy* to have me. You joined my forces willingly. Bowed and simpered and kissed my ass—"

"No." The word is a venomous spit. "I didn't join your Okhwang siege, god, because it was clear to any eye that you would miserably fail. And you did. While I stayed behind in Gamangnara," the demon inhabiting Hyun-tae's body whispers, "you threw away the key to my home. The Dark World was raided, and despite my incorporeal form I was *dragged* down to Jeoseung, made to slave under that depressing administration as a torturer of the dead."

A dull pounding has started to bludgeon Seokga's temples, possibly from the caffeine but more likely from this demon's fucking *monologuing*. He struggles to maintain his composure as the eoduksini, clearly incensed, throws his hands into the air. "Do you know how *boring* that is? They're already dead! There's no point!" He shakes his head, and Seokga is unnerved to see that his lips have twisted into a hungry smile. "But this plane brims with life. You may have taken Gamangnara from me, trickster, but I'll create it anew. Your energy will be delicious, I'm sure. I have never taken the life of a god before. Or such a prolific gumiho," he adds, turning his gaze to Hani. Seokga can barely breathe through his fury. "Finally, Seokga the Fallen, Seokga the Trickster, I will have my revenge on you. Finally, after all these centuries, you will die by the hand of Eodum, devourer of worlds, monster of shadows, and reaper of chaos!"

There's a beat of silence.

Hani and Seokga exchange confused glances, and Seokga blinks. "Who?"

Hyun-tae—Eodum—gapes at him. "Who?" he echoes shrilly. "*Who?* What do you mean, *who?*"

"I mean," Seokga replies coldly, "that I don't even know who you are." He lifts his sword. The silver flashes as he raises it into the air. Seokga's other hand is still in Hani's. He dreads the moment he must let go.

Eodum snarls, quivering with rage. The shadows around them grow deeper, darker. "I will *kill* you, Seokga," he hisses. "You will know my name, then. I may not be able to drag you into unconsciousness," he adds, stepping off the car and landing on the concrete gracefully, "thanks to your little caffeine trick."

Seokga utters a curse. "You," he seethes, voice trembling with rage as he recalls opening the cabinet door to find an empty space where his coffee should have been. "I *knew* I had some bags left—" Out of all the crimes Eodum has committed, throwing away Seokga's precious caffeine is by far the worst. Violence brews in Seokga's blood.

The demon smirks. "And then you went to the store. Did you enjoy the plague demon? Imagine my disappointment when the two of you returned, alive and well. Honestly, though, I didn't think the coffee would work. I thought it was—like your Okhwang siege idea—incredibly stupid. But alas. It appears I am wrong. No matter. There are other ways to kill a god and a gumiho. As my little messenger said, your story does not have a happy ending. But first, I'm in the mood for another . . . appetizer. Somi," he says, clucking his tongue, "show our friends a lovely little welcome, will you?"

"No," Hani whispers. Her hand trembles as she withdraws it from Seokga's. "Somi, don't do it."

The other gumiho silently steps from the car. "You lied to me," Somi says in a voice trembling with ire as she focuses on

Hani. "You deceived me. You made me into this. You gave me these Cravings, this bloodlust. I'm like this because of *you*."

"Somi—"

"It's true, isn't it? Say that it's not, Hani. *Say that it's not!*"

Hani is silent.

"I see. You still haven't told him, have you?" Somi glances in Seokga's direction. He tenses as his mind stumbles slightly in confusion, even as he keeps his eyes on the eoduksini, who has begun to grin. He is trying not to listen to the babbling gumiho, but her voice carries. "I thought so," she scoffs bitterly. "You're exactly as he says that you are."

"Darling, you've been manipulated—"

"And now I can't stop," Somi pants. "I can't stop. Did you know I'm able to kill in masses now? Without even a kiss? I bet you never even figured out how to do that, Hani, but I did. *I did* because of what you made me. It's simple, really. You just have to kill them halfway, first. That's when their soul starts rising into the air. If you're quick, you can suck it in. Snatch it. Like catching a butterfly in a net." A manic, fervent glint shines in her eyes. "I have consumed so many souls, Hani."

Eodum laughs softly. "It's what makes us the perfect pair," the demon says. "We're always hungry for more."

"Shut up," Seokga snaps, heart beating wildly in his chest and sweat dribbling down his spine. Fucking caffeine. "Shut the fuck up."

Somi raises her hands, golden power brewing in her palms. "I should have known from the moment you gave me those livers. You were planning to use me as your scapegoat all along."

She takes a step toward Hani, visibly shaking. Her hands, Seokga notices as he looks to her, are stained with dried blood. Her mouth is crusted with it, and it splatters her cream-colored sweater.

Livers.

What *livers*?

The eoduksini is chuckling, and Seokga yanks his mind away from the subject. He will not allow himself to be distracted—

"Somi," Hani says, and her voice is pleading. "That's not true. Remember that I buried the evidence for you. The recordings, the bodies, I got rid of them all. Would I have done that if I am as awful as you say?"

The other gumiho falters, and so does Seokga. His mind spins with anxiety and confusion. Hani has known all along that Somi is the Scarlet Fox? She is the one who got rid of the bodies at the university, and the footage? His mouth tightens. Is it not just coincidence that Hani had spent an abnormally long time in the washroom just minutes before Shim had called Seokga to alert him to the missing evidence?

How many times has he brushed off these coincidences, too wrapped up in his changing feelings for Hani? Too reluctant, deep down, to consider what they might mean? Too frightened to be betrayed again? To be left alone?

Seokga's sword wavers, dropping to his side in confusion.

Bewildered, he glances to Hani, unable to stop his chest from clenching in betrayal. She would have kept him from becoming a god once more? All for an Unruly who happens to be her co-worker?

But what does Somi mean by *scapegoat*?

And *what livers*?

"You did what?" he asks quietly. He will give her the benefit of the doubt for now, but when this fight is over . . . He has many, many questions for Kim Hani.

Hani's eyes are wide, but she ignores him, focused only on Somi—who bunches her fists together, claws *snick*ing out. "Then tell him," she pants. "Tell him the truth, *right now*." She points to Seokga with a violently trembling finger. "Tell him, Hani."

A horrible suspicion begins to creep along the ridges of

Seokga's mind. He shoves it away. No. Not her. Not Hani. "What is she talking about?"

"I . . ." Hani turns to him, her eyes brimming with tears. "I . . ." But she cuts off with a curse, turning back to Somi, whose eyes narrow to slits.

"I see," Somi says as Eodum watches with an expression of delight and a ravenous grin. Somi is white with fury, pink-tinged tears spilling down her bloodied face. "I was right. I'm nothing but your scapegoat."

"Somi, please, listen to me. Let me explain—"

"No. No. I won't be the one to die," Somi says, steel threading through her voice. "I *can't* be the one to die." She strides toward Hani, every movement filled with purpose. Seokga once more lifts his sword into the air, but in the seconds that it takes for him to do so, the two gumiho are already in the heat of battle, a blur of claws and golden flame.

Hani dodges Somi's hurl of power, and sidesteps her punch. "Somi, you don't understand—"

"I understand just fine," Somi growls, lobbing another burst of power at Hani. Hani dodges it nimbly.

"Stop using your power." Seokga watches with his heart in his throat as Hani ducks another flare hurling toward her. "You're going to burn yourself out."

"Stop holding back!" Somi shrieks, attacking with a new frenzy. *"Fight me!"*

But Hani continues to dodge and block, never going on the offensive.

Seokga searches for a way into their battle, but if he aims for Somi, there is a great chance that he will end up striking Hani instead. There is nothing for him to do but turn toward the eoduksini, hatred strangling his vocal cords as he seethes.

"You."

Before he can think his actions through any further, Seokga

is launching himself at the eoduksini, his sword cleaving through the air—and hitting metal as Eodum easily sidesteps away from the car, looking bored. Seokga stares as protuberant black veins begin to slowly snake up the jeoseung saja's porcelain skin, curling around his arms, his neck, and creeping across his cruel face. The evidence of the darkness within Hyun-tae's body moves, slithering across his form like live serpents, as Eodum chuckles.

"Come now, god," he says, pulling shadows toward him until he holds strands of darkness in his hands like whips. "Surely you don't truly believe that you stand even so much as the slightest chance." With a sharp, fluid movement, Eodum flicks his wrist. Seokga bites down on a cry of pain as shadow—cold, sharp shadow—pierces his skin and sends him flying backward. Blood seeps from the wound in his chest as he climbs to his feet, panting. Eodum sighs. "Your fight is for naught."

Behind him, Seokga hears Hani grunt in pain. But he cannot take his eyes off the eoduksini, not now. "Foul, sniveling creature," he sneers, reaching for his power, emerald magic snaking toward the demon, cutting through its shadows. *Restrain him,* he orders it, sweat dribbling down his temples. *Restrain him.* It is easier to access this magic than usual, thanks to the caffeine—but it also makes it harder to control. Seokga fumbles to guide it to where it must go, but his mind is an eddy of anxiety, and his bloodstream runs hot with something close to panic. "I am a god—"

Eodum waves off the emerald threads as if they're vaguely annoying fruit flies. "Perhaps you could have bested me when you were Seokga the God. But now, Seokga the Fallen . . ." He smiles and sends a wave of darkness tearing toward Seokga. "Well. This is almost too easy."

Seokga chokes as he drowns in the shadow, pain bursting through his limbs as what feels like thousands of honed knives dig into his flesh, thousands of fists beat at his skull. Eodum's voice is cruelly amused as it whispers along the planes of his consciousness.

"Accept your fate, Seokga the Fallen, and perhaps I will let the gumiho live."

Seokga sputters on his own blood, blind, utterly trapped—

A flare of vicious, burning light blinds him. Shatters the darkness into pieces like shards of glass exploding from a fallen wineglass. Seokga gasps, wheezing, as he meets Hani's eye from across the warehouse. She is still occupied with Somi, her face cut and bruised, but one golden-glowing hand is outstretched toward him as the other fends off Somi's attacks.

How? Seokga thinks, dragging himself to his feet with his sword. *How does she have enough power to do that?*

Hani has been wielding her fox bead for too long now. And somehow—she has not burnt herself out. For a gumiho to possess this much power, she'd have to have consumed thousands of souls.

Not now. Focus. Seokga attacks, slicing through the air with as much speed, as much strength as he possesses. But another blow of black has him blinded, gritting his teeth as Hyun-tae's chuckle weaves around him in a sinister caress. He swipes blindly with his blade to no avail. It is only when Hani's power shatters the darkness again that he is able to strike, drawing blood from Hyun-tae as he slashes his sword across his chest.

For a moment, neither creature moves, both staring at the blood dripping from the gash. But then the eoduksini snarls, all humor disappearing from his face. "That was a mistake."

A maw of roaring darkness swallows Seokga whole.

CHAPTER FORTY-FIVE

HANI

SEOKGA IS SCREAMING.

Screaming, his voice broken and raw and full of pain as the eoduksini sends wave after wave of darkness crashing down upon him. There is too much shadow—enough that Hani cannot manage to fend off the gloom while also fending off Somi.

His scream shatters something inside of her.

Hani has been holding back. But not anymore.

"You get one chance," she warns, flicking her wrists. The scarlet daggers slide into her hands, their ruby red gleam reflecting in Somi's eyes as she gapes, faltering in her attack. "You have one chance to leave this warehouse, Somi. Because if you don't, I cannot promise you that I will not hurt you. Not while your new friend is hurting *him*." Something has snapped, some primitive creature of wild wickedness finally rising to the surface, freed from the bonds that have kept it in place for the last one hundred and four years. "Know, Somi, that I'm sorry for the harm that I caused you. I *am*. But the eoduksini plans to do far worse. I won't stand by and let this world burn to the ground." She twirls her daggers as Seokga's screams grow desperate. Every part of her aches to run to him, but she must tend to this first—this friend turned foe. "So leave now, or I will not be held accountable for what I choose to do next."

Somi visibly swallows, her eyes darting from Hani's daggers to her face and back again.

"You have three seconds," Hani says, her voice lethally soft. "One."

The other gumiho takes a small step back.

"Two."

Hani watches as something in Somi's expression shifts. As apprehension turns to bloodlust. As her lips pull back from her teeth, contorted in hatred.

Fine, then.

There is no going back—no mending the shredding ties between them—as Hani breathes, *"Three."*

Somi flinches even as she raises her fists. As if she has realized that the creature looking at her from behind Hani's eyes is no longer her coworker from the Creature Café.

No, it is the Scarlet Fox.

And Somi never stood a chance.

One blow to the stomach from Hani's foot. An uppercut to the jaw. A hard slam on the head by the hilt of Hani's dagger.

The gumiho crumples to the ground, unconscious but alive, as Hani sheathes her weapons back underneath her sleeves and turns toward Eodum, who gleefully attacks Seokga's limp figure. Between the flashes of darkness she can just barely make out his face as it knots with pain, and his back as it arches off the ground.

Fury like she has never known before fills her blood as Seokga's screams die, replaced by whimpers of agony.

Whimpers.

Seokga, god of deceit, god of mischief, god of malice, is *whimpering.*

Hani grits her teeth and lets power siphon from her bead into the palms of her hands, her skin searing as she summons more. More. *More.* Centuries of accumulated energy gathers as she stalks toward Eodum, the rapid beating of her heart and the thumping of her boots against the ground a battle song.

"Hey," she snarls, as her palms scream in pain from the white-

hot power burning within them. Eodum falters, looking up—and she unleashes herself.

An ocean of golden energy crashes toward the inky darkness, molten flame crackling as it pounds against the shadow, shattering it into a million obsidian shards. It's less precise than it could be, after drowning herself in caffeine and subjecting herself to shaky limbs, but it's effective enough.

She sneers as Eodum makes a noise of choked fury, gathering whips of darkness into his hands. "Don't even fucking *try*," she growls, sending another energy explosion toward him. The warehouse shakes as the golden power meets its mark, more debris tumbling from the broken rooftop. Eodum hits a cement pillar, groaning as he staggers forward. His eyes blaze. Blood drips from a gash on his forehead.

Hani grimaces, still gathering more power from her fox bead. "I'm not done yet," she warns, even as a rational part of her mind begs her to slow down. Depleting one's fox bead results in death, and the amount that she's gathering now is dangerously close to all of it.

Eodum laughs, but there is no amusement in his tone. Nothing but vehemence and violence. "You'll regret doing that."

"Maybe," she pants. "Or maybe not. And I'm leaning toward *not*."

As Seokga groans on the ground, the demon stalks toward her, shadows lashing through the air. Hani chokes as one shadow-whip meets her side, its bite icy-cold and cutting deep.

More, she demands of herself. *I'll drain my fucking fox bead if I have to.*

Eodum sneers, a wave of darkness looming behind him. "It seems I underestimated you, Kim Hani."

She smiles sweetly even as her arms blister and boil with the amount of power she has begun to collect in her palms. "You did," she purrs.

And as the wave of darkness roars toward her, Hani channels the entirety of her focus on the darkness demon inhabiting Hyun-tae's body.

Pure, undiluted power stolen through centuries of devouring souls boils through her blood. Pain strangles her as she bites back a scream. It hurts—oh, gods. It burns. It really, really burns.

But Seokga is wounded. And even whole, even at his full strength, he is still no match for the demon. He is no longer a god, and she is the only one left standing. She has to try—has to at least *attempt* to put an end to the eoduksini's terror on Iseung.

So as the darkness approaches her, Hani aims for Eodum, her fingers splayed, her skin bubbling with burns.

And Kim Hani explodes.

Brilliant, bright power erupts from her hands, blazing through the darkness with unadulterated strength and, in a rush of molten gold, cleaves through the eoduksini's chest.

Hyun-tae staggers, smoke unfurling from where a burning, gaping hole smolders.

Again. Gritting her teeth against the agony, Hani sends another flare of earthshaking power toward the eoduksini. It hits its mark. Eodum falls, but does not turn to ash.

The eoduksini is still alive.

She cannot allow that.

And neither can she stop the cry of pain that bubbles up in her throat as she summons the last dregs of her power, the collection of centuries of killing, of her London feast. Her arms are bright and red, the skin blistered beyond repair, as she sends the final flames of her golden energy soaring toward Hyun-tae's body, ripping through the air, a gilded blade.

She does not see if Eodum turns to ash or not. She does not see if he becomes nothingness, flecks of dark dust floating to the ground. She hopes, but she does not see.

For Kim Hani's eyes are squeezed shut as she screams in

agony, her arms smoking. She collapses on the ground as a terrible, fiery pain wracks her every nerve, her every cell, every single molecule of her being. Her back arches from the ground. She is being shredded to tatters, burning and burning and burning as molten needles peel her skin from her bones. She knows that if she attempts to summon her fox bead, there will be no answer. It is gone, only smoldering embers that will never light again in its place.

She has burned herself out.

And that means . . . That means that she is dying.

Somewhere, through her ragged screams, a small part of Hani is able to think. To reflect. *Dying.* It's an odd word, carrying with it the connotation of a closing chapter. The end of a line. She can't be dying—there is so much more she must do. Needs to do. She needs to apologize to Somi. To apologize, with every ounce of her being, with a raw, wounded sincerity. She needs to show Seokga how to make gimbap. Needs to wake up in his arms and study his serene, sleeping face. Needs to taunt and tease him until his scowl melts into a smile.

But she's dying.

Dying.

It's strange, dying.

At least it will end soon, a voice whispers wryly against the pain. *That's the beauty of dying. It can't last forever . . .*

Somewhere, Hani is vaguely aware of a groan. Seokga is crawling toward her, blood trickling from his mouth, his nose. "Hani," he is rasping. "Hani."

She struggles to open her eyes, to shut her mouth against the cries. She only partially succeeds, able to open her eyes, to study Seokga's face as she sobs. He, too, is weeping, weeping in agony and heartbreak as one of his dirty, trembling fingers grabs her ruined ones. "Hani—no. No, you *cannot.*" Some of that old, cruel fury twists his mouth. "You *cannot* die. You *cannot* . . . " He doubles over on his side, scarlet splattering the pavement.

Seokga is wounded. Badly.

And he is dying, too.

It is evident in the pallor of his skin, the dismal dullness in his emerald eyes as he turns to her again. The fallen god is dying, and he knows it.

"I will admit," a voice rasps, "that your efforts were . . . valiant."

No . . . Impossible.

Across the warehouse, Eodum is standing, one hand pressed to the wound on his chest and a terrible smile stretching his split lips to show bloodied teeth. Shadows slither up his body, patching the wounds with inky darkness. "But as I . . . said," he continues haltingly, wincing as he cracks his neck once. Twice. "The story of the god and the gumiho does not have . . . a happy ending."

Hani's screams die in her mouth, her pain trumped for a brief moment by horror. Horror and shock. And fucking *fury*.

The eoduksini lives.

Despite everything, the eoduksini *lives*.

No. No. Hani fights to breathe, clinging on to life with every breath remaining in her lungs. She will stay to see this through . . . somehow.

There must be a way.

There *has* to be a way.

Her eyes frantically move from Hyun-tae as he lifts his arms, shadows flocking to his command, to Seokga, limp and dying.

Seokga the Fallen, dying.

No—there is a way. There *is* a way . . . if Hwanin so allows it.

Her mouth has begun to fill with blood.

Somehow, she knows that Hwanin is watching, that the emperor of the gods' strange eyes are fixated on the scene in the warehouse from his throne in Okhwang. On his brother, who, despite everything, he does not want to die. She can feel them, ancient and watchful, trained on the three figures in the Iseung warehouse.

I do not want you to die, little brother. Those had been his parting words in the restaurant that day. Hani's eavesdropping ears had picked them up well.

I do not want you to die.

So as she chokes on scarlet copper, for the first time in her life, Kim Hani prays to Hwanin, the god-king. Hwanin, Seokga's older brother.

Hwanin, she thinks through the fog of agony, of death, *I know that you are listening. I know that you are watching.*

And I know that you see that your brother is balancing on the brink of death.

For a few brief moments, the silence in her mind is deafening. But then—

The warehouse seems to fall away, scattering in the wind, swirling into nothingness. Hani drifts along the stream of nonexistence, wondering worriedly if she has passed through the veil separating life and death. If she is taking the Hwangcheon Road to Jeoseung, if she is floating atop the Seocheongang River toward Yeomra's halls. A small part of her marvels at this nothingness. She has never seen nothingness before. Everything else before this has been somethingness. But . . .

Surely this means that she is dead.

"Not dead," a cool voice says as she is pulled through the void. "I wish to speak to you, Kim Hani." And out of the fascinating nothingness steps Hwanin, his expression somber, his eyes dotted with millions of stars. "For you have come to bargain."

CHAPTER FORTY-SIX

HANI

THE VAST NOTHINGNESS IS REPLACED, ALL AT ONCE, BY somethingness.

Hani stands in the middle of a lavish throne room, her muddied combat boots glaringly out of place atop the glossy black floor that is so polished she is able to see her reflection in it. Scarlet pillars hold up a cavernous ceiling of rich red wood swirling with golden paint depicting stars, moons, and suns.

She is, somehow, in Okhwang. The heavenly kingdom of the gods.

Before her sits an impressive dais, a flight of ruby stairs leading to a wide, high-backed throne on which sits Hwanin. With a jolt, she realizes he is watching her.

He observes her impassively, his chin tilted slightly upward, his hands laced together in his lap. Hwanin wears a traditional, flowing hanbok of the deepest blue, a sash of pure white ribbon around his waist. By his side stands a younger god with the same long silver hair, although his eyes are different, dark blue yet lacking the star-dotted depths. This, Hani knows, must be Hwanung. Hwanin's son.

Hani gives a bow of great reverence, kneeling on the ground, clasping her hands before her forehead, which nearly touches the floor. Her arms, she realizes, lack the awful burns that she acquired only minutes ago. Hani does not try to ponder this, not when her mind is already drowning in an ocean of panic. Only when Hwanin says quietly, "Rise," does she do so.

"So," Hwanin, emperor of the gods, says softly. "Kim Hani."

Hani juts out her chin, unable to help the defensiveness that rises within her at his disapproving tone. "That's me," she retorts sharply. *And what about it?* Hwanung stiffens, but Hwanin seems unfazed.

As Seokga's older brother, it is likely that it will take much more to throw him.

"I heard your prayer." Hwanin tilts his head. "It was very loud, Kim Hani. You practically screamed it at me. It was not very easy to ignore. My ears are still ringing."

"The eoduksini—"

"Yes, I'm aware of the events currently occurring in the warehouse." Hwanin sighs. "Yeomra needs to keep his employees more in check. This rogue eoduksini has given me my first migraine in six hundred and twenty-eight years."

She doesn't care about his *migraine.* "Seokga is dying," Hani snaps. "And so am I. Nothing is standing in the way of the eoduksini doing as he so wishes. I call upon you, Hwanin, to loan your divine intervention—"

"I am not currently interested in facing the eoduksini," Hwanin replies evenly. "Let's see how Seokga fares, first."

She barely bites back a string of insults and instead quivers with rage. "You would leave Seokga to fend for himself? He'll die within *minutes* if you don't act." Perhaps she has overestimated Hwanin's willingness to save his brother. Perhaps all of this—the eoduksini, his deal with Seokga—was a ploy to get rid of the fallen god once and for all.

As if sensing her suspicion, Hwanung frowns at her. "Let my father continue."

Hani bites down on her tongue and glowers at the two gods.

"On the contrary." Hwanin leans forward in his seat. "Seokga will die within minutes if *you* do not act, Kim Hani."

She falters. "What—"

"A bargain," Hwanin replies, gesturing at Hwanung. "A compromise."

Hani waits, every passing moment feeling like an eternity. *What is happening in the warehouse? Is Seokga still conscious?*

"My original deal with Seokga may be familiar to you," Hwanin continues. "Should Seokga the Fallen kill both the Scarlet Fox and the eoduksini, he will be reinstated to his former position as a god. Well. I am willing to modify it—just slightly."

"What do you mean?" Hani breathes. "What do I have to do?"

"I know your secret, Kim Hani." His eyes glitter. "You are the Scarlet Fox."

She stiffens. "Yes." She shouldn't be surprised that Hwanin knows. At this point, who *doesn't* know?

Seokga doesn't, she reminds herself bitterly. *He doesn't yet know. Right?*

"I am willing to fulfill this bargain halfway. I see now that Seokga will not be able to best the eoduksini in his current state. It's grown too strong too quickly. That is something I didn't account for. I expected for him to find it immediately, battle it, and kill it. This was not the case. So, let me make an adjustment to my promise." He glances to Hwanung. "Modify the bargain as this, son: Should Seokga kill one of the two Unrulies formerly mentioned, he will immediately regain one half of his former power. Should he kill the other one of two Unrulies formerly mentioned, he will immediately regain the other half of his former power and be reinstated to his former position, effective immediately. On Hwanung, god of laws and kept promises, I so swear this."

Should Seokga kill one of the two Unrulies formerly mentioned, he will immediately regain one half of his former power.

Hwanung closes his eyes, clasping his father's hand in his. "It is done," he says a moment later, opening his eyes. They glow azure for a moment before flickering back to their normal dark blue.

"You can do that?" Hani rasps. "You can modify promises sworn on Hwanung?"

Hwanin smiles a tight, bland smile. "I'm his father. I'm able to pull some strings. It is easiest to do when the newly modified promise requires more pain and sacrifice than the first." He holds her gaze. "I think, Kim Hani, you know the deal that I am offering."

She does.

And she manages, just barely, a slight nod.

"And before I send your consciousness back to the mortal realm, Kim Hani, let me ask you this." Hwanin's voice, although steady, carries an undercurrent of uncertainty. "My brother . . . cares for you. It is hard for me to discern why. I do not know if he cares about you enough to mourn what follows, but that is Seokga's nature. He loves only himself, nobody else."

That's not true. But Hani only scowls at the clear insult and folds her arms. "What are you trying to say?" she snaps. "Spit it out."

Hwanung stares at her. "You dare—"

"How did you do it?" Hwanin glowers right back at her, finally shedding his calm façade. "How did you convince him to care for you?"

He's jealous, Hani realizes slowly. *Jealous that Seokga has chosen me to see the side of him that is kind. That is . . . loving.* The realization seems irrelevant in the face of what she knows she must do next, but she still somehow senses that Hwanin's envy is a monumental sign of a new life ahead of Seokga. A new life in Okhwang. A life of peace.

Without her.

Hwanin glares at her, waiting for an answer.

But Hani just shrugs and gives him a wicked grin. "Let me reincarnate after my death," she says, "and I'll tell you everything you need to know." There's no way that she won't be sent to Jeoseung's torture chambers and seven hells, but it's worth a shot.

The heavenly emperor coughs. "You've killed more people than any gumiho in history."

"Thank you."

"You're not reincarnating. And I see that you don't plan to inform me of your strategies. Fine." Hwanin scowls, and for a moment, the family resemblance between him and Seokga is clear. "Goodbye, Kim Hani."

Before she even has time to blink, the god snaps his fingers and the world goes white.

CHAPTER FORTY-SEVEN
SEOKGA

"Hani," Seokga rasps, tasting tears and blood as he bends over her, as if to shield her from the approaching eoduksini. The gumiho is limp, unmoving. Her arms are burnt beyond repair. He cannot tell if she is breathing.

A wine-brown gaze, heavy and dull with pain, meets his as her eyes fly open. Alive—she's alive. But for how long?

"Hani," he whispers as the warehouse grows darker. Eodum is summoning the darkness to him as he makes his way toward Hani and Seokga, his rage palpable as he uses his shadows to pull Hyun-tae's flesh back over his wounds. This is it. . . . This is the end.

She blinks up at him through a glaze of tears. "Seokga," she whispers. Seokga barely notices that one of her ruined hands is moving, fumbling in her pocket for something. "This world will . . . see the morning dawn again." She reaches for his hand, and he lets her take it. They will go together.

Hani gazes up at him, blood leaking from her mouth. "I need you to know," she whispers, "that it wasn't all . . . a lie. I . . . promise."

She's delirious, the color leeching from her skin with every passing second. "Hani," he whispers, "just close your eyes." He glances behind him at the approaching eoduksini only a few feet away. Shadows circle his arms, darkness flowing behind him like a cape. Seokga struggles to stand. He will make a final attempt—

But Hani pulls him back down with what must be the last of her strength, her eyes wide. "Seokga," she whispers. "Seokga."

He shakes his head. No. This cannot be the last time that she says his name.

She smiles up at him, a bright, beautiful thing even as blood dribbles from her mouth. "Make him suffer," she whispers, and presses something cold into his right hand.

It happens so quickly that Seokga does not have time to realize that it is a hilt of a dagger—a scarlet dagger—before she is gripping his hand in hers and dragging the tip of the blade downward to her chest.

Hani guides the dagger they both hold through her heart.

CHAPTER FORTY-EIGHT

HANI

I HAD TO, HANI THINKS AS SHE STARES UP AT SEOKGA, her own scarlet dagger embedded in her chest. His face is stricken with horror, and she thinks he might be screaming her name . . . But she cannot hear anything anymore. Can barely even see.

I'm sorry, she wants to say, but her tongue is limp and useless in her mouth. *I'm sorry, I'm sorry.*

But this is my sacrifice.

For you.

For Somi.

Hani's lashes begin to flutter shut.

All my life, I have been selfish.

I want my ending to be selfless.

As Hani closes her eyes for the last time, a final tear streaks down her bloodied cheek.

CHAPTER FORTY-NINE
SEOKGA

Seokga watches that final tear slip down Hani's still, lifeless face.

The world has never been so silent.

It is as if he has been sucked into a vacuum where nothing exists but the pounding in his skull and the icy horror that has begun to freeze over his bones.

"Hani," he thinks he might be saying over and over and over, but the noises spilling from his mouth are guttural, animalistic, lacking all semblance of speech.

She is dead.

Dead, by his own doing. Seokga stares at his hands. Horror and betrayal dim his vision to black. He doesn't understand. He doesn't *understand*.

This is a nightmare, he thinks through the growing roar inside his head. *This is a nightmare brought upon me by the eoduksini.*

It is not real. It *cannot* be real.

Kim Hani cannot be dead.

Dead, with a scarlet dagger embedded in her chest.

A scarlet dagger.

Realization knocks the remaining breath out of Seokga's lungs. His vision clears in a flare of light. His horror doubles tenfold.

A scarlet dagger. A scarlet *fucking* dagger.

. . . Look to one with the eyes of the teary . . .

As Hani's last teardrop finally splatters to the concrete floor, the sound of it seems to echo through the warehouse. Through Seokga's soul.

It was never Nam Somi.

. . . The ones you seek are closer than you imagine, but you are alone, god, in a sea of deception . . .

No. *No.*

Seokga cradles Hani's head in his hands. Her skin is cold, like stone. A shard of pain stabs at his stomach as her hair falls into her face. As he sees, for the first time, the small patch of red at the very top of her scalp.

. . . Let your mind not be fooled by surface perceptions . . . Verity, hidden beneath insincerity . . .

"*Arrgghh!*" Seokga's back arches as his blood heats, boiling, a transformation wracking his body. Something ancient and potent surges through his veins, singing through his bloodstream as it floods his body. *Back. Finally, finally back.*

The pain inflicted by the eoduksini's attacks fades. In its place is a familiar thrumming. His muscles spasm as electricity shoots through them, sparking a fire in its wake.

His power.

It is back.

Not all of it, Seokga realizes dimly as Eodum approaches, shadowed whip lashing through the air. Not all of it, but a good portion. With the rush of magic running through his veins, it almost seems as if the demon is moving in slow motion. He reaches for those emerald threads, finding them solid. Whole. An arsenal of weapons at his disposal.

His eyes linger on Hani's dead body. On the lips that will never smirk again, never bite out a witty retort. On the eyes that will never alight with that sparkling, sunny laughter.

Seokga looks once more at that scarlet dagger and as a sob pushes its way up his throat, it occurs to him that he has suspected her identity for a while, now. More so than he has even allowed himself to realize, pushing the suspicions from his mind, unable to confront the possibility. Wishing to remain in a reality that was always too good to be true. Echoes of memories flit through his mind, carrying with them the sweet scent of citrus, and the sharp sting of betrayal that he is all too familiar with.

What would you do? If it was me instead of Somi? He remembers her face in those moments as she posed that question, so hesitant and wary. And afraid. *Would you kill me?*

He shirked away from that hypothetical that wasn't a hypothetical, after all, unable to face the truth—or even allow himself to ponder whether there was something more behind her words because . . . because . . .

Even if it meant wandering Iseung for an eternity more, Seokga would not have been able to kill Kim Hani. Would not have been able to kill the Scarlet Fox.

But she is *dead*.

Fuck all matters to him now.

A wrath unlike anything Seokga the Fallen has ever known rears its head, an ugly monster with a gnashing maw, thirsty for blood.

As the darkness comes for him, Seokga turns.

And he *fights*.

CHAPTER FIFTY

SEKGA

South Korea will later announce New Sinsi's violent trembling as an earthquake. Startled civilians will avoid high places for the next few weeks, terrified of another incident. But the truth is that the city shakes as a god and a demon battle for the fate of the world.

Seokga dodges a wave of darkness with ease, stepping from one point of the warehouse to another, jumping through space in little more than a half second. Teleportation. Oh, how he's missed it.

His sword sings in his grip as he stalks toward Eodum. The demon has committed a multitude of sins. Should he wish to, Seokga can control him.

Hani had wanted the eoduksini to suffer. And compulsion is not suffering.

Pain is.

Seokga snarls as he aims to plunge the blade of his sword into Eodum's side. The eoduksini whips away and sends another wave of hungry shadows toward him. Seokga transports himself so that he stands directly in front of Eodum, the darkness failing to reach him. *"You,"* he growls hoarsely, leveling his blade at the eoduksini's throat, *"took everything from me."*

Eodum grins, but it is a grin filled with pain. Hani's attacks weakened him considerably. His chest bubbles with burns, even underneath the sinewy darkness patching his wounds. "I see you've regained a few of your powers," he rasps. "How fascinating." The shadows of the warehouse dim as Seokga's blade caresses his neck, the flesh beneath it shivering. "I wonder what sort of deal the gumiho struck with your brother."

Seokga's hand trembles with grief and fury. The blade nicks the eoduksini's neck, drawing blood. He can end it here, end it now. But—

I wonder what sort of deal the gumiho struck with your brother.

Hani. Hani, the Scarlet Fox, who died by his hand. The bargain between Seokga and his brother. The power that he possesses that feels, beyond a doubt, as if it is half of what it once was. Exactly half.

Half of a bargain fulfilled.

Half of my power returned.

Seokga closes his eyes and listens to the sound of his own heart breaking, over and over and over again.

The eoduksini coughs. The sound is wet and bubbling in his throat. "I just want to go back," he rasps, glossy blood slipping through his lips. "I want my home again. I could have remade it here."

Bitter, acidic self-hatred sears Seokga's throat like sickness. If the Dark World hadn't been locked, the eoduksini would not be here. Hani would be alive.

Hani . . .

"I will take my time on you, I think," Seokga whispers, hardly able to breathe as he stares at the creature looking through the jeoseung saja's eyes. "I will make you scream before the end of this."

Eodum pales.

And Seokga keeps true to his word.

CHAPTER FIFTY-ONE

HANI

IT IS AN ODD THING TO BE A SOUL WITHOUT A BODY.
As Seokga stands over the heap of ash that was once the eoduksini, Hani's soul steps out of the shadows of the warehouse. The sky above is tinged with sunlight, casting a soft yellow glow into the abandoned building. Dawn has come, sweeping away the darkness from the city of New Sinsi with slender, rose-tinged fingers. The light has broken, beautiful and bright.

The eoduksini is dead, and the world is at peace.

Hani walks, her feet barely brushing the ground, to the god's side. Even from there, she can feel it. The power rolling from him in waves. He is a god once more, free to go to Okhwang.

But he does not leave.

Seokga stumbles to Hani's body and sinks to his knees, silently sobbing. Hani stares at herself, dead and cold, with an odd feeling of detachment. That is her, and yet it is not.

It is nothing without her soul in it. It is not *her* without her soul in it.

Hani places a raw, ruined hand on Seokga's back. It drifts through him, translucent, but somehow, Seokga still senses it. Senses *her*.

He raises his head, his bloodshot eyes finding hers. "Hani," he whispers.

"The jeoseung saja will be coming for me soon," she says quietly and swallows hard. "To . . . take me to Jeoseung." *To take me to the seven hells.* Hani will never be reincarnated, not with the blood on her hands. The gods, unfortunately, do not share the belief that gumiho are meant to kill. She glances toward Nam Somi's unconscious body, lying limply feet away. "Do not hurt her, Seokga. I turned her into what she is. I . . . She's right. I corrupted her. She was never the Scarlet Fox. It was me, all along." The confession spills from her lips, and it tastes like bitter cloves.

Seokga is shaking his head fervently, his eyes wide and lips thin. She knows that he does not want to hear of this treachery, but he must. He *must* understand.

"I took the job as your assistant to steer you in the wrong direction. I heard Hyun-tae speaking of it with Shim in the Creature Café. I saw the opportunity, and I grabbed it by its throat." Hani glances back to Seokga, to his pain-wracked expression, his reddened eyes. "Let Somi go. She will learn, in time, to manage her Cravings." She hopes, desperately, that she speaks the truth.

Seokga is silent, and she cannot tell if the brokenness within his gaze is one of betrayal or grief. His cheeks are stained with tears, and he leans on his sword as if without it he would crumple to the ground—a puppet cut free of its strings. The horrible words continue to roll from her tongue, gaining momentum and speed as she rushes to explain, to make him understand. "Hwanin offered me a solution. He modified your bargain. It had to happen, to defeat the demon. Without your power, you would have died, and Iseung would have been transformed into the Dark World."

"But you died," Seokga snarls. His voice cracks, and his snarl gives way to a tremoring whisper. "You *died,* Hani."

She manages a small smile. "I did," she says, hardly believing it herself. None of this feels real. It's as if she is in another nightmare, one that she can never wake from. "But you have what you wanted—"

"What I wanted," Seokga retorts, holding a hand to his chest where his heart still beats, "was *you.* I wanted for the sun to shine on us again, Hani. I made you a promise. A promise on Hwanung—"

"Look." Hani lifts her head up to the sky. The dawn has spread now, creeping along the sky in a flush of Midas gold tinged pink. "The sun shines on us, Seokga. We've won."

"That isn't what I meant," he rasps. "Hani, that isn't what I meant at all."

She shakes her head. "Sometimes, promises are fulfilled in strange ways." Hani swallows tears as she cups Seokga's face between her hands, trying not to sob at the way they pass through his skin, utterly inconsequential.

"You will be reborn," Seokga insists, breathing unevenly. "I will find you, Hani, wherever you go. Whoever you are."

"Seokga," she murmurs, "rebirth isn't an option for me."

"No." His eyes widen. "No."

Hani shrugs, even as her stomach clenches at the prospect of an eternity of torment. Perhaps Eodum will even be the one inflicting it. But she must act strong—for Seokga. "If hell has visiting hours, you can find me there."

As if on cue, the sound of tires crunching on gravel sounds from the outside of the warehouse. A jeoseung saja has come for her.

The other Unrulies turned to ash when they died, flitting to Jeoseung without the luxury of an escort. Yet here Hani stands— the most Unruly of them all—with her body lying whole and intact on the floor. With a hearse waiting outside.

She does not quite know what this means.

Perhaps . . . perhaps the Scarlet Fox died a hero. Not enough to absolve her of her sins, but just enough to descend into the hells with dignity and honor.

"I'm sorry," Hani whispers, staring up at Seokga—the god

whose scowls melt into smiles, whose eyes are capable of thaw-
ing from a frigid ice to a sparkling warmth. "I'm so sorry. For
everything."

"No," he whispers. "Hani, no. I am the one who is sorry."

"You have nothing to apologize for."

"My hand"—the trauma in his voice is thick and ragged—"it
killed you."

"It was my choice," Hani says firmly. "My decision. My hand
guiding yours. And I am glad that it did." She doesn't turn as she
hears the padlock binding the warehouse's door being broken,
nor as the doors groan open. "Go to Okhwang, Seokga. Go back
to your palace. Live as you've longed to for years. I'll be fine."

A blatant lie. Hani is going to suffer for an eternity, and she is
very much not looking forward to it. But she keeps her smile,
gentle and reassuring, pasted on her lips as she brushes a ghost of
a kiss against Seokga's. Their lips do not touch, not really, but
even so—there seems to be a flicker of warmth against hers as she
pulls away. "Maybe you can convince Yeomra to go easy on me."

"Kim Hani?" a new voice calls. A jeoseung saja steps into the
warehouse, his somber eyes going to Hani. "Age one thousand
and seven hundred years. Died from depleting fox bead and a
wound to the heart. Is this you?"

The word sticks to the back of Hani's throat, but she forces
it out with difficulty. "Yes."

"No." Seokga whirls toward the grim reaper, his eyes bright
with pain and his sword raised. "You can't take her," he warns,
voice little more than a snarl. "You *won't* take her. Stay back." He
steps in front of Hani, who easily passes through him. She turns
to look at him one last time.

"Goodbye, Seokga," she whispers, tracing the planes of his
face, memorizing their sharp angles and cold contours. She will
keep this memory of him close to her when she is enduring her
eternal punishment.

"Hani . . ."

As her heart shatters, she leans forward. Her phantom lips brush over his and he trembles, shaking his head. Hani pulls away, and he reaches for her, fingertips passing through her shoulder. Never to touch her again.

As glorious sunlight creeps over New Sinsi like an egg yolk seeping out from its shattered porcelain shell, Hani turns and follows the jeoseung saja out of the warehouse. Follows him into the sleek black hearse.

She does not look back.

Hani doesn't know whether to be relieved or disappointed that Seokga does not follow as she begins her descent into Jeoseung.

CHAPTER FIFTY-TWO

HWANIN

The doors to the throne room slam open with enough force that the walls of Cheonha Palace shake.

His brother's temper tantrums tend to start like this. In an ever-changing world, the door-slamming performance put on by his sibling is the one constant.

Oh, great, Hwanin thinks, exchanging a wary look with his son. *Here we go.*

Seokga strides into the throne room, his eyes bloodshot and wild, his sword swinging through the air as he fends off the cluster of royal guards that have attempted to prevent his entry. His hair is matted with blood, his skin dappled with cuts and bruises. Hwanin suppresses a sigh as his brother sends the guards crashing to the ground and starts toward him. *"Brother,"* he growls, storming up the stairs to the throne. *"What have you done?"*

"Hello and welcome to you, too," Hwanin says, waving a hand at Hwanung in dismissal.

"Father," Hwanung protests under his breath, "I do not think that I should leave you alone with Uncle—"

"Go," Hwanin insists gently. He is fairly certain that he can handle Seokga, even in his rage, quite well by himself. If worse comes to worst, he'll simply banish him. Again.

Glaring, Hwanung begins to dematerialize, no doubt scampering off to sulk with his newest female friend. Hwanin cuts his gaze to the guards pulling themselves to their feet and groaning in pain. "Out, all of you."

Seokga is breathing heavily. Hwanin tilts his head. He has never seen his younger brother so . . . panicked. So . . . emotional. Even when he was sentenced to his punishment on Iseung, he was more collected than this.

"Did you know?" Seokga demands, his voice tattered with rage and grief and fury. "Were you watching all this time? Did you know that Hyun-tae was the eoduksini? That Hani was the Scarlet Fox?"

Hwanin sighs thinly through his nose. He has been expecting this question. "The knowledge of the heavens is mine," he says slowly. "Yes, Seokga, I knew about Kim Hani. But Eodum escaped my notice. He transferred bodies in Jeoseung, where the heavens are blind. But he was still clever about it. Even Yeomra did not see." Tricky, awful creature.

Hwanin had known Kim Hani, the Scarlet Fox, was eavesdropping in that New Sinsi restaurant the day he summoned Seokga to make him his offer. But it was Hwanin's wish to see Seokga struggle to uncover the Unruly gumiho's identity, to see him struggle to reclaim his title of a god.

And a small, spiteful part of him had chosen to remain silent as he'd watched the girl join Seokga's side as his assistant, and then friend, and then lover. Hwanin had desired to see him betrayed as he had been, six hundred and twenty-eight years ago. But as he'd watched Seokga begin to . . . care for the gumiho, he'd found himself enraptured. The man Seokga became around that woman was so different from the brother he has known.

He had been both confused and fascinated by it. So he said nothing, merely continuing to observe. At one point, he sent Hwanung down to Iseung to bring him a box of movie-theater popcorn with extra butter. The story of the god and the gumiho was an addicting drama.

Yet Hwanin does not feel the need to explain himself and his reasonings to Seokga. Instead, he simply says, "This was your fight, brother. I did not see any reason for me to intrude, nor to guide you."

"*You,*" Seokga snarls, and Hwanin is taken aback to see that his brother is . . . *crying.* Tears are rolling down his bloodied cheeks, undoubtedly stinging his cuts and wounds. "You told Hani that—"

Indignant, Hwanin straightens at his lack of gratitude. He has expected thanks, not these ungrateful attacks. "That if she died by your hand, half of your powers would return? Yes. I did. And I kept to my word. The eoduksini has returned to Jeoseung, where Yeomra has taken it upon himself to ensure it never again escapes. Iseung is saved from becoming a Dark World. You are a god once more. You have returned to Okhwang. What else do you want?" Hwanin frowns. "Do not tell me that you mourn for this woman." Is his passion for the gumiho not fleeting? Does it remain with him, even after death? Impossible. "She was going to die, anyway. I gave her death meaning. You ought to be thanking me."

He watches as Seokga flinches. "You made me kill her," his brother rasps. "You—you made me fucking *kill her.*" His voice sounds as if he is in a choke hold. He sways in his spot, unsteady. "I-I *killed her.*"

Hwanin calmly crosses one leg over the other, annoyed by Seokga's lack of *understanding.* Can he not see that all of this was done for him? "Your ingratitude, Seokga, is astounding. It's impressive, even for you."

"I made her a promise. A promise on Hwanung. That we would share a sunrise together once more." Seokga points a trembling finger at Hwanin. "You pulled her into this game. You and the eoduksini both."

Anger straightens Hwanin's back and has him lifting his chin in fury. "Do not compare me to that demon—"

"Prove me wrong, then," Seokga demands. His chest is rising and falling rapidly, and his entire body is shaking as violently as a leaf in the wind. "Prove me wrong, brother. Allow Kim Hani to be reincarnated. Allow her to walk upon Iseung once again. Allow her to be reborn."

"No. You know the procedure—"

"Hani saved Iseung." Seokga is climbing the steps of the dais now, his eyes flashing. "She drained her fox bead and weakened the eoduksini. Without that, I could not have killed him. She saved this realm you love so much from eternal darkness and horror. Does that not outweigh everything else? Let her be reborn. And she did not turn to ash when she died, as other Unrulies do. Does that not say anything, brother?"

Hwanin bites the inside of his cheek. "Seokga—" He cuts off abruptly as he watches Seokga do the impossible. Before the foot of his throne, Seokga *bows,* placing his forehead to the ground in submission.

"Please," Seokga whispers. "Hwanin, please."

Seokga has never said *please* to him in his life.

Seokga has never *bowed* to Hwanin in his life.

But for this gumiho, he does both.

How did you convince him to care for you? Hwanin had asked Kim Hani, unable to stop his curiosity. His envy. She touched a side of Seokga that sibling rivalry has always prevented him from reaching. Sibling rivalry, envy, and the small matter of that attempt at a coup.

The gumiho had given him a wry little half-smile, before shrugging and requesting the same thing that his younger brother now requests. Reincarnation.

Hwanin knows, deep within his soul, that if he says no now, the Seokga he's watched on Iseung will disappear. The god of deceit will once again be cold and unloving, as bitter and biting as a winter wind. He will be closed off to him forever, the door to his heart locked by the unbreakable bonds of hatred.

But if he says yes, *this* Seokga could remain. And perhaps, one day, the two brothers could . . . reconcile.

And with that revelation, the decision is made.

Hwanin closes his eyes. "Rise, Seokga."

His brother shakes as he drags himself to his feet. "Please," he whispers again. "Please, Hwanin. I will do anything. I will give you *anything*."

He opens his eyes and fixes them upon Seokga's pale visage. "She could be reincarnated at any time," Hwanin says slowly, trying to ignore how Seokga nearly crumples to the ground in relief. "It could be a minute from now, a day from now, a year from now, or centuries from now. I have no control over that, and neither does Yeomra. But, fine, brother. I will send notice to Yeomra to put Kim Hani through the reincarnation process. And since I'm feeling *generous*," he says pointedly, expecting a great display of appreciation once his speech is done, "she will be given a form in which you can find her. She will have the same eyes. Fox eyes, wine-brown. This is what I offer you in exchange for . . ." Hwanin falters. He cannot ask Seokga for friendship— he does not want a forced camaraderie, a forced brotherhood. So instead, the emperor of Okhwang says, "In exchange for your pledge to stand loyal by my side. Another coup, brother, and this bargain is null."

"Swear it on Hwanung," Seokga breathes, eyes wide. "Swear it on your son."

Hwanin inclines his head.

And for the first time in six hundred and twenty-eight years, when their hands meet, both grips are warm. Gentle.

"I swear it," Hwanin says quietly. "For you, brother, I swear it."

GODLY GOSSIP

ISSUE #92814

BROTHERS REUNITED!!

FORMERLY ESTRANGED BROTHERS HOTTIE HWANIN AND SEXY SEOKGA REUNITE!

by Suk Aeri, editor in chief

The world was shaken this past Chunbun when we learned via an official announcement sent directly to our unsuspecting doorsteps that formerly estranged brothers Hwanin and Seokga have reconciled.

Can you *believe* it?

Banished to Iseung some 628 years ago (but who's counting, right?) after he (pathetically) tried and failed to instigate a coup, the fallen god has finally returned home to the realm of the gods and been reinstated to his former godly position.

"I am pleased that Seokga has rejoined our pantheon," Emperor Hwanin (king of the gods, emperor of Okhwang, stand-in ruler of Iseung, son of Mireuk, son of Mago, beautiful beyond belief, virtuous upholder of moral standards, winner of the Sexiest God of All Time award) told *Godly Gossip* on March 21. "His actions against the eoduksini proved his worth. We welcome him back with open arms."

When reached out to for a comment on his recent re-ascent to godhood, Seokga (former not-god, two-faced liar, longtime winner of *Godly Gossip*'s Hot But *Not* award, and infamous elderly dog-walker dater) shape-shifted into a wolf and bit the leg of our reporter. (Said reporter is currently in the Magical Mishaps Unit at New Sinsi Hospital and accepting donations.)

Here on Iseung, we will certainly miss the green-eyed god and his many shenanigans . . . but we hear whispers on the wind at *Godly Gossip* that he won't be able to stay away for long.

After all, there's no place like home.

EPILOGUE

NEW SINSI, SOUTH KOREA 2018

FOR THE FIRST TIME IN TWENTY-SIX YEARS, THE CHERRY blossoms have bloomed early.

A not-mortal walks the length of the petal-covered sidewalk, a cool March wind ruffling his dark hair as he slowly follows the winding path through the city park. In his slender hand he holds a cane, glossy and black with a silver snake coiled around the long length of it. Its mischievous eyes stare up at its owner as he tilts his head to the early spring sky, savoring the warm glow of the sunlight.

On a nearby tree, a small cherry blossom is torn from its home amongst the other flowers, swirling upward on the same wind that caresses the not-mortal's face. It dances on the gale, tumbling and twisting, spinning in delight as it rises up, up, up . . . before slowly fluttering down to the sidewalk below, aiming for a nice spot amongst other fallen blossoms. Yet the cherry blossom does not land where it has aimed. It instead flutters to the man's narrow shoulders, resting atop the soft black fabric of his suit.

Seokga sighs and flicks the flower from his shoulder, holding back a sneeze. Jacheongbi is still clearly miffed by the practical joke he played a few days ago, using his gift of creating illusions to bring one of her flower pots to life. It chased her through

Okhwang until Hwanin ordered Seokga to cease creating a racket. Reluctantly, he obeyed. But the goddess was clearly less than pleased at the absence of an apology.

This, it seems, is Jacheongbi's revenge. Shaking his head, Seokga continues on his way throughout the city park, passing by couples strolling hand in hand through the display of sweet, pink cherry blossoms. Many pause to take pictures, pressing their cheeks together and grinning. Seokga watches them with a heavy heart. *Perhaps,* he thinks, finally turning away, *if things had turned out differently . . .*

He pushes the thought down. It has plagued him since 1992. Dwelling on it is useless. Instead, he chooses to visit this city, hoping in vain to catch a glimpse of a girl—or a boy—with angular, wine-brown eyes.

Statistically, it is unlikely that his lost love has been reborn into the same city where their story both began and ended. But he cannot stop himself from visiting New Sinsi every few months, scouring the streets for her. For Hani.

New Sinsi has changed rapidly in the years since 1992, growing and expanding with an almost alarming speed. No longer is New Sinsi the grimy city it once was; now it is a glittering hub of culture and style, the streets nearly unrecognizable. Apartments like Hani's old hovel have been upgraded with sleek skyscrapers that glitter down upon the city in the sunlight.

Sometimes, for old times' sake, Seokga visits the precinct. Chief Shim has long passed, but he left this world as Seokga's friend. The crushing hug Seokga received from him after stopping Eodum is a memory that Seokga still cherishes. The late chief's grandson, Shim Jung-kook, has become the haetae chief. He supposes that he is grateful there have been few Unruly gumiho attacks. Nam Somi, the gumiho from so long ago, does not appear to be in New Sinsi. In the aftermath of the battle against Eodum, Seokga had honestly forgotten about the curly-haired gumiho from the warehouse, so fixated was he on returning to Okhwang and demanding Hwanin allow Hani reincarnation. Yet the handful of Unruly gumiho attacks from Seoul to Montreal—those, he thinks, must be Nam Somi. He does not bother to track her down, though. Hani's last wish had been for Somi to go free, and so she shall.

Sometimes, Seokga and Shim Jung-kook go for drinks. It is ... nice to have somebody to share a bottle of soju with. Somebody to have entertaining, meaningless conversation with. He does not speak to the other divinities often in Okhwang, with the exception of communicating through (mostly harmless) pranks. This morning, he stole into Cheonha Palace and plucked all the feathers out of Haemosu's crow-feather headdress before replacing them with ludicrous pink ones from an Iseung craft store. He fled before Haemosu could alert Hwanin to the occurrence.

Seokga has kept to his promise of remaining loyal to his brother. Yet Kim Hani is nowhere in sight.

Fighting back another sneeze, Seokga makes his way to a park bench. He will stay for a while, watching the comings and goings of mortals, and the falling of cherry blossoms. And then he will return to his palace in the sky.

Seokga closes his eyes and breathes in the spring air. It is peaceful here. Perhaps he will grab a coffee before his return to the heavens. Okhwang does not have coffee.

Like its home city, the Creature Café has grown exponentially since 1992. It is a chain now, with four locations in New Sinsi, six in Gwangju, seven in Seoul, and eight in Busan and Incheon. Sometimes Seokga orders his typical coffee. Other times, he orders hot chocolate.

Actually, a hot chocolate sounds appealing right about now. Seokga glances around for any watching eyes before stepping through space and time to stand outside the original Creature Café.

The bell chimes as he enters, breathing in the smell of roasted beans and brewing tea. Despite himself, he looks around for Kim Hani at the register, only to be met with disappointment as always. It is a slouching bulgasari taking the orders, chewing on a strip of metal like bubblegum. She flicks her eyes up disinterestedly as he steps to the counter. Her eyes, Seokga notes, are a plain brown. Seokga quickly orders his hot chocolate and, cupping the warm paper cup in his hands, exits the café onto the street outside.

He takes a sip, savoring the overwhelming sweetness. It reminds him of that day in Busan, waking up to hot chocolate and strawberry egg buns. He smiles into his cup as he walks. Hani would be so pleased with him—drinking this infernal drink and *enjoying* it.

He is, in fact, enjoying his hot chocolate so much that when the red thread first appears—tying itself around the pinky finger tilted slightly out from the café's cup—he doesn't even notice it. He's still savoring the rich depth of the chocolate, the airy sweetness of the whipped cream, the way Hani's face swims in his memory . . . laughing as she teases him, scowling as they argue, blushing furiously as her eyes trace the contours of his body. Unable to hold her body to his, he instead often holds her face in his mind, fervently recalling every detail—every freckle, every dimple—lest he one day lets her slip away.

He isn't sure, at first, what pulls him from his reverie. Perhaps it's the cool spring breeze that brushes against his face as he wanders underneath the cherry blossom trees. Perhaps it's the laughter of nearby children, young and happy and bright. Or perhaps it's that curious sensation around his little finger . . . almost like something has been *tied* there . . .

The trickster god's green eyes narrow as he glances downward.

And in that moment—that singular, formerly inconsequential moment—Seokga's heart stops cold in his chest.

The thread is thin and glitters faintly underneath the sunlight, light dappling the rich scarlet hue. It has been tied around his pinky in a complex knot, an intricate pattern that almost resembles a small flower. From there it flows, like a river of winding red, through the flowering trees. It curls and loops around the smiling couples, who are unaware of its presence as it whorls deeper into the heart of the city, connected to something—someone—far in the distance.

Seokga's hot chocolate falls and splatters on the sidewalk in an explosion of cream and sugar and cocoa. He does not notice. He does not care.

Nothing else matters but *this*.

Trembling with wonder and hope, Seokga raises his hand higher, tilting it this way and that. Studying the string, the small fibers that compose this physical manifestation of destiny.

Of true love.

He knows, with a certainty that is absolute, there is someone else at the end of this thread. Someone who is waiting for him.

And he knows that there is only one person that the Red Thread of Fate would connect him to. Only one person that he is destined for, in heart and body and soul.

As the late morning sun shines over New Sinsi in its brilliant, beautiful glow, Seokga begins to follow the thread.

Toward Hani.

ACKNOWLEDGMENTS

A heartfelt thank-you to my agent, Emily Forney. Sincere thanks as well to my brilliant editor, Sarah Peed, and to the rest of the incredible team at Del Rey Books. Thank you to Ayesha Shibli and Tricia Narwani in editorial, as well as Scott Shannon, Keith Clayton, and Alex Larned in publishing. Thank you to Ashleigh Heighton, Sabrina Shen, and Tori Henson in marketing, as well as David Moench and Jordan Pace in publicity. Thank you to Nancy Delia, Pam Alders, and Paul Gilbert in production, as well as Edwin Vazquez in interior design. Thank you to Belina Huey and Regina Flath in the art department. I must also thank the talented Sija Hong, the artist of this gorgeous cover.

Thank you to Molly Powell and the team over at Hodderscape, as well as Kuri Huang, who illustrated the beautiful UK cover. Thank you also to Anissa and the team over at FairyLoot (a dream come true).

I wouldn't be the storyteller I am today without my family's encouragement. Thank you to my mom and dad for always supporting my dreams, no matter how big. Thank you to my lovely brothers, who find creative ways (insults) to keep me humble. Thank you to my grandmother and grandfather. Thank you to my 할머니 and 할아버지, to whom this book is dedicated. Thank you to Serena Nettleton, my best and oldest friend. I love you all.

Finally, I'd like to thank you, the reader. I hope to see you for another adventure soon.

ABOUT THE AUTHOR

SOPHIE KIM has a penchant for writing stories that feature mythology, monsters, mystery, and magic. Her work includes young adult novels such as the Talons series and books on the adult spectrum such as *The God and the Gumiho*.

ABOUT THE TYPE

This book was set in Requiem, a typeface designed by the Hoefler Type Foundry. It is a modern typeface inspired by inscriptional capitals in Ludovico Vicentino degli Arrighi's 1523 writing manual, *Il modo de temperare le penne*. An original lowercase, a set of figures, and an italic in the chancery style that Arrighi (fl. 1522) helped popularize were created to make this adaptation of a classical design into a complete font family.